FOR MY WIFE, NICOLA

She read out to me the content of the original BBC Magazine news thread 1913: When Hitler, Trotsky, Tito, Freud and Stalin all lived in the same place, as published online:18 April 2013, and said,

"That would make a great idea for a new book"

Cover (edit) & Page 3 (full). Ferdinand Schmutzer -1926

Photograph of portrait: Nicola Miller

Freud is quoted by the artist to have loved his portrait. He wrote -"It gives me great pleasure and I should really thank you for the trouble you have taken in reproducing my ugly face, and I repeat my assurance that only now do I feel myself preserved for posterity."

Buy here: shop.freud.org.uk/products/schmutzer-colour

Rear cover: Café Central c.1900. Photographer unknown

COPYRIGHT EXISTS
©Brittunculi Records & Books 2023

One Lump Or Two, Mister Hitler?

Imprint: Lulu
ISBN: 978-1-312-43204-8

This Book is licensed for your personal enjoyment only. This publication may not be resold or given away to other people without the express consent of the publisher. If you would like to share this publication with another person, please purchase an additional copy for each person you share it with. If you are reading this book and did not purchase it, or it was not purchased or supplied for your use only, you should return it to the publisher and purchase your own copy.

Jonathan R. P. Taylor

JonathanTaylorBulgaria@gmail.com
www.lulu.com/spotlight/britunculi
www.soundcloud.com/jonathantaylorbulgaria
www.facebook.com/jonathantaylorbrittunculi

ONE LUMP OR TWO, MISTER HITLER?

Freud, Tito, Trotsky, Stalin & Hitler

VIENNA: 1913

Jonathan R. P. Taylor

Foreword

The Vienna of 1913, the capital of the Austro-Hungarian Empire, is likened to a cultural soup that attracted those with ambition from faraway lands across the empire. An empire which then exceeded a population of 50 million and consisting of no less than 15 nations. The Emperor, Franz Joseph, presided over all of this from the luxury and security of the Hofburg Palace. His heir, Archduke Franz Ferdinand, who resided in the Belvedere Palace, eagerly awaited his time on the throne. Balkan nations that flexed their muscles through land grabs following the collapse of the Ottoman empire vied for greater control and this led to his assassination (during a Royal visit to Serbia) in 1914, and would ignite WW1.

The intellectual community was small; it was a city where everyone knew one another. A city of 2 million where less than fifty percent were native born Viennese. A quarter of its population were from Bohemia and Moravia and Czech was spoken as a dominant language, alongside German, this was the norm. It was a city that spoke countless languages and where army officials were required to issue orders in at least 12 different mother tongues. The state was losing control and one could easily hide away, unnoticed, and unchallenged. A political climate where all was perfect for the political dissident and/or others who found themselves to be on the run from someone or something, elsewhere. In 1913, almost 1,500 Viennese committed suicide, out of desperation to escape the vast filthy and crawling slums of the time.

As history now informs us, we know that the Soviet dictator Joseph Stalin (Iosif Vissarionovich Dzhugashvili) arrived in Vienna for one month during the year 1913. He was there alongside Leon Trotsky and Nikolay Bukharin to author the political work: Marxism and the National Question. Stalin and Trotsky were both in political exile, fleeing Czarist Russia.

First attempts at a Russian revolutionary in 1905 had failed. Leon Trotsky had now founded the ideological newspaper: Pravda. He lived in the city of Vienna, writing, between the years 1907 - 1914. A young metal worker, Josip Broz, was also found to be there, residing amongst the city's quarters, before he was later drafted into the Austro-Hungarian army. We know that man today as the former Yugoslav leader: Marshal Tito.

At this time, Sigmund Freud was a respected practitioner, and well established in Berggasse. Fleeing persecution, he left Vienna in 1938, this as Austria became annexed by the Nazi's. The leader of which, Adolf Hitler, was also known to be in Vienna during the year 1913, and pursuing the dreams of any would be young artist of the time in wishing to join the Vienna Academy of Art.

At the end of WW1, 1918 would witness the Austro-Hungarian Empire crumble, shattered into pieces and become redundant on the greater world stage. Whilst Freud himself now lived in Great Britain (1939), as a refugee, the great though historically infamous dictators; Stalin, Hitler, Trotsky and Tito would all soon rise to power. Their beliefs and ideologies would lead to the killing of untold millions.

There is no historical account of the time that factually clarifies that Hitler met Trotsky, or if Stalin knew Tito, or if Freud knew any of them at all. Maybe they never did but let's just imagine for a moment that they did. For the purpose of this book, the question now becomes - what on earth would they have found the time to talk about...

Introduction

At the beginning of the 20th century, Vienna was noted to be the world's sixth largest city. As the notable European centre for arts and culture, it afforded itself a renowned global reputation. And here, political agitation and demonstration for the cause of Socialism gained great pace and popularity as nationalist and ethnic conflict within Austria-Hungary were coming to a fore. Many felt that war was imminent and the breakup of the Empire quite predictable.

The former home of the Archduke Franz Ferdinand, the Upper Belvedere, is today an art gallery. Its impressive collection of Gustav Klimt has over post-WW2 years, found itself, today, significantly decreased in size and value. The Portrait of Adele Bloch-Bauer 1, valued at over $100 million now confiscated from the Austrian state, this after 60 years on display. Now, returned to its rightful heir, former Austrian and now Los-Angelino - Maria Altmann. After much legal wrangling it was eventually proven that the portrait of Altmann's aunt, The Woman in Gold as known affectionately, and one of Klimt's greatest masterpieces, was in fact acquired by the Austrian state, post WW2, as part of a collection of Nazi-looted Artworks.

If one leaves the gallery behind and heads further down road into downtown Vienna, you will soon discover a small apartment museum, a humble but middle-class home, and one that housed the private practice and living quarters of the psychoanalysis, Sigmund Freud.

Among a commendable modern host of talent, the city also gave birth to, or to the careers of, the composers, Beethoven, Mozart, Schubert, Brahms, Bruckner, Haydn, Mahler and Strauss. The great names in science beyond Freud include Wittgenstein, Popper, Schrödinger and Mendel. Alongside Klimt other notable artists established themselves in Viennese history, such as Schiele and Hundertwasser. Vienna's streets and walls are found to be adorned with commemoration plates for anybody who was anybody, and at every opportunity. The city's well-maintained cemeteries now all bear the names of an endless record of talent and achievement that we all, today, recognise as among the greatest masters of their unique expressive fields.

These great minds of their time would all frequent Vienna's wide array of popular Coffeehouses. The Wiener Kaffeehaus reached their peak in popularity at the turn of the 19th century. Historical legend records that they were born of the Turkish-Ottoman retreat, this as soldiers of the Polish-Habsburg army liberated the city during the second Turkish siege: 1683. A huge quantity of what was then initially believed to be abandoned camel food was later identified as sacks filled with roasted coffee beans.

The Polish King, Jan III, granted consent to his officer, Jezry Kulczycki, to open the cities first Viennese coffeehouse. Though, this is the talk of legend and, beyond this legend - it is believed that coffeehouses had actually existed in the city for at least a year beforehand. If we stick with legend, for now, we find that Kulczycki added sugar and milk – and thus, the Viennese coffee traditions were born. It is believed to be of more accurate fact that a Catholic priest, Gottfried Uhlich, created the legendary stories in his written accounts of the siege; in his work of 1783. For what reason we do not know, but, among many other coffeehouse traditions, visitors to the city today will always find a picture of Kulczycki hung upon its coffeehouse walls.

A second legendary account also exists. One in which Kulczycki, an Ottoman captive for two years, knew exactly what coffee was and its true value and popularity to the Viennese. He tricked his commanding officers into giving him the sacks which he had reported to them as - quite worthless.

In truth: Vienna's first coffeehouse was opened by Johannes Diodato. He was a businessman and, an Armenian by birth. Business soon boomed and many coffeehouses sprang up across the city, akin to mushrooms overnight, all supplying the middle-classes with this new and well received Beverage. Unlike Starbucks of our modern era, the various blends did not have names and preference was selected by pointing to a simple coloured-card chart.

Stefan Zweig, an Austrian writer of noted literature penned the following narrative: *"The Viennese Coffee House is an institution of a special kind, actually a sort of democratic club, open to everyone for the price of a cheap cup of coffee, where every guest can sit for hours with this little offering, to talk, write, play cards, receive post, and above all consume an unlimited number of newspapers and journals."*

The coffeehouse was all about social practices and Viennese culture. The pinnacle of which was to create a space to meet others sociably, in an atmosphere of grandeur. Among a wide range of coffee and international newspapers one also enjoyed the magnificence of Vienna's famed pastries.

News, correspondence, and gossip would spread as quickly throughout the coffeehouses of the city just as fake news on Facebook spreads today. The socialite would find themselves surrounded by marble tabletops, Thonet upholstery and a rich tapestry of historicism in interior design. The evenings afforded live music in large appreciative environments. In the summer one could sit out amongst the beauty of the Schanigarten eating one's Apfelstrudel, Millirahmstrudel, Punschkrapfen or Linzer torte.

Certainly, one of the most popular facilitations of the Viennese coffeehouse was the regular delivery of literature readings upon which attached themselves the leading writers of the time. They would meet and exchange ideas and even sit down quietly to write amongst the calm presence of the intelligentsia. Karl Kraus' Die Fackel (The Torch) is known to have been written in such a way thus gaining it the nickname, Coffee Literature.

The poets: Arthur Schnitzler, Alfred Polgar, Friedrich Torberg, and Egon Erwin Kisch would also compose their great works within this environment. It is believed that Peter Altenberg, a most reputable and highly regarded writer, and poet of the day, would spend so much time in his local coffeehouse that he even had his post redirected there. That particular coffeehouse was called the Café Central and I see no better place from where to start this story. But before we do: we must surely afford ourselves time to examine some of the anti-Semitic material published in Vienna, and across a wider hostile Europe at that time, works that directly impacted on the ideological core of so many.

A young Adolf Hitler would, in 1926, use his experiences of Vienna (from as early as 1908) as excuse for his tirade of hatred, this as penned in Mein Kampf. We know today that this 'dire, boring tome' is not historically correct: It is all part of the Hitler myth. In truth Hitler's anti-Semitism was not to be formulated or surface until some 10 years later - upon defeat of Germany in WW1. Hitler wrote of nothing new. There were no great revelations or testaments born of this self-appointed prophet, it was all borrowed from other sources readily available elsewhere at the time.

In the 11th chapter of Mein Kampf (Vol: 1) he reveals his true self. It is basically that of Günther's Racial Science of the German People. Hitler uses the words of other established anti-Semites too, such as Henry Ford and Wilhelm Marr, and borrows extensively from the Houston Stewart Chamberlain anti-Semitic classic: The Foundations of the 19th Century. We find in Hitler's words analogies to Richard Wagner's essay: Judaism in Music. Wagner wrote: *"The Jew can naturally but echo and imitate and is perforce debarred from fluent expression and pure creative work... all revolutionary overthrows have been staged by Jews"*. We also know today that it was the writer Heinrich Class who had previously advocated the colonisation of the Slavic regions to the East, emulating the crusades of the Teutonic Knights.

With all of this in mind, surely, Hitler's work becomes one of blatant plagiarism. And the seed of land grabs existed in countless literature sources long before 1918 when WW1 actually broke out. No; there was nothing new from Hitler concerning the belief that the mixing of races would lead to decline and sterility. The anti-Semite Theodor Fritsch wrote, whilst addressing what he viewed to be the

"Jewish question", and identified the character of his savior of the race as follows: To be a *"sublimely brilliant mind with unlimited courage, the real dragon killer, the true Siegfried"*. Now doesn't that sound familiar, ah, yes, this is Hitler's narcissistical description of himself we read of in Mein Kampf.

In Vienna of 1913, all of what we now know to be true today, was yet to be. Sigmund Freud wrote at the time: *"What pathetic nonsense this young artist is full of, at times I find him to verge on pathetic drivel. Both Trotsky and I agree: he considers himself to be a great artist, but we fear he is nothing more than* laughingstock".

The year is 1913. The place is Vienna.

Leon Trotsky sipped from his cup as he enjoyed today's newspaper. Café Central was a regular haunt for the young revolutionary. He would scrutinise the text hoping that he could understand the minds of those who contributed to the printed literature now placed upon his lap. Pouring over his words, he assimilated his ideas concerning the united international worker's struggle: Communism. These were radical times of great upheaval and political change in Europe; and none more so than found here in the minds of the Viennese.

Austria was a good place to be. Lenin, Trotsky's close friend was also in exile, though he was living in Krakow (then a city of the Kingdom of Galicia and Lodomeria). He had now established wide circulation of his new revolutionary work: Pravda (Truth). The first Russian print run had taken place on 5th May: 1912. Trotsky had contributed greatly to the newspaper which had long been established in Vienna, but now today, the first legal and 'Russian' based St. Petersburg edition was on sale. It was most popular upon Russian city newsstands. Under Lenin's leadership, it was the first time Pravda was published as a mainstream political publication. The days of secret underground editorials and covert distribution of its former Austrian origin were now a thing of the past. The revolutionaries were serious, and they were now very well organised.

Trotsky would sit in the coffee house for hours, patiently compiling his radical propaganda. He would never miss a deadline for inclusion in Pravda's next assault on the political establishment, and its royalists. The Czars, at any cost, would be removed from power. His revolutionary counterpart, Joseph Stalin, had now also arrived in Vienna. It was January: 1913. Stalin had disembarked from his train, routed from Krakow, Poland, carrying only a basic wooden suitcase at his side. Leaving Vienna's north terminal on route to a meeting with Trotsky; he would soon announce his arrival.

The two had never met previously. Seated at his favourite table, Trotsky soon felt a cold chill as the draft of the coffee house door opened and the warm, smoky air exchanged with the bitter cold of the street outside. A short man entered. He had greyish brown skin, which was covered in pockmarks, and notably he was sporting a large peasant's moustache. This figure, of dark complexion, was not at all as tall as Trotsky had expected, quite short in stature in fact. Trotsky, aware of his vulnerability, as an intellectual Russian dissident, saw nothing in this man's eyes that resembled friendliness. Though, they were now for the first time, both introduced to each other. After the usually expected social pleasantries customary of the day, the two men soon sat down to engage in political dialogue.

Stalin would soon be busy and on task writing the work: Marxism and the National Question, this with comrade: Nikolay Bukharin. Trotsky's advice was much sought after as he was held in the highest regard and trust of his counterpart: Lenin. After today's initial meeting both Trotsky and Stalin would often be found seated together formulating their ideas, this as Bukharin eagerly scribbled away with pen to paper. Picking up on their ideological threads of thought, ones he would later use.

Following one now regular political Central Coffee House gathering, just a handful of days after Stalin's first arrival, the group caught the attention of a young metal worker seated across the room from them. Bukharin had by now left the table, like a whirlwind, and had rushed off to his apartment, to now put some of his conclusions to print. As he left, saying; *"I will see you next week gentleman with a first draft – in the interim I shall be engaged with my typewriter, you know where to find me if needed"* – he closed the door most noisily behind him. The modestly dressed figure that had taken their eye took the opportunity to utilise the free seat now available and walked over to them, inspired, as a manual worker, by the words of revolution he had overheard.

Stalin initially maintained a skeptical silence, his need to control things coupled with his obvious distrust of others was by now, all too apparent to Trotsky. The metal worker introduced himself to the pair as Josip Broz. He informed them that he worked at a local factory: Daimler automobile of Wiener Neustadt. In a small town south of the city. He explained that he shared many of the views he had overheard and was in the city centre today seeking other work that would pay better, and with no intention of rudeness or presumption, expressed his eagerness to join in and talk with other like-minded socialists. *"By all means, take a seat"* – Trotsky said to the young man as he offered his hand in greeting. *"Thank you"*, Josip replied - "My friends call me Tito."

It was now fast approaching midday. The streets outside were bustling with life as the city workers paused for dinner. An artist had set up and sat himself across the road, on the pavement opposite, painting a landscape of the famous central arches, street, and city life as it now unfolded before him. This young man, equally, appeared to be quite poor, the three men would glance out of the window and make a regular reference to him, as they talked of an internationalist movement in which all would be fed, housed and educated.

Just as Tito had then uttered the words: *"an end to poverty and free health care for all"* and Stalin had most forcibly added; *"yes, a Soviet Union of states based upon central control akin to the United*

States of America" – they heard laughter unfold into the room. A man at the counter, ordering a sandwich to take away had felt the need to express his dismay at such a notion. From a few feet away he added to the conversation: *"America is a most grandiose experiment gentleman, but I'm afraid it will never work."* Given the unnatural shattering of the discussion hastened by his interruption, he went on to explain. *"Freud, Sigmund Freud; I'm a psychoanalyst and I'm afraid I don't subscribe to your belief in human nature gentlemen"* ...

Stalin, most put out by Freud's laugher felt humiliated. He beckoned Freud to join them. *"Why don't you pull up a chair and tell us all why not then or would that be beneath you to join the table of the common worker?"* he snarled. *"No offence was intended sir, I assure you, I just didn't agree, and if you did not seek my engagement then do keep your voices down – this is a coffee house you know, not a public gathering for political rally!"* Freud asserted. Trotsky calmed the waters by leaving the table and pulling up a spare chair he removed from another, he placed it amongst them all as an invitation to be seated. *"Join us sir, no offence is taken"*, he delivered to the room in a softly spoken and welcoming tone - *"I have heard good of you, Sigmund, by all accounts you are very popular amongst the fragilities' of the ruling class. I'd be very happy to take coffee with you if you feel able.*

Freud replied: *"Then that I will my fellow. I have some time to kill this afternoon. One of those frail ruling classes of ours, your words not mine, has now canceled our planned home call. Too scared to open the door I believe. They are so hysterical women, don't you think? - But first I must take this Salami sandwich to the impoverished young man across the street. He's only 24, completely down on his luck and his delusional dreams to become a master of our fine Vienna Academy of Art are not quite going as well as he intended. Chap's hungry, I offered him lunch but he's busy painting away and doesn't want to interrupt his genius, as he put it - I'll be back in a tick".*

As they waited for his return, the three men, Trotsky, Stalin and Tito discussed this new strange encounter. Stalin was concerned that this man would add no valuable input to the discussion. Trotsky was more open-minded about that matter. He believed that the revolution was one in need of both the bourgeoisie and the proletariat mind, and not just a matter of seizure of power from the elite. Tito, the quietest member of the group, and lacking in political awareness and confidence, wanted to learn more. He was there to grasp at ideas and had no intention of preaching to his older, much wiser peers.

Fresh coffee arrived at the table and a menu was secured for later civilised perusal. The overconfident Freud soon returned saying: *"That's that then, he's fed and watered – poor chap finds himself living in a Danube-side dosshouse in Meldermannstrasse".* As he drew up the chair to the table he added: *"What's the coffee like then? – I usually only frequent the Café Landtmann. I've invited the artist to join us; he said he'd be finished soon, I told him the coffee would be very good, but without having first tasted it I fear I may have lied to him..."*

Both Stalin and Trotsky confirmed in unison that the coffee was found to be of the highest standard and there should be no concern on that political front. *"Wonderful"*, chuckled Freud, "unlike that poor young man's paintings then..."

Stalin soon took back control of the conversation by explaining that Trotsky and he were working on political texts and incites, revolutionary material, and that he personally had no time for chit-chat. Freud, as ever quick off the mark and notably the sharpest mind amongst them replied: *"You'll enjoy one of my publications then, Die Traumdeutung, the interpretation of dreams, - as a neurologist I would always encourage my fellow compatriots to dream..."* It was quite apparent that the newcomer had much to say and wasn't going to be backward in coming forward with it. Tito didn't quite know what to make of this uncomfortable exchange, Trotsky on the other hand took an immediate liking to him, and a wide smirk broke out across his face. Stalin was not amused.

Time soon passed by on this chilly dank winter's Monday afternoon. The four men, in between folly, disagreement and even some agreement too had enjoyed themselves; they soon agreed that they would take lunch together, every day, for the remainder of the week. Stalin was quick to impress that that would have to be it, as Nikolay Bukharin would return next Monday, with the first draft chapters of Marxism and the National Question. Stalin had but one month only to deliver to Lenin in St Petersburg something of political viability, for the party. For education of the Bolshevik faction of the Russian Social Democratic Labour Party formed the year before: 1912. Sarcastically Stalin informed Freud that: *"You, as a man of privilege are free to live in your world of dreams, but to beat your enemy you must first learn how to hate him, dreams will not change the world – it is bloodshed that is needed"*.

Silence fell. The awkwardness of which was only broken by the sudden entry of the young artist bursting in through the street door and announcing at the top of his voice, to Freud across the room: *"My masterpiece is finished: look, look, it's finished!"* Freud issued a courteous reply: *"So you finally come to join us do you young man? - Find yourself a chair. Is it one lump or two, Mister. Hitler?"*.

Sigmund Freud's Journal

Freud spent the evenings, long into the early hours, sitting in the armchair of his study penning his journal, after the day's encounters of that specific week. Without such empirical writing it would be true to say that these conversations would never have come to light today, in these later years. Freud's journal: A most accurate and noteworthy historical document that would warn us of what was to become. Divided into sections with named titles, he introduced each member of what we now know to be, and as simply called, The Sugar Lump Club. The relevance of sugar will become clear to us later. In the journal Stalin is referred to as Dzhugashvili, his name at the time in 1913, but for clarity I use Stalin in this text as this is the name as known today. However: there is a claim by some scholars that by 1910 he had already started to use his new – "Stalin" (man of steel).

He was born in Georgia, a country that would later be annexed by the Soviet Union, this when he became supreme ruler of the new Soviet Union from 1924 – 1953. Appointed General Secretary of the Communist Party's Central Committee, he had come to power in 1922 following Lenin's death. History informs that he suppressed all criticism of his leadership.

Freud wrote much about Stalin and noted in his journal: *"Whilst the two new men work on the book, I feel a sense of rivalry between them, both seem to contradict each other in matters of control and state; at times they are most hostile to each other's contribution"*. It was obvious to Freud that Stalin had visions of a new enlarged socialist federal union that expanded beyond Russia's present lands. In contradiction of both Lenin and Trotsky. He talked frequently of Russia becoming part of a greater Russian Empire. Freud noted: *"This fellow is an opportunist, deeply distrusting of Trotsky, manipulative, and I feel not sincerely committed to his socialist cause. He believes that should war break out Russia should seize the moment to expand but unlike others in the club, he has never made any reference to 'world domination'*. It was obvious that Freud considered Trotsky and Stalin to be odd bedfellows, none more so than when he wrote: *"Stalin believes that a Socialist state could operate independently and trade directly in association with other Capitalists states– though Trotsky dismisses this outright in favour of an internationalist movement uniting all workers of the world. I can't imagine how they will ever manage to agree long enough to ever finish that cursed book"*.

These are telling words as we know because as the historical record provides, after Lenin's death, Stalin dismantled and destroyed all of the new economic policies of Lenin, instigated in 1920, and replaced it with a highly centralised command economy. His rule was one of industrialisation and agricultural collectivisation, seeing rapid transformation from an agrarian society into an industrial power.

Freud seemed to hold a greater respect for Trotsky, writing *"Whilst I sit for hours listening to his utter nonsense to the point of boredom at times, I do feel a sense of genuineness within his belief. A sincere fellow who concerns himself only with the liberation of the workers - though has no wish to be in control. Whilst I do enjoy his company, I cannot say the same for the other. Trotsky expresses his views of a world rid of rulers and monarchy and a cooperative movement controlled by the workers, a redistribution of power from the top to the bottom as it were. It is guided by a true ideology, no matter how inconceivable this is to me, but Stalin, he just seems to hate, an angry man who I sense wants blood".*

We know that Trotsky advocated violent world revolution but was Freud trying to explain in these words that this was born out of a revolutionary necessity and, not for the want of purposive violence. Stalin clearly wanted revenge. This anger, his need for that pound of flesh, perhaps, born out of the failed 1905 Russian Revolution that had sent both men sent into political exile abroad. Freud summed his feelings up clearly when he noted: *I'm not surprised that the revolution failed, they have no sense of political direction or agreement – a fixation on blaming all but themselves for this. With such distrust between them I feel one or the other must concede to the dominant personality, but I have no incline at this venture who this will be".*

Following the death of Vladimir Lenin on January 21st (1924), Lenin's close friend Leon Trotsky had become the de-facto Russian leader. Stalin, who Lenin had come to dislike and distrust immensely, now vowed to be in power; he began eliminating any political opposition in his way. As Trotsky fled for his life, Stalin's thugs soon caught up with him in Central America, where he was in political exile, killing him with a single blow of an icepick to his head. Trotsky had fled into exile as he had criticised Stalin's new cult of personality and was infuriated when the new Soviet National Anthem was now to include Stalin's name.

During his power grab and subsequent leadership, Stalin would go on to kill millions of people through starvation in the process, holding tens of thousands more in correctional labour camps, the disruption to food production caused the catastrophic Soviet famine of 1932–1933. Further, the Holodomor famine of Ukraine. During the years 1926-1934, an estimated 10 million people starved to death, almost all of whom were peasants. He was responsible for ordering the Great Purge of the party, government, armed forces and intelligentsia. His opponents or so-called enemies of the Soviet people were imprisoned, exiled, or executed. From 1936 to 1939, the Old Bolsheviks, supporters of Trotsky, and most of the Red Army Generals, were convicted of plotting against Stalin and summarily executed, this without any right to appeal. They were quite simply - 'taken outside and shot'.

Freud wrote positively of Tito. He said of him in the journal: *"A charming man with polite manner, a worker lacking in education and many airs and social graces but of pleasurable company"*. He viewed Tito as the student, as separated from the delusions of the other's – the two would be revolutionaries of Russia as he had called them. There were many references to the "would-be's" – clearly indicative of an unsettling feeling toward Trotsky and Stalin. *"He does not contribute political knowledge of foresight to the club, but when he speaks it is of his feelings, there is wisdom about this mind that I don't gain elsewhere from the wider conversations"*. Freud was clearly most positive about his interactions with Tito, adding:

..." As a citizen he is not hiding or fleeing and has no indicators prone to violence. Working in the laborious and demanding Daimler plant has taken its physical toll on many, and his focus is one of political education and unionisation of the workers at the plant. His concern is the conditions at the factory, and he never considers socialism beyond the necessities and essentialist needs of his inner world. Though, I fear his new interactions with others amongst us may politicise him beyond this. He is not in search of power but there is a revolutionary zeal beginning to surface - sympathetic to the communist cause".

There were many interesting points that I discovered whilst reading Freud's journal in research for this title, but none surprised me more than his underestimation of the young Adolf Hitler. He noted that: *The would-be's consider themselves to be loyal patriots, as does the young Hitler, but with startling difference. For Trotsky and Stalin, patriotism means a love of one's country, they see the benefit of unity of humanity, and they refer to anti-Semitism as against party rules. Though when discussion about such comes up at the table Stalin does not contribute but remains solon and indifferent. It is not what he says on the topic but what he does not. Trotsky informed that he could never become a leader due to the nation's distrust of his Jewish background, one he shares with myself, and I would have expected a degree of support from his comrade – but this was notably absent.*

When Freud refers to Hitler on the subject of patriotism, we discover a compelling difference. *"For the artist patriotism is not based on what is good for one's nation but only for one's own race. Though he controls what he says among the group you feel he is insincere in his acceptance of Trotsky and I as Jewish – this comes to the fore when we describe ourselves as citizens. He almost develops a range, flicking his hair back and tossing his nose around into the air with a lunge back of the neck. Indicative of deeply censoring his true deep loathing I suggest. When I remind him of my kindness, he informs me that it is my duty to support his great work – and he is only in a place of desperation and charity because of the conspiracy of others. He truly believes that one day he will achieve great things – but I see nothing of this in him".*

He talks of Hitler paintings as follows: *"One's sees leadership quality in the Russians, but this is quite lacking in Hitler. A weak and at times quite pathetic man: he is delusional. He talks of his art and masterpieces, but I am aware that this is not true – the Academy have already informed me that he has been knocked back twice. I had bought two portraits of this young artist as I felt quite sorry for his pitiful circumstance. A patient of mine, one employed of the Academy, had recognised the work hung upon my hallway and informed he is not of the standard, but this is not what you hear from the man himself. Quite the opposite – he informs that he is too good for such study now and wishes to become a fine art painter, possessing an exceptional talent that the academy cannot cater for.*

Although Freud had never previously met Hitler until that first meeting by chance outside the Central Coffeehouse that day in January, and having purchased the paintings thereafter, we find there is a reference in a later entry that indicates Hitler had been a visitor to Freud's local: the Café Landtmann. He wrote: *"There is much talk of a young Austrian artist in the café tonight: much laughter and folly among the gentlemen. This young fellow had asked for the menu, not for fine foods or beverages but for the bedrooms above. However, he was unable to be catered for in that department as he found the young ladies who abode here to be too old for his personal taste. He was of the belief that "If they are old enough to bleed then they may be slaughtered". It is the talk of the whole house. The man had embarrassed himself and soon left tail between his legs. I am quite sure that it is the young Adolf that they talk of, which surprises me greatly as I had thought of him to be possessed with the decease of homosexuality".*

Visitors today, to the small downtown museum and former apartment of Sigmund Freud can see the journal on display, and as I found, by written request to the trustees, it will be opened to those curious scrutineers of its content. Though a work born only of a handful of some 163 pages, it does speak volumes about what was to become, and the relationship and bond kindled between the men of the Sugar Lump Club of Vienna: January 1913.

It is better that we now approach the journal again by continuing to put its content back into the dialogue as originally spoken at the time. It's also quite impossible to know exactly which particular point of conversational topic took place on each individual day during the course of the men's meetings, those of that week in January. The journal does not always specify the time, day or date, it is at best considered to be nothing more than a random collection of Freud's recollections. Therefore, I continue, for ease of reading and understanding, to create for you now, the wider conversation as if it was delivered as one.

What is known to us as an indisputable fact is that as Hitler rose to power, and during WW2, up to 6 million Jews, 7 million Soviet civilians, 3 million Soviet prisoners of war and around 1.8 million Polish civilians would become victims. Both purposeful and collateral damage of Hitler's insanity and his wider vendetta of hate. A further 312,000 Serbian civilians, 250,000 disabled persons, 196,000–220,000 Roma and around 1,900 Jehovah's Witnesses, and 70,000 'criminals' (which included homosexuals) would also meet this heinous end. There is no reliable figure for the countless dead of the German political resistance, those who opposed the Nazi regime in Axis-occupied territories. We must also remember that the first country to become occupied by the Nazi regime was Germany, itself.

The World According to Sugar

The sugar lump, long before the days of the finely diced and most precise dimensions of the sugar cube we know today, would be found on all tables of all Viennese Coffeehouses. A large rock of sugar would be broken into lumps, accordingly as desired, as if cracking a walnut in the jaws of a nutcracker. The sugar cracker, however, would not only break down the larger lump into small manageable pieces to be dissolved in one's coffee, but would also come to symbolise the fractious minds of those sat around the table. The future of Europe would be decided by fractions of sugar lumps which moved strategically around that table as if part of a larger game of draughts and/or checkers.

Greed could be determined by the quantity consumed. Freud never took sugar in his coffee, just a splash of milk, and Tito desired just one small lump to sweeten the taste. Trotsky had a very sweet tooth. A man that would always take three lumps, stirring it into his drink slowly, around and around whilst talking. Stalin had an equally sweet tooth and would crack several lumps away from the rock at once, more than required or deemed to be necessary, adding to taste through prolonged pauses, but always placing a few shattered fragments upon his napkin as if a squirrel would harbour nuts and seeds to see it through winter later. Occasionally, dropping another one or two into his cup midway, though the coffee by now would often have gone cold. Hitler would always ensure that the rock was beside his cup, as if a dog were guarding its bone. A man who desired all of the sugar at once but didn't yet have the confidence to fight for it, a reservation born out of fear of objection from the others. *"Will you be keeping the sugar to yourself"*, Stalin had uttered.

Freud noticed that Hitler did not consume the same quantity of sugar as the others. Often, he would just sprinkle it into his drink from above, crumbling it between thumb and forefinger, just a brief powdering as if peppering his salami was all that he required. It was more about possession. Every time the gentlemen asked him to pass the sugar over, he would politely comply, immediately. But there, afterward, would again slip the bowl gently back toward him, as if not to be noticed, to his cup and saucer quarter side. He didn't want the sugar, but the need of the others to be forced to have to continually ask for it stood out to Freud. Often, these subtle silent interactions or gestures bear more weight on his thoughts than the words of the conversation itself.

"Why do you persist in hogging the sugar, Mr. Hitler?" – Freud eventually asked.

"*Am I?*" – Hitler replied: "*How rude of me, sorry, I was merely keeping it out of harm's way. No offence was intended of it.*"

"*What harm?*" - interjected Stalin.

"*You know full well sir - every time you say anything it is followed by a mighty thump of the tablecloth under the weight of your fist. Can you not see that when you do this the cutlery rises into the air with embarrassing clatter? If I leave the sugar in the centre of the table, it is certain to go everywhere*".

"*Ridiculous*" – blasted Stalin, as he rose up to the challenge of the day's new argument. "*You just want to control the sugar; you seek to control the conversation too...*". And all soon started to become very personal.

"*How dare you, what use of I for this sugar, I don't even want any. And you, look, there on your napkin, 5 lumps already at hand, you don't want it either*". Hitler then tossed his nose into the air with belittling effect causing Stalin to explode into rage.

"*The milk is mine, then. Let's see how you like having to ask for it every time you wish to use it*". With a mighty grab Stalin lunged forward, then gripping the milk jug handle so tightly as if he would never let go, pulled the jug away from the centre of the table toward him. This with such force that much of it sloshed out onto the tablecloth, and thus now wasted.

Trotsky, ever aware of the wider embarrassment of the behavior at the table as the silence that had followed throughout the coffeehouse became most evident, started to laugh aloud. Aware that this laughter would at the very least defuse the moment and lead others of the Central Café to believe that matters were not quite so serious, then said: "*I suggest you find a way to share. After all: if you have all the sugar and he now has all the milk, neither Freud, Tito nor I shall no longer have any coffee left to enjoy for ourselves*".

The moment was further diffused by the arrival of the waitress, keen to replace the soiled linen with a fresh adornment, and in doing so felt the need to comment: "*What a fine mess you have all made of it today gentlemen...*"

Freud seized the opportunity for analysis. It was evident that such petty quarreling was indicative of deeper routed disturbances and born out of a clash of personalities. He recognised that the issue was one born out of power and control and not for the need of sugar at all. He noted that whilst Hitler's coffee was already sweetened sufficiently to taste, he would want it all, and nothing less than future possession of the whole bowl would suffice. Stalin, though in possession of adequate sugar reserves already, needed to know that future quantities would be made available on demand and without question. Freud sat back whilst Trotsky continued to reason with them.

"This is the problem as I see it gentlemen, communism in one country cannot work. For here, Hitler, you see, we are in possession of all of the milk, are we not?"

"Indeed, you are, Trotsky, but I have all of the sugar".

"Yes, young Adolf – this is truth, and whilst you control the sugar, representative of another country, as if it were beyond the control of ours, we will always depend on you before we can drink our own coffee".

"And I too on you" replied Hitler – *"You now have all the milk".*

"Indeed: and whilst we rely on each other within this mutually agreed gentleman's agreement over the supply of milk and sugar, as, shall we say, raw resources for our nation's needs, the sugar the Austro-Hungarian Empire and the milk, the Russian Empire, will there not always be friction between us?" – Trotsky ended.

Hitler paused before reply, lost in thought and about to speak, until and when Stalin then interrupted his mind's direction.

"Trotsky – I don't agree", he said, *"If Mr. Hitler supplies Russia with the sugar, and Austro-Hungary supplies Russia with the milk, where is the problem?"*

"The problem is this Stalin, you have milk and Hitler has sugar but, neither of you have possession of the coffee!"

Trotsky clarified his point. And it was a simple though effective one. Whilst both men agreed to share their natural resources all would be well, but both independent Empires, Russia and Austro-Hungaria, would always have to rely on the others cooperation, both were at the whim and control of the other, whilst Hitler would share his sugar and Stalin his milk, it wouldn't be all of it, but just enough, a controlled supply used to influence and control each other's foreign policy. A nation's best interest could never be fulfilled in such a manner as one must never rely on anything that can be taken away from it. An independent socialist economy could never prevail where it was deemed necessary to rely on the supply of goods and resources from the capitalist economies of the west. Sugar is sugar and milk is milk, both of equal value but on their own they are quite useless as milk and sugar do not make a coffee. Iron is iron and coal is coal, but they do not make a train…

Trotsky's vision, quite at odds to that of Stalin's, was of an internationalist movement of workers, a global cooperative that would share the milk, sugar and coffee equally, each according to need: a socialist utopia. There would be no central state in control but a collective of nations working together for the greater good of humanity. A world in which all would be free to drink an abundant and uninterrupted supply of coffee: with milk and sugar.

One would have thought that Stalin would have found Trotsky's analogy, and confrontation of his belief in a one party centrally controlled state to be quite objectionable – but this was not to be the case. Stalin was soon to play his hand and, as the dialogue between the men developed further, this became most apparent.

"It appears that what Leon is saying gentlemen is that both of you seem to think that you are in a position of power and position over the other, that is, in actual fact, nothing of the truth" – Freud said. "The real centre of power is over there, on the other side of the room, the waitress that we see to be in possession of the coffee jug, and all the coffee in it". He continued: "I think you put that very well, most learned Trotsky, neither Hitler with all his sugar nor Stalin with all his milk have anything of value at all, we still have no coffee on the table. And you fail to see the obvious: I don't take sugar in my coffee and I'm more than happy to skip on the milk as well. You see, you cannot negotiate without the credibility of force gentlemen, and your position is quite untenable. Whilst I have no need of your resources, those on the table before you, I will always be independent of you".

Stalin, enraged with angry, threw his chair back outward from beneath him as he then stood bolt upright. He turned on his heels and headed forcibly off across the room toward the young waitress who was pouring her coffee for an older man, seated alone. Startled by his aggressive manner she froze. *"I'll have that now,"* he shouted – *"Can't you see we have none, am I required to wait all day on your stupidity?"* So shocked was she by this wholly unwarranted and quite unexpected rage attack forced upon her, she fled the bar in tears, to then sob in the kitchens to the rear. He returned just as forcibly back to his table.

"I fear that was a step too far" - protested the startled Freud, to which Trotsky soon added his dismay at such hostility toward the poor young girl, as well.

"What on earth's got into you", Tito, usually always quiet and reserved, had then demanded to know of Stalin, adding; *"She's just a poor worker like the rest of us, trying to make ends meet, trying to feed her family out of poverty like the rest of us. She is not our enemy. The enemy is outside, those she is forced to service..."*

"It was not my desire to frighten her; I merely sought to make my point clear. The one you all seem to miss. That my decisiveness, manner and stature terrified her".

"And the point of that point was what then, Mr. Stalin?" – Tito enquired, angrily. Stalin stared back, piercingly, straight into Tito's eyes, as if possessed by the evil of a cruel headmaster now challenged by a schoolboy's insolence.

"That a powerful state can demand of it subordinates anything it so desires: after all, who has the coffee now?"

"Then yes, your point is made very well then, Mr. Stalin, but I see I am the only one of us that requires just enough sugar to sweeten the taste, and not so much more that it then ruins the drink for us all". Stalin slammed the coffee pot down onto the table with such force

that its content now splashed outward from the rim. The linen tablecloth now soiled for the second time, and as if blood had been shed upon a battlefield.

"*Well: what do you think about it Mr. Hitler? – Have I made the point clear or not? You have sugar, but I now have both milk and coffee*". Stalin concluding his outburst with the words: "*Which one of us has the most powerful Empire now? – Is It Russia or Austro-Hungaria?*"

Hitler just sat there, head down, looking deep into the sugar bowl in front. After a brief moment, one taken to gather his thoughts, he responded thus:

"*Do you see what has happened Stalin, you have spilt coffee onto the sugar. Look how it has dissolved and discoloured, spreading like a cancer across it. Infected and polluting it. The sugar is no longer pure: it is contaminated. If this sugar were representative of Austro-Hungaria, then it is an Empire no longer worthy of fighting for*".

Stalin turned to Trotsky and then demanded an answer of him instead: "*And so then it falls on you my dear comrade, do you think that my coffee jug is worth fighting for?*" Freud sensed that Stalin was attempting to flex his muscles and was sparing for a fight, with anyone, and as Hitler had not taken the bait, perhaps Trotsky would. Trotsky complied:

"*I would yes, I'd just snatch that jug right from your hand*". And this he did, as if David was fighting against Goliath, catching his 'superior' quite by surprise. Freud bemused by Trotsky's direct challenge to authority, smiled, as he then smugly asked of Stalin:

"*So, you no longer have a coffee jug Stalin - what plight will befall your Empire now?*"

Stalin's reply was immediate and unequivocable: "*One man one problem: no man no problem*".

Just a Hint of Anti-Semitism

We now know today that Tito returned to Zagreb later in the year, this, where he enlisted in the army. Stalin had already left Vienna by February. He returned to Siberia, remaining in political exile, though he escaped many times. At the outbreak of WW1, the following year: 1914 - Hitler, having dodged his initial draft had by now fled to Munich. He later enlisted in the Bavarian army. Trotsky fled the war in Austria and headed for Switzerland. Freud remained in practice in Vienna, that was until the outbreak of WW2.

Freud's journal does not state anywhere that Hitler was a redemptive anti-Semite. Surprisingly his notes are quite at odds with the common Hitler myths and false narratives we have come to believe today. These myths were born out of Hitler's autobiographical work of 1924: Mein Kampf. Within the text Hitler explains that he became an anti-Semite following his experiences in Vienna. In actual fact, his anti-Semitism was born out of Germany's defeat in WW1. 1918 being a period of his life that was yet to unfold. Many false claims, mistruths and outright lies, hundreds, layered one upon another would later be made into that infamous biographical book of Adolf Hitler - all of which we know today are untrue. They are the latter creations of fantasy, of Hitler's deluded and fanatical ideals, these mixed within his egocentrically and narcissistical need for attention. In 1912: Freud's conversations with him portray a very different story.

It had been a crisp, cold January morning, one that had followed the tensions of the previous meeting, today had led the conversation in a very different direction. One may have thought that such testation's expressed beforehand would have isolated the group from one another, driven a wedge in between them, not just politically but socially, but this was not the case. It appears that a relationship born of inflexible will and bloody-mindedness had actually glued the group more closely together, and at a central core of this adhesive bound, politics and the new world order. It was a meeting of intellect rather than of intellectual minds, this was clear, but a friendship and a common bond seems to have cemented the sugar lump club together, and with ever closer ties.

This particular morning, noted to be 10.00 am (day unknown), Freud as ever, and as the first to arrive, sat and enjoyed his coffee. The press of today focusing on the tensions between the Austro-Hungarian ruler, Franz Joseph, and the demands of separatism as desired by Serbia. War was imminent, but yet, it still seemed many years away. These were deeply troubled times, a political climate of extremes and the new ideals of the socialists gaining ever daily in popularity. Tito had not found recruitment to his worker's union to be objectionable to most, and this inspired the young metal worker's loyalty toward the other members of the sugar lump club. The Habsburg dynasty was on the verge of losing its grip on power and should that happen then surely, it would be war. Austria and Germany both sought to prevent Serbian isolationism from the Empire and had agreed to intervene as united forces should this prevail, but there was little will for real actual conflict. Smoldering ash was best left to smolder alone as long as it did not possess a flame that could burn the entire house down. The Empire was on the verge of imploding: but no spark had as yet blown across onto the other's dry tinder.

Hitler, Tito, Stalin, and Trotsky soon arrived. All excited by the find of today's newspaper headline: *"Ferdinand keen to replace Joseph on Habsburg Throne – Could it be War?"*

"Good morning gentlemen", Freud said, as the four walked into the Central Coffeehouse together, almost in unison. *"It's a beautiful morning for conversation but I'm not sure it's a good day for war"*, added Freud, and having then laughed turned his newspaper overleaf.

"The four of us have just been buying a copy from the corner stand, sorry for the tardy arrival, but we could not help but take a moment to share the headline, how's the coffee this morning?" Tito enquired.

"As good as it gets, I believe, with milk and sugar too" – Freud acknowledged Tito with a wide smirk as if mocking the others with his new gained possession of the world, adding: *"The early bird gets the worm gentlemen, no need for conflict at all"*. And then in addressing Hitler enquired: *"I see you've lost your copy already then Young Adolf?"*

"Not lost Sigmund old chap, just put to a better cause, stuffed in my sack – I'll use it to clean my paintbrushes later if I may". Hitler's tools of the trade now noticed to be hung over his shoulder. A small black wooden paint box hanging from his right shoulder, a smudged multi-colored wooden palate tied across the lid with string, and both covered over by a cloth sack bag for his brushes, hung from his left across his chest.

"You look quite the part today young man, anything particular in mind?" Freud asked.

"Oh, the usual, child portrait, started last night but no need to be finished until this evening" – Hitler confirmed. Freud was about to ask of his easel but soon realised it must be still at the portraitures commissioner's home. It made perfect sense not to carry it around all day, after all, and Freud was never one to ask the obvious.

"How's the art going these days sir, still managing to earn a crust or two?" Freud felt the need to ask out of politeness and to show a greater more enthusiastic interest in the young fellow's endeavors.

Though he had already purchased the two prints off Adolf, and in truth, had no desire to own a third, whenever the subject of additional purchase arose, he would simply suggest that his clinic wall did not have the necessary free space and that a third would, inevitably, take away take from the grandeur of the two already appreciated by his patients as now on proud display.

"*I drink my bottle of milk and eat my morsel of bread*" – Hitler volunteered as Trotsky then interjected rudely, interrupting the polite flow between the two.

"Hitler, seriously! – Are you still trying to sell Sigmund that old yarn? You're among friends now, we're not your potential customers anymore, so can we finally move on from that old street buskers treat…"

Hitler too then laughed and joined in the folly of the others as Trotsky slapped him across the back of the shoulders to indicate his unconditional acceptance alongside them today. Tito addressed Freud and explained the origins of this new humour as expressed between the pair upon this fine January morning.

"*I was in the Café Landtmann last night, handing out Pravda, said I'd help Trotsky out across town, anyway, regardless, all quite boring but – our young Hitler, he isn't as nearly as poor as he likes to make out. He inherited an orphan's pension from his mother and has a healthy interest free loan on top of that from his aunt*".

"Ah, so my mistake was to frequent the Landtmann too then was it Tito?", stated Hitler, now caught at somewhat of an awkward juncture. Hitler was not upset by the revelation as it was abundantly clear that all of the men had found it, such gossip gained from the reliable sources of the Landtmann, as indeed - most hilarious. Freud continued the joke:

"So, all your talk of the young struggling painter from Braunau am Inn, and Vienna being the saddest period of your life, the misfortune and misery you sold me, is all twaddle then, is it? Perhaps I'll have my money back."

Hitler, un-phased, immediately replied: "No, not at all, a lie is only a lie if it's found to be a lie. I am from Braunau, true, and when they failed to acknowledge my talents at the Academy of Fine Arts, I was for a long time sad and miserable, all still truth sir!"

"And of the admittedly meager living painting postcards then?"– Freud asked, as he now probed further.

"All true Sigmund, it was and is, just didn't mention the money I had elsewhere. Nobody wants postcards anymore, it's all about the portraits these days, and there's not enough money in that either!"

Freud, almost in tears by now, and with Trotsky and Tito doubled up with laugher at either side of the young painter, to the point of pain, finished off with one final question:

"And: you didn't have any work for an entire year and spent it wondering the city in misfortune?"

"I didn't, but that was when I came here in 1908, I didn't have to work for an entire year... the misfortune came later, when I realised, I'd have to get a part-time job so I could continue to stroll around the city, going to bars and concerts".

Hitler had shown Freud up to be somewhat gullible in faith he'd put in the words of others. Trotsky on the other hand couldn't resist having the final word on the matter:

"Perhaps all of those hysterical young ladies of yours you spend so much time psychoanalysing were telling the truth after all?"

The gentlemen finally calmed down and sat together for coffee. The conversation soon turned back to one of the impending wars.

"So, gentlemen, item one on today's agenda, shall we? If war breaks out, what are you going to do about it?", asked Sigmund of the others, and Tito contributed first:

"I'd return home to Zagreb immediately and enlist, obviously. I am not in favour of war but how could I stand by, and watch Austria and Germany attack my fellow Serbs? It would be a call of duty to take up arms against any oppressor of one's homeland, wouldn't it?" Hitler, with newfound post folly confidence immediately disagreed - adding:

"Normally, yes, Tito my friend, but how does one truly define one's homeland? Are your fellow Serbs countrymen of a nation state or are they pollutants as we find here within the Empire?"

"I'm not sure I fully understand Adolf – surely all countrymen are one and the same?"

"One and the same is an illusion! - Hitler exclaimed. Thumping the table with a mighty blow of his right clenched fist, a habit he had by now acquired from Stalin, one that had always served well to control the attention of the table. Hitler continued:

"Do you seriously believe that just because someone is a Serb, they all want the same thing? No! As soon as Serbia would gain any incline of independence from the Empire then all would come forward out of the woodwork with true intent! Divide and conquer, remove the Empire from the equation and Serbia would be defenseless against any interior tensions and non-more so than the Marxists!"

"The Marxists!" – shouted Stalin. "You mean to reference Trotsky and I as communists in that personal slight, do you?"

"No! – Hitler asserted. "I have no objection or aversion to social democracy, there are many aspects of communism I fully engage with, but one really has to question in whose best interests it serves". Trotsky was also keen to hear more and asked Hitler to finely pinpoint what his objection to Marxism actually was.

"Trotsky: As a revolutionary you have already made it clear that you would never be accepted as a leader alongside Lenin in your would be Socialist Russian state – why? Because you are Jewish:

these are your words sirs, not mine! And when you said this what happened – did anybody at this table disagree? No!"

It was true of the time to say that anti-Semitism was rife across Europe. Deeply ingrained in all European societies of 1913. A fact that Trotsky had long accepted as a barrier to his potential leadership. Following the failed 1905 Russian revolution that had led both him and Stalin into political exile, he and Lenin had discussed this very issue. Lenin was not convinced that Trotsky was right - indeed, anti-Semitism was against party discipline, and Lenin wanted to see a fully representative party based on multi-ethnic lines controlled by the proletariat. Stalin had not agreed. As an ethnic Georgian and a Roman Catholic, he remained to be convinced. Orthodox Christianity was after all – the established faith within the Russian Empire and the people were certain to be more trusting of one they saw as one of their own: Even if such a figure himself would afterward be required under Marxist-Leninist ideals to denounce Christianity itself.

Hitler continued to explain: *"It's not a matter of I being an anti-Semite or not gentlemen, for if I was, I would surely not waste my time in conversation here. Freud – you are a Jew too are you not? I have sold my paintings to you. I drink, dance and frolic with Jews just as if they were my own Volksgemeinschaft* (ethnic community). *You sit and talk about revolution, but the fact is Marxist theory was written by a Jew, the man your talk of daily as if he were a God: Karl Marx. It's a matter of trust, that's all I am trying to say".*

"So, you are suggesting, Hitler, that the workers see communism as a Jewish conspiracy and not one of an internationalist movement of united workers, one free of the chains of exploitation, but not the shackles of their xenophobia?", asked Freud, and Hitler continued to labour his point. He explained that he believed that Karl Marx had created, in the Manifesto of The Communist Party and Des Capital, the world's most dangerous books, which were, ideological wars on capitalism - and that all that the House of Habsburg and the elite ruling classes had to do to maintain the stereotyped beliefs of the workers was to ridicule it, and this was to done by creating a so-called "Jewish conspiracy".

"If you sincerely wish to succeed and not fail again you must convince the proletariat that they are losing more than their labour: convince them that they are losing their heritage, culture, and, more importantly, their identity. Then they will soon rise up to fight alongside you. You need more than political voice gentlemen; you need to identify an enemy worthy of the cause." Silence befell and Hitler paused to sip from his cup. In a manner as if so proud of his words and to suggest that he had suddenly turned from a naïve young artist to the status of a new respected revolutionary.

Stalin and Trotsky had found a bittersweetness within these words. The Russian secret police, on direct order of the Tzars, had already published the work, "The Protocols of the Elders of Zion" (1903) in Russia. Its sole purpose was to discredit Marxism and revolutionary action. It was a remarkable piece of Russian propaganda that convinced many in playing to the ingrained field of anti-Semitism of its time and convinced many that this was an original and ancient Jewish manuscript. Here was found the evidence of a global Jewish conspiracy that sought to control world economics. It was in fact a work of pure contemporary fiction, a forgery, and a disgraceful work that would gain a false sense of dignity alongside those of Homer, Plato, the Bible and the Talmud.

"So, Mr. Hitler", again asked Freud: "Given such passionate and eloquent delivery - if war broke out tomorrow, who would you fight for? After all, you have still most successfully managed to avoid the question".

"To be honest and frank with you Sigmund, I would not. I have no interest in being a soldier, any more so than being a revolutionary leader. Do you think God would have chosen me to paint if he then required of me that my hands be blown off within the trenches of warfare?" replied Hitler.

"You would not? You'd have to do something, or they'll execute you for treason in avoiding your draft. The question requires an answer of you, young Hitler". Freud insisted that the question be answered.

"Then that be the case, I would join a Bavarian regiment. He answered.

"But you are Austrian", stated Trotsky. "Surely you would fight for your homeland as much as Tito would fight for his?"

Hitler did not answer, and Tito then found desperate need to intervene. "I would, yes Adolf, I would enlist, but it would not be a Serbia created out of the darkness that you suggest. Why must the workers be separated along ethnic lines? That's utterly ridiculous of you - a preposterous notion. It's a common fight against a common oppressor, a single enemy, the ruling classes. A strong state can unite its peoples – regardless of ethnic tensions. Strong leadership and free education are all that is required to unite us all. Anti-Semitism is just a weapon like any other used upon the battlefield of our oppressor, to turn worker against worker".

The gentlemen talked about what they referred to as the British example. A United Kingdom of four separate nation states, coexisting together and ruling the most powerful Empire on earth – The British Empire. Both Trotsky and Tito agreed that power could be shared in such a way. Whilst they were both open in their condemnation of slavery, they believed it to be a good example of a controlling central power sharing its wealth equally. That after all, Scotland had benefited more financially from the colonial slavery of Africa than had the English: profit that Scotland had used to buy up vast lands in occupied Ireland and to trade globally with the America's. Hitler soon reminded them that it was this profit that had directly funded the mill towns of the industrial revolution. And through profiting out of the sales of slaves to other nations, all that had been achieved was slavery of one's own: the workers.

"*Perhaps it would have been better advised to make the Negros work in the mills of England whilst the Aryans enjoyed more leisure time to play*", he had said unashamedly. "*Had that been the case then Britain would surely be the first to succeed with its socialist revolution. Didn't Karl Marx - your prophet say: that England would be the first to thirst for revolutionary change against its rulers – but it wasn't was it? Do you see what I am saying now, Trotsky?*" - Hitler concluded.

Freud observed that both Tito and Trotsky were quite at odds with Hitler's remarks, but a sense of uneasy agreement prevailed of Stalin. None more notably so, when Stalin asked of Freud his option on the Negroes being enslaved within the mills of England. He had replied that such logic would throw mankind, along with its humanity, into a darkness from which he feared it would never recover. Stalin gleefully reminded him: "*Wasn't it you that said upon our first meeting that America was a most grandiose experiment, but you feared it would never work? Perhaps an Empire must be ruled by the dominant master race of its own kinsmen - the young painter may have a valid point*".

Freud was annoyed by the apparent twisting of his original words. He had said it, yes, but this was now a practice of sophistry on the part of Stalin, undoubtedly designed to impress his understanding of the wider social problem upon Hitler.

Stalin continued: "*Reading between the lines I would suggest that young Hitler here would fight for a German Empire but not the one he currently lives under - a Germany under the control of foreign blood. But of you Sigmund, would you enlist should war break out – you are an Austrian citizen too, are you not?*"

Freud thought for a moment and then gently replied. "*Well, I am too old for the draft so I would have to volunteer. And that being the case, my choice would be not. And I would point out gentlemen that I was born in Freiberg in Czechoslovakia, it seems to me that this is an Austrian problem, and not a Czech one. Battlefields are created by old men for the young to die upon*".

Hitler burst into uncontrolled laughter. "*The point is made clear gentlemen; you are an Austrian Freud - but first you are a Czechoslovakian Jew. You will sit at home drinking wine and eating pheasant, carrying on your uninterrupted life's daily routine as if completely untouched by the war, all whilst others die to defend your country for you"*.

Freud remained silent, unable to fully absorb, to comprehend the magnitude of the dark disturbing words now spoken, a stillness in the air then broken by Stalin's incessant need to have the final word, this on any matter. With perfect timing, as if a comedian delivering the punch line to his joke, Stalin uttered:

"What a shame you have no desire for political leadership Adolf – you've certainly got a mouth I could use".

Hitler: The Foundation of a Myth

We know that Adolf Hitler would later, upon his rise to power, consistently connect all political matters with those of his delusional theories on ethnicity and race. He would, during WW2, set out to destroy the Soviet Union with his new weapon of mass destruction: anti-Semitism. His delusional ideals leading to catastrophic war with Russia and, the mass extermination of millions through genocide and extermination during the inhumanity and onslaught of the Shoah: The Holocaust. It must be noted, however, that within the autobiographical work of 1924, Adolf Hitler does not make a direct reference to a planned systematic Holocaust and its systematic decimation of millions. It is, however, most certainly there – hidden between the lines of hatred in creating an environment where genocide becomes predictable.

He states: *"If twelve or fifteen thousand of these Jews who were corrupting the nation had been forced to submit to poison gas, just as hundreds of thousands of our best German workers from every social stratum and from every trade and calling had to face it in the field, then the millions of sacrifices made at the front would not have been in vain. On the contrary: If twelve thousand of these malefactors had been eliminated in proper time, probably the lives of a million decent men, who would be of value to Germany in the future, might have been saved".*

What Hitler refers to here in the text of Mein Kampf is the focus of blame he places on 'the Jews' for Germanys defeat of 1918 in WW1. The quote does not offer any hint of death camps or factories of extermination - This paragraph was reference only to his desire to have seen Jews die upon the Western Front. Hitler, and his supporters had originally vowed by 1941 to expel all Jews from all areas under German rule. A systematic campaign of murder and terror would ensure this would happen more efficiently. The Holocaust, as death camps, was born out of consequence in the later war against Joseph Stalin's Soviet Union.

Within Freud's journal we note a remarkable shift in attitude within the benevolence bestowed of Sigmund toward Adolf that becomes apparent mid-week. His original notes of the week never identified the young artist as the redemptive anti-Semite, racist and xenophobic mass murderer that we can identify with today. Indeed: originally Freud seemed to welcome the contributions of all parties at the coffee table, seeing it as a way to enlighten his enquiring understanding of others. He noted: *"I do not agree with what you say gentlemen, but I will defend your right to say it".* But this frank openness would soon begin to falter as Freud came to view and reflect upon the true horror of the words spoken and began to understand what both Stalin and Hitler where capable of if given a position of power: They both, equally, he felt, craved and desired it. Tito's opinion was more in tune with Freud's own: *"I believe that power should never be given to those who seek it"* – The man who would later become known as Marshall Tito, the leader of the post war Yugoslavian state, had remarked. Trotsky saved no punches at all in his acceptance of violence as a means to revolutionary ends, but he was at least honest and predictable. What Freud felt he saw before him was indeed what Trotsky was*: "A committed principled left-wing ideologist"* – he noted. But before we address the next chapter, the conversations which certainly caused Freud the most personal anguish and discomfort are found whence we take a look at Freud's notes from a much later Period. These found penned on A4, loose leaves, and slipped into the back of the original journal as if an afterthought. Though an afterthought that certainly took place after Freud fled the Nazi-Germany's annexation of Austria and now found himself to be living in exile, fleeing for his life to the United Kingdom. He wrote:

"Hitler's autobiographical work: Mein Kampf (My Struggle) maintained a remarkable openness that was at best naïve, though by March 1933, there was no doubt within the minds of the German masses what the Nazi leader's future intentions were. 52 percent of Germans voted for the Nazi's and their new coalition government. This gospel of a new era was now accepted as the bible of National Socialism. His hatred of Jews and Communists prevailed throughout".

Borrowing on the foundations of International Socialism, National Socialism was not based on a worldwide international movement to free all from the bounds of manual work and slavery, but Socialism based on the interests of his single controlling nation state, and one created of its pure bloodline: the belief in the dominance of Aryanism. He despised democratic process and self-governance as corrupted: He was a dictator that created an unquestionable and unaccountable totalitarian Germany. Upon taking power all democratic processes were dissolved. Germany, as was the case with Stalin's Soviet Union, would become a single party state.

He portrayed himself as the worker, one of the ordinary people, himself a victim of unscrupulous employers who had little respect or dignity for the routine labourious chores and achievements of the manual class. He claimed to have been a casual labourer whilst residing in Vienna, predominantly in construction. Though, he equally tried to separate and distance himself from them as the deep-thinking intellectual who had divine words of wisdom to offer the German masses. In Mein Kampf one reads that he later comes to believe that he is a chosen prophet of God. He claims that he over-heard terrible things on the construction sites, this concerning;

Kinsfolk, the Fatherland, religion and morality, writing: *"The Social Democrats dragged all through the mud".* He claimed that when he challenged the men he was told to: *"Get lost or else be thrown down from the scaffolding".* The reality in truth is that the young Adolf Hitler had never worked a single a day on any construction site, not ever in his life, anywhere.

Hitler did not introduce any new thinking of his own, and the complete lack of sourced footnotes within his autobiographical work, deliberately absent, is a shallow attempt to portray his radical views on the purity of the German kinsfolk as something new now in the offering to his people. His volkisch-conservative biologistic world was born of the reactionary mainstream of the time. The would be "Führer" was not alone in his contempt for Slavs, Marxists and Jews, and his ideas on natural selection and Darwinist theories concerning the law of the jungle. They were reprints derived from popular and pseudo-scientific knowledge of his day and none more so than that of social Darwinism. But Mein Kampf, as a monotonous and boring tome, was unique in the way it presented integrated key elements of German political culture: All greatly exaggerated for the purpose of installing hatred and fear of non-Germans among his followers.

Mein Kampf is built upon lies and half-truths, manipulated and radicalised for effect. The Austrian Jewish critic, Karl Kraus, would regularly condemn the poor literary work of other Jewish playwrights at the same time that Hitler apparently put his own pen to paper. Hitler mirrors this and states that: *"Jewish theatre critics went easy on productions by Jewish authors".* Hitler also claims that *"nine-tenths of all literary filth"* was created of Jewish hands. Though, no matter how many other counter-examples that destroy this argument be presented for scrutiny, the far-right maintain them to be exceptions to the rule. Mein Kampf is a work of deliberate distortion of the truth and equally the creation of very poor research. Factual errors alone are noted to be in the hundreds. Hitler writes that the Habsburg dynasty of Franz Joseph and Franz Ferdinand spoke Czech: they did not, they spoke German.

Of the text itself, it is correct to say that Hitler possessed a broad range of rhetorical and stylistic tools. He was not an incompetent writer and was undoubtedly aware of how best to deliver his text for maximum impact. Subtly drawing the corrupted mind of the anti-Semite ever closer in by not offering anything new, but merely confirming to the mind of the reader what they had already chosen to believe in beforehand. Mein Kampf reinforced what readers already thought and subscribed to. Hitler noted in 1924 that: *"I am not a man of the pen, and I write poorly".* Not one ordinarily for self-criticism, he expressed his feeling that the book was not particularly competent linguistically. But such apologist rhetoric can surely be dismissed as an attempt to gain sympathy and thus increase sales: the poor down and out artist who now finds himself thrown into the chaos of the political world in a selfless attempt to save one's own nation. It is not so much poorly written, but a boring tome of self-pity, and certainly of a strange style that many at the time did not find to be off-putting.

Unsurprisingly the right-wing press praised the work, whilst left wing reviewers condemned and reviled it. The later president and former diplomat, Ernst von Weizsäcker, wrote to Adolf Hitler to thank him for his: *"Warm-heartedness toward social suffering"*. A pastor thanked God *"For the hours in which I was able to study Adolf Hitler's book"*. It is not true to say that terms deemed to be of Nazi provenance such as: *"Volksgemeinschaft"* (ethnic community) and *"Entartung"* (degeneracy) were creations of the Nazi movement. They were also frequently in use by the wider democratic movements of the time. They were in common usage, and also in keeping with the political spin of the day, recalls Freud.

Germany of 1920 was a hotbed of delusional ideas, a nation of wild uncontrolled political despots and desperados. A Germany that had sent 13 million soldiers to fight in the trenches of WW1 - 2 million of which never returned. Germanys defeat on the battlefield blamed on the Jews, Social Democrats and Communists was the foundation stone of Hitter's "stab-in-the-back legend". Everyone else was to blame for Germanys defeat except for those of 'true' German origin - themselves. For many, it was the only plausible explanation for how else could such a great nation have failed had it not been betrayed from within? Many Germans simply could not recover from such defeat. The armistice that had sealed the Fatherlands fate was to fall squarely at the door of blame upon German society, democratic consensus had discredited itself. The centre-right parties, the SPD midfield and those of the centre-left (along with large segments of the wider population) were all to be held accountable for their actions. In Hitler's disturbed warped twisted mind, the issue was quite simple - Germany had not been defeated but by accepting the Treaty of Versailles, an act of treachery and treason had been undertaken.

The left-wing soon took full advantage of Germany's economic collapse with radical right-wing militia groups counteracting their every move. Germany was now on the verge of civil war. A judicial system, hostile to the republic, stood back from it all as the murderous activities of both sides soon became the daily routine. With left preoccupied by fighting right, and vice-versa, it was now time for a broader conservative national spectrum to absorb politicalised anti-Semitism. The German Empire was to be saved. Social Darwinism, not merely sympathetic to the ideology of Nazism, but others, were following the hyperinflation of 1923's collective mainstream thought. *"The year 1923 wore Germany out",* wrote Sigmund Freud, adding: *"...and it prepared it not for Nazism in particular, but for any fantastical adventure. The thing that gave Nazism its streak of insanity developed at the time: The cold madness, the imperiously self-indulgent, and the blind determination to achieve the impossible".*

Hitler, recovering in a military hospital in Pasewalk following blindness born of a Mustard-gas attack searched desperately for someone to blame, and he soon identified the *"Gang of despicable criminals who were to be fought tooth and nail",* as he penned within his work: Mein Kampf. Now known as Lance Corporal Adolf Hitler, obsessing over his stab in the back legend, he announced: *"For my part, I then decided that I would take up political work".*

We do not know when the young artist, recovering war veteran and nationalist, actually in truth made the decision to seek political office, but Freud is doubtful that this event occurred as early as 1918. Bavaria at this point was in chaos due to the consequences of the new Bavarian Soviet Republic. Plunged into chaos by left-wing uprising for several months, and, in Hitler identifying of this that a handful of these new Socialist leaders were Jews, had convinced himself of an inextricable link that bound Judaism and Bolshevism together - at the helm. It was for him one and the same thing. Marxism was a Jewish conspiracy.

It is more likely that the decision was made after the events of summer 1919, when transferred from military hospital by his radical right-wing superior officer to Reichswehr camp near Augsburg (Bavaria). Hitler, the fledgling propagandist, was now put in a position where he could turn like-minded and revenge enthused soldiers into an army of dedicated nationalists through his strident tirades of professional rhetoric delivered, often talentedly, in hatred against Jews and Communists. Soon Hitler would find himself in the presence of larger audiences where he continued to vituperate against The Versailles Treaty and the social democrats.

The Jewish communities soon became known as the vanguard of Communists traitors, now often referred to as simply – *"Jew bloodsuckers".* The Nazi movement now renamed the National Socialist German Workers' Party had quickly fallen into his reaching grasp. As head of the party, he now felt invincible, and plans were soon hatched with the intention of over-throwing the ruling government. Inflation rose to unprecedented levels: One kilo of bread now cost 200 billion marks. He would organise and conquer, dealing a lethal death blow, now orchestrated from headquarters that were well established in Munich, a place at the very heart of the Weimar Republic.

He had neither sufficient support in terms of armed combatants at his disposal, nor the necessary knowledge and expertise of military strategy to succeed. It was logically speaking, a most amateur affair, one doomed to failure from the get-go. With many of his militia recruited from local beer halls, with a handful of local and loyal police officers sprinkled amongst them, power in Berlin was never going to be succeeded to him. The coup of November 8th, 1923, was little more than a propaganda stunt and a political fiasco. The man to his side was killed by a bullet that had missed Hitler by centimeters and though the coup attempt failed, it did succeed in propelling Hitler further into the attentions of public political arena. Sentenced to five years in prison at Landsberg am Lech, most certainly furnished in relative luxury alongside a permitted handful of loyal supporters, his cell was more akin to that of a middle-class apartment. He was not in power but had already started to win over the minds and hearts of the German people. He put pen to paper and addressed his need to settle the old scores of the war with others. Hitler the inmate was now Hitler the writer.

Mein Kampf was never dictated to his Nazi inmate Rudolf Hess - this is a complete myth. Adolf Hitler typed the work himself, engaging in role-play and impassioned re-enactments along the way. Hess noted in a letter sent home to his mother of May 17th, 1924: *"I can hear his voice in our joint living and dining room, he appears to be in the midst of reliving wartime experiences. He is imitating the sounds of shells and machine guns, and he is jumping wildly around the room, transported by his fantasy"*. So intoxicated by his own words, whilst describing his first deployment to the front, Hiter had burst into tears whilst reading the passages out aloud.

The self-appointed demagogue argued that: *"The magic power of the spoken word would now set in motion great historical avalanches of religious and political movements"*. Adding*:* *"An outstanding speaker is rarely a good theoretician and organiser at the same time... a combination of both talents in a single individual created a great man"*. Reading between the lines there was no doubt where this 'great man' was now to be found – Himself. From his first days of poverty in Vienna to the misery of alcoholism amongst fellow workers, he claimed that *"Hunger was the faithful guardian which never left me"* and having like most *"consumed the breadwinners wage within just three days"*. He reinforced his life of squalor to readers and none of which was truth.

Vienna was claimed to be *"the school of his life"*. Claims of life as if: *"like a maggot in a putrescent body"* - was all complete fabrication. Adolf Hitler the construction worker probably never existed. His experiences in Vienna were solely responsible for his change in thinking he claimed, previously he had had nothing against Jews, parliamentarianism or Social Democrats. In Mein Kampf he devotes only a few pages that describe his journey into anti-Semitism and in doing so expresses his admiration for the anti-Semitic Viennese Mayor of the day: Karl Lueger.

He describes his offence at Eastern European Jews he found on the streets of the city writing: *"The odour of those people in caftans often used to make me feel ill"*. For Hitler, his objective realisation was scribed to be: *"Was there any shady undertaking, any form of foulness, especially in cultural life, in which at least one Jew did not participate? On putting the probing knife carefully to that kind of abscess, one immediately discovered, like a maggot in a putrescent body, a little Jew who was often blinded by the sudden light"*. For Hitler, Judaism had as he claimed, a devastating impact. He adds to his narrative of Vienna: *"The occasion of the greatest inner revolution that I had yet experienced"*.

His hatred of Jews permeates in feverish rants throughout the flow of Mein Kampf. Judaism is the source of all evil and growing vehemence is evident as he writes. Though, and according to Munich historians, Hitler's testament is a fable. His anti-Semitism developed in Munich 10 years after he first claimed it to be the case. It was not until after the end of the war in 1918, affected by defeat and revolution, that we see the true development of the *"dogmatic racial anti-Semite"*.

Hitler was certainly further inspired by the 1922 literary work: "Racial Science of the German People", a title penned by Freiburg eugenicist Hans F. K. Günther. In it Günther claims that: *"The Nordic person has a tendency toward solitariness, and is forbidding, hard and relentless, highly talented but usually a poor student"*. A description that Hitler uses in Mein Kampf, almost verbatim, to describe himself. Hitler neither refers to patrons nor to friends in his attempt to establish systematic incompleteness. He set out to stylise himself as the unknown individual, the everyday anonymous worker, offering his followers an especially large serving of potential with which he would use to manipulative others of similar fate to now identify with him and his remarkable self-defined qualities as their future leader.

Freud later considered Hitler to be a man both consumed by and inhibited by fear, which he describes as a *"plague of fears"*. He remarks of: *"Sticky pubertal passages that fabulate about prostitution"*. He notes that: *"Procreation is the only purpose for the union of marriage where the female psyche is influenced less by abstract reasoning than by a vague emotional longing for the strength that completes her being"*. Notably Freud describes the tale of the black-haired Jewish youth who, in Hitler's words, *"Lies in wait for hours on end, satanically glaring at and spying on the unsuspicious girl whom he plans to seduce"* as *"A classic Adolf Hitler rape fantasy"*. Found scattered across several chapters he notes that: *"Behind a chaotic panorama, there lies a misanthropic set of concrete ideas"*.

Mein Kampf, through the eyes of Sigmund Freud, is a story about the survival of a species - the Aryan. A species that exists within the events and historical accounts of Hitler's construct of an Aryan nation. For Freud, Mein Kampf is: *"A fantasy born out of a misguided sense of a great and eternal struggle for existence, the natural results of the effort to conserve and multiply the species and the race"*. It is Hitler's altered reality, a disconnect with the truth in a world where pacifism leads to - *"barbarism"* Where humanitarianism leads to *"chaos"*. A book that describes peace and the rule of law not as the achievements of a civilised homogenous and open embracing secular society but the signs of a civilisation in decline. Freud further remarks on the words of Hitler - *"When the courage to fight for one's own health is no longer in evidence... then the right to live in this world of struggle also ceases"*, with the following guidance, *"The man found to be writing these words is someone for whom the war never really came to an end"*.

"Of course," - writes Freud: *"He anticipates the outcome of the competitive struggle in which every manifestation of human culture is almost exclusively the product of the Aryan creative power. And it is the duty of their noblest representatives, namely the Germans, to perform the historic mission to stop the Jews who, as "The international maggot in the body of the nation", seek to control the whole world and its order"*.

Jews would weaken the world through a covert conspiracy of mass racial *"crossbreeding"*. Within this global takeover, Aryan powers of resistance will weaken. Upon establishing their fake democracy, they as Marxists would then establish: *"The dictatorship of the proletariat"*. Hitler describes the circumstances of the *"Great, last revolution"* indicating that it had already begun within the "*Jewish Bolshevism"* of the Soviet Union. Of Hitler, Freud noted on later reflection: *"Hitler's ambition to create a new world order, one rid of the disease of Judaism, was limited only by time that was now running out"*.

Tito & The Snail

Tito was in a refreshing mood one following yet unknown day, Freud had penned. It appears that Freud thought admirably of him at the time and referred to him in one later paragraph of his journal as: *"the storyteller"*. The encounter that day had been summed up in fine reflective detail and clearly demonstrated the impression made on the psychoanalyst's probing mind. The men had joked together, Freud asking: *"Are you too prepared to give up your life as a revolutionary as Stalin and Trotsky declare?"* – *"I've no fear of death"*, replied Tito: *"I just don't want to be there when it happens."*

Tito had told Freud a story. They had been alone together awaiting the arrival of the other three. Unusually and without reason, they were noted to arrive quite a bit later than usual. Passing time by, the story unfolded.

"I was outside the Daimler factory a few weeks back", Tito has stated. *"I was talking to the men about Karl Marx. General chit-chat and nothing special"*, he informed. *"Just trying to recruit for the trade union, you know, stuff like that, the norm"*. Having been asked about Marx by a fellow worker, one he did not know, he had explained that Marx had been born in Prussia, 5th May 1818, in Trier (Brückengasse). Today: a small town found on the border of western Germany. He'd studied at the University of Bonn but had lived in Manchester with his good friend Fredrick Engels, as journalists, writing on the mills of England's industrial revolution and the desperate plight of the workers now enslaved there. Within many notable ideas of the time, history, philosophy, political theory and economics: his work – The Manifesto of The Communist Party: 1848.

It was the first party-political manifesto ever written Tito had told the interested worker. *"I was doing all the usual speak, key facts, names, dates and places, just to demonstrate that I had knowledge worth sharing before discussing the key concepts of surplus value, class struggle, exploitation and materialism when he suddenly interrupted me, stopped me dead in my tracks in fact, as he then just randomly started to tell me a story"*. Tito explained to Freud. *"He just gave me his entire life story, it went on forever, to say an hour is an under-exaggeration Sigmund, - I must tell you"*.

The man's story had begun on one unknown Christmas Eve. Tito, quite unsure which Christmas Eve the worker was referring to, explained that it had been recently, past few years, but that that lack of fine detail did not impact on the story. Freud had listened patiently to Tito's recollections and was, according to his journal, quite bored and frustrated with the slow pace of delivery at many points.

"It was all quite surreal" – Tito imparted. "I kept interrupting him and continually tried to get his focus back toward me, and the revolution, the words of Karl Marx, but he just wasn't interested – he just rambled on and on and on".

It seemed liked the story had already gone on forever before Tito had even managed to begin to tell the story itself, finally getting down to explain that the man had been at home with his family. The man had had a comfortable home and what was, by all accounts, a good life. He had been an engineer. He, and family, had lived in the affluent suburb of Esterhazy Park and had all the modern trappings and worldly goods beyond others of the time.

"Silver candlesticks, gas lighting and a grand piano, among many other nice things" - Tito continued to explain. "They had just finished Christmas dinner, he had put his three children to bed at eight, and was sat in an armchair, beside the fire, his wife and he reading whilst listening to the calming tick-tock of his grandfather's old inherited Grandfather clock". Upon finishing this sentence Tito then randomly started to explain that there was plenty of wood in the house for Christmas, even telling Freud how many logs were placed beside the fire. 7 he had recalled the man telling him.

Frustrated with the over and unnecessarily continued great depth and detail of the story, we see that Freud had become quite bombastic with Tito. After one hour, he said: "Am I ever going to hear this blasted story or are you just going to continually waffle on abut it..." to which Tito had replied: "If the finer detail was not important, I wouldn't be telling you all about it, would I?". Freud despaired of it, and Tito continued plodding over his words just as before, quite unaffected by his friend's apparent and obvious state of boredom and ever-increasing lack of disinterest.

And of you, the reader, I am certain that you are here with me now, surely you are equally frustrated by such unnecessary overuse of text, but I assure you it does have important significance. The story finally began.

There was a knock on the door; it was exactly the stroke of midnight; the clock had just announced to the second the arrival of Christmas Day. It was a cold frosty night, but they had eaten well and with the warm glow of the firelight flickering out across the room, they did not feel cold at all. He thanked his lucky stars for his fortunate life as he walked to answer. "Who could it be at such a late hour" - he thought. It was not a night that one wanted at all to be without warmth, sleeping on the streets amongst the many homeless peasants of Vienna's slums. "It must be the poor" - he concluded, "They've come to ask for food again and food they shall eat" – he decided. He was a good honorable man and, that was important to note insisted Tito.

As he'd risen from the comfort of his armchair, he had put down his book: "A Christmas Carol" by Charles Dickens, a work that many in middle-class circles had read since the first publication in 1843. He was utterly bewildered by Ebenezer Scrooge's absolute meanness and lack of humanity to those of lesser social strata placed unkindly below him. Upon opening the door, he found no-one. He looked round about, left to right and up and down. He found only a snail on the doormat to his feet. Without thinking, he gave the snail a swift though gentle kick with the tip of his slipper, and off into the night's air it flew - far away out of site.

"I'm a farmer's boy you know", said Tito. "From a peasant family in Croatia, Kumrovec actually. I was born in 1892. My father was an alcoholic; he borrowed so much money from the banks that he used to send me to negotiate with his creditors, so they wouldn't take our land. I think he thought they would take pity on me, a child and..."

"And this has got what to do with the story?" – asked Freud.

"Nothing really", replied Tito: "Only to say that I've had a really hard life and thought you might show some interest in my own story first – the banker's used to ridicule and mock me. I always wanted to be so much more than I am today. When I was child, I dreamed of being a waiter, or a tailor – running away to the USA, or something grand like that".

"Then why didn't you" asked Freud: "Life is what you make of it you know".

"Actually, I don't agree with you on that point, Sigmund, my father spent the family's travel money on booze, broke our hearts at the time. Promised us a new life overseas and then drank our hopes and dreams into oblivion: mother's particularly. She was a good hard-working farmer's wife but... well, fate had its way, I guess".

The door sprung open and in walked the three gentlemen with a spring in the heel as expected but somewhat late. *"Thank God"*, cried Freud. *"Forget the revolution today, just save me from this never ending story first please gentlemen?"* Though after Freud had said this he did chuckle somewhat. He wasn't really desperate but just, kind of desperate, I think.

"Well don't let us interrupt you", Trotsky said - and after some friendly banter, both Hitler and Stalin too seemed keen to know what the story was all about.

Just as Freud stated to utter the sentence: *"I fear we will never find out sirs, the snail got kicked and that was it so far"*- Tito seized the moment to recap on the entire event from beginning too thus far. In his journal Freud notes that this is the period of his life in which he felt had prompted his first hair loss. Noting: *"For a man of such charisma and personality, he can at times be utterly boring. Women seem to flock to him; he's informed me of a string of young fillies... and his reputation for virility and affairs is well established amongst the coffeehouses. What on earth do they see in him? I just wanted to pull my own hair out by the roots at the end of it all".*

The story, again after much delay, now regained direction and pace. Tito explained that after the man had kicked the snail, everything had gone downhill from there. As he'd gone to answer the door his wife had fallen asleep with her book, knocking over a candle in the process. The chair had ignited, and after failed attempts to dowse the flames, having first awoken the children – his home had been raised to the ground by fire.

"That's awful", said Trotsky. *"I know"*, replied Tito, adding: *"But it all gets much worse I assure you"*. Tito then explained that he had been born the seventh of fourteen siblings, and, that he was lucky to reach the age he is today, that being 21 years old. Only six of his siblings had lived into adulthood. And then equally randomly he started talking about how A Christmas Tale had at first been published by Chapman & Hall of London in 1843.

This time it was Stalin who managed to get Tito to return and re-engage with the story.

"So, he kicked the snail having answered the door thinking it was the poor and then the house burns down and what? Tito accordingly continued the story at Stalin's request.

After Christmas, the following year they had found themselves in the poor house. The man had gone from riches to rags within an instant, but they weren't yet aware of it. It seemed that every month thereafter a new horror would befall him. His life was now in ruins, a complete and total disaster.

"So, what happened next then?" - Stalin asked. The relationship between the two was an uneasy alliance but overall, Stalin liked young Tito and would often refer to him as a good man. He was most interested in hearing more.

Following the fire, the house next door had caught, it too being gutted along with several other adjoining apartments and tenements. The engineer had been forced to sell his business to settle multiple compensation claims. Left without home or company, the family then took up temporary rented accommodation. Though he had secured work in a local factory for himself and was in the process of obtaining a loan to start afresh. It would be a smaller, more modest affair, but in remaining creditworthy he realised that he would soon be back on his feet again.

"Do you know why I wanted to be a tailor or even a waiter when I was a child" - Tito asked the group. Hitler and Trotsky were by now laughing their heads off at the random remark, yet again, mid-flow, and in witnessing Freud's utter despair with him, made the laughter even greater. And of course, Stalin couldn't see what was funny at all, as cold as ever, impatiently waiting on the next installment of the story.

"What the..." bellowed Stalin: as Tito had then explained that he'd always wanted to wear nice clothes. It appeared to him that waiters of the day had the best cut cloth. If he couldn't be a waiter then as a tailor, he would at least then learn how to make his own bespoke fits instead, and that was the reason.

Eventually calm returns and so does the story. Later, during January, having borrowed cash up to the hilt, he lost his job. And in losing his job, he could not only pay his rent but also his children's school fees. The bank foreclosed on his loans, and, now quite unworthy of credit, he relied on the generosity of friends. *"So, you would think that things couldn't get any worse wouldn't you"*, Tito said, *"But I assure you they did"*.

Hitler recapped: *"So in December after he had kicked the snail his house burnt down, and then in January he lost his company to bankruptcy, followed by homelessness in February – is that correct?"* he asked. *"Not quite that bad yet"*, stated Tito, *"His best friend became a guarantor for the families rent, so jobless yes, but homeless no"*. Tito divulged.

"Thank God for that" - added Freud". *"It's a terrible story: I do hope he finds some happiness at the end of it... for I fear you will upset my delicate sensitivities if I hear much more of this sorrow and sufferings"*.

"You see, capitalism is the enemy of us all, we are all victims of a brutal system"- Tito said, and again, returning to his random thought and output. *"That's why I was trying to tell this man of the words of Marx the day we met. The system plays us all off against each other, we are not enemies and it's all too simplistic to say that the bourgeoisie are our enemy... they can suffer terribly too"*.

"Absolutely," interrupted Trotsky: *"After all, had he not gone to the door to feed the poor none of this would have happened"*. And as Trotsky then finished speaking Stalin concluded: *"I'm not so convinced that it was a misguided attempt to help other less fortunates that led to this unfortunate set of circumstance, personally, I think the snail had something to do with"*.

"Are you suggesting that the snail possessed evil, Stalin?" - asked Freud.

"Do you not think it possible Freud? He was problem free until he kicked it. Keep your friendly snails close and your enemy snails even closer, that's what I would have suggested to him". The men soon realised that this was one of Stalin's poor attempts at humour, though they all laughed out of an acknowledged politeness.

"I used to have a beautifully cut suit, once upon a time, before I arrived in Vienna that was. I bought it in Prague". Tito rambled. *"I was forced out of desperation to bed down for the night in a cattle shed, woke up the next day to find a cow had eaten it, well, most of it - at any rate"*.

"Tito! Seriously! Can't you just stay focused for a moment – what happened next, we're in March now; yes?" Trotsky demanded to know, he was by now as frustrated as Freud with this endless tiring story which appeared absent of the necessary and much needed conclusion. Freud noticed that only Hitler and Stalin remained patient with Tito's offering and put this down to the fact that they had never showed any interest in anybody else but themselves previously so why would they change today, though observed that they too were now changing. Stalin wanted to know everything. Hitler, however, by now, was doodling with charcoal on a linen place mat.

"Actually gentlemen, I owe all that I know today, my entire education that is, to the Communist Party" - Tito said: before eventually getting around to March.

March had been appalling too. The man having now borrowed extensively from the friend who had become the willing guarantor of the families rent tuned out to be not so much of a friend after all. He had taken liberties with his wife.

"You mean he was, shall we politely say, taking personal liberties of the flesh in romantic ways with his friend's wife?" enquired a confused Stalin.

"That's exactly what I am saying", Tito replied, *"And in April, he had not only moved into the apartment with her but was now suing his former friend for the sums outstanding".*

Freud was sickened to the core by this latest revelation, he demanded to know what happened next. Tito continued to elaborate. *"Well, of course, he couldn't pay it back Freud, the borrowed money that is, and in May he found himself incarcerated in a debtor's prison".*

The room fell silent as not one of the sugar lump club could find any words of further expression that could possibly be used to express their utter shock and dismay at this poor man's suffering. Tito, keen to break the silence and lift the heavy depressing atmosphere, then continued. Unsurprisingly, nothing to do with the story, but an exchange of dialogue with young Hitler, sat opposite, and concerning the men's joint love and appreciation of dogs!

"Hunting, fishing and horse-riding, that's the life I hope for Adolf, walking with my dogs in the countryside - and most of all I'd like to do this whilst living on an island". Tito informed.

"Yes, dogs, it's the German shepherd breed for me on that score, not so keen on the hunting though, trying to reduce my meat intake. Not so good for the body these days". Hitler replied. *"I'm more of a mountains man personally, but I agree, living on an island does appeal to the senses somewhat. I like to call my dog Blondie; I knew a girl called Blondie once – quite the dog herself".*

Stalin and Trotsky then shouted-out in perfect unison: *"June! What happened in June man? – For Christ's sake Josip Broz!"* Interrupting, and using Tito's formal birth name as a means of asserting some greater authority over him as a teacher would assert over one's unruly pupil.

"I was trying to avoid June gentlemen. Terrible, absolutely terrible. Obviously, the new love affair didn't work out – how could it? I mean, you can't build happiness on someone else's unhappiness, can you? It haunted the new relationship – the debtor's prison that is".

Tito continued: *So, he left her after just a handful of weeks, and she, the ex that is, well – took to the oldest profession in the world: sadly".*

It was Freud who interrupted the story's flow this time - saying: *"It's a symptom of arrested-development, it signals that the individual is quite unable to integrate inner conflicts. It's all about low self-esteem, her overall view of life's value and of course a good dose of poor self-esteem. If I were to treat such a wretched woman as this for the condition of prostitution, I would at first seek to resolve internal and external conflicts – focusing on her childhood relationships, that to her parents".*

"Don't need to worry about all that now, Freud", Tito exclaimed. *"She's dead!* And then continued to explain to the exasperated gathering silent before him - that: *"Concerning the milk, sugar and coffee debate yesterday, I believe that economic self- sufficiency is what a nation requires most, any dominant member of an Empire will always seek to make its lessor member's contribute more of the fair share to the greater nation among them, that seems logical, doesn't it? Yes, terror as a weapon must end, we all need to find a new way, a different kind of approach – what do you think Stalin?"*

"Dead! – What do you mean Dead? Stalin's dismissive retort.

"Dead, yes, quite dead I'm afraid. Tito revealed as he explained the circumstance of such as: *"Yes, in June her neck was broken – she'd gone to visit her husband in debtor's prison and..."*

"And? – and what? Freud insisted on knowing more, ever infuriated by yet another quite unnecessary aside pause in the dialogue between them.

"And? – well and indeed, he'd lost everything now, hadn't he?" Tito started to publicly evaluate the poor man's life. *"And the family's name and honour were a step too far for him. Even from within the pitiful conditions he found himself incarcerated in, his reputation would save him, upon settling his later debts, well at least he had hope of a fresh start. But now – who would touch him? All hope had been taken away from him by his wife's treacherous act. He lunged forward; arms stretched out from the void of his cell bars and snapped her neck!" Such was his rage, instantly it was, dead, yes, there was no doubt about that".*

Tito then informed that as a result of this heinous violent act, June had been the month in which he was sentenced to death by hanging.

"It's the snail" – snarled Hitler. "You can't trust them! – They move around with their homes on their backs, like a horse and cart, transients, gypsies all of them!" Hitler became ever more increasingly obsessed with his snail theory. "He needs to find that snail and deal with it! That's what I'd do".

Stalin, not quite convinced if Hitler was joking or not, used his previous phrase with perfect comedic timing: "So, we're back to milk, sugar and coffee again then are we Hitler? "One snail one problem, no snail no problem!" – Even Freud found time to laugh uncontrollably at the refined comment, now presented in a humorous fashion, one that had caused some degree of reflection and concern to him previously.

Freud added: "An apology is needed I feel, after all, if all this stated as a result of a mere flick of the toe, one dreads to think what would have happened to this poor blighter had he chosen to stamp on it instead. I'd apologise, that's what I'd do – sorry snail!" He concluded.

"Can this desperate man's plight get any worse, Tito?" - Trotsky asked: "Surely not, please say no!" - And without further ado Tito continued to deliver his sad narrative. "Yes, - it now worsens for him. His circumstances do not improve, for in July he was told that his children, desperately poor, unwashed, unfed and unclothed, now on the street and uneducated among the squalor of the city - they were sent to the workhouse by the old back-stabbing friend. His interests were in the loins of the fairer sex, not of the children. He wiped his hands of it all".

Hitler continued to insist on a snail conspiracy. Becoming more and more convinced of a cult of insects who worked covertly to undermine the wealth of the state. Freud on the other hand had spoken in depth about madness, testifying that certain conditions had provoked this man to violent act, and as such, insanity surely made him do it – he could not surely be held accountable for his actions and be executed at the end of a long rope atop of a very big drop.

"You've hit the snail on the head there, Sigmund old chap". Tito joked as he explained the nail to snail pun was merely a "Freudian slip" – Again explaining the slip / sip part - due to their presence in the coffeehouse.

"Jokes don't work if you have to explain them, surely you know this Tito": Trotsky informed and concluded: "Anyway - do you really think that this venture is appropriate a time for joking?"

"You're right, Trotsky, it's all very sad isn't. I'll resist and do apologise - now, where were we..."

"It's August now I believe" – said Freud.

"Ah, yes, August. Well in August..." and then he suddenly stopped and started to tap his fingers upon the tabletop. "I love playing the piano", he informed: "Just freeing up my joints a little if you don't mind gentlemen. Too much typing last night I fear, never leave Croatia without my typewriter: never know when one will need it next to knock up a one sheet for the revolution..." he ended. He was keen to ease his joints and later explained that he was meeting a friend across town where the two would play a piano duet together, later that day.

"If you don't get to August soon, I'll have you shot in the bloody street in front of your damned typewriter" – Stalin yelled!

"Shot Stalin? – shot? That's not very democratic of you, is it? You're starting to sound like a fascist. That's the problem with the nationalist mindset – they don't see the need for alternate opinion - But then again, I suppose there is no need for a multi-party democratic platformed state as the Communist Party represents all the workers, doesn't it?" Though: after saying this Tito did impart further on the key facts concerning August.

"The whole trial had been based on the notion of his insanity, you are correct Freud, and he had suffered a total catastrophic collapse of the mind. And Adolf, you too are correct to some degree as much discussion concerning the 'apparent curse of the snail' was put forward to the judge by the man's defense team" Tito explained.

"So, some good news at last then Tito" – said Trotsky. "He didn't get hung after all".

Freud interjected: "Actually, it's hanged, Trotsky and, well it's bloody obvious to me that he didn't get strung up – had he been so he would never have lived to tell Tito his tale – would he?"

"I'd missed that point completely, went straight over the top of my head" – uttered Stalin. "Yes, so it must finally be good news then, Tito?

"Not exactly good news" - Tito continued. "He still had no money; his defense team consisted of his brother; he was a local book shop owner. A clever man yes, but no experience of the legal system, especially the defense skills needed to defend a man from the crack of the noose. The insane defense all backfired, hoping to be freed he was not, and found that in August he was sent to the asylum – for life!"

Tito then drifted off topic again: "Live and let live I say, I'm not above a deal with the devil – What do you think about freedom of the press gentlemen? And of free movement too? – I'm all in favour myself... should war break-out I'd like to see an independent Yugoslavia free of its ethnic conflicts. I understand the nationalist debate but once it starts it cannot be stopped, can it? Where does all that division end?"

"*September Tito – September – please! Can we finish the blasted story!*" - Stalin again snarled. And interestingly: Freud's journal later noted that the story had in fact taken over three hours to deliver - at this point of the dialogue! A frustration that I sense that you too, as readers, - now share in.

"*I was going to say that we make our own history, and I wanted to discuss the need to overthrow the monarchy, but given such tense mood of yours Stalin, I will hurry, just for you!*" Tito had become aware of the lack of patience now with him and decided that if the story was ever going to be finally concluded - time was now of the essence.

September arrived and Tito informed how the man had found out that his oldest son had died of consumption whilst in the workhouse that month. October informed him that his second youngest, also a son, was also now critically inflicted with that same dreadful, fatal condition.

And in November, the poor helpless fellow now confined for life through his insanity, heard a devastating rumour passed on to him from his brother. "*It was a credible one*", his brother had told him during a brief fleeting visit to the asylum. That is, his youngest, his only daughter, a precious beautiful young girl, was to be sold as an apprentice to Mrs. Viene, a notorious brothel owner, who, without any doubt was left of her fragile mind, and had notorious intent for her. Mrs. Viene would often recruit from the workhouse by means of a subtle backhander that settled the outstanding financial accounts of her purchase's siblings, and also, paid for silence of the worker's.

The room was silent, all of the men and, after quite a degree of pause reached for the coffee jug simultaneously. None had any idea of what to say – it was certainly the worst and most tragic story that they had ever heard. Pouring coffee would at the very least break, they collectively assumed without a single word, Tito's attention of them. What was there to say but, nothing. They were all crushed by this bitter revelation and the cruelty of life's blow inflicted upon this poor unknown man. "*Gentlemen, I see that you are quite distressed, do you wish me to continue into December or shall we call it a day there?* - Tito said as a means to merely break the uncomfortable silence and savage tale.

"*In all honesty, I'm not sure I can hear any more*" - Trotsky, almost whispering had said: "*I have nothing to say other than that*". He looked down into his coffee cup and blessed the life he had led so far. Stirring his coffee around and around in contemplation.

"*I have not witnessed such tragedy and distress since 1905, when the Cossacks stormed the lines of demonstrators and butchered the people with swords*" – added Stalin.

"*I'm not sure that Mrs. Viene is such a bad person*" – noted Hitler, "*After all, the girl would now be saved from the fate of consumption, wouldn't she?"* His views on women as mere procreators, and his need born of local reputation for frequent paid comfort of the younger girl, surely impacting on his inappropriate, misguided, caught off-guard words.

Freud summed up: *"I fear what we hear for December will be the worst revelation of all, and I'm not sure that I have now the psychological stamina or personal resilience necessary to absorb the full impact of it but, I sense that you will impart that it is the brother who told you of this tragic story – after all is said, how would you have come to know of it? Yes - the brother tells you, doesn't he?* Said Freud. *"And this poor desperate fellow is himself found deceased, perhaps he found some peace in the end and..."*

Tito interrupted Freud at this point. Speaking in a newly found, kind softened tone, as if reading a bedtime fairy story to a child, a manner of which to ease the men's discomfort as he now finished the tragic story off. Finally putting to sleep a most grotesque tale of human suffering, throwing it to the past where it now belonged.

"Do not try to over-analyse the outcome my friend. I will explain". He said. "Yes, the brother did become involved, but he was not the one who told me the tale. For in December the brother hatched a plan to break his kin out from the confines of the asylum. He had raised enough money from his new book sales, about the story itself, to slip the guards just enough to provide freedom and silence. In December his brother was free, but on the run, homeless and hungry. *'If only I could return to the old family home and just collect enough to sell – I could pay for the treatment of my son, and for the return of daughter'* – The escaping man had said to his brother. *'We could flee together, abroad, a new start".* He knew the risk of being caught was considerable for he would soon be recognised amongst the neighborhood of his former street and abode, and thus returned to the asylum with short swift - but what was his freedom worth, its true value beyond the happiness of family?" - Tito then paused to sip slowly from his coffee cup.

"I need to know" - demanded Freud. "Is it a happy ending? Does he succeed? Does he get caught? Tell me Tito – tell us all, please? – And accordingly, Tito obliged the men further. He explained that he had waited for the cover of darkness before creeping away from the protection and security of his brother's bookshop where he had hidden in the cellar below. The entrance to which and steps down below were hidden from public view by an old wooden bookcase pushed across. The brother had collected the worst of all unsellable literature he possessed and placed it upon the shelves knowing that customers would now not bother to pay attention or scrutiny to it. It was true to say that his hide-way would never have been found. Though: against his brother's advice, he felt he could not remain there.

"He arrived at his former home late in the evening, about 11.30 pm, it was on the following Christmas Eve. A year to the day that all of this tragedy had started. He thought about the previous year's encounter with the snail as he brushed aside the ash from the fire that had raised most of the house to the ground. He dug though the filth and debris looking for anything he could sell. But all was gone, what hadn't been destroyed by fire had by now been looted: there was nothing of value to be found" – Tito informed them all as they silently awaited the final outcome, and as the perfect storyteller he continued to narrate to his audience.

"He sat down in the earth, sobbing, a broken man – he took a glance at the pocket watch his brother had lent him. It was almost midnight – within seconds it would be Christmas Day. He thought back to the days of his former life and happiness, but he could not find any joy now. At the very pinnacle of human anguish and of despair he..."

"He what?" - Demanded Hitler – *"He killed himself, didn't he? That's what I'd have done!"* Hitler had interrupted again, most inappropriately, and as if lacking in the very basics of human compassion.

"No!" – returned Tito. *"He was indeed contemplating such an act but was broken from his moment of despair by a strange feeling that suddenly came over him. Somehow unable to end his own sad bitter life, he had felt an overwhelming sense of purpose born in his suffering. That he must live to spend his entire life of his sufferings, for his sins, for kicking the snail you see, that's what he thought. An act that had doomed him to his pathetic, lonely existence. Yes: he became redemptive and sorrowful for what he had done the former year – he knelt down upon his knees and began to pray for the very first time in his life".*

"Oh yeah, that's right, God'll save him – what God?" - Trotsky declared. It was Freud's interpretation that this aesthetic remark was directed at Stalin, who had of course, trained previously as a Priest. The God issue was always a problem between the two men and Trotsky would often dig at Stalin's vulnerability on this point. Whilst Stalin pretended to non-believe these days, for the party's benefit, he would often creep off to attend a secret but obviously not so secret - religious mass.

Tito summed up what had happened next by saying that at exactly midnight, 12 months to the day, 12 months to the precise very second, and as his watch struck exactly the stroke of midnight as Christmas Day arrived: he heard a knock at his burnt and off the hinge, front door.

"And" – asked Freud.
"And" – asked Trotsky.
"And" – asked Stalin.

"And" – asked Hitler: all in turn and one by one, raising their heads high, above, and moving upper bodies forward, closer into the centre of the table toward Tito, as if a set of nodding dogs on a car windows back parcel shelf.

"And?" – Replied Tito to his now most attentive cohort: *"Well: he had assumed his presence had been discovered. He gave in, emotionally, psychologically, he answered the door expecting to be arrested and returned to dire conditions of the asylum, locked away for the rest of his life. Suffering for his sins as he had now resolved himself to do – but there was no-one there, not a person or cat or fox in sight, the streets were completely deserted. He looked down and there it was: he saw the snail!"*

<u>That very same snail</u> had returned exactly a year to the day - at midnight of Christmas Eve, to the very second. The man looked down at the little helpless creature. The snail raised its head, and in extending its fragile eyes at the end of its tender tentacles upward and outward toward him: and in a soft pathetic, squeaky little voice, which was not one as expected of great prophetical revelation – it said: *"What did you do that for?"*

Of all those present, Sigmund Freud would later write: *"It was the man we would come to know as Marshal Josip Broz Tito who revealed himself to be the master manipulator"*.

:

Workers of All Lands Unite

By all accounts, Hitler had believed Tito's story to be one of good versus evil. He had fixated on the idea that a dark force of satanic elements was in control. For him, the story was no more than a fable in which a very sinister warning was present. Stalin, on the other hand, saw the tale as more straightforward. *"He should have stamped on the cursed thing the first time he saw it"* – he had remarked.

Indeed, the two discussed at length the need to eradicate the snail to prevent the subsequent anguish and suffering of this poor fellow. Hitler was not contented. *"How would you know if that was the only one?"* - he had asked. Concluding: *"You'd have to stamp on them all, surely?"* – *"No! I don't believe so"*, Stalin had replied. *"An example of might is all that would be required to send a very clear warning to any would be terrestrial pulmonated gastropod molluscs agitator! – Stamp on one and you'll soon find that you've already stamped on them all"* he added.

For Trotsky the story was testament of the absence of God. *"Religion, you see gentlemen, the opium of the working class – they turn to God in the hope that their poor sad existence will somehow miraculously become better: but we all know it won't."* He had continued: *"See: he turned to God in his hour of greatest need and God sent a snail..."*

Tito had interjected by saying. *"Actually Trotsky, that's a bit of a misquote. I think you'll find what Marx really said was; religion is the sigh of the oppressed creature, the heart of a heartless world, and the soul of soulless conditions. It is the opium of the people"* - he concluded that Trotsky's' rendition was, if not a misquoted interpretation of the original metaphor, then, it was delightfully simplified beyond original context to such a degree that it was pure sophistry. The common expression we know today was probably attributed to an overzealous Trotsky, as ever, keen to dismiss the notion of a God, that God would save humanity. No – for Trotsky it was socialism that would prevail as the savior of humankind.

Freud also noted in his journal that, he had said that day, and in no doubt an attempt to demonstrate his linguistic superiority over the others, that the quote itself was founded in - *"Die Religion ist das Opium des Volkes" of the 1844 work: A Contribution to the Critique of Hegel's Philosophy of Right"*.

To which Tito had merely replied – *"It was a joke gentlemen..."*

"A joke? But it's not funny" – added Hitler.

"Yeah, I agree" thus contributed Stalin – *"That's about as funny as Adolf's Oedipus complex..."*

"What Oedipus complex" – A startled Hitler had demanded to know.

"Yours" – blurted out Stalin.

In a fit of laughter, Trotsky had apparently said in between his bouts of uncontrolled giggling, and in response to Stalin's tenacity, said – *"I think he's referring to your mother obsession..."* Stalin turned to Freud at this moment and issued a cheeky wink across the table; just to let the intellectual amongst them know that he, Stalin, had done his homework. Stalin would always keep one eye on the ball and one on the referee, just to let you know that he knew more about others than they at first believed. He would not play the game without first having learnt his opponent's rules.

"What mother obsession?" – Hitler responded to all present at the table, before then turning to Freud and asked: *"Sigmund - What's an Oedipus complex? Anyway..."*

We do not know if the young Hitler had taken up Freud's invitation that day, but we do know that the offer was made, for, in his journal Freud had commented: *"The young artist demonstrates all classic symptoms of Oedipal within psychosexual stages of development. He clearly desires his mother and denigrates his father. One senses within our conversations that the child Adolf competed with his paternal role-model for possession of the matriarch, this same-sex parent is a rival to mother's attentions and affection. A theory that I closely examined in my 1899 thesis: The Interpretation of Dreams - though I did not coin the phrase Oedipus until 1910. This young man formulates perfect research material. Asked that day what an Oedipus complex was, I could do little more than offer a more private discussion... In addressing the question that day, in avoiding bitter confrontation between the two men, I merely suggested that Stalin was making folly of Adolf's continuing need to write to a young woman by the name of Geli Raubal, a half-niece. I did not impart that I observed certain sexual attraction to his opposite sex parent and the hostility noted toward the same-sex parent, which has, I believe, manifested into frustrated and inappropriate sexual fantasy toward this younger near-sibling".*

We can only conclude that Hitler did not partake of any therapy sessions under Freud's directions, for had this been the case, evidence of it would certainly have been discovered in the journal. We are left only with this brief paragraph as a record of the discussion of the Coffeehouse that day. Much more of Freud's journal as found is dedicated to the wider discussion that preceded, and this concerned the work of Karl Marx.

Tito had explained that according to Marx, the capitalists exploit the labour force by taking advantage of the difference between the labour market and whatever the system can produce for sale in that market. All successful industry followed the simple equation of surplus value: *"Input unit-costs are lower than output unit-prices and the creation of surplus labour is the difference between the costs of keeping workers alive against the costs of what they can produce"* – he had concluded.

"Yes, indeed, you understand correctly," a supportive Stalin had added, noting: *"Marx believed that capitalists are vampires sucking the worker's blood".*

Trotsky eagerly contributed: *"But Marx says that the creation of profit is no means an injustice – he held a dual view of capitalism, and capitalists simply cannot go against the system".* To which Freud added: *"Yes, it is surely not property and equipment that define capital, but the relationship between worker and owner".* Hitler described this relationship as a *"Cancerous cell"* adding - *"It is a problem of the economic system in general, I believe".*

The men discussed how Marx had described capitalism as unstable – a system undoubtedly prone to periodic crisis in which only the workers would truly suffer. With investment in new technologies a reduction in the labour force would follow. This surplus value and corporate profit would fall as economies grow. A system of growth followed by collapse, more growth and further collapse, and so on, would lead to ever increasing economic severity. Ultimately, as the workers did not own their means of production, only the capitalist class would become enriched and empowered.

"The workers were better off under Feudalism" – Trotsky remarked. *"Under capitalism they are destined to remain impoverished".* Tito elaborated: *"Yes, I think they were Leon, they were poor but free, they had land and food a plenty. Pre-industrial Agrarian societies simply complied to the land-owners quota, once done by the end of the week, at least they could work and rest at their own leisure, but now they live ten to a room in filth and squalor, working sixty-hours per week, for what? An ever-increasing reduced mortality rate and countless deaths and injuries.*

"Indeed", noted Stalin, *"The Communist Manifesto has much to offer the proletariat, but it is only a diagnosis and not the cure".* – *"Yes! Stalin!* Trotsky immediately shouted out in publicly administering his loyal support to the cause: *"As if a doctor were to identify the illness without prescribing a cure"* - he said.

"So, you think that the feudal foundation stones of the past that the bourgeoisie class built itself in developing today's capital will endanger the existence of bourgeois property today, Trotsky?" – Freud inquired.

"Yes, I believe so, no-one is better placed to understand this phenomenon than the Russian, is that not true?" – He replied to Freud. *"The means of production and of exchange and of the conditions under which feudal society produced and exchanged are no longer compatible with today's developed capitalist productivity.*

The Manifesto offers us all a social and political constitution adapted from it, the means of production have become too powerful, and they are now at the workers' disposal.

"All we need to do is take control, Freud", added Stalin. "Bourgeois society may believe that the system brings order into the whole, but 1905 disproved that didn't it? They may execute us, imprison us or exile us, but their greed has produced the perfect conditions for their own downfall – and that is one of workers revolution".

"But the revolution of 1905 failed Stalin, you are in exile, I guess that makes you one of the lucky ones, doesn't it?" - Freud enquired.

"We must teach the proletariat how to hate, to educate the masses and show them who their oppressor is. Yes, to beat your enemy you must first teach others how to hate their enemy. Prison makes the ideal school of crime for the criminal, just as it does the revolutionary; the sheer number of political prisoners ensures only that the 'lesser' learns from the 'greater' - both directly and indirectly!" - Stalin had answered before continuing with: "A prison inmate that enters only with a basic knowledge of Marx and Lenin soon finds he will leave with an extensive one, should he first survive the ordeal of course. What else is there to do all day but to educate oneself in communist philosophy? – The more they brutalise us the more we revel in their downfall", - he concluded.

Tito elaborated: "*Propaganda is smuggled in Freud, and shared by the more knowledgeable amongst the faithful, it is then distributed by horse or mouse*".

"*I don't follow your meaning*", Freud said as he questioned Tito further – "*By horse or mouse, what do you mean?*" He asked. Tito eagerly explained: "*A horse is a small cloth sack or sock tide with string, easily swung from adjacent cell to cell, the mouse is a small stick, a split to one end where pages can easily be inserted and passed at reach through cell bars opposite with equal efficiency. There is the kite too, because of its triangular shape, a piece of paper folded so small it can be easily passed hand to hand, or mouth to mouth if visits are afforded – they may think they are breaking us but in reality, they have sent us to the greatest university of all*".

Leon Trotsky summed up: "*Whilst the rich live in palatial opulence and abundant luxury and the poor live on the streets like rats of an infested sewer, they serve only to radicalise us: even the minor criminal has the capacity to become a great communist leader*" - he said before concluding with: "*Marx believed that the industrial workers would rise up, and this would be an internationalist global uprising, around the whole world. The structural contradictions of capitalism will necessitate its end, from this post-capitalistic era will be born socialism within a truly equal communist utopia*".

Stalin then interjected: "The *bourgeoisie are their own gravediggers, the fall of capitalism and the creation of squalid urbanisation will lead to the victory of the workers – this is inevitable! 1905 was not a failure, Sigmund, but merely the beginning of a new mass consciousness. It is the awakening!"

Tito joined in: "*Communism is now a real movement; we will abolish the exploiting classes and deal with the present state of things. The workers of all lands will unite, of this I am sure, we need but one nation to collapse, to implode upon itself and the rest of the world's great empires will then all fall thereafter, like dominoes*".

Upon a momentary pause, Freud then turned to Hitler, addressing him directly with the following words: "*Marx argued in his paper: The German Ideology of 1846 - that capitalism will end, this is true gentlemen but, where will that end begin? We have not seen it of the workers of the British Empire as he first penned it to be, but of Germany, he said he was uncloaking these sheep, who take themselves and are taken for wolves; of showing how their bleating merely imitates in a philosophic form the conceptions of the German middle class; how the boasting of these philosophic commentators only mirrors the wretchedness of the real conditions in Germany – I wonder Hitler, is this new democratic society Marx predicts, enfranchising an entire population, to be born of Germany first?*".

Hitler replied. "*I don't see that as plausible Freud, no, the conditions for revolution may be ripe, yes, German workers surely want to end their self-alienation and be free to act without bondage to the labour market, but the notion of all united workers is surely a false premise.*

"*Why do say that Hitler*" - Freud probed further. "*United by what? Look at the world's greatest economy shall we, the United States of America, born of colonial wars of occupation and then a war of independence, and then after that a civil war. Where today the colonialist working classes live in relative comfort whilst the Negroes as slaves sow the seeds and harvest the crops in absolute poverty: and yet today its output per capita is the world's highest. It didn't need socialism to make it a flourishing, economically advanced country did it... Are you advocating slavery Adolf?*, asked Freud.

"*No Freud, but the whole idea that workers are only separated by the shackles of their labour is utter nonsense. What I'm saying is that whilst Marx may argue that all men are equal, clearly in America they are not. Some are more equal than others: and it works does it not? Has ever before so much prosperity been attained by such a comparably large population?*", Hitler concluded.

Freud was about to reply to Hitler when Stalin rudely interrupted. "*I think you're being really naïve Adolf; you clearly know nothing of the desperate plight of the average American worker not to mention a nation that builds its wealth on slavery and child labour, the greed and excess of the American capitalist is boundless".

"I didn't say it was perfect, I'm just using it for example" - Hitler replied to Stalin before continuing to elaborate on his point. "Here you have a United States but no central bank or federal tax system and..."

It was Freud who interrupted this time by commenting – "Yes, that is correct, but there are moves I understand to change this later this year". - "Whatever" – acknowledged Hitler: "But we're talking about America now, today, as it stands, the wealthiest nation in the world. And should war break out tomorrow who do you suppose they would support – their trading allies, that would be the single foremost decision. Worker will gun down worker on the battlefield to protect their nation's wealth, to fight alongside their so-called capitalists, side-by-side, not the workers of other nations. What I am saying gentlemen is that the needs of the nation will come before the needs of the worker – there is no international untied workers struggle, only..."

"So, you're saying that American workers will turn on, say, German workers, or German workers will turn on Russian workers, or Russian workers will turn on the French or British worker to protect the wealth of the Tzars and ruling elite, the bourgeois who all treat them like filth before they will fight for the rights of each other?" - Asked Freud.

"Yes gentlemen, that is exactly what I am saying. And America is the best example of this. A country where the Jews continually condemn us, the Europeans, as anti-Semitic but condone their own racism. A country where the Negros cannot attend a white school, or travel on a white bus, walk on the same side of the road or eat in the same restaurant as the white – where the act of romance between the two races result in the lynching only of the black man!"

Hitler had started to become ever increasingly gripped by anger – and it was evidently he who was now thumping the table as he addressed his attentive cohort, and it was Trotsky who now again challenged the young naïve artist's disparity of the socialist cause.

"Hitler, you don't understand anything of Marx, do you?" - He said in a most sarcastic patronising tone, as if to belittle his words, and continued: "Marx understands this point, that the proletariat is ignorant, that's why we as the intellectual Marxists must educate them, to give them the knowledge the elite deny them so that they may break their bonds, that they will identify their common oppressor, a common cause that unites them all and..."

"And nothing" - Hitler interrupted. "You're living a pipe dream, and you are the one who seeks to patronise me? War, yes war, that inevitable war we all talk of, if this war broke out tomorrow what would it be over? The Workers' rights? No – ridiculous! It will be based on ethnic divisions and not the division of labour, and no doubt it will be the Slavs who..."

"Slavs Hitler? – asked Tito. "What of the Slavs?" - he demanded to know of him. Hitler had paused on the word 'who' and now sipped in silent defiance from his coffee, before replying after some degree of pause.

"Yes, the Slavs Tito. Isn't it Serbia who seeks independence from the Austro-Hungarian Empire? Isn't in Serbia who will bring the Empire to war? You want Slavic independence based on ethnic lines before socialism - isn't that the fact of the matter?"

"No!" - replied Tito most adamantly: "I want to see the end of the Empire, yes, but I want to see the creation of a socialist union, not an ethnic Slavic elite. You are wrong!"

"Wrong, Tito? What do you think will happen if Serbia declares independence? War, that's what! And you seriously believe that the workers of this great Empire of ours will unite behind you? No – Germany will align itself with Austria as Germans and it will be a war between the workers, they will run to fight without question because it is not an attack on a nation but an act of war against all non-Slavs – an attack on the both the proletariat and the Tsars – and they will all fight happily together, and not for your new socialist utopia!"

Freud interjected: "So what of the Jews then Hitler? Will they fight the Slavs too?"

"You're asking the wrong question Freud; the question should be not with whom will they fight or whom they will fight against - but for what they will fight for?" – Hitler replied.

"They would fight for their nation, undoubtedly, they would unite against the common aggressor regardless of ethnic or religious difference, of course they would, should war break out Austrian, German or Jew would fight in the same trenches – this is certain". Freud asserted.

"And there it is again Freud, Jew, not German? Isn't the whole purpose of the Zionist mindset to establish an independent Jewish state based on a perceived racial dominance, built on a superiority of others?" Hitler asked.

"Utter nonsense" Freud replied forcefully: "You surely don't subscribe to that garbage, I don't want to live in a Jewish homeland any more than you want to live in a Christian homeland and, regardless, if you have not discovered Judaism within your own family tree – then I'm afraid, Adolf, you simply haven't gone back far enough".

Hitler accordingly replied in a much calmer tone as if he felt that he had been misunderstood. "Sigmund, I don't intend to appear offensive, I am just addressing the conversation and expressing my opinion. I have no fight or quarrel with any of you, and there are many aspects of socialism to which I wholeheatedly adhere. And I most certainly don't want to be a leader or a politician, so maybe I am the wrong person to ask for an opinion on such things. But if I were, I would see nothing abhorrent in the creation of a Jewish state, or a Slav state – and suspect that both you and Tito here would both want to live in them. Whether they are communist, or capitalist is not the central issue. I am merely saying that one's identity will always come before one's political persuasion and that the workers will kill other workers based on this single point. The capitalist nations will send their cannon fodder to the trenches, and they will keenly go: King and country will always prevail".

Both Freud and Tito acknowledged this, but Trotsky had remained unconvinced, saying: *"If a Russian revolution should succeed, all others will see us as their vanguard and the dominoes will topple Hitler, of this I am certain. If war is inevitable then I believe it will unite us and not divide us"* – He had said, though Stalin took a more inquisitive attitude.

"The means will justify the end and if part of that process involves a lower tier of social class as; I won't say slave but cheap labour, then yes, given the American example it has its uses..." – *"Yes",* laughed Freud, in surprisingly offering a hint of his own subtle racism, joking: *"I don't care whose Negro they are as long as they are my Negro!"* He had noted this joke in his own journal that day. Apparently causing much light-hearted laughter. Stalin had then continued:

"Are you sure you don't want to be a leader? I think you have political potential". He concluded before later adding: *"So the question left in the air is one of; machines will replace manual labour, and new, even greater more efficient machines will soon replace the old machines, but men will still have to make those machines – so just who will those men be?"*

"No thank you", replied Hitler. *"I am an artist and that is my passion, I believe that God has chosen me for greater things, and I have no interest in being the one that makes those machines. God has given me a unique gift and I intend to use it. I have my greatest works to yet complete; maybe one day I'll even write a book too, like you gentlemen".*

Freud's journal informs us that it was Tito who had again made the greater impact on the conversation and on his reflective thinking. The journal entry ends with Tito's words:

"The end justifies the means gentlemen only when the means has an end".

The Tsar & 1905

Much discussion had centred around the work of Karl Marx and of his counterpart and great friend: Friedrich Engels. Marx's wife, Jenny, had died during the December of 1881. Developing a serious bronchial condition and overcome with grief, Marx himself would only live for just 15 months thereafter. What had initially started as catarrh developed into bronchitis and later: pleurisy. He died on 14th March 1883 at his London home aged 64 years. Marx was buried by family and friends in Highgate Cemetery: as a stateless person. 11 mourners were present at the funeral of 17th March in which his closest friends gave eulogies: including Friedrich Engels & Wilhelm Liebknecht. Liebknecht's political career had combined Marxist revolutionary theory with legal and practical political activity. As leader of the German SPD, the new political party became Germany's largest political party of its era. Engel's eulogy included the passage:

"On the 14th of March, at a quarter to three in the afternoon, the greatest living thinker ceased to think. He had been left alone for scarcely two minutes, and when we came back, we found him in his armchair, peacefully gone to sleep - but forever".

The initial family burial plot was later relocated to a new plot nearby where a new memorial to his life and work was erected and inscribed with the words: *"Workers of All Lands Unite"* - The last line of the Communist Party Manifesto. Also inscribed are the words: *"The philosophers have only interpreted the world in various ways - the point however is to change it"* – of the 11th *"Thesis on Feuerbach"* – as edited by Engels. In 1970 a portrait bust by Laurence Bradshaw was added to the memorial by The Communist Party of Great Britain.

Eric Hobsbawm, an eminent Marxist historian said of Marx: *"One cannot say Marx died a failure"* - As within 25 years of Karl Marx's death the socialist movements of both Germany and Russia had gained between *"15 and 47 per cent"* in representative democratic elections. Continental European socialist parties all acknowledged their Marxist origins though Marx's philosophy was, as a whole, mostly rejected in Britain. Notably, unable to secure work, Marx had spent his later years relying on loans and the charity of friends in order to make ends meet.

Discussions on Marxism had inevitably led to the Russian Revolution of 1905. Much of this we also find recorded in Sigmund Freud's journal of 1913. A journal simply titled by Freud as – "The Sugar Lump Club".

"What had been the causes of the revolution in Russia" – Freud had asked Stalin. To which Stalin had replied: *"There were many"*.

As Freud put, he had answered whilst - *"Most gracefully, eloquently in fact sipping his coffee"*, later elaborating: *"The peasants were starving, emancipated, wages were pitiful, and they were forbidden to sell or mortgage their allotted land. And then the Russification policies of the Tsars compounded this, the state brutally oppressed ethnic minorities, the repression and discrimination put them on the streets. They were forbidden to serve in the army or navy, refused schooling and denied the vote. The peasants revolted and were soon met with bans on strikes and protest – they then banned trade unions, they brutalised any worker who stood up against them – and we had a government who did nothing to protect them".*

Trotsky added to this by saying: *"...But the educated classes, the intellectuals and the students at our universities developed a new social consciousness, the more the peasants became hungry the greater the thirst for socialism and an end to the monarchy developed – 1905 was a most radical time for Russia"* – he concluded.

"I guess for Vladimir Lenin it was all about milk, sugar and coffee then?" - Freud stated, and to which Trotsky enquired – *"I'm not sure I follow you Sigmund..."*

"Well: didn't Lenin in his work 'Imperialism' blame certain conditions on Russia's dependence on overseas nations, did he not agitate the major powers, did he not cause all this rivalry that would ultimately lead to war?" Freud had expanded the point.

Stalin explained: *"I'm not sure that war is the appropriate definition of Lenin's intent Freud, but if violent overthrow and revolution is what you refer to then I accept that we are at war - yes".* Tito then intervened: *"I don't think we can look at the causes for 1905 individually, but together as a whole, surely they all created a perfect storm for revolt".*

And Hitler too then interjected, saying: *"I would agree Tito, yes, it was born of overall discontent with the dictatorship of the Tsar's and monarchy, it was inevitable given such conduct that their overthrow would be manifested in the minds of the poor".*

"Of course Adolf" – Trotsky then commented: *"It all led up to greater and great political protest that then ultimately led to rioting, all they wanted was better wages and better conditions, we as revolutionaries all sought to encourage mass strike activity and to radicalise the minds of students, and to encourage student demonstrations and..."* Stalin then interrupted with the words: *"And as revolutionaries that included the assassination of government officials".*

"Didn't Plehve, the minister of Russian interior say in 1903: The most serious ones (problems) *plaguing the country was those of the Jews, the schools, and the workers?"* asked Freud. Stalin replied: *"Yes – and it was in that order".* To which Trotsky added – *"That's why I as a Jew Freud would never be leader, anti-Semitism is as*

much ingrained in Russian cultural identity as it is here in Austria". – "And the people saw prolonged problems in Russia that were not as severe in the Western economies" – Tito also explained, continuing with - "The Russian economy was so intertwined with others, fixed into European finances, Russia's industrial recessions lasted much longer than elsewhere, 1900 plunged Russian industry into prolonged depression, Freud. This all fanned the flames of the agrarian problem that led up to the revolution of 1905".

Freud listened intently to the men's explanations. Trotsky had explained that so great was the nation's debt and desperation that even the *'nobles'* who had all previously remained loyal to the monarchy were now forced as well to sell their estates, either too the Noble Land Bank or to whoever else would buy them. And this had even included tenant peasant farmers now able to secure their own homes. The government had hoped that the peasants recently freed from the slavery of serfdom would now become a new land-holding class. They financed small repayment schemes in the hope that they would become politically conservative – but it all happened far too late. Whilst the nobility had now sold off one-third of its lands and the government had enacted new laws alongside those mortgage schemes for peasant farmers – the train had already, uncontrollably, started to run away. Socialism was by now well established as an ideology and gaining ever more and more momentum as it travelled.

Stalin was keen to elaborate: *"This was allotment land Freud, and the peasants saw through it immediately. They wouldn't actually own their own plot but an assignment under an open field's agreement. They weren't buying their freedom from serfdom, the land would not be owned by them but by a community of peasants, a cooperative if you wish, but they could not resell the land or renounce any rights to it. Instead of being enslaved to the nobles, they became enslaved by themselves. Forever: they would have to pay their fair share of rent and tax to the newly established village commune".*

"Do you know that by 1904 peasant arrears to the communes amounted to 118 million rubles, Freud?" – said Trotsky. *"Their wages were so small they could buy neither food nor pay taxes, a policy that aimed to prevent the proletarianisation of peasants had now done quite the opposite. They roamed the countryside, travelling hundreds of miles to find new work. They were desperate people who would do desperate acts and their anger soon turned into violence"* – Trotsky concluded.

"Violence" asked Freud, *"So who was responsible for this violence?"* Trotsky continued in explanation to him, that – 'These weren't single acts but organised masses, those who now totally ignored the restraints of authority. When you have nothing left what else have you to lose but your life? And if that life holds no value, you will easily sacrifice it. It wasn't Lenin who inspired violence but the

cruelty of a system that simply didn't care". And Tito too had been keen to demonstrate his knowledge of the events by adding to the conversation that: *"During 1902 thousands of peasants had destroyed and looted noblemen's properties in the provinces of Kharkov and Poltava. The rebellious crowd was later brought into submission by troops who brutally punished them".*

Trotsky was impressed by the young novice's knowledge of such things and asked where he had learned of this truth. Tito merely laughed before replying: *"From you Trotsky my friend, I read about it in Pravda!"* Stalin slapped Tito hard across the back in congratulatory appreciation and in turning to a most surprised Trotsky commented: *"Well done Leon, you see, I told you someone was reading it!"*

Hitler now joined in: *"And what did they do to try and solve the agrarian crisis Freud? I'll tell you; they blamed the Jews for it. Whilst the Tsars tolerated other faiths and culture, they never showed respect for it. They enforced that Christianity was true and progressive, they created an ethnic hierarchy. They created the myth that Jews were a special problem, enemies of Christendom, that they were the ones who exploited the peasantry and that they were the vanguard of a genuine Jewish conspiracy to over-throw the crown: they the Jews were the ones that were really in control of the revolutionary Marxist movement".*

"Yes, it's that deflection technique again isn't. To solve a problem, invent another one, and blame someone else entirely..." Frued said as Hitler then went on a rant about the art of propaganda...

"Since I became an artist, I have always taken a tremendous interest in propagandist activity. Especially the way poster art can deliver powerful messages. And I see gentlemen that the Socialist-Marxist organizations have mastered this art too and have applied it as an instrument to your cause with astounding skill. I think that the correct use of propaganda is a true art that has remained practically unknown to the bourgeois parties. I believe it is a weapon of which is owed many of your success in Russia...." Hitler stated.

Trotsky soon regained control of the conversation and led the table back to the discussion on the 1905 revolution. *"It wasn't just the Jews that became targeted, but all national and religious minorities. Russian administrators couldn't even agree on a definition of Pole: well not a legal definition anyway. They have made identity a matter of one's birthplace and always use the phrase 'of Polish or Russian descent' these days. They have striven to make non-Russians inferior, their propaganda is designed to aggravate feelings of disloyalty, nothing less"* – Trotsky concluded.

"Yes, indeed" - added Stalin. *"You see, post 1861, given the emancipation of the Serfs, they were forced to take into account all wider public opinion, but they failed outright to gain the peoples'*

consent and support. Russification policies directly led to the Polish uprising of 1863. *"Of course,"* interjected Stalin as Trotsky then continued, *"The uprising was brutally crushed, in the eyes of the Tsar the stability of the Empire was at threat".*

"And distrust of Germany too", added Hitler. *"During the 1870s Russia objected to the unification of Germany by Otto von Bismarck, though by blood and iron he achieved his aim. Should you have had such character on your side in 1905 gentlemen, your revolution would have succeeded!"* – *"Yes, Hitler, a great man indeed"* - Tito confirmed. *"Germany, from a defensive standpoint, needed control over Prussian lands around the Rhine to the west, that is if a German Empire was ever to prove viable. And the small principalities were already destined for their own independence. What was Prussia then is now central Germany, it was great strategic thinking on Bismarck's part we must surely agree?"*

"And that all started the process of Russification" - Stalin said in reply. *"This upset in the balance of power between us led the Tsars to only one conclusion: Germany would use its new strength against us"*. And Trotsky then added to this: *"They needed to turn the new borderlands into Russia proper, not just in land mass but in cultural heterogeneity. Those of true Russian character, they thought, would be more likely to rise-up in defense of their motherland"*. – Again, *"Yes"*, contributed Trotsky, *"And it was this identity crisis amongst the minorities, the so-called nationality problem, that would later plague them"*.

"In understanding the revolution, Freud" - Trotsky continued to explain: *"You must first understand the social, political and demographic conditions the Tsars themselves had created for their own downfall. It was a grim picture of laissez-faire capitalist policies that achieved nothing. Agricultural production was stagnant, but elsewhere, in Europe, the west, internationally, the peasants saw their grain prices fall, we needed imports, and our national debt was out of control. As the people starved, they spent even more money on military preparations for war. The famine became even more widespread than ever before..."*

"Do you know how many died of starvation in 1891?" - Stalin asked Freud. Freud just gestured with his right hand, palm upward, to signify that he did not.

"We're talking about 900,000 square miles, the previously rich fertile lands of the Volga and Nizhni-Novgorod, Riazan, Tula, Kazan, Simbirsk, Saratov, Penza, Samara and Tambov. We're talking about the malnutrition of twenty million people, all hungry and in need of food. 400,000 Freud, yes, 400,000 died from starvation and disease..."

Freud noted in his journal later - *"It was here, at this exact point, as Stalin finished expressing the word 'disease' that Trotsky raised himself up as he slung his right forearm hard across his chest, the sound so firm it could have been the beat of a drum, and delivered the following as if he were now attending a political rally. Such was his eagerness to stand bolt upright that the chair shot back out from underneath, at some speed I say, this drawing much attention from others around us."*

"These people's efforts were in vain, who with unchanged lives, desired to come to the people's aid by distributing the wealth they have first taken from them" – Trotsky had delivered in an impassioned poetic manner".

"Yes, yes!" - Shouted out an over excited Hitler, himself now rendering the attentions of the on-lookers round them. *"You deliver your words to perfection":* he blurted, almost rendering himself an orgasm.

Trotsky turned to face Freud as he now smiled, though indignantly. As if asking Freud to offer the fundamentals of at least a basic literary education to the young artist amidst them.

"No, *young* Adolf", Freud said to him – *"They are the words of Lev Nikolayevitch Tolstoy".*

Trotsky demanded a round of spirit of the waitress to which she immediately complied. "За здоровье! (za zda-ró-vye: to your health)" - Trotsky said as he raised his glass a high and to which the room now fell into collective loud applause.

After the impromptu toast, Stalin continued to explain that a process of industrialisation had led to the spread of peasant urbanisation. Their new informed ideas for social reform returning with them to the farmlands. Marxism spread like wildfire back home to the peasant communities. The industrialised workers were dissatisfied. The government tried to quell their dissatisfaction, just as the efforts of the Tsars to provide food relief for the famine, these were seen as too little too late (and included the theft of farmers grain that was rightfully not theirs to take). New regulatory labour laws offered little change.

Children under the age of 12 years were relieved from factory work, except in the case of night shift glass manufacturing. Those between the ages of 12 to 15 were no longer required to work on Sundays and holidays. Workers had to be paid at least once per month and limits were introduced to reduce fines for worker tardiness. Employers were prohibited from charging their employees for electricity that was used as a part of their employment, such as nighttime lighting. Despite attempts to challenge unfair and unhuman working practice and conditions, by the end of 1900 they still worked a six day week: eleven hours a day. Though 'only' ten hours was required of them on Saturdays.

Most employers remained stalwart in refusing such concessions. Workers were still fined for poor work; they continued to work excessive grueling shifts and attempts to unionise were denied. They remained the lowest paid workers in Europe.

"*Dissatisfaction quickly turned into despair and their strikes were banned*", Stalin had informed. "*Impoverished workers were now sympathetic to radical socialism. The workers revolted with revolutionary protest and countless illegal strikes soon became the vanguard of revolution*".

"*The Russian progressives, the Union of Zemstvo Constitutionalists and the Union of Liberation both demanded a constitutional monarchy*" explained Trotsky. "*But that was not enough for us*" added Stalin. "*We, as the two other main groups, the Socialist Revolutionary Party and the Marxist Russian Social Democratic Labour Party - wanted much more. The liberals were calling for freedom of religion, political reforms and a constitution, full freedom of the press, an elected national legislature. The Tsar, that scoundrel Nicholas II, sat on his arse in the grandeur of his palace only offering token improvements. They all soon started to listen when Vyacheslav von Plehve was assassinated*", Stalin concluded.

"*I'm not sure I know who Plehve was?* asked Tito. "*He was the Minister of the Interior, a terrible man, a Tsarist*" – Trotsky informed. "*After the assassination they appointed a new minister, Pyotr Sviatopolk-Mirskii, he was more liberal, an attempt to appease the people's demands, but the crucial demand for a representative national legislature was still ignored*".

Stalin elaborated further: "*In 1902 the strikes started in the Caucasus', the pay disputes on the railways encourage others, we had the general strike of Rostov-on-Don and we were soon addressing crowds of 20,000 with revolutionary speeches, but they, the Cossacks, continued to butcher us. Political demands soon became economic ones; by 1903 the south was ready for a total over-throw of the elite ruling classes. Following city wide wage strikes in Tiflis, workers found that their working day was reduced, they got a new taste for the power they held in their own hands – we the people held our own destiny*" – This; Stalin had informed almost without a pause for breath, and as predicable, Trotsky would always continue to contribute, adding:

"*The strikes had spread to Odessa by spring of 1904, then St. Petersburg, Baku and Kiev, by 1905 there was no stopping us*" – Trotsky had said.

"*It was Putilov that tipped the scales I believe*", added Tito, eager to get more involved and demonstrate his historical understanding in this most informed, enlightened gentleman's exchange as he then explained that: "*Four workers were sacked for their membership of a workers assembly*".- "*Yes Tito, at the Putilov ironworks, the railway and artillery supplier, yes, 1904, St. Petersburg, they refused to reinstate the four so workers downed tools, a strike was called, the*

Putilov strike then spread like wildfire, now we had 150,000 strikers from 382 factories on the streets – the whole city came to a standstill. And by the 8th of January 1905 – St. Petersburg fell into darkness without its electricity!" Trotsky informed him. Smiling in a calm friendly way in recognition of the political potential this young informed new friend had to offer, Trotsky added: *"No electricity, no newspaper production and all public areas were closed – By January 1905 we were unstoppable!"*

…The Cossacks would charge at us, cutting us down with their swords, slicing us up like meat, trampling us below horse charge hooves, they were relentless, but we stood our ground - but Bloody Sunday changed everything that day Freud", Trotsky said. *"If you want to understand you need to be there with us in Russia on January 22nd, it was carnage."* He continued as he addressed the increasingly inquisitive Sigmund, and then went on to explain how the events of bloody Sunday that day had had huge consequences on imperialist Russia.

He continued: *"Allowing tens of thousands of peasant agitators to starve, brutalising and cutting down Marxist sympathisers, all legitimate responses of a brutal regime, but to shoot down 1000 unarmed demonstrators led by their own church was quite another. All Father Georgy Gapon wanted to do that day was deliver a petition to Tsar Nicholas II at the Winter palace, and his response was to order his Imperial Guard to kill them. The Tsar had turned on his own church"* - Leon Trotsky had summed up.

A quiet Adolf Hitler had remained sat impassively on the fence, doodling on the tablecloth for most of the dialogue until eventually feeling the need to contribute. *"And here you both are"* – he uttered.

"Here we both are what Young Adolf?" - Stalin asked. Hitler elaborated: *"Well you're both alive and well, living in exile having fled a failed revolution…"* He had spoken with some degree of disdain.

Stalin was, obviously, somewhat angered and replied: *"We didn't fail, we're banished Mister Hitler, the Tsar is terrified of us!"* – *"Whatever you sell it is as, you lost, didn't you? The Tsar and Imperialist Russia remain".* Hitler said. Freud had noted in his journal; *"As if wanting to provoke an argument."*

"We may have lost the battle, but we will win the war" – Trotsky forcefully stated in a most defiant manner. *"This is just the start; it cannot be stopped!"*

Freud had interjected. *"Now, now, gentlemen, we are all reasonable fellows are we not? Let's not get into argument or bogged down over technicalities, shall we?"* It was clear to Freud that the impassioned delivery of their historical account of 1905 by the others had not been appreciated by the young artist and, thus much to the annoyance and utter contempt of the two revolutionaries.

Freud had also noted, later in his journal, that a fractious atmosphere had developed but did not go into greater detail.

He did write however that Hitler had questioned the true unity of the workers movement, saying: *"All Russification served to do was annoy the ethnic nationalist groups amongst you. Be it the Finns or Poles or Baltic provinces, the Muslims, or the Jews, they all want the opposite to what you foresee: they want their own autonomy just as those of the Austro-Hungarian Empire today. They won't unite with you but will merely seize the opportunity to settle old scores"* – He had stated before concluding: *"As your mass movements now stagnate all you will witness is a rise in terrorism upon which many more thousands will die".*

"And what would you have us do then Adolf?" demanded a now quite aggressive Stalin. Hitler replied: *"I've already told you, all I want to do is paint, but I will say this: The world is not there to be possessed by the faint-hearted races".*

Hitler & The Crumbling Empire

Freud had never identified categorically what was said on each particular day of that week during 1913. Block paragraphs of textual recollection and reflection are therefore a matter for this author's interpretation. Ultimately, some content, however, is easier to associate with specific conversation than others. One becomes aware when studying the journal how the week developed given the closeness and relationship that developed between the members present, those present at the Sugar Lump Club gatherings. One can see that as confidence to challenge each other grows, the lightheartedness and shallowness of previous conversations fades. This must demonstrate a greater awareness of familiarity amongst the group. Often sequence is gauged by its reference to previous conversation, accordingly it must have occurred later on in the week - and this is certainly the case with this chapter.

When Freud writes without reflection of fact that could only have been established afterward, of a later historical event, it is evident that that entry was almost a fact of immediacy, that very same day perhaps. When he reflects *'as later or after'* it could indeed have been spoken of, days, weeks, many months or even years after the fact, this was the case maybe. It is my opinion, a humble opinion, that entries to the journal could not have been completed after he fled Austria for Britain in 1936: this as the journal was discovered amongst belongings much later found of post WW2 years. The journal had remained in Vienna amongst many other works, hidden by friends. More on this can be read about in this book's appendix.

Both Stalin and Trotsky would frequently taunt the young artist, it would appear, by regular attempts to seek his opinion, this despite his indifference to both politics and of their leaders. Though Hitler would, from time to time, demonstrate his degree of understanding on key facts that others were not quite so aware of. Freud noted that he had a degree of political astuteness when he had informed Tito that: *"The Manifesto of The Communist Party had been written in the central library of Manchester: Britain"*. Tito, despite being able to quote almost verbatim most of the manifesto's text, had not known this. Freud also noted that the two Russian revolutionaries had pretended to be aware of this fact, but Freud had not been – *"Convinced of their sincerity"*.

Conversations had again soon turned back to the possibility of war within the Austro-Hungarian Empire. Hitler had said: *"The conflict in the Balkans is the powder keg of Europe, should war breakout I believe it will start there, a war that will drag us all into a wider conflict"*.

Tito had been the one to ask for greater clarification, Hitler had continued to explain: *"Well: when Austro-Hungaria annexed the former Ottoman territories of Bosnia and Herzegovina during the crisis of 1908 -1909 it served only to anger the Kingdom of Serbia. After all, the Ottomans had occupied it since 1878, and, of course, this was met by Russian political interference, the Pan-Slavic and Orthodox Russian Empire, you must see that this shattered any hope of peace gentlemen?"* he'd said.

"Yes", replied Tito, adding: *"But, the Ottoman territories are shrinking by the day. The Balkan League is numerically superior and, most importantly, strategically advantaged, you must see that? We will see the occupied lands of the former yoke return to European hands. The League is achieving rapid success".*

"Do you think that Britain and France will stand by and allow the spoils of this conflict to be divided without their interference?" Uninterrupted, Hitler then continued: *"Do you think that had Austro-Hungaria not annexed Bosnia and Herzegovinian that Serbia would not have flexed its own muscles? It was the Treaty of Berlin that freed Bosnia and Herzegovina in the first place, and following the Empires later annexation, the Ottoman's soon sought to restore their suspended Ottoman constitution, didn't they? The great nations will always seek to maintain the status-quo and protect their Christian populations"* - Hitler had explained.

"But the Ottoman's surely don't have the strength to win, it's just implausible Adolf" - Tito argued. *"I'm not suggesting that at all, as the league wins, they will then turn on one another, that's inevitable. There will be land grabs to restore former territories; the united will become the divided. Those minorities caught up in the middle of it will all seek their own independence and there will be yet another treaty that represents only the interests of the greater majority. All of the great Empires will want a slice; Russia, Austro-Hungaria, the British and French".*

"I still don't see how this Balkan League War can affect the rest of us – the Balkan war has nothing to do with the actions of the Austro-Hungarian Empire?" – Tito enforced. And now in an attempt to direct him to the central issue, Trotsky then afforded his 'superior' advice to the group.

"I believe that what young Adolf is suggesting is that any new treaty will enlarge the territorial borders of Bulgaria, Serbia, Montenegro or Greece - and in doing so what will become of the former Ottoman lands of Rumelia, Thrace or Macedonia? Someone, but just who we don't know yet, yes, will want to claim it!" – Tito had clarified.

"I think even a monkey could have predicted this conflict" – Hitler added to Tito's words. *"That may well be",* suggested Tito and continued: *"But even that monkey wouldn't be stupid enough to*

threaten the stability of Austro- Hungaria, especially given Germany's allegiance to it. It's just not possible for the Balkan conflict to spread – I simply don't see that as militarily viable – it would never succeed – total suicide".

"Generals may win battles, but it is people who win wars" – Hitler said. "When a population becomes intoxicated with hatred of another, they will soon jump as lemmings from a cliff top, that you'll see, it's an ethnic problem as much as it is a geographical one". – "Nonsense", Trotsky scathed back at him, "Soldiers win battles, but it is logistics that win wars".

'Given the hindsight of history we possess, we now know much of this to have come true. Bulgaria attacked both Serbia and Greece on the 16th of June 1913. As a result, it again had lost huge sways of its former borders to both nations and further, the territory of Southern Dobruja, to Romania, in what was referred to as the Second Balkan War lasting just 33 days. The great Empires had managed to keep the conflict contained, an independent Albanian state was established, but it would not be long before the localised conflict would have a huge impact on the rest of Europe.

Hitler had been noted by Freud to have challenged the two revolutionaries thinking. Freud wrote: *"The Young Turks had tried to encourage the Muslim populations of the region, especially Bosnia-Montenegro, to re-settle to the south in northern Macedonia in Ottoman controlled lands. Leon and Joseph seem to lack the significance of last year's Albanian uprisings* (Spring: 1912) *in which the Albanian Muslims and existing populations of Ottoman immigrants, united together. Even Albanian military officials and soldiers have now switched allegiance to the Ottoman forces. This is surely to be a catastrophe for the Empire* (Austro-Hungarian). *Especially as a policy of re-populating Macedonia where few Muslim minorities exist today is now prevalent. The Committee of Real Muslims has issued the Kararname decree. They have proclaimed that all Muslim peoples of northern Albania, Epirus, and Bosnia all fight. To instigate all possible means against the forces of the Bulgarian, Serbian and Montenegrin Kingdoms. It instructs all Muslims to defend the territorial integrity of their own* (Ottoman) *Empire".*

In reading the journal one does not gain a simplistic sense that Sigmund Freud is sympathetic to the nationalist focus of the young Adolf Hitler, but he does seem to understand the wider complexities of Empire building. There is one tell-tale sentence that particularly stands out: *"Whilst Stalin and Trotsky are educated and most informed, principled to an honorable degree I feel, they remain somewhat naïve in such endeavors, Hitler is more realistic - though clearly quite uneducated in such matter"* – The journal states.

Freud had quizzed Hitler on his cultural identity, this the journal also stipulated. *"Who are you?"* – Freud had asked him. *"I'm not quite sure I fully understand the question" - Hitler had replied. Freud elaborated. *"Well, you talk like a nationalist and engage in theories of Darwinist evolution, survival of the fittest, yet on the same token you say you are a Christian? And that's all a little perplexing to me. – you're a very contradictory young fellow at times, aren't you?"*

"Not at all Freud, there's only one race of people's and that's the human race" - Hitler had replied, and thus, Freud had probed further; *"But there's the very issue, if you are acknowledging that we are all of the same species why do you insist on talking of racial divisions – different races?"*

"I think that one's race or identity is something that we create for ourselves, it's not necessarily purely a genetic thing but a cultural or religious badge of identity we mostly choose Freud".

"Exactly, so let me ask you again – who are you?" Freud continued to push the question. *"Well, I guess I am Bavarian then – does that answer the question?"* - *"It does but then again it asks a bigger question and that is, what is a Bavarian?"* - *"Then the answer to that wider question would be I'm a German then – surely?"* Hitler said proudly. *"So, what's a German"* - Freud then asked, persistently remaining on focus.

The two men, much to the other three's amusement and enjoyment then engaged in seeking to acquire such a definition. Toing and froing with each other as if they were playing table tennis. They had started in the Paleolithic era, and both agreed that The Alps were totally inaccessible during the Ice Age period, therefore human habitation of Austria could not be dated to be earlier than Middle Paleolithic. Evidence of Neanderthal settlement in the region had never been discovered. Remains of rock shelters at Lake Constance and the Alpine Rhine Valley had been found but were minimal, and of the Mesolithic era. Though, and with discussions that included the funeral site at Elsbethen, and just a hand full of microlithic artifacts found, they were not significant enough to substantiate the theory of an original regional populace. The Neolithic period had proven, more interestingly to Freud than Hitler, evidence suggesting most of those areas known today as Austria were amenable to Neolithic agriculture. Of this there was evidence.

The Copper Age had provided archeologists with traces of early Copper Age settlements (Chalcolithic era) in the Carpathian Basin hoard and other finds at Stollhof, Hohe Wand, and Lower Austria, and of course artifacts recovered from an array of other hilltop settlements were known as common finds in eastern Austria.

"So, are you a Neolite or a Copperite?" Freud joked.

"Don't be ridiculous", Hitler had replied. *"How can anyone know that?"* he asked, sarcastically.

"Well, how far back in one's family tree can you realistically go Adolf?"

"There will be a definite problem on my father's side Freud - I don't know who my grandfather was..."

"Exactly my point, there you have it!" lambasted Freud: *"You could be a Slav, a Jew or a Pole then?"* Adding, in a most humorous manner: *"At least as a Jew I can go as far back as Moses!"*.

Immediately, Hitler was found to be equally as quick of f the mark with his wit, imparting the words: *"I don't really care, Freud, as long as I'm not French"*, he chuckled.

To say that by now both Tito and Trotsky were pissing themselves with laughter – *"...would have been the understatement"* - Freud had noted. Elaborating on the fact that: *"Stalin just didn't get it at all"*. For Stalin the entire conversation had appeared to be a complete waste of good time. The men then moved on to the Bronze Age.

They agreed that Bronze Age fortifications were appearing across Austria during this era, and these had to have been erected to protect something: perhaps commercial centres for mining or copper and/or tin processing. Trade was evident in a flourishing culture reflected by grave artifacts found at Pitten. The Iron Age too had later represented the creation of Austria's Hallstatt culture, this had succeeded the Urnfield culture. The influence of both the Mediterranean civilisations and Steppe peoples on the region was undeniable, and later of course, arrived the Celtic La Tène culture...

The Hallstatt cultures of 800 BC had been named after salt mine settlements. The Hallstatt to the west had direct trade routes to Greek Colonies on the Ligurian coast. In the Alps, the Hallstatt cultures maintained contact with the Etruscans of Italy. And The Steppe Peoples had arrived via the Carpathian Basin from Russia.

Both men also agreed that the first tribal villages and settlements that they could describe as ethnic minorities of sufficient quantity and size to realise a 'civilisation' in the region was probably the La Tène (Celtic) culture. It was after all, as both acknowledged, that the earliest place names known in the region had after all been born of them.

"So, let's just agree that you're a Celt for the time being then shall we, Adolf?" – Freud insisted. Hitler had by now become rather irritated with the whole conversation and replied – *"I think it's you Sigmund who fails to see the wider picture. Race is not something you can prove, no more than the existence of a God, the same God that we both choose to believe in, though it be from quite different perspectives. Race is just something that is, you know who you are and to what you identify yourself as. Ask our revolutionary friends here if money exists? It doesn't, it's just pretty little pieces of printed paper with pictures on, it's of no more value than what we chose to wipe our own rear-ends with, but we believe in it because of the guarantee of payment we place on it."* – *" Go on then"*, Freud asked.

"If money doesn't exist why are those three all prepared to die fighting over it? Hitler then concluded with: *"Race doesn't have to be a scientific fact for you to believe in it, Freud – it may be a social construct, but we all know what it is, and I am a true German!"*

"Is now a good time to suggest that you're black then, Adolf?" – Tito Joked. *"After all, if we go with your God theory then we all evolved from Eden, and that's now proven to have been in Africa".* Hitler was not amused and merely responded: *"If you're going to keep forcing the issue gentlemen then I'll choose to be a Roman. Why? Because Noricum and Rome were active trading partners of the Roma era with fixed military alliances from as early as 15 BC. As Austria was annexed to the Roman Empire and endured for 500 years of so-called Austria-Romana, I guess that's a pretty healthy race to have descended from!"* – Feeling that he had gained the upper hand, he had continued:

"History is always written by the winning side" he said, *"And if I were to sum up what is wrong with the Empire, I think I could do it very easily. Look around us gentlemen, there are many signs of decay which ought to be given serious thought, don't you think? As far as economics are concerned, that is, you spend far too much time concentrating on reform, if you want to win the hearts and minds of the people then you need to understand them".* The young painter, somewhat out of place amongst his newfound intelligentsia, was most encouraged to continue by all concerned. And this he did so.

"Well let's take the increase of population in Germany and the question of providing their daily bread. Why do we consider the idea of acquiring fresh territory such a deplorable idea? It seems to me that the world's Empires are all seeking commercial conquest of the world over each other and at the cost of each other. This must surely lead to unlimited and injurious industrialisation. The obvious being that by weakening the agricultural classes, there is a proportionate increase in the proletariat moving into urban areas, and this can only upset the natural equilibrium and order of things. The great divide between rich and poor becomes apparent as luxury and poverty now live side by side and the deplorable consequences, the creation of slums which are infected, as a rotten apple to its core, with unemployment. This is what's causing havoc. And this is what we see in Russia isn't it? You intend to take them from the land and turn them into industrial machines, do you not?"

Stalin was not in agreement: *"Rapid industrialisation creates wealth, Adolf, wealth that we as the state share equally amongst those that have created it. We need factories, but there will be good conditions, good pay, short hours and generous holidays and health care too. By creating wealth, we create leisure time for all the people"*, he stated.

"Yes", - replied Hitler: *"But the population inevitably becomes divided into political classes. Social discontent and unrest versus commercial prosperity. Surely - things cannot go on as they are?"* He continued to explain his discontent with the system as he saw it.

"Commerce has assumed definite control of the State, and money has become the new God whom all now serve and bow down to. We've forgotten our heavenly Gods, religion is old fashioned, and all we do today is worship mammon in a state of utter degeneration".

Freud interjected. *"I don't believe this to be true Adolf. In this day and age, with science and understanding, where man created God in 'his' own image, very few people really subscribe to such nonsense".* Sigmund explained that his identity as a Jew had little more significance in his life other than being a historical or cultural identity. *"I certainly don't accept the existence of a monospherical God",* he explained. Laughing before adding: *"And, if there were I'd certainly be asking him who elected him to rule".*

Hitler didn't persist as if reluctant to engage in debate about theology with his vastly superior and well-armed opponent and soon moved on to other topics.

"Our Majesties make a mistake when creating representatives of new finance capital to the ranks of the nobility" - He said, continuing: *"Ideal virtues have become secondary considerations to those of money. The nobility of the sword now ranks second to that of finance. The nobility has lost more and more of the racial qualities that those who created this Empire stood for. Disruption is being brought about by the elimination of personal control; the whole economic structure is being transferred into the hands of joint stock companies. The workers are now degraded into an object of speculation in the hands of unscrupulous exploiters who are assuming control of the whole of national life. We have given way to money-grabbing capitalism. Surely, now, national life is dependent on commerce rather than ideal values.*

"Welcome to Marxism", Trotsky stated: *"I had been starting to wonder how long it would take you to engage with us".* Tito was also inspired to see that Hitler was now thinking through the greater ideals of the Socialist cause.

"Marxism isn't enough Trotsky" - Hitler announced, developing a broadening sense of self confidence in the attention he was now receiving. *"You may seek to fill the pockets of the poor and redistribute the wealth of the rich amongst them, but you create a secondary void. People want more than their daily bread on the table – they want something to believe in, something to live for".*

Stalin was the first to address Hitler's negativity. *"Are you suggesting that Socialism isn't a worthy enough cause to fill that spiritual void? It seems to me that working for all, a collective sense of duty beyond self will prevail".*

"I've no desire to argue with you", Hitler replied adding: *"But it seems to me that the Bolsheviks see themselves as replacing God. You offer the people nothing more than work and death. They as individuals just became another cog in the very machines, those mechanical apparatus they spend a lifetime servicing".*

"Utter nonsense" – Stalin stated aggressively as he thumps his fist down onto the table - though this was in a manner to reassert control of the conversation rather than as a gesture born out of personal aggression toward Hitler's words. Stalin went on to explain his training in the Priesthood, and suggested, most arrogantly, that if anyone was to know anything of the existence of God, it was he. And all this education had done for him was assert that humanity was all alone in the world.

Trotsky took up his sedentary position between the two. *"I see the issue of religion as a means of oppression, though I accept that it is so ingrained in human culture and identity that I fear it can never be truly exorcised".* And followed this with what Freud would later describe as a further dig into Stalin's public hypocrisy. *"You may have trained as a Priest, and I concede you have a greater knowledge of Theology than I, but you still have that overriding need to pray – don't you?"* Stalin was angered by what he saw as a public betrayal. *"Trotsky, do you believe that I too am immune from Bourgeoisie conditioning? I am a product of the working classes and I too have been brainwashed into such thinking. That life is designed for the purpose of suffering and inner turmoil, that subservience on earth will be met upon death by the greatness and grandeur of heaven. I may have at times a personal need of God, but that doesn't mean to say that I would ever want to meet him!"* he concluded and Trotsky backed down.

"If you feel the spiritual need to talk with God you must surely believe in him" - Freud posed the question to the now irate Stalin, adding: *"And if you do believe then I find it hard to understand why you would never want to meet him – If God exists, then you have somewhat of a conundrum on your hands don't you Stalin?"*

"He doesn't, there is no God, and it's up to us to fill that void with Marxism, that's what people will now live for. I'm merely speaking aloud. If you were to put all of the sins of the Tsars and Monarchy and of the ruling classes together in one basket, that would not equate to one tenth of the sins of God. If God exists, then it is he who is the most deplorable sinner of them all, a heinous, despicable detractor who allows nothing but suffering and servitude of the poor".

Hitler, realising that the conversation was now being taken away on matters beyond his control now regained the attention. *"This is the problem, not whether there is a God or not, but the fact that we as people only deal with what is necessary, we live our lives born out of essentialism - our worst sin is in the decadence and habit of only doing things by halves".*

"And you are suggesting what Adolf? That we create a merger between God and Marxism just to fill the ignorant minds of the narrow-minded and uneducated? – Freud asked. Stalin remained in quite agitated contemplation at the question. It was Tito who now broke the awkward silence at the table, saying: *"It seems to me that's what Marxism already is – Christianity, but without the resurrection."*

Trotsky was more jovial and suggested that*: "Maybe Lenin should become the new God then!"* He joked. Freud joined in the newfound humour and asked: *"Are you sure he's up the job? He's only 5 feet tall and is rather too partial to violence for me!* Trotsky had joined Freud in now laughing aloud.

Stalin, himself only 5 feet tall and very self-aware of his shorter right arm, due to illness in childhood, and potted facial figure due to chickenpox, turned to Trotsky and demanded to know - *"So if you believe that Lenin is too short to be of Godly stature what are you suggesting about me?"* – *"I'm not suggesting anything, it was a joke amongst friends",* Trotsky replied, now realising that the gentlemen through joint humour had hit on a rather soft spot in Stalin's character. *"It was Sigmund who made the joke, not I – I have nothing but respect for the fine qualities of our leader, you know that".* He ended, in defense of his behavior and folly.

"I think you're suggesting that you are the man for the job?" - Stalin said abruptly and lacking in any humorous tone what-so-ever. *"So; Marxism is to become the new God, to construct it's own temples of splendor and awe, and if I am to understand the thinking of our young artist correctly, half-heartedness will not suffice - Do you want the top job, Trotsky?"* Stalin asked.

Trotsky replied and continued with great effort to make light of the tension now found to be present between the two of them. *"I'd rather have an icepick to the back of the head"* – he joked.

Rise and Fall of the Austria-Hungarian Empire.

In piecing together key aspects of history as referred to within the journal, I found that the construction of a historical timeline aided my understanding greatly. I have included it here in offering further insight into the complexities of the situation – It will help.

When the Archduke Franz Ferdinand was assassinated the following year in 1914 - we know that the Sugar Lump Club of Vienna had by now - long parted ways. The murder of Austria's heir to the throne triggered the First World War. It was the final spark to the touch paper of an already highly explosive powder keg. Ferdinand was killed in Sarajevo by a Yugoslav nationalist: Gavrilo Princip - on 28th June 1914. This was 18 months after the conclusion of the gentlemen's meetings at the Central Coffeehouse: Vienna.

Austria-Hungaria delivered an ultimatum to the Kingdom of Serbia which led to many entangled international and historical alliances being invoked. Major world powers were now at war with one another - a conflict that soon spread across the globe.

Russia, Serbia's ally, mobilised her forces in an effort to avoid invasion on 25th July. It failed, and by the 28th of July, the Austro-Hungarian Empire had declared war on Serbia. In response, Germany demanded of Russia that it demobilise, it refused to do so and on 1st August, Germany and Russia were now at war.

Russia was outnumbered on its Western Front and called on its Triple Entente ally, France, for help. In 1870, the former French territory of Alsace-Lorraine had been lost to a now unified Germany and the Second French Empire was over due to the Franco-Prussian war. Hostility toward Germany had remained, it had featured over time, France was determined to retake Alsace-Lorraine. All it needed was an excuse. Coming to the aid of Russia did just that.

Germany and France maintained heavily fortified borders (Known as the Schlieffen Plan). Germany would invade France from the north (entering neutral Belgium). Germany broke her existing treaties, in order to protect neutral Belgium from Germany's aggression - the United Kingdom now came to its defense.

Russia continued to fight on its Eastern front and in doing so made significant gains. However, it was soon halted by German forces at the Battles of Tannenberg. Its desire to take East Prussia also crumbled following the battles of the Masurian Lakes. The war offered land grab opportunities to others. In November 1914, the Ottoman Empire joined the Central Powers; this opened up new fronts in Mesopotamia and the Sinai. In 1915, Italy joined the allies. Bulgaria had chosen to remain loyal to the Central Powers, it had lost large swathes of land during the 1st & 2nd Balkan Wars, it wanted them back. Romania joined the Allied Powers in 1916 and in 1917, so too did the USA.

Little did the men of 'The Sugar Lump Club' know at the time, but the Russian government would collapse in 1917. The subsequent revolution led to the signing of the Treaty of Brest Litovsk. Russia was now out of the war, its new deal with the Central Powers (to stop fighting) was much to the delight of Germany. A Germany that now became very confident of success, a series of offensives along the Western Front of 1918 would bolster this opinion. Germany was never defeated on the battlefield – it was forced to sign the armistice due to its political and revolutionary unrest at home. Germany signed on the 4th October, 1918. The war was now over and within months of this the world as the men had known it, Freud, Tito, Trotsky, Stalin and Hitler, would change forever. The great empires of Germany, Russia, Ottoman and Austro-Hungaria would all cease to exist.

The National borders of the smaller and now independent nations were restored, new borders were created, and Germany lost her colonies to the victors. The Paris Peace Conference of 1919 saw Britain, France, the United States and Italy impose their own terms. A series of new treaties were signed, and the peace-keeping efforts of the League of Nations were born. History tells us that through economic depression and global humiliation, a renewed but more extreme form of nationalism would now arise in Germany: Within the next 20 years the Second World War would break out. 'According to sugar' - The world of Stalin and Hitler lay just around the corner.

CE: Historical timeline.

100 – 500 : Barbarian invasions begin.

300 – 500: Goths & Vandals. Völkerwanderung - The Great migration that sealed the fate of Roman Austria.

500 – 700: Slavs and Bavarii. The second phase of the Austrian Migration. The Langobardii (Lombards) appear in the northern and eastern quarters. Driven south (567 CE) to northern Italy by the Avars. The Avars and Vassal Slavs settlements stretch from the northern Baltic Sea to the southern Balkans.

717: Bavarian and Franks co-exist but Bavarian independence is temporary, subjugated by Charles Martel. The last Agilolfing duke is deposed by Tassilo III.

788: Carolingian control removes all non-hereditary Bavarian kings.

800: The Duchy of Bavaria Austria comes under direct rule. The King of Franks: Charlemagne. 800 - 814. As Emperor, the Kingdom of the East (Österreich) is now part of the Holy Roman Empire.

862: The Hungarian displacement begins in the eastern territories.

896: Hungarian raids against Frankish domains is commonplace. They settle on the 'Hungarian Plain'.

955: Magyars by Otto I is defeated. Austria comes under German rule.

962: Otto I of Germany is crowned Emperor by the Holy Roman Empire.

976: North-eastern Austria is gift to the Babenberg family by Otto II.

1020: Habichstburg, as erected by Count Radbot (Hawks Castle – Zurich) gives birth to the Habsburg dynasty.

1242: The last duke of Babenberg dies without leaving a male heir to succeed him. His Austrian territories become the property of King Ottokar of Bohemia.

1273: Absent of a German Thrown the Great Interregnum begins. Habsburg Prince Rudolf becomes King.

1278: King Ottokar II of The Holy Roman Emperor at Dürnkrut is defeated by King Rudolf I. All Austrian territories are now under the Habsburg domain.

1291: To resist Habsburg domination the Swiss forest districts of Uri, Schwyz and Unterwalden sign the Everlasting League in Rütli meadow.

1315: The Swiss defeat the Habsburgs at Morgarten.

1320: The independent cantons become the Swiss confederation.

1356: Charles IV establishes seven electors, four hereditary German rulers and the archbishops of Mainz, Cologne and Trier.

1438: Habsburg dynasty adapts the office of Holy Roman emperor as a hereditary.

1477: Maximilian as heir to all Austria marries Mary the heiress to Burgundy, this and following alliances form the Habsburg empire.

1485: Vienna is seized by Matthias Corvinus, the king of Hungary. He makes the city his new capital.

1490: The Habsburgs recover Vienna from the Hungarians following the death of Matthias Corvinus: 1490.

1496: The heir to Austria, Philip, weds Joanna. She is the daughter of Ferdinand and Isabella of Spain. This is the second great Habsburg alliance.

1500's: Austria is invaded by the Ottoman Empire (Exact date unknown).

1516: Spain becomes part of the Habsburg empire following the death of Ferdinand II under the rule of Charles V (Charles I of Spain).

1519: Charles V bribes the seven permanent imperial electors with finances borrowed from the from Fuggers. It amounts to 852,000 florins.

1547: An agreement made between the Turkish sultan Suleiman I and the Habsburg ruler Ferdinand I sees Hungary now divided between the pair.

1556: Charles V abdicates. The Netherlands and Spain are passed to his son Philip. The title of Holy Roman emperor succeeds to his brother, Ferdinand.

1556: Following the division agreement of Charles V there are now two Habsburg empires, being 1) Austrian and 2) Spanish.

1600's: Defeated, the Ottomans leave the Austrian regions.

1618: Habsburg regents are thrown from the windows of Prague Castle by Bohemian nobles. The Thirty Years' War begins. Bohemia Protestants revolt against the Catholic Habsburg emperor.

1619: Elector palatine of the Rhine (The Protestant Frederick V) is elected king by the Bohemian nobles.

1620: To the west of Prague the battle of the White Mountain ends the brief reign of Bohemian Protestant Frederick V as king.

1648: Thirty Years' War ends with the Peace of Westphalia. The Habsburgs declare Roman Catholicism as the official Austrian religion.

1683: As the Turkish army now approach, the royal court of Vienna is abandoned by the emperor, Leopold I.

1683: The Polish king John Sobieski drives the Turks away from the city walls. A historic turning point for Vienna.

1687: The Hungarian Diet grants the Habsburg dynasty a hereditary right to the crown of St Stephen in Austria.

1700: The death of the Habsburg King of Spain.

1701: War soon breaks out between French and Austrian claimants to the Spanish throne: The War of the Spanish Succession.

1701 - 1714: Austria gains Belgium and the Spanish lands in Italy.

1713: The War of the Spanish Succession ends upon the signing of the treaties of Utrecht.

1714: The treaties lead to the Spanish Netherlands becoming transferred to Austria.

1723: Charles VI, as emperor, allows Hungary to be ruled as a separate kingdom within the empire.

1740: Charles VI dies. His eldest daughter, Maria Theresa (aged 23) becomes the new Habsburg empress.

1740: The king of Prussia (Frederick II) invades the Habsburg province of Silesia. It triggers the War of The Austrian Succession.

1741: Frederick defeats the Austrians at Mollwitz. He secures Silesia as his own. French and Bavarian armies join the war against

Austria, attacking upper Austria into Bohemia. As an ally of France, Spain joins the war. Britain, as ally to Austria, is fighting the Spanish in the War of Jenkin's Ear and now joins the wider conflict. French and Bavarian forces enter Prague, the jewel in the crown of the Austrian empire.

1742: The Bavarian capital, Munich, is captured by Austrian forces.

1746: Maurice de Saxe now occupies the entire Austrian Netherlands as the French commander.

1748: The War of the Austrian Succession ends with the signing of the treaty of Aix-la-Chapelle. However, hostilities will soon continue as the Seven Years' War.

1756: France and Austria sign a treaty of alliance - the Diplomatic Revolution.

1762: Maria Theresa, the Habsburg Empress, hears a 6-year-old child play music for the first time in her presence. This child was Wolfgang Amadeus Mozart.

1763: As signed by both Prussia and Austria, the Treaty of Hubertusburg increases their power and, also the power of the separate states: Including Germany.

1772: The first partition of Poland is divided between Russia, Prussia and Austria.

1781: First lawful Protestant worship in Habsburg territories follows the 'Edict of Toleration' by Joseph II. He also emancipated the serfs of Habsburg territories.

1786: Mozart's Marriage of Figaro premieres in Vienna. This is followed by Mozart's huge successes in Prague. The emperor Joseph II is said to have told the young prodigy – "It has 'too many notes".

1789 – 1799: The years of the French Revolution.

1790: In the court theatre of Joseph II in Vienna, Mozart's opera, Così fan Tutte, now premieres.

1792: Europe plunges into 20 years of conflict following the declaration of war on the Austrian emperor by France.

1797: Austria cedes the Austrian Netherlands and northern Italy to Napoleon of France under the Treaty of Campo Formio. In return the free republic of Venice, as created by Napoleon, is ceded to Austria.

1805: The Austrian and Russian armies are defeated at Austerlitz and Napoleon now enters Vienna.

1806: To protect it from Napoleon, Francis II disbands the 1000-year-old Holy Roman Empire.

1810: Napoleon marries an Austrian archduchess, the daughter of Emperor Francis I, Marie Louise.

1815: The Battle of Waterloo, fought on Sunday 18th June 1815, now ensures Napoleon's defeat.

1848: Following the Vienna uprising, chancellor Klemens von Metternich resigns from office. A second uprising resulted in the emperor Ferdinand I fleeing to Innsbruck. Martial law is imposed in Prague as a result the Pan-Slav congress (radical Czech students). A third uprising occurs following the suppression of unrest in Hungary. Ferdinand I flees Innsbruck for Olomouc. He is forced to abdicate and passes his thrown to his 18-year-old nephew, Francis Joseph.

1849: The deposition of the Habsburg dynasty and independence for Hungary is announced by the nationalist leader: Lajos Kossuth. The Habsburgs soon recover both Austria and Hungary.

1856: <u>Sigmund Freud is born (Příbor, Czech Republic, 6th May).</u> He is known to have spoken 6 languages - fluently.

1859: Austria declares war on Sardinia. Austria is defeated by Italy and France. The French liberate Piedmontese (Milan) from Austrian rule. With the aid of France, Piedmontese forces now defeat the Austrians at Solferino.

1864: Schleswig-Holstein is captured by joint Prussian and Austrian forces. A military alliance that is short lived.

1866: The Seven Weeks' War begins when Prussia invades neighbouring German states. Known as the first blitzkrieg, Prussia defeats Austria. The treaty of Prague ends the war, Austria loses control over Germany to Prussia. Austrian rule also now ends in the

Venetian territories. Venetia becomes part of the new kingdom of Italy.

1867: The emperor of Austria, Francis Joseph, is crowned king of Hungary. A 'dual monarchy' of Austria-Hungary is established. The Prussian Zollverein (customs union) includes all German states except Austria.

1878: Joseph Stalin is born (Gori, Georgia. 18th December). This is the same year that the Berlin congress allows Austria to become 'administrator' of Bosnia-Herzegovina. A former province of Turkey.

1879: Leon Trotsky is born (Bereslavka, Ukraine 7th November).

1889: Adolf Hitler is born (Braunau am Inn, Austria, 20th April).

1892: Marshall Tito is born (Kumrovec, Croatia, (7th May).

1905: The first Russian Revolution. It fails to cease control.

1908: Bosnia-Herzegovina is annexed by Austria in response to Istanbul's policy of the Young Turks.

1913: Freud, Tito, Trotsky, Stalin, and Hitler are all known to now reside in Vienna. Freud is an established psychoanalyst. Tito works as an engineer at the Daimler factory. Austrian-born Hitler seeks admission into the school of arts. Trotsky and Stalin live here whilst in exile from Russia.

1914: The assassination of Archduke Franz Ferdinand in Serbia (Heir to the Austrian throne) ignites World War I. Franz Ferdinand is assassinated in Sarajevo by a Serbian nationalist, Gavrilo Princip. Austria and Germany unite against the Allies. Austria-Hungary plans to attack Serbia and seeks a guarantee of German support. Germany promises its support which now provokes war with Russia. With German support war is now declared on Serbia, the bombardment of the Serbian capital, Belgrade, begins. On the 30th July the 30th Russian forces mobilise. On 1st August, Germany declares war against Russia. 10th August, France declares war on the empire of Austria-Hungary, Britain joins France with her declaration of war: 12th August.

1915: Italy declares war against Austria-Hungary: 23rd May. It does not declare war on Germany. Austria-Hungary troops capture

Belgrade. Serbia is abandoned in October to Austrian and Bulgarian forces.

1916: The emperor Francis Joseph dies 21st November. He had ruled on the thrones of Austria and Hungary for 66 years. He is succeeded by his great-nephew, Charles I.

1917: During February through to October the second Russian revolution begins – and succeeds. The Russian political landscape had been fragile and violent since 1905 and by the end of 1916, Russia, having lost two million soldiers in the ongoing war was collapsing into economic and political turmoil. The Bolsheviks were now in power.

1918: Austria-Hungary signs an armistice with the Allied powers: 7th November. In Padua and in the absence of Germany. Six centuries of Habsburg rule now end with the deposition of the emperor Charles I. With the end of the Habsburg Austro-Hungarian Empire, German-speaking Austrians declare their own independent republic. Czechoslovakia is established as a new nation from the ashes of Austria-Hungary. Tomas Masaryk is it's first president. Prime minister Mihaly Karolyi proclaims the republic of Hungary. At 11am 'Paris time' on 11th November, the Allied Forces announce victory and complete defeat for Germany, Germany signs the Armistice of Compiègne. The Treaty of Versailles takes six months to negotiate.

It would not be until 1925 when 'that book' would first be published, Hitler's: Mein Kamp (My Struggle). A date that is beyond the scope of this book but none-the-less at least some fleeting recognition of it is required. The UK Freud Museum, which is faithfully situated in Freud's final residence, primarily relates to the 1930s and thereafter. This is the decade in which Sigmund left Vienna for the safety and security of London. Mein Kamp is presented as the 'Black Book' – an art installation where the words in entirety are redacted. It is an appropriate and most powerful way to sanitise a tome of utter vulgarity and hatred. Freud, alongside his maternal grandparents are known to have 'only just' escaped Nazi persecution in Vienna: The family had fled to Romania in the nick of time during1939, eventually arriving in Great Britain.
I had the great honour of meeting Leon Greenman, author of 'An Englishman in Auschwitz, and a survivor of the Shoa. He had been incarcerated in the death and was the only 'known English Jew' to have survived such a horrific experience. His family did not. He asked me to visit the camp, and to tell the world of its horrors, a

cause that he had dedicated the remainder of his life to. I had met Leon during one of his many university talks. He asked me to write to him of my experience, and this I did some 6 years later. I composed the song 'The Holocaust Denier'. With great sadness I then discovered that he had died, peacefully, during the previous year. I know he would have approved.

It is hard to know what to do about Mein Kamp, the reality is the simple fact that it is not going to go away. I wanted to include, at least in part, some of it within this title, but I cannot. I find it utterly repulsive, and I am not prepared to have such hateful, venomous words sitting side-by-side with my own. Equally: I do recognise that it has historical value. I have compromised, this is perhaps against my better judgement as some may rightfully argue. I created the audiobook: Words At War - with reading of the translated English version of James Murphy: 1939.

I will endeavour to explain my rational so do let me please sow this seed. I didn't want people who held a genuine historical curiosity in reading it to be fooled by charitable versions. Whilst (some) retailers may shake responsibility for 'dirty profits', handing over their financial cut to charities; the publisher (in the vast majority of cases) remains paid in full. Do we even stop to think who that publisher or 'random uploader' is? And do these 'charities' ask themselves just where has this donation come from? Let me put it another way. Ian Brady (the infamous Moors Murderer & child killer) also published his own horrific autobiographical work. Though banned in the UK, it is still easily available elsewhere. While there may be genuine interest in reading that too from a psychological perspective, others may want to read it for more sinister reasons.

Inspired by the hate and vitriol toward Jewish ethnicity as expressed in "Mein Kamp", the murderous couple's 'first date' was to watch the film 'Judgment at Nuremberg'. Many sources state that Myra Hindley (Brady's lover) recollected that it was 'King of Kings'. So, I would ask you, should Brady's book too be sold for charity? Can you imagine 'a child welfare trust' accepting the proceeds of its sale. Isn't that the most abhorrent thought!

In publishing my 'anti-fascist' audio version, I expected a tirade of hate from the far-right. I expected the liberal minded amongst us to sit on the fence; as if awaiting 'consent' before they felt able to comment on it. And too; I expected criticism from like-minded anti-fascists who do not share in my point of view. My view is simple, banning books means we are scared of their content, that somehow, they keep a truth too dangerous to be known. Has banning Mein Kamp for over 70 years in Germany led to the reduction of fascist post-war sentiment? No, the neo-Nazis and far right amongst us has today increased substantially. Mein Kamp should be published but it must be de-financialised: profit must not be made from the genocide of millions. When published it must be annotated, the truth presented alongside Hitler's blatant fabrications and lies.

In commencing this 'audio work' my motives were, and remain so, true and honourable. That profit should not be made out of the genocide and cruelty of the Nazi regime. Within the introductory passages of this version, the IfZ Germany and controversies of the republished title are discussed in detail. I agree wholeheartedly that 'in the ideal world' all copies of Mein Kamp must contain annotations that expose the Hitler myth for what it is. The rantings of a deeply manipulative anti-Semite, a genocidal lunatic, who created death camps to 'cleanse' whole 'races': Jews, Romani and homosexuals', the disabled and countless others (over 11 million peoples) who were sent to their deaths on state orders and with total state complicity.

I accept that I do not live in an ideal, I live in a reality where 'the book of hate' is being republished countless times without argument and annotation. This fails to serve the task of 'defusing the bomb' that now again sits amongst us after the original copyright restrictions expired. My work approaches the balance of annotation by adding to it a substantial amount of 'counter-balanced material' from within the public domain, additional material that far counterweighs the words of hate as read, and material that debunks the Hitler myth and Nazi ideology. It contains over 42 hours of reflective antifascist literature. Within the main narration, is 'hours upon hours' of historic rare radio broadcasts that allow the listener to 'understand the enormity and magnitude' of the Second World War as it develops.

The IfZ Edition (Germany) has done this far more effectively than I, though it is a work that I cannot offer you as it is protected by copyright. I did write to the IfZ and ask that I be allowed to use their work as annotations within the public domain, and at the time of publishing, a reply had not been received. It appears to me that even when governed by the most righteous of reasons the power of profit remains the driving force within the 'wider industry.' In meeting my ethical considerations, you will also find a substantive appendix: US Military film footage as audio (1945) submitted as evidence during The Nuremberg Trials. Audio 'interjection' is further supplied by audio soundtrack of the 1960 Erwin Leiser film: Mein Kamp (legally defined as an orphaned work). This is found as a precursor to Chapter 11 (Race & People).

It is correct to say that the narrated appendix is compiled from the public domain works of Wikipedia. Some may feel that, given the circumstances of its (Wiki's) creation, it may be viewed as inaccurate. This is not the case. Indeed, Mein Kamp 'as an industry published work' would be given more academic credence if we subscribed to that argument. Most, I feel certain would agree, that such a debate here, would become laughable. Though edited for this work, I have not altered the substantive content or sentence construction.

Contained within my audio version is a substantial collection of rare historic WW2 radio broadcasts & reading of the Holocaust testimonial (Chapter 3 only) of the work of Leon Greenman: An Englishman in Auschwitz. Remembrance is given with further inclusion of the narrator's work: The Holocaust Denier. Recommended Holocaust awareness reading concentrates on The Library of Holocaust testimonies as provided by Yad Vashem (The World Holocaust Remembrance Centre). Additional bonus audio material includes the Old Time Radio Broadcasts (1943-1945 / 83 x 30 Minute Broadcasts). Produced in cooperation with the Council on Books in Wartime by the NBC (USA), episodes of Words at War were based on literature created during the war by a variety of authors. Words at War is a glimpse of the beliefs (with a sprinkle of wartime propaganda), and fears of (predominantly) American authors during WW2.

A collection of broad casts by Lord Haw Haw are also included (15 Broadcasts c.1939-1945). Lord Haw-Haw was a nickname applied to the wartime broadcaster and traitor: William Joyce. He is remembered for his propaganda broadcasts that opened with "Germany calling, Germany calling", spoken in an upper-class English accent. The same nickname was also applied to some other broadcasters of English-language propaganda from Germany, but it is Joyce with whom the name is now overwhelmingly identified. There are various theories about its origin. The English-language propaganda radio programme Germany Calling was broadcast to audiences in the United Kingdom on the medium wave station Reichssender Hamburg and by shortwave to the United States. The programme started on 18th September 1939 and continued until 30th April 1945; it stopped when the British Army overran Hamburg. The next scheduled broadcast was made by Horst Pinschewer (aka Geoffrey Perry), a German refugee serving in the British Army who announced the British takeover. Pinschewer was later responsible for the capture of William Joyce. Joyce was executed and is buried in Galloway, Ireland.

And finally; you will hear a collection of Charlie & His Orchestra (11 Broadcasts c.1940-1944). Charlie and his Orchestra (also referred to as the "Templin Band" and "Bruno and His Swinging Tigers") were a Nazi sponsored German propaganda swing band. Jazz music styles were seen by Nazi authorities as rebellious but, ironically, propaganda minister Joseph Goebbels conceived their use in shortwave radio broadcasts aimed at the United States and (particularly) the United Kingdom. British listeners heard the band every Wednesday and Saturday night at about 9 pm. The importance of the band in the propaganda war was underscored by a BBC survey released after World War II, which indicated that 26.5 percent of all British listeners had at some point heard programmes from Nazi Germany. The German Propaganda Ministry also distributed their music on 78 rpm records to prisoners of war.

'If we held a minute's silence for every victim of 'The Holocaust,' we would stand in silence for eleven and a half years'.

The Vienna Circle

The Vienna Circle was a name given to a collective of great Viennese thinkers of the time who proposed that matters of God, ethics and aesthetics were meaningless. They asserted that testable assertions about such things were wholly unverifiable, therefore, a complete waste of time. The conversations amongst the coffeehouses would focus on substantive facts – known proven existence. However, one particular event that week would question this way of thinking and that event was the Skandalkoncert.

Freud would often refer to himself as Dr. Max Liebermann, a pseudonym used when referring to himself as one of his own former students, and a new persona being somewhat of a crime sleuth. Freud had a passion for solving mysteries and was quite a fiction novelist himself. The mystery of the Skandalkoncert had fascinated him, gossip had spread like wildfire across the city.

The Skandalkoncert (Scandal Concert) was also often referred to as the Watschenkonzert (Slap Concert). Hitler, being an admirer of Wilhelm Richard Wagner, had attended this concert, one performed by the famous Jewish conductor: Arnold Schoenberg. A member of the Vienna Concert Society. Buschbeck, the event's organizer was a member of a different society: The Viennese School of Composer's and, if nothing else, he was keen to experiment. A riot had broken out with one man being slapped across the face by Buschbeck, it would come to light that the injured party was none other than Adolph Hitler himself. Buschbeck yelling at the time: *"If its art, it is not for all, if it is for all, then it is not art."* A most put out Hitler had complained of this remark the following morning to the gentlemen of the coffee house where upon hearing this, Tito had laughed at the young Adolf's pompous attitude, and merely chuckled: *"Hearing you get slapped must have been the most harmonious sound of the evening, then".* The concert had taken place in the Muzikvein (Great Hall), and by all accounts not at all to Hitler's personal tastes.

Trotsky, having joined in with Tito's folly, was met with wrath. *"I don't know why you're laughing, Trotsky"* – Shouted Stalin. *"You're nothing more than a paper tiger, nothing more than a noisy champion with fake muscles."* Adding: *'At least Adolph has a principle at stake, he's anything but your beautiful uselessness".* Trotsky was enraged and Hitler, seeing this change of mood, jumped in, and attempted to clarify the event. *"Let me explain, I went with that Klimt fellow, the one who published that series of filthy filly drawings, twenty-five of them, in the Fünfundzwanzig Handzeichnungen. So, I'm anything but narrow minded, Tito, if that it was you attempt to portray."* Gustav

Klimt was a leader of the Vienna Secession, an art movement which together created a number of iconic paintings that we have all come to dearly love and appreciate, today.

"I'd been advising him on a new style, from last year" – Hitler added. *"A Portrait of Adele Bloch-Bauer II, I told him, more gold Klimt, more gold"*. No stranger to controversy, Hitler would then put himself across as Gustav's mentor, which at the very least diffused the mood between Trotsky and Stalin, especially when he stated - *"Without my talent he would never have got that one finished in time"*, then continuing without a breath; *"His Vienna's International Exhibition of Prints and Drawings this year is my doing, not his"*. Freud, neither fooled nor impressed replied; *"I know the chap well, very well, Hitler, I appreciate that he has a rather dodgy chest these days, I keep telling him to wrap up before he catches something, but to suggest he is your apprentice now is way too far beyond the pale"*. History informs us that Klimt died of bronchial complications resulting from Spanish Flu in 1918. Hitler took back control of the dialogue.

"I'm not here to argue with you, Freud, the truth is truth, and we'll leave it there" – *"Truth? I think if you tell a big enough lie enough times it becomes your truth,"* Freud muttered below his breath as Hitler ranted on. *"I went to the concert last night as invited, with Gustav and his on again off again mistress, Alma Mahler. She's written dozens of books and songs, if she invited me then that alone is testament to my superior creativity, she knows everybody, and those she does not know are not worth bothering with"*. Maintaining centre stage, Hitler explained that at the concert they had shared a table with Oskar Kokoschka, a poet and playwright. Hitler then, in underpinning his intellect, proceeded to recite the names of dozens of world-famous works of art. *"If war breaks out gentlemen, Oskar and I will both sign up. Me because I am a patriot, he because Alma wants rid of him, she told me so. If I am so talentless, why would she seek my guidance and companionship?"* – *"Pray tell then"*, asked an inquisitive Trotsky. Freud however, attended to the obvious detail: *If Gustav is meeting with Alma behind Oskars back, I suggest you give such company a very wide birth in future, young Adolph."*

"I'll quote her, gentlemen, shall I? She said - He alone seeks my destruction. One cannot cleanse what is soiled. What foul fiend sent that one to me, Adolph?" Freud did not break confidentiality but did remark later in the journal that he knew all too well of this 'notorious' pair and of their 'Vienna couplings'. Writing: *"He (Oskar) has created a life size doll which Alma informs is called – 'Alma Doll'. She alleges it to be a true to real-life Alma, intimate in every detail and he carries around with him wherever he goes, she told me, even to parties and the opera...* Freud knew at the very least that this part of Hitler's narration had now contained at least in part, some truth.

"So, yes, of course I wanted to impress Gustav, Oskar and Alma, that is why I invited them there and we were seated in anticipation of a brilliant concert. I was aware that it could not compete with the brilliance of Wagner but I did expect music, gentlemen, and they were all amateurs, and what did we get for our pennies? Garbage, gentlemen, utter garbage. Not even the worst of tropes and cliches that would remotely appeal to the masses" - Hitler had ranted on.

"So, you hit the organiser because you didn't like the music" suggested Tito, then in quoting Freud's dear friend and protégé, Carl Jung, he explained choice: *"It is not for you to decide what is or what isn't music, Hitler. Buschbeck had neither sought nor asked for your advice, it is subjective only, it was his concert"*. Tito was aware that his knowledge of Jung would impress the great psychoanalyst seated beside him. *'I wasn't the only one, Tito, everybody there hated it, it was a riot, the whole place got smashed to pieces. We paid for music and what we got was noise"*, and in turning to face Stalin, finished – *"Yes, Stalin, it was the principal of it"*.

Freud again picked up on the obvious; *"So, nothing to do with the fact that Arnold Schoenberg is a Jewish conductor then, Hitler?"* – Hitler was now the enraged one and Freud continued. *"You seem to think that you can talk on informed behalf of everyone present last night, these matters of aesthetics are meaningless. Whether it was or wasn't and who did or did not is not testable, you make assertions about taste based on your own opinions, ones that are wholly unverifiable, and frankly, Hitler, a complete waste of my time this morning"*.

"How dare you", a most put out Hitler demanded to know. *"I got slapped because that man was an odious fool, an ignorant oaf who knows nothing of culture. I'll tell you this, Freud, Franz Lehar was experimental, but he managed critical success. There's nobody like him, my taste is much broader and more educated than you prescribe"*. It was Lehar who had inspired the likes of the Italian opera composer - Giacomo Puccini. Hitler was keen to stress that whilst not mainstream at the time, he was seen by many as the greatest composer of Italian opera. *"I like and respect a genuine composer that pushes his boundaries"*, Hitler added. *"Puccini on the influence of Franz Lehar tried his hand at creating Operetta's, Freud, and he succeeded, pure genius at every level, and what about La Rondine, one of the biggest events to take place this year, a new and pure creation, Freud, he has created an operetta of perfection"*.

"Yes, pure" replied Sigmund. *"Lehar's father is an Austrian bandmaster in the Austro-Hungarian Army, and his mother, Christine Neubrandt, a Hungarian woman of German descent"*. If one was ever to find themselves quizzed, it was always Freud who would be found on the winning team. *"How can you remember all this historical detail?"* - Stalin asked as Hitler, now frustrated, finally shut up.

"That's easy" said Freud, *"Always keep one eye on the ball and one on the referee".* Hitler was not going to remain silent for long - *"So hate the player, not the game, is it? - And what have you recently achieved Mister Sigmund Freud, a book about dreaming that finally, yes finally, got published in English only this year, and a book that you wrote over 14 years ago. You're all the same, you chosen ones', you know nothing Sigmund Freud".* Adolph Hitler had then by all accounts of the journal, got up and left, slamming the door of the Central Coffeehouse behind him. His last words upon exiting: *"You're a kwakzalver".* A *'kwakzalver (quacksalver)' is a Dutch word and the origin of British slang: Quack. It is applied to those who secretly sell dubious medical cures of an uncertain origin.*

Tito, as ever the source of immediate quick humour turned to Freud and reassured him – *"Worry not, Freud, you won, they're all the same these Austrians, nothing but *unts and crybabies".* - *"He'll be back tomorrow",* added Trotsky. *"He told me earlier that his Creditanstalt bank loan application had been turned down, yet again, apparently, it's their fault now, that's why he can't get into college. I suspect that the concert was his Achilles heel. It reminded him that art challenges and changes, and what he has to offer has been left behind. He's nothing more than an inadequate postcard seller".* – *"I fear that we will never hear from him again",* Freud suggested to the others, feeling that perhaps he had gone a little too far with Adolph's fragile mind today... *"You most certainly will",* remarked Tito, *"Not that I want to be cheeky to my elders but who else is going to pay for his coffee. I'd say bollocks to him, personally, but rumour is - he only has one!"*

We know that the Rothschild family were Jewish, extremely wealthy, and originally from Frankfurt. Their banking empire, Creditanstalt Bank, was spread across Europe. Salomon Mayer von Rothschild was the first to move to Vienna establishing the first Viennese branch of the family and, by 1913, the Rothschilds firmly established Vienna as <u>the</u> European centre of finance. Louis Nathaniel de Rothschild owned the huge Vienna Palais Rothschild. The family homes would later be ceased, looted and destroyed - as 'Aryanised' by the Nazi's. The Austrian Government held on to over 200 art works belonging to the family until as late as 1998 – when they were finally returned. Later, being sold at Christie's auction house (London -1999).

It is without doubt that Freud's later work: A seminal paper - The Ego and the Id - was published with Hitler and Stalin in mind. Even though this was not completed until 1923. As the journal now informs, he was fascinated by the psyche of these two men, and to a lesser degree, the others. In this seminal paper that uses quotes from the 1913 meeting, he describes what he sees as the psychodynamics of the id, ego and super-ego. Had Freud not met

Tito, Trotsky, Stalin and Hitler, psychoanalysis as a theory would never have been developed. The id is a set of uncoordinated instinctual actions based on Hitler's idiocy. We know that the ego is the organised and realistic part, his findings based on Trotsky and Stalin, who at the very least owned a successful newspaper. And, accordingly, the super-ego, based on his assumptions of the young Tito in playing the critical balancing act.

Both Carl Gustav Jung, the founder of analytical psychology and Sigmund Freud, the founder of psychoanalysis, were the greatest of friends. They would regularly meet at the Café Landtmann for group gatherings within the Vienna Circle. The Vienna Circle conducted lengthy meetings and correspondence, all discussing their joint visions in regard to contemporary human psychology. Though, of them all, whilst Freud may have become the most famous it was Jung who is highly regarded today as the most influential. For Sigmund, Jung was his heir to 'new science' beyond psychoanalysis. We do know that Freud had invited Jung to meet the young artist and the other three revolutionaries of the Sugar Lump Club, but it was an invitation that was never taken up. Freud having noted: *"Carl would rather feed his penis into his coffee grinder than waste time on that lot"*.

Carl Jung found it difficult to follow his older mentor's doctrine at times, and as history informs us, we know they later parted ways. Jung establishing his own branch: Analytical psychology which was quite separate from Freud's original theories on psychoanalysis. Jung's 'individuation' concerns the matter of a lifelong psychological process of differentiation. An understanding of one's 'self', based on both conscious and unconscious forces. He focused on human development, describing this as: *"Synchronicity, archetypal phenomena, the collective unconscious, the psychological complex and extraversion and introversion."* It was not that he was averse to meeting the others, Trotsky, Tito and Stalin, that he had declined Freud's invite – no, not at all, he liked to be intellectually challenged. The fact is, Jung was also an artist, a craftsman, and a prolific writer. He had met Hitler on a handful of occasions already, they had painted together, seated side-by-side, passing time and chatting. Both evidently had very different techniques and styles.

Jung had said to Hitler: *"As a human being, the artist may have many moods, and a will, and personal aims, but as an artist he is 'man' in a higher sense - he is 'collective man' - one who carries and shapes the unconscious, psychic life of mankind."* He had gone on to share one of his many books with Hitler, but soon discovered that he was not quite as enlightened as himself. On returning the book the following day, as agreed, Hitler had said: *"You'll be dead before you'll ever get that pulp coffee literature published"*.

Yes, his decline of the invitation was personal, coming to light much later on and not born of Freud's journal. It was a much later publication, The Freud/Jung Letters: The Correspondence Between Sigmund Freud and C. G. Jung (Princeton University Press, 1974). We know that most of Carl Jung's books were published posthumously and still to this day, many remain unpublished.

Freud's investigations into the unconscious mind led him to believe that Adolph Hitler's sexual and aggressive impulses were in perpetual conflict. His need for a sense of supremacy over others were his defense mechanism. Yes, Adolph Hitler was Sigmund Freud's raw material.

War of The Boxes

Freud never said: *'Time spent with cats is never wasted"*. This is a misquote wrongly attributed to him, and as we deal with fact not fiction here, it is important to say that. However, whilst there is absolutely zero evidence of that quote ever being attributed to him, he did write in a letter to his friend Arnold Zweig, quite the opposite: *"I, as is well known, do not like cats"*. Freud was more of a dog person, and this was due to what he had penned within a brief paragraph as; *"The war of the boxes"*.

One of his former patients was Sabina Nikolayevna Spielrein, she would herself later become one of Vienna's first female psychoanalysts. As a Russian physician she was already well established. She went from patient to student and then to colleague of Carl Jung. We read in her diaries of 1908 –1910 of an intimate relationship soon developing between the pair whilst working together. Apparently, Spielrein had three cats, and from time-to-time Freud and Jung would have supper together at Spielrein's apartment.

They were young cats, siblings, one male and two female, found to be abandoned kittens. Their names were Бронте (Bronte), Осен (Autumn) and Зигги (Ziggy). The origins of these names are unknown and quite irrelevant as what really mattered to Spielrein, Jung and Freud was their behaviour. The cats had a box each, all three boxes placed side by side and to no advantage over the other, with adequate bedding beside the warmth of the fire. As siblings, peace and harmony co-existed, until that was, one would attempt to sleep in its box. The war of the boxes brought much joy to the psychoanalysts as they would all eat together, watching, and fascinated by what would always unfold.

The cats would only want to sleep in the boxes when one or the other had already attempted to do so. Occupation of all three boxes simultaneously was never witnessed. Whichever box the first cat chose to climb into, then, the other two cats would seek to occupy that same territory, and whilst usually most playfully, one would soon conquer. Countless experiments demonstrated that even when two of the boxes were moved far away from the heat of the fire, should a cat climb into one of them, the conqueror of the fireside box would abandon its luxurious position to regain this alternate substandard box. Freud had noted: *"Cats are a ridiculous species, dogs would never abandon the heat of the fireside, they would fight to defend it, but of these cats, the priority seems to be - I only want what somebody else has got, even when it is to its own disadvantage and against the norms of survival instinct"*. We know that Carl Jung had

2 adult cats of his own, a male (Poe) and a female (Skyla) and in comparison, behaved in much the same manner.

In reading the journal this brief paragraph is clearly intended to link to his feelings about the impending war. He goes on to say: *"This will be nothing less than an opportunity to land grab, Empires who seek to flex their muscles, just like those stupid cats, they want what others possess, and to great cost and suffering when they have all they require, already"*. From the analogy we can only assume that Tito was a dog, Hitler, Trotsky and Stalin were cats. Freud seems to be suggesting that dogs fight to protect, whilst cats fight to occupy. I found no evidence of Hitler's return to the Coffeehouse again that year within the journal. It is hard to decipher at times as previously discussed but I fear it is accurate to suggest that Hitler's last words to Sigmund Freud do appear to have been, quite simply: "You're a kwakzalver".

Upon Hitler's final words as noted by Freud (upon storming out of the coffeehouse) we see that Tito too also now disappears from the texts, as they occurred in that week of 1913. Freud offers no explanation as to the subsequent whereabouts of both Tito or Hitler. He does note that Trotsky would meet up regularly with his revolutionary comrade, Nikolay Bukharin (The Russian writer whom Freud had met on the first day). This would be to finish their work on Marxism and the National Question. There is recognition in the final pages of the journal, however, of a significant exchange that took place between Freud and Stalin. In conclusion it is now shared with you.

Freud had felt he had somehow failed Hitler. He noted: *"Upon examination, that was not handled as well as one would expect, I do feel somewhat guilty, it is true to say that this has disturbed my sleep to a degree that makes me feel uncomfortable with my retrospective actions"*.

We know that his enduring idea of personality (human psyche) held more than one aspect for Freud. Binary principles (life and death) make what we are as human. The Ego and the Id develop our reasoning, working out the equation of right and wrong, a pair of psychological conditions that lead to secondary reasoning. Pathological and non-pathological alike, for Sigmund, it was these conditions, pathological and non-pathological alike, that laid life's groundwork.

"The id is the primitive and instinctive" – that is, present from birth. For Freud, a source of all psychic energy as a primary component of who we are, our personality. "It is the impulsive and unconscious... it responds directly and immediately to the instincts". Beyond this, the direct influence of our external world creates the ego. The ego is the modifier of the id – it regulates our instincts; it makes us human. *"The id is driven by the pleasure principle...*

immediate gratification of all desires, wants, and needs", however, the ego brings us back to reality, the consequences of our conduct, a realistic and socially acceptable way to behaviour in satisfying the ids needs. The ids 'I want it now' versus the ego's - 'don't do it'.

We find our values and morals formed within the super-ego, the education supplied by our scholars, parents and community. The ids 'I want it now' versus the ego's - 'don't do it', but now enhanced with the super-ego's – 'don't do it because of... the reason why'. "For Freud, the super-ego functions to *"control the id's impulses... those which society forbids...* (Our instinctive need for) *sex and aggression."* He presents these opposites as *"simultaneously engaged in conflict by repressed thoughts".* At any level of the human psyche an; *"interplay between the love instinct and the death instinct can manifest itself".*

Freud had asked Stalin a simple question, it centred on his disturbed sleep, he asked; *"All I have done is slight the fellow, I confronted him with the realities of his misguided values and morals, and it is I who know lacks sleep. He has all the makings of a monster, Stalin, how is it that he sleeps at night?"* Stalin offered his advice in saying that Freud thought too much about such things and answered: *"Given everything we have come to know of Hitler this week, Mister Freud, it is clear, he doesn't drink coffee after 7pm".*

Stalin would then go on to offer more sound advice as we read within the journal, this would be referred to as 'the cognitive gap'. Freud summed this up as an emotional conflict between his actions and the interpretation of what others thought of his actions, the stress caused when he felt that he had let others down. *"Most of you Europeans believe we only drink Vodka"* Stalin had started, adding; *"But that's not true, you know. As Bolsheviks we prefer a fermented beverage, we call it Kvass, Freud, but these days, it's almost impossible to find a decent pint of it anywhere in Russia... that's why Vodka is taking over, it's cheap, quick, and cheerful".*

Stalin explained that Kvass, as an old and traditional beer had been produced in Russia for well over 1,000 years, and that it was known to be the favourite beverage of Peter the Great (As Russian Emperor: 1682 - 1725. *"To make a good Kvass, Freud, you'll need rye bread, the darker the better and then season it with herbs and fruits, apples or berries are the best for flavouring, but the key ingredient is the amount of birch sap, it is this that separates the master form the novice",* – *"That does sound rather delicious in wetting one's palette, I rather fancy some of that, you never know, it might help me to sleep",* Freud chuckled.

"Oh, yes, it'll do that my friend, but it's a sweet drink, given the amount of sugar you put in your coffee, none, I'm not sure if it is the most perfect for you. It is the aroma's that does it for me, just like the coffee here does in dragging one from the street, it smells best when

made with pumpernickel, brown sugar, and prunes, you should try some". – "Have you found any of it in Austria" Freud asked. "No, just mediocre versions, low in alcohol, suitable for children only, I tried one and it tasted just like a cheap soda".

Stalin continued: *"You'll only find the real thing in Russia, Moscow is best, the Yar, they say it was opened as far back as 1826, popular these days with the Russian elite but don't let that spoil the taste. I've met many famous poets, actors, writers and artists there, Friday evenings are better, for both music and for the company of..."* Freud interrupted: *"Is it a brothel? Stalin".* – *"None more so than this very coffeehouse, if you want it, it is there for the taking, but most come here for the coffee as I feel certain you would agree, Freud".*

Sigmund Freud, in offering his hand in friendship explained that one day, when Trotsky and Stalin were able to safely return home again, from exile, that perhaps he could meet with them again and enjoy a pint a Kvass together. He was most keen to do this, this is certain as he noted the address of the Yar within the journal. He was shocked by Stalin's reply. *"Not possible, not now or ever, Freud, I'm banned".* – *"Banned? Then why build me up with all this excitement, Stalin, in my head I was already there, what a disappointment, I'm most perturbed"* he said. *"I wasn't offering you a holiday, Freud, the Yar and Kvass are quite irrelevant, it is the story I wished to share with you. It is your stress that requires of my attention, not your aperitifs'.* As reported, Stalin had gone on to share his story, and as history also informs, we know that after leaving Vienna, he would remain in Siberia, in exile, and would not return to Russia until the revolution of 1917.

Stalin explained that the story he wished to share had begun in 1910. *"I told Lenin I was arrested in March of 1910 for political agitation, Freud, but that wasn't quite true. I was sent back to Solvychegodsk, following an incident, you could call it a brawl it that helps to clarify, it had occurred one drunken evening, I was just young and fool hardy, and yes, I was in the Yar".* – *"You lied to Lenin?* – had asked Freud. *"Yes, not proud of it, it certainly creating a sense of distrust between us when he found out the truth, perhaps to the extent that our trust in each other may never fully recover, but I wasn't trying to big myself up, absolutely not, I was genuinely too embarrassed to admit to what I had done, Sigmund, it was shameful of me, unforgivable in fact".*

Freud noted how Stalin had told him of this 'shameful' night on the town, one where he had been drinking to excess, and one where he would return to his favourite hord for his final beer of the evening – this, to the Yar alehouse. Stalin had demanded to drink the best pint of Yar in Moscow, and an all too eager to please landlord had served him just that. The landlord had by his account been so thrilled with Stalin's appreciation of his brewing talents, and duly served him with a pint of the best Kvass ale in Moscow. *"This is a pint of the best ale in Russia, if not the whole world"* the landlord was noted to say. Stalin had savoured the powerful arousing aromas, the taste. The texture, he congratulated the barkeeper, he was the master, of that there was no doubt. It had taken Stalin an hour to drink as so much conversation had been shared between the patron and proprietor in exchanging views on how such perfection had been created.

Upon finishing his drink, he had then climbed onto the bar, dropped his trousers, and urinated 'literally - everywhere'. *"Why would you do such a thing"* – Freud had asked, and was most shocked by this appalling conduct and confession. *"I don't know to this day"* – Stalin replied, adding; *"I just did, I was bursting, I felt like I was going to explode, if you have ever paid attention to the horses of Vienna, Freud, you know that it was not a halfhearted attempt, I pissed over the whole bar, soaked it, pissed like a horse and it stank".* There was no plausible reason for him not venturing outside to empty his bladder, this he accepted, for some strange reason unbeknown to himself, he had freely chosen to do this.

'So, what happened next" - 'Well, unsurprisingly, Freud, the Cossacks were summoned, and they beat the living daylights out of me, and as you can imagine that wasn't the first beating of the evening, they were my desert. With every punch the landlord had demanded to know why I had done such a thing, I could only reply, I don't know, I must have a problem, I begged him to stop, but no. That's really why I got arrested and sent back to Solvychegodsk". Gossip soon spread throughout Moscow's back streets and Lenin would soon come to hear of the true circumstances of that evening's events. It would not be for an entire year that Stalin would develop the strength and stamina he needed to return. *"Did you actually go back'*, enquired Freud. *"I did indeed",* the reply, *"At the very least my intention was to apologise, I felt so terribly awful about it, for the whole 12 months, I needed to get the guilt and shame of it all finally off my chest".*

Stalin explained: *"I went in, it took quite some doing, believe me, but I mustered up the courage eventually and I said, a pint of the finest Kvass in Russia please landlord"* – *"And..."* Sigmund's single extended word of encouragement as he was so eager to know more. "He took one look at me and then punched straight on the end of my nose". Graphic details followed concerning both the copious amounts of blood lost and the agonising pain experienced. *"He screamed and screamed at me, and all I wanted to do was apologise. Every time I tried, I got a swift swing toward my chin, backing up with every avoidance until I soon found myself outside in the street again. I walked around the block, gave it about an hour until I was too cold to stay on the street no more, and went back in".* Freud had noted down in his texts how the landlord had finally accepted Stalin's apology. We read that the landlord had recognised him immediately, saying - *"Do you think that I don't remember you, last year I gave you a glass of the best beer in the entire world and in return for all of my efforts, you pissed on my bar".-* " *I did",* had replied Stalin, *"It was me and I don't deny it, you did nothing wrong, you were nothing but kind to me, and yes, it was the best beer I have ever tasted in the entire world, but please, please, please accept my humble apology, sir".*

Yes, after calming down, the landlord had indeed accepted that apology. Stalin had explained how shameful his behavior was, the guilt that he had felt and held on to for the last 12 months, and of his genuine and sincere need to apologise in person for such abhorrent thuggish behaviour. Stalin had accepted that he had a problem, and with his nose swollen and blooded, had told the landlord his actions were wholly unforgivable. *"I want to start afresh, that's what I am here to do, I was wrong, and you were right. You are a good man, landlord, forgive me for my previous conduct – I must taste your ale again, for if not, my life is not worth living, I was a priest at one time, sir, I know what the wages of sin are".* What else could the landlord have done, here in front of him a priest begging for his forgiveness, of course he forgave. Stalin had accepted all responsibility for 'his problem', unconditionally, and as a Christian, the proprietor had forgiven him. He would be served not one but three beers, a Kvass to which there was no equal.

"Isn't forgiveness the most beautiful of actions"- Freud said with a smile beaming from his face. "I'm so pleased to hear it all ended so well for you, Stalin, a happy end is a pleasure to hear, it must be so wonderfully to have finally released yourself of all that ill feeling and guilt you had carried for so long". – *"Well, Freud, not exactly",* Replied Stalin as he elaborated further. *"I'm not the tallest man on the planet as you well know, and three pints, well, that was it. I jumped up on the bar, but this time it was different - as I only pissed in his face.".*

Stalin had filled in all the gaps for the bemused and rather confused learned psychoanalysts, we know thus as Freud had reported on this discussion in vivid detail within his journal. Whilst the landlord had attempted to wash the urine from his face in utter disgust, Stalin had fled into the dark damp of the cold night, he escaped and hid. *"As he was mopping his face with a towel, I released immediately it was now or never, I knew what was about to unfold given my previous beatings, so I fled the Yar as if my life depended on it, and, Freud, I had no doubt it did".* Stalin had clearly had a serious behavioral problem for which he had eventually sought treatment. *"I couldn't carry this pain around with me, anymore, Freud",* he had explained, continuing; *"I went to a clinic in Poland, somewhere I wouldn't be recognised, I had weeks and weeks* of aversion therapy, even electricity applied to my skull, I went to confession and mass, I did everything I could to recover, but recover from my shameless condition I did, it took months but yes, eventually, I recovered...".

The journal tells us that Freud learnt a great deal from the revolutionary concerning the many positive aspects of that journey to recovery, the need to accept and fully embrace one's condition and that recovery is possible. He also came to fully understand why Stalin had discussed such personal circumstances with him. A story he was so very keen to share with his dear friend Carl Jung and the others of the Vienna Circle and that is why the story contains so much accurate detail as Freud had penned to Jung, *"I learned so much from him, about my true inner self, my own psyche and negative emotions', the reason why I had felt so broken for insulting that young painter, my guilt."*

Stalin had written over 12 letters, one per month, over yet another 12-month period to the proprietor of the Yar. He had become obsessed with his need to again apologise and to inform of his cure. *"I was ill sir, I know this may be impossible for you to understand, but my illness had taken over me, to behave in such a way for a second time, I have no words to offer, but I do tell you this, if it were not for those events I would have remained ill and controlled my by an inner disease, a parasite that took over me".* Stalin did not receive a reply to any of those most intimate letters until the very last was sent. Within his twelfth letter he had enclosed a certified conformation as signed by his psychiatrist – *"I can confirm that this man is cured"*, it read. *"Without your forgiveness for a second time I fear he may relapse; I stress the utter importance of this..."* Only then had he received a reply to his correspondence, and within it an invitation to return to the Yar.

"You see, good people do exist, Freud, imagine that, how kind and compassionate that man must have to be to forgive me again, and to invite me back, I was over the moon, the best day of my life it was". – *"Did you go back",* asked Freud, *"Did you not feel it to be a trap?"* – 'No, not for a second, I had borne my soul to him, poured out my heart, his letter was so genuine, it was pure human-to-human love, he understood me now, we both understood that we had nothing to fear of each other".

Stalin continued: *"The day came, and I walked confidently back into the Yar, another full year had passed me by, and I was greeted with smiles and the warmth of the fire, he beckoned me over and offered his hand. I took it and shook it firmly, I told him just how much his forgiveness had meant to me, that life was not worth living without his finest ales a part of it. His wife made me the most delicious soup, I sat beside the fire nourishing my meal, I was in heaven."* The proprietor had walked over bringing Stalin's drink to his table as he had seen how much the warmth of the fireplace heat was being appreciated. *"This brew has just won the award of best Russian Kvass, Tsar Nicolas III has personally endorsed it, we are to become the official supplier to His Majesty the King"* he proudly divulged.

"I'm not sure most people would have been so forgiving, Stalin, forgiveness for me isn't a religious position but a practical action, I've always viewed it akin to removing your hands from around the other fellow's throat, it's about letting go and finally moving on, isn't it?" – 'Yes, Freud, and I more than anyone had finally moved on. I finished my soup, Borscht it was, both parsnip and hogweed, absolutely delicious, perfect in every detail, a poor man's meal but a poor man I was. I savoured the King's pint, that too was perfect but just the one this time, stood up, adorned my cap and coat and thanked him again for his kindness. As I was leaving, I caught a glimpse of his wife working hard away in the cookhouse, I turned and waved to her a fond farewell".

Sigmund Freud was most impressed with Joseph Stalin's recovery, this was obvious by the excitement of his words, especially when he finally understood how this linked back to his feelings toward Hitler. As Stalin was leaving he noticed 4 Russian men playing cards, Preferans, and large sums of money were at stake. Intuitively he walked over, introduced himself and then – pissed all over their table. As one would expect, all hell broke out, Stalin, without anytime to pull his trousers back up was punched to the floor – he was now being beaten and kicked by four very angry men. *"They were pulverising me"*, Freud, he explained. 'The landlord bellowed – 'get that sick, lying scoundrel off my premises, throw that garbage of a man out of here and never let him return' - and I was dragged into the street where the beating continued".

The landlord had now, by all accounts, assisted the others with the beating, and his wife too, striking Stalin to the legs with a steel poker. It was noted that had a gang of Bolsheviks not recognised him and had they not intervened in pulling them all off him, Stalin would have most certainly been beaten to death that evening. *"You are a liar and a cheat, cured my arse, you are a *astard of a man"*, - The insanely irate publican had shouted as Stalin now stumbled back to his feet.

"You can call me many things, of that I am guilty, but a liar is not one of them" – Had retorted Stalin, adding: *"I told you I was cured and cured I am sir – I no longer feel guilty".*

-The End-

ONE LUMP OR TWO, MISTER HITLER?

Your Supplementary Stage Adaptation

Newspaper:
Vienna_konzert_Karikatur_in_Die_Zeit_vom_6._April_1913.
Public domain.

Genre: Dark Comedy

Cast: 8

Words Spoken: Waitress: 3806 (Regina Wiener)
Trotsky: 3345
Bucharin: 1107
Tito: 4524
Stalin: 3823
Freud: 3966
Hitler: 4721
*Hawker: 1289

Additional cast: Unlimited Coffeehouse Patrons.

The stage is set for one single location: The interior of the Central Coffeehouse (Vienna). To the far left of stage is Freud's writing bureau, chair, a rug and tall floor lamp, to the far right of stage is Hawker's newspaper vending stand (Possibly a hand-pulled cart). Centre back is the coffee house entrance door, a single 'open' window is to the left of it. To the right of the doorway is the coffeehouse serving counter.

The role of ***Hawker** can easily be merged into that of Bucharin reducing the <u>essential cast to 7</u>. However, it is my humble opinion that this should be avoided as Hawker adds what I feel to be essential flow and direction by bouncing off 'the waitress'.

Scripts can be hidden in multiple locations to reduce the burden on the speaking cast, behind the counter for the waitress, and/or within newspapers / menus etc. for the gentlemen. The script can also be shared out at the Director's discretion amongst the 'unlimited number of coffeehouse patrons', if preferred. Accordingly, repeating the gentlemen's words as 'overheard conversation'.

NOTE: Generally speaking, women were not permitted entry to the coffeehouse of 1913. Further humour is carried when the cast of 'Unlimited Coffeehouse Patrons' effortlessly becomes a cast of women secretly dressed as men. The role of Adolph Hitler can equally be presented by such a woman. Whilst Freud, Tito, Hitler, Trotsky, and Stalin are all considered to be quite young in 1913, I would encourage directors to use their own discretion in presenting this play with an older cast. The characters are best portrayed as visually aged in line with historical recollection and audience familiarity.

PROLOGUE:

Opening: Waitress as dual role narrator reads to audience as she tidies, cleans tables and prepares for the day's business.

Waitress: In the Vienna of 1913, all of what we now know to be true today, was yet to be. Sigmund Freud wrote at the time: What pathetic nonsense this young artist is full of, at times I find him to verge on pathetic drivel. Both Trotsky and I agree: he considers himself to be a great artist, but we fear he is nothing more than laughingstock.

Waitress unlocks door and greets customers. Leon Trotsky arrives first, Now seated, he sips from his cup as he enjoys today's newspaper.

Waitress: Café Central was a regular haunt for this young revolutionary. He would scrutinise the text hoping that he could understand the minds of those who contributed to the printed literature now placed upon his lap. Pouring over his words, he assimilated his ideas concerning the united international worker's struggle: Communism. These were radical times of great upheaval and political change in Europe; and none more so than found here in the minds of the Viennese.

Trotsky enters. Seated at his favourite table in front of the central window, and after a brief atmospheric pause, Trotsky soon feels a cold chill as the draft of the coffee house door opens and the warm, smoky air exchanges with the bitter cold of the street outside. He addresses the waitress.

Trotsky: There's quite a chill in here, my dear, I suddenly feel rather cold.

Bucharin enters alongside a short man. He has greyish brown skin, pockmarks, and notably he is sporting a large peasant's moustache. This figure, of dark complexion, takes Trotsky by surprise – particularly his height, he is not at all as tall as Trotsky expects. The men's reaction to each other is indifferent – unfriendly. The waitress introduces the stranger.

Waitress: Leon, these gentlemen are asking for you.

Stalin, carrying a small wooden suitcase and Bukharin carrying his cased typewriter, join Trotsky at the table.

Trotsky: *Thank you my dear, yes, I've been expecting them.*

Trotsky stands politely to greet Stalin and Bucharin. They shake hands.

Trotsky: *You must be Joseph Stalin and Nikolay Bukharin, welcome to Vienna Comrades. I've been expecting your visit today, what a pleasure to finally meet you both.*

The waitress now narrates as the three men 'mime and gesture' as if in detailed pollical conversation.

Waitress: *They were now for the first time, all introduced to each other. After the usually expected social pleasantries customary of the day, the three men soon engage in political dialogue.* Stalin had come to meet Trotsky in Vienna to write his work: Marxism and the National Question, this with comrade: Nikolay Bukharin. Trotsky's advice was much sought after as he was held in the highest regard and trust of his counterpart: Lenin.

Lights slowly fade as if to imply significant passing of time. Audio volume slowly increases, that of 'general coffee house chatter' to imply that hours are now passing. Tito enters silently whilst the stage lights are down, he sits himself at an adjacent table. Bukharin also enters in darkness, he is to be found 'scribbling away, seated with Trotsky and Stalin.

Waitress: *After meeting, both Trotsky and Stalin would often be found seated together formulating their ideas, this as Bukharin eagerly scribbled away with pen to paper. Picking up on their ideological threads of thought, ones he would later use.*

Bukharin: *"I will see you next week gentleman with a first draft – in the interim I shall be engaged with my typewriter; you know where to find me if needed.*

Tito enters to stand at the serving counter. After a brief pause Bukharin leaves, closing the door most noisily behind him. The modestly dressed-looking figure, Tito, catches their eye, he walks over taking the opportunity to utilise the free seat, now available to him.

Waitress: *Tito was inspired, as a manual worker, by the words of revolution he had overheard.*

Stalin initially maintains a skeptical silence, he conveys a natural distrust toward Tito, Trotsky becomes aware of this, facial expressions express dismay. The metal worker introduces himself to the pair.

Tito: *Gentlemen, if I may join you, my name is Josip Broz. I work at the Daimler automobile works, of Wiener Neustadt. A small town, south of the city.*

Waitress: *He explained that he shared in many of the views he had overheard and was in the city centre today seeking other work that would pay better, and with no intention of rudeness or presumption, expressed his eagerness to join in and talk with other like-minded socialists.*

Trotsky: *By all means, take a seat, sir.*

Tito: *Thank you - My friends call me Tito.*

Background 'cityscape' audio builds as it is now approaching midday. The streets outside are bustling with life as the city workers start to pause work and head out for dinner.

Waitress: *An artist has set-up and sat himself across the road, to the pavement opposite this coffeehouse. He is painting a landscape of the famous central arches, streets, and city life as it now unfolds before him.*

Freud now enters to stand at the serving counter.

Tito: *An end to poverty and free health care for all...*

Stalin: *Yes, a Soviet Union of states based upon central control akin to the United States of America...*

Waitress: *As the men debate, laughter is heard to unfold into the room. A man at the counter, ordering a sandwich to take away had felt the need to express his dismay at such a notion.*

From a few feet away Freud seeks to interject into the gentlemen's conversation. Freud laughs aloud. He addresses them.

Freud: *America is a most grandiose experiment gentleman, but I'm afraid it will never work.*

Stalin, Trotsky and Tito stare at him conveying the rude and unnatural shattering of their discussion. Stalin conveys humiliation.

Freud: *Freud, Sigmund Freud; I'm a psychoanalyst and I'm afraid I don't subscribe to your belief in human nature gentlemen ...*

Waitress: *Obviously, Stalin beckoned Freud to join them.*

Stalin: *Why don't you pull up a chair and tell us all why not then or would that be beneath you to join the table of the common worker?*

Freud: *No offence was intended sir, I assure you, I just didn't agree, and if you did not seek my engagement then do keep your voices down – this is a coffee house you know, not a public gathering for political rally!*

Trotsky calms the mood by leaving the table and pulling up a spare chair, one he removes from another table, he places it amongst them all as an invitation to be seated.

Trotsky: *Join us sir, no offence is taken - I have heard good of you, Sigmund, by all accounts you are very popular amongst the fragilities of the ruling class. I'd be very happy to take coffee with you if you feel able.*

Freud: *Then that I will my fellow. I have some time to kill this afternoon. One of those frail ruling classes of ours, your words not mine, has now cancelled our planned home call. Too scared to open the door I believe. They are so hysterical women, don't you think? - But first I must take this Salami sandwich to the impoverished young man across the street. The painter - He's only 24, completely down on his luck and his delusional dreams to become a master of our fine Vienna Academy of Art are not quite going as well as he intended. Chaps hungry, I offered him lunch but he's busy painting away and doesn't want to interrupt his 'genius as he put it - I'll be back in a tick.*

The waitress prepares and brings fresh coffee to the table and a menu is secured for later civilised perusal. In doing so she says...

Waitress: *As they waited for his return, the three men, Trotsky, Stalin and Tito discussed this new strange encounter. Stalin was concerned that this man would add no valuable input to the discussion. Trotsky was more open-minded about that matter. He believed that the revolution was one in need of both the bourgeoisie and the proletariat mind, and not just a matter of seizure of power from the elite. Tito, the quietest member of the group, and lacking in* political awareness and confidence, wanted to learn more. He was there to grasp at ideas and had no intention of preaching to his older, much wiser peers.

The overconfident Freud returns.

Freud: *That's that then, he's fed and watered – poor chap finds himself living in a Danube-side dosshouse in Meldermannstrasse.*

Sigmund Freud draws up the chair to the table as he now sits.

Freud: *What's the coffee like then? – I usually only frequent the Café Landtmann. I've invited the artist to join us; he said he'd be finished soon, I told him the coffee would be very good, but without having first tasted it I fear I may have lied to him...*

Stalin: *The coffee is most adequate, Mister Freud.*

Trotsky: *The coffee and the company are found to be perfect, Freud.*

Tito: *A pleasure to meet you, sir.*

Freud chuckles in uncertain approval.

Freud: *Wonderful to hear, gentlemen, unlike that poor young man's paintings then... He comes across as rather down and out, I fear I know why.*

Stalin: *Trotsky and I are working on new political texts and incites, revolutionary material, I hope it is not chit-chat you seek, Freud.*

Freud: *Well as a political scholar then, Mister Stalin, you'll enjoy one of my publications then, Die Traumdeutung, the interpretation of dreams, - as a neurologist I would always encourage my fellow compatriots to dream...*

Waitress: *It was quite apparent that the newcomer had much to say and wasn't going to be backward in coming forward with it. Tito didn't quite know what to make of this uncomfortable exchange, Trotsky on the other hand took an immediate liking to him, and a wide smirk broke out across his face. Stalin was not amused.*

Stalin: *You, as a man of privilege are free to live in your world of dreams, but to beat your enemy you must first learn how to hate him,* *dreams will not change the world – it is bloodshed that is needed. Nikolay Bukharin will return next Monday, Freud, with the first draft chapters of Marxism and the National Question. I have but one month only to deliver it to Comrade Lenin in Krakow, for St Petersburg later, it needs to be something of political viability, for the party.*

An awkward silence falls, it is then broken by the sudden entry of the young artist bursting in through the street door and announcing at the top of his voice...

Hitler: *My masterpiece is finished, Freud: look, look, it's finished!*

Freud: *So, you finally come to join us do you young man? - Find yourself a chair. Is it one lump or two, Mister. Hitler?*

ACT TWO:

The stage is in darkness except for one spotlight that focuses on a writing bureau/desk, where Freud is seated and scribbling away. From the darkness unseen, the waitress' voice continues to narrate.

Waitress: Freud had spent his evenings, long into the early hours, sitting in his armchair. in his study penning his journal, after the day's encounters of that specific week. Without such empirical writing it would be true to say that these conversations would never have come to light today, in these later years. Freud's journal: A most accurate and noteworthy historical document that would warn us of what was to become. Divided into sections with named titles, he introduced each member of what we now know to be, and as simply called, The Sugar Lump Club. The relevance of sugar will become clear to us later. In the journal Stalin is referred to as Dzhugashvili, his name at the time in 1913, but for clarity I use Stalin in this text as this is the name as known today. However: there is a claim by some scholars that by 1910 he had already started to use his new: Stalin (man of steel). He was born in Georgia, a country that would later be annexed by the Soviet Union, this when he became supreme ruler of the new Soviet Union from 1924 to 1953. Appointed General Secretary of the Communist Party's Central Committee, he had come to power in 1922 following Lenin's death. History informs that he suppressed all criticism of his leadership. Freud wrote much about Stalin and noted in his journal...

Freud looks up from his desk and speaks immediately continuing the sentence above.

Freud: Whilst the two new men work on the book, I feel a sense of rivalry between them, both seem to contradict each other in matters of control and state; at times they are most hostile to each other's contribution.

Audio again plays; Hawker shouting; "Read all about it! War imminent. Read all about it! Austro-Hungaria readies for war." After a brief pause, a glance down, Freud continues.

Freud: This Stalin fellow is an opportunist, deeply distrusting of Trotsky, manipulative, and I feel not sincerely committed to his socialist cause. He believes that should war break out Russia should seize the moment to expand but unlike others in the club, he has never made any reference to 'world domination'.

Waitress: *It was obvious that Freud considered Trotsky and Stalin to be odd bedfellows, no-more so telling than when he wrote...*

Freud: *Stalin believes that a Socialist state could operate independently and trade directly in association with other Capitalists states– though Trotsky dismisses this outright in favour of an internationalist movement uniting all workers of the world. I can't imagine how they will ever manage to agree long enough to ever finish that cursed book.*

Waitress: *Freud seemed to hold a greater respect for Trotsky, Freud wrote...*

Freud: *Whilst I sit for hours listening to his utter nonsense to the point of boredom at times, I do feel a sense of genuineness within his belief. A sincere fellow who concerns himself only with the liberation of the workers - though has no wish to be in control. Whilst I do enjoy his company, I cannot say the same for the other. Trotsky expresses his views of a world rid of rulers and monarchy and a cooperative movement controlled by the workers, a redistribution of power from the top to the bottom as it were. It is guided by a true ideology, no matter how inconceivable this is to me, but Stalin, he just seems to hate, an angry man who I sense wants blood.*

<u>A brief pause as Freud now clips and lights his cigar.</u>

Freud: *I'm not surprised that the 1905 revolution failed, they have no sense of political direction or agreement – a fixation on blaming all but themselves for this. With such distrust between them I feel one or the other must concede to the dominant personality, but I have no incline at this venture who this will be".*

Waitress: *Freud wrote more positively of Tito. He said of him in the journal: A charming man with polite manner, a worker lacking in education and many airs and social graces but of pleasurable company. He viewed Tito as the student, as separated from the delusions of the other's – the two would be revolutionaries of Russia as he had called them.*

Freud: *He does not contribute political knowledge of foresight to the club, but when he speaks it is of his feelings, there is wisdom about this mind that I don't gain elsewhere from the wider conversations.*

<u>He pauses to draw on his cigar in contemplation.</u>

Freud: *As a citizen he is not hiding or fleeing and has no indicators prone to violence. Working in the laborious and demanding Daimler plant has taken its physical toll on many, and his focus is one of political education and unionisation of the workers at the plant. His concern is the conditions at the factory, and he never considers socialism beyond the necessities and essentialist needs of his inner world. Though, I fear his new interactions with others amongst us may politicise him beyond this. He is not in search of power but there is a revolutionary zeal beginning to surface - sympathetic to the communist cause.*

Waitress: *There were many interesting points that are discovered later on in Freud's journal, but none is more surprising than his underestimation of the young Adolf Hitler.*

Freud: *The would be's consider themselves to be loyal patriots, as does the young Hitler, but with startling difference. For Trotsky and Stalin, patriotism means a love of one's country, they see the benefit of unity of humanity, and they refer to anti-Semitism as against party rules. Though when discussion about such comes up at the table Stalin does not contribute but remains sullen and indifferent. It is not what he says on the topic but what he does not. Trotsky informed that he could never become a leader due to the nation's distrust of his Jewish background, one he shares with myself, and I would have expected a degree of support from his comrade – but this was notably absent.*

<u>Hawker leans through the window.</u>

Hawker: *Freud said that for the artist patriotism is not based on what is good for one's nation but only for one's own race. Though he controls what he says among the group you feel he is insincere in his acceptance of Trotsky and I as Jewish – this comes to the fore when we describe ourselves as citizens. He almost develops a range, flicking his hair back and tossing his nose around into the air with a lunge back of the neck. Indicative of deeply censoring his true deep loathing I suggest. When I remind him of my kindness, he informs me that it is my duty to support his great work – and he is only in a place of desperation and charity because of the conspiracy of others. He truly believes that one day he will achieve great things – but I see nothing of this in him.*

<u>Stage spotlight fades whilst another now refocuses on the waitress, now behind the serving counter, busying away.</u>

Waitress: *He talks of the artist Hitler as follows: One's sees leadership quality in the Russians, but this is quite lacking in Hitler. A weak and at times quite pathetic man: he is delusional.*

<u>Reversal - Stage spotlight fades from her whilst another now refocuses on Freud, still at his desk</u>.

Freud: *He talks of his art and masterpieces, but I am aware that this is not true – the Academy have already informed that he has been knocked back twice. I had bought two portraits of this young artist as I felt quite sorry for his pitiful circumstance. A patient of mine, one employed of the Academy, had recognised the work hung upon my hallway and informed. He is not of the standard, but this is not what you hear from the man himself. Quite the opposite – he informs that he*
is too good for such study now and wishes to become a fine art painter, possessing an exceptional talent that the academy cannot cater for.

Waitress: *There was much talk of a young Austrian artist in the Café Landtmann, yesterday, and much laughter and folly among the customers here too. This young fellow had asked for the Landtmann menu, not for fine foods or Beveridge but for the bedrooms above. However, he was unable to be catered for in that department as he found the young ladies who abode there to be too old for his personal taste. He was of the belief that: If they are old enough to bleed then they may be slaughtered. It is the talk of the whole house. The man had embarrassed himself and soon left tail between his legs.*

Freud: *I am quite sure that it is the young Adolf that they talk of, which surprises me greatly as I had thought of him to be possessed with the disease of homosexuality.*

ACT THREE:

The waitress is busying away cleaning tables as the lighting now returns to the full stage. All are now present at their table.

Waitress: *The sugar lump, long before the days of the finely diced and most precise dimensions of the sugar cube we know today, would be found on all tables of all Viennese Coffeehouses. A large rock of sugar would be broken into lumps, accordingly as desired, as if cracking a walnut in the jaws of a nutcracker. The sugar cracker, however, would not only break down the larger lump into small manageable pieces to be dissolved in one's coffee, but would also come to symbolise the fractious minds of those sat around the table.*

Stalin: *Will you be keeping the sugar to yourself, Hitler?*

Tito, in an address to the audience says…

Tito: *Hitler does not consume the same quantity of sugar as the rest of us. Often, he just sprinkles it into his drink from above, crumbling it between thumb and forefinger, just a brief powdering as if peppering his salami was all that he required. It was more about possession. Every time we ask him to pass the sugar over, he politely complys, immediately. But there, afterward, he will again slip the bowl gently back toward him, as if not to be noticed, to his cup and saucer quarter side. He doesn't want the sugar, but our need of it forces us to have to continually ask for it.*

Freud: *Why do you persist in hogging the sugar, Mr. Hitler?*

Hitler: *Am I? – How rude of me, sorry, I was merely keeping it out of harm's way. No offence was intended of it".*

Stalin: *What harm?*

Hitler: *You know full well sir - every time you say anything it is followed by a mighty thump of the tablecloth under the weight of your fist. Can you not see that when you do this the cutlery rises into the air with embarrassing clatter? If I leave the sugar in the centre of the table, it is certain to go everywhere.*

Stalin: *Ridiculous – You just want to control the sugar; you seek to control the conversation too…*

Stalin thumps the table with a mighty blow.

Hitler: *How dare you, what use of I for this sugar, I don't even want any. And you, look, there on your napkin, 5 lumps already at hand, you don't want it either.*

Stalin: *The milk is mine, then. Let's see how you like having to ask for it every time you wish to use it".*

Stalin lunges forward, then gripping the milk jug handle so tightly as if he would never let go, pulls the jug away from the centre of the table toward him. This is done with such force that much of it is sloshed out onto the tablecloth, and thus now wasted.

Trotsky: *I suggest you find a way to share. After all: if you have all the sugar and he now has all the milk, neither Freud, Tito nor I shall no longer have any coffee left to enjoy for ourselves.*

The waitress seizes the moment, it is defused by her arrival at the table.

Waitress: *What a fine mess you have made today, gentlemen...*

Tito, in an address to the audience says...

Tito: *Freud seized this opportunity for analysis. It was evident that such petty quarreling was indicative of deeper routed disturbances and born out of a clash of personalities. He recognised that the issue was one born out of power and control and not for the need of sugar at all. He noted that whilst Hitler's coffee was already sweetened sufficiently to taste, he would want it all, and nothing less than future possession of the whole bowl would suffice.*

Stalin: Though in possession of adequate sugar reserves already, he needed to know that future quantities would be made available on demand and without question.

Trotsky: *This is the problem as I see it gentlemen, communism in one country cannot work. For here, Hitler, you see, we are in possession of all of the milk, are we not?"*

Hitler: *Indeed, you are Trotsky, but I have all of the sugar.*

Trotsky: *Yes, young Adolf – this is truth, and whilst you control the sugar, representative of another country, as if it were beyond the control of ours, we will always depend on you before we can drink our own coffee.*

Hitler: And I too on you. You now have all the milk.

Trotsky: Indeed: and whilst we rely on each other within this mutually agreed gentleman's agreement over the supply of milk and sugar, as, shall we say, raw resources for our nation's needs, the sugar being the Austro-Hungarian Empire and the milk, being the Russian Empire, will there not always be friction between us?

<u>Hitler pauses before reply, lost in thought.</u>

Stalin: Trotsky – I don't agree - If Mr. Hitler supplies Russia with the sugar, and Austro-Hungary supplies Russia with the milk, where is the problem?

Trotsky: The problem is this Stalin, you have milk and Hitler has sugar but, neither of you have possession of the coffee!

<u>Tito again addresses the audience directly.</u>

Tito: Trotsky clarified his point. And it was a simple though effective one. Whilst both men agreed to share their natural resources all would be well, but both independent Empires, Russia and Austro-Hungaria, would always have to rely on the others cooperation, both were at the whim and control of the other.

Freud: It appears that what Leon is saying gentlemen is that both of you seem to think that you are in a position of power and position over the other, that is, in actually fact, nothing of the truth. The real centre of power is over there, on the other side of the room, the waitress that we see to be in possession of the coffee jug, and all the coffee in it.

Tito: Well, I think you put that very well, most learned Freud, neither Hitler with all his sugar nor Stalin with all his milk have anything of value at all, we still have no coffee on the table. And you fail to see the obvious: I don't take sugar in my coffee and I'm more than happy to skip on the milk as well. You see, you cannot negotiate without the credibility of force gentlemen, and your position is quite untenable. Whilst I have no need of your resources, those on the table before you, I will always be independent of you.

<u>An older man enters and goes to be seated alone. Stalin becomes enraged with anger; pushing his chair back and standing bolt upright. He turns on his heels and heads forcibly off across the</u>

room toward the young waitress who is pouring her coffee for this older man. Startled by his aggressive manner she freezes.

Stalin: *I'll have that now – Can't you see we have none, am I required to wait all day on your stupidity?"*

So shocked is she by this wholly unwarranted and quite unexpected rage attack forced upon her, she flees. She is heard to be sobbing in the make-believe kitchens to the rear of the stage. Stalin returns just as forcibly back to his table.

Freud: *I fear that was a step too far!*

Trotsky: *What on earth's got into you?*

Tito: *She's just a poor worker like the rest of us, Stalin, trying to make ends meet, trying to feed her family out of poverty like the rest of us. She is not our enemy. The enemy is outside, those she is forced to service...*

Stalin: *It was not my desire to frighten her; I merely sought to make my point clear. The one point you all seem to miss, gentlemen of this table. That is, that my decisiveness, manner and stature proved to be terrifying her.*

Tito: *And the point of that point was what then, Mr. Stalin?*

Stalin: *The point is this, that a powerful state can demand of its subordinates anything it so desires: after all, who has the coffee now?*

Tito: *Then yes, your point is made very well then, Mr. Stalin, but I see I am the only one of us that requires just enough sugar to sweeten the taste, and not so much more that it then ruins the drink for us all.*

Stalin slams the coffee pot down onto the table with such force that its content now splashes outward from the rim. The linen tablecloth is now soiled for the second time.

Stalin: *Well: what do you think about it Mr. Hitler? – Have I made the point clear or not? You have sugar, but I now have both milk and coffee. Which one of us has the most powerful Empire now? – Is it Russia or Austro-Hungaria?*

Hitler sits there, head down, looking deep into the sugar bowl in front. After a brief moment, one taken to gather his thoughts, he responds thus...

Hitler: *Do you see what has happened here, Stalin, you have spilt coffee onto the sugar. Look how it has dissolved and discoloured, spreading like a cancer across it. Infected and polluting it. The sugar is no longer pure: it is contaminated. If this sugar were representative of Austro-Hungaria, then it is an Empire no longer worthy of fighting for.*

Stalin: *And so, then it falls on you my dear comrade, do you think that my coffee jug is worth fighting for?*

Trotsky: *I would yes, I'd just snatch that jug right from your hand.*

This he does - as if David is fighting against Goliath, catching his 'superior' quite by surprise. Freud is bemused by Trotsky's direct challenge to authority, he smiles as he then smugly asks of Stalin...

Freud: *So, you no longer have a coffee jug Stalin - what plight will befall your Empire now?*

Stalin: *I say this, Freud, One man one problem: no man no problem.*

ACT FOUR:

It's a fresh day, the waitress having returned to work busying away.

Waitress: *Freud's journal does not state anywhere that Hitler was a redemptive anti-Semite. Surprisingly: his notes are quite at odds with the common Hitler myths and false narratives we have come to believe today. These myths were born out of Hitler's autobiographical work of 1924: Mein Kampf. Within the text Hitler explains that he became an anti-Semite following his experiences in Vienna. In actual fact, his anti-Semitism was born out of Germany's defeat in WW1. 1918 being a period of his life that was yet to unfold. Many false claims, mistruths and outright lies, hundreds, layered one upon another would later be made into that infamous biographical book of Adolf Hitler - all of which we know today are untrue.*

Bucharin enters, he walks to the front of stage, and narrates.

Bucharin: *This particular morning is noted to be 10.00 am, the day is unknown, Freud as ever, and as the first to arrive, would sit and enjoy his coffee. The press of today is focusing on the tensions between the Austro-Hungarian ruler, Franz Joseph, and the demands of separatism as desired by Serbia. War is imminent, ladies and gentlemen, but yet, it still seems to be many years away. These are deeply troubled times, a political climate of extremes and the new ideals of the socialists gaining ever daily in popularity. Tito does not find recruitment to his workers' union to be objectionable to most and this has inspired the young metal workers loyalty toward the other members of the Sugar Lump Club.*

The Habsburg dynasty is on the verge of losing its grip on power and should that happen then surely, it will be war. Austria and Germany will both seek to prevent Serbian isolationism from the Empire and will agree to intervene as united forces should this prevail, but there is little will for real actual conflict. Smoldering ash is best left to smolder alone as long as it does not possess a flame that could burn the entire house down. The Empire is on the verge of imploding: but no spark has as yet blown across onto the others dry tinder.

Bucharin exits the stage as Freud arrives. After a brief pause, Hitler, Tito, Stalin, and Trotsky arrive. All excited by the find of today's newspaper headline.

<u>Hawker leans in through window.</u>

Hawker: *Read all about it! read all about it! Ferdinand keen to replace Joseph on Habsburg Throne – Could it be War? Read all about it!*

<u>The waitress takes a copy, pays the Hawker, and takes it to Freud.</u>

Freud: *Good morning gentlemen, it's a beautiful morning for conversation but I'm not sure it's a good day for war, how are one's moods today?*

<u>He turns his newspaper overleaf.</u>

Tito: *The four of us have just been buying a copy from the corner stand, sorry for the tardy arrival, but could not help but take a moment to share the headline, it'll never come to war, how's the coffee this morning?*

Freud: *As good as it gets, I believe, with milk and sugar too. The early bird gets the worm gentlemen, no need for conflict at all.*

<u>Tito, Stalin, Trotsky and Hitler take their seats. They peruse their newspapers – all but Hitler who does not have a copy.</u>

Freud: *I see you've lost your copy already then Young Adolf?*

Hitler: *Not lost Sigmund old chap, just put to a better cause, stuffed in my sack – I'll use it to clean my paintbrushes later if I may.*

<u>Hitler's tools of the trade are hung over his shoulder. A small black wooden paint box hanging from his right shoulder, a smudged multi-colored wooden palate tied across the lid with string and both covered over by a cloth sack bag for his brushes, hung from his left across his chest.</u>

Freud: *You look quite the part today young man, anything particular in mind?*

Hitler: *Oh, the usual, child portrait, started last night but no need to be finished until this evening.*

Freud: *How's the art going these days sir, still managing to earn a crust or two?*

Hitler: *I drink my bottle of milk and eat my morsel of bread.*

Trotsky: *Hitler, seriously! – Are you still trying to sell Sigmund that old yarn? You're among friends now, we're not your potential customers anymore, so can we finally move on from that old street buskers treat…*

Tito: *I was in the Café Landtmann last night, handing out Pravda, said I'd help Trotsky out across town, anyway, regardless, Freud, all quite boring but – our young Hitler here, well, he isn't as nearly as poor as he likes to make out. He has inherited an orphan's pension from his mother and has a healthy interest free loan on top of that from his aunt, isn't that so?*

Hitler: *Ah, so my mistake was to frequent the Landtmann too then was it Tito?*

Freud: *So, all your talk of the young struggling painter from Braunau am Inn, and Vienna being the saddest period of your life, the misfortune and misery you sold me, is all twaddle then, is it? Perhaps I'll have my money back.*

Hitler: *No, not at all, a lie is only a lie if it's found to be a lie. I am from Braunau, true, and when they failed to acknowledge my talents at the Academy of Fine Arts, I was for a long time sad and miserable, all still truth sir!"*

Freud: *And of the admittedly meager living painting postcards then?*

Hitler: *All true Sigmund, it was and is, just didn't mention the money I had elsewhere. Nobody wants postcards anymore, it's all about the portraits these days, and there's not enough money in that either!'*

<u>Freud, Trotsky and Tito double up in laughter at either side of the young painter.</u>

Stalin: *And: you didn't have any work for an entire year and spent it wandering the city in misfortune?*

Hitler: *I didn't, but that was when I came here in 1908, I didn't have to work for an entire year… the misfortune came later, when I realised, I'd have to get a part-time job so I could continue to* stroll around the city, going to bars and concerts.

Trotsky: Perhaps all of those hysterical young ladies of yours you spend so much time psychoanalysing were telling the truth after all – Freud?

The gentlemen finally calm down, they are reading their newspapers.

Freud: So, gentlemen, item one on today's agenda shall we? If war breaks out, what are you going to do about it?

Tito: I'd return home to Zagreb immediately and enlist, obviously. I am not in favour of war but how could I stand by, and watch Austria and Germany attack my fellow Serbs? It would be a call of duty to take up arms against any oppressor of one's homeland, wouldn't it?

Hitler: Normally, yes, Tito my friend, but how does one truly define one's homeland? Are your fellow Serbs countryman of a nation state or are they pollutants as we find here within the Empire?

Tito: I'm not sure I fully understand Adolf – surely all countrymen are one and the same?

Hitler: One and the same is an illusion!

Hitler thumps the table with a mighty blow of his right clenched fist, a habit he had by now acquired from Stalin, one that had always served well to control the attention of the table.

Hitler: Do you seriously believe that just because someone is a Serb, they all want the same thing? No! As soon as Serbia would gain any incline of independence from the Empire then all would come forward out of the woodwork with true intent! Divide and conquer, remove the Empire from the equation and Serbia would be defenseless against any interior tensions and non-more so than the Marxists!

Stalin: The Marxists! – You mean to reference Trotsky and I as communists in that personal slight, do you?"

Hitler: No! – I have no objection or aversion to social democracy, there are many aspects of communism I fully engage with, but one really has to question whose best interests it serves.

Freud: Pray tell young man, go on then…

Hitler: As a revolutionary, Trotsky, you have already made it clear that you would never be accepted as a leader alongside Lenin in your would be Socialist Russian state – why? Because you are Jewish: these are your words sirs, not mine! And when you said this what happened? Did anybody at this table disagree? No!"

Waitress: It was true of the time to say that anti-Semitism was rife across Europe. Deeply ingrained in all European societies of 1913. A fact that Trotsky had long accepted as a barrier to his potential leadership. Following the failed 1905 Russian revolution that had led both him and Stalin into political exile, he and Lenin had discussed this very issue.

<u>Hawker enters to sit at his vending stand – Addressing the audience directly, explains…</u>

Hawker: Lenin was not convinced that Trotsky was right - indeed, anti-Semitism was against party discipline, and Lenin wanted to see a fully representative party based on multi-ethnic lines controlled by the proletariat. Stalin had not agreed. As an ethnic Georgian and a Roman Catholic, he remained to be convinced. Orthodox Christianity was after all – the established faith within the Russian Empire and the people were certain to be more trusting of one they saw as one of their own: Even if such a figure himself would afterward be required under Marxist-Leninist ideals to denounce Christianity itself.

Hitler: It's not a matter of I being an anti-Semite or not gentlemen, for if I was, I would surely not waste my time in conversation here. Freud – you are a Jew too are you not? I have sold my paintings to you. I drink, dance and frolic with Jews just as if they were my own Volksgemeinschaft. You sit and talk about revolution, but the fact is Marxist theory was written by a Jew, the man you talk of daily as if he were a God: Karl Marx. It's a matter of trust, that's all I am trying to say.

Freud: So, you are suggesting, Hitler, that the workers see communism as a Jewish conspiracy and not one of an internationalist movement of united workers, one free of the chains of exploitation, but not the shackles of their xenophobia?

Hitler: If you sincerely wish to succeed and not fail again you must convince the proletariat that they are losing more than their labour: convince them that they are losing their heritage, culture, and, more importantly, their identity. Then they will soon rise up to fight alongside you. You need more than political voice gentlemen; you need to identify an enemy worthy of the cause.

<u>Silence befalls and Hitler pauses to sip from his cup. All present stare at him. He sips in a manner as if so proud of his words and to suggest that he had suddenly turned from a naïve young artist to the status of a new respected revolutionary.</u>

Freud: So, Mr. Hitler, given such passionate and eloquent delivery - if war broke out tomorrow, who would you fight for? After all, you have still most successfully managed to avoid the question.

Hitler: To be honest and frank with you Sigmund, I would not fight. I have no interest in being a soldier, any more so than being a revolutionary leader. Do you think God would have chosen me to paint if he then required of me that my hands be blown off within the trenches of warfare?

Freud: You would not? You'd have to do something, or they'll execute you for treason in avoiding your draft. The question requires an answer of you, young Hitler.

Hitler: Then that be the case, I would join a Bavarian regiment.

Trotsky: But you are Austrian, surely you would fight for your homeland as much as Tito would fight for his?"

Tito: I would, yes Adolf, I would enlist, but it would not be a Serbia created out of the darkness that you suggest. Why must the workers be separated along ethnic lines? That's utterly ridiculous of you - a preposterous notion. It's a common fight against a common oppressor, a single enemy, the ruling classes. A strong state can unite its peoples – regardless of ethnic tensions. Strong leadership and free education are all that is required to unite us all. Anti-Semitism is just a weapon like any other used upon the battlefield of our oppressor, to turn worker against worker.

Waitress: The gentlemen talked about what they referred to as the British example. A United Kingdom of four separate nation states, coexisting together and ruling the most powerful Empire on earth – The British Empire. Both Trotsky and Tito agreed that power could be shared in such a way. Whilst they were both open in their condemnation of slavery, they believed it to be a good example of a controlling central power sharing its wealth equally.

Hitler: Perhaps it would have been better advised to make the Negros work in the mills of England whilst the Aryans enjoyed more leisure time to play, had that been the case then Britain would surely be the first to succeed with its socialist revolution. Didn't Karl Marx -

your prophet say: that England would be the first to thirst for revolutionary change against its rulers – but it wasn't was it, it's Russia? Do you see what I am saying now, Trotsky?

Stalin: *And... Wasn't it you, Freud, that said upon our first meeting that: America was a most grandiose experiment, but you feared it would never work? Perhaps an Empire must be ruled by the dominant master race of its own kinsmen - the young painter may have a valid point.*

Freud: *Sophistry, Stalin, pure sophistry. You're twisting my words to suit.*

Waitress: Freud was annoyed by the apparent twisting of his original words.

Stalin: *Reading between the lines I would suggest that young Hitler here would fight for a German Empire but not the one he currently lives under - a Germany under the control of foreign blood. But of you Sigmund, would you enlist should war break out – you are an Austrian citizen too, are you not?*

Freud: *Well, I am too old for the draft so I would have to volunteer. And that being the case, my choice would be not. And I would point out gentlemen that I was born in Freiberg in Czechoslovakia, it seems to me that this is an Austrian problem, and not a Czech one. Battlefields are created by old men for the young to die upon.*

Hitler bursts into uncontrolled laughter.

Hitler: *The point is made clear gentlemen; you are an Austrian Freud - but first you are a Czechoslovakian Jew. You will sit at home drinking wine and eating pheasant, carrying on your uninterrupted life's daily routine as if completely untouched by the war, all whilst others die to defend your country for you.*

Stalin: *What a shame you have no desire for political leadership Adolf – you've certainly got a mouth I could use.*

ACT FIVE:

Darkness: Single stage spotlight focuses only on Bucharin as he continues with his narration.

Bucharin: We know that Adolf Hitler would later, upon his rise to power, consistently connect all political matters with those of his delusional theories on ethnicity and race. He would, during WW2, set out to destroy the Soviet Union with his new weapon of mass destruction: anti-Semitism. His delusional ideals leading to catastrophic war with Russia and, the mass extermination of millions through genocide and extermination during the inhumanity and onslaught of the Shoah: The Holocaust. It must be noted, however, that within the autobiographical work of 1924, Adolf Hitler does not make a direct reference to a planned systematic Holocaust and its systematic decimation of millions. It is, however, most certainly there – Hidden between the lines of hatred in creating an environment where genocide becomes predictable. He states...

Second spotlight now focuses on Hitler seen to Bucharin's right.

Hitler: If twelve or fifteen thousand of these Jews who were corrupting the nation had been forced to submit to poison gas, just as hundreds of thousands of our best German workers from every social stratum and from every trade and calling had to face it in the field, then the millions of sacrifices made at the front would not have been in vain. On the contrary: If twelve thousand of these malefactors had been eliminated in proper time, probably the lives of a million decent men, who would be of value to Germany in the future, might have been saved.

Spotlight fades as we now refocus only on Bucharin.

Bucharin: What Hitler refers to here in the text of Mein Kamp is the focus of blame he places on 'the Jews' for Germany's defeat of 1918 in WW1. The quote does not offer any hint of death camps or factories of extermination - This paragraph was reference only to his desire to have seen Jews die upon the Western Front. Hitler, and his supporters had originally vowed by 1941 to expel all Jews from all areas under German rule. A systematic campaign of murder and terror would ensure this would happen more efficiently. The Holocaust, as death camps, was born out of consequence in the later war against Joseph Stalin's Soviet Union.

Within Freud's journal we note a remarkable shift in attitude within the benevolence bestowed of Sigmund toward Adolf that becomes apparent mid-week. His original notes of the week never identified the young artist as the redemptive anti-Semite, racist and xenophobic mass murderer that we can identify with today. Indeed: originally Freud seemed to welcome the contributions of all parties at the coffee table, seeing it as a way to enlighten his enquiring understanding of others.

Spotlight now focuses on Freud to Bucharin's left.

Freud: *I do not agree with what you say gentlemen, but I will defend your right to say it.*

Spotlight now focuses on Tito to Bucharin's right.

Tito: *I believe that power should never be given to those who seek it.*

Spotlight fades as we now refocus only on Bucharin.

Bucharin: I believe that power should never be given to those who seek it, those, the words of the man who would later become known as Marshall Tito, the leader of the post-war Yugoslavian state. Trotsky had saved no punches at all in his acceptance of violence as a means to revolutionary ends, but he was at least honest and predictable. What Freud felt he saw before him was indeed what Trotsky was…

Spotlight now focuses on Freud to Bucharin's left.

Freud: *A committed principled left-wing ideologist.*

Spotlight fades as we now refocus only on Bucharin as he continues his address to the audience.

Bucharin: *Hitler's autobiographical work: Mein Kamp (My Struggle) maintained a remarkable openness that was at best naïve, though by March 1933, there was no doubt within the minds of the German masses what the Nazi leader's future intentions were. 52 percent of Germans voted for the Nazi's and their new coalition government. This gospel of a new era was now accepted as the bible of National Socialism. His hatred of Jews and Communists prevailed throughout'.*

Spotlight now focuses on Hitler to Bucharin's right.

Hitler: *The Social Democrats dragged all through the mud. When challenged they can only reply: Get lost or else be thrown down from the scaffolding.*

Spotlight fades as we now refocus only on Bucharin.

Bucharin: *Mein Kampf is a work of deliberate distortion of the truth and equally the creation of very poor research. Factual errors alone are noted to be in the hundreds. Hitler writes that the Habsburg dynasty of Franz Joseph and Franz Ferdinand spoke Czech: they did not, they spoke German.*

Spotlight now focuses on Hitler to Bucharin's right.

Hitler *I am not a man of the pen, and I write poorly.*

Spotlight now focuses on Waitress to Bucharin's left.

Waitress: *But such apologist rhetoric can surely be dismissed as an attempt to gain sympathy and thus increase sales: the poor down and out artist who now finds himself thrown into the chaos of the political world in a selfless attempt to save one's own nation.*

Spotlight fades as we now refocus only on Bucharin.

Bucharin: *The year 1923 wore Germany out, wrote Sigmund Freud, adding: ...and it prepared it not for Nazism in particular, but for any fantastical adventure. The thing that gave Nazism its streak of insanity developed at the time: The cold madness, the imperiously self-indulgent, and the blind determination to achieve the impossible.*

Spotlight now focuses on Hitler to Bucharin's right.

Hitler: *For my part, I then decided that I would take up political work, somebody had to stop those Jew bloodsuckers who stabbed Germany in her back. The magic power of the spoken word would now set in motion great historical avalanches of religious and political movements. An outstanding speaker is rarely a good theoretician and organiser at the same time... a combination of both talents in a single individual created a great man.*

Hunger was the faithful guardian which never left me, I consumed the breadwinner's wage within just three days. Vienna of 1913 was the school of his life. It was like a maggot in a putrescent body. The odour of those people in caftans often used to make me feel ill.

Was there any shady undertaking, any form of foulness, especially in cultural life, in which at least one Jew did not participate? On putting the probing knife carefully to that kind of abscess, one immediately discovered, like a maggot in a putrescent body, a little Jew who was often blinded by the sudden light.

<u>Spotlight now focuses on Waitress to Bucharin's left. Bucharin remains in darkness.</u>

Waitress: *Apparently, Vienna was now the occasion of the greatest inner revolution that Hitler had yet experienced. The new Hitler, the dogmatic racial anti-Semite.*

<u>Spotlight now focuses on Freud to Bucharin's right.</u>

Freud: *He anticipates the outcome of the competitive struggle in which every manifestation of human culture is almost exclusively the product of the Aryan creative power. And it is the duty of their noblest representatives, namely the Germans, to perform the historic mission to stop the Jews who, as - The international maggot in the body of the nation, seek to control the whole world and its order. Hitler's ambition to create a new world order, one rid of the disease of Judaism, was limited only by time that was now running out.*

ACT SIX:

The stage returns to the normal hustle and bustle of the coffeehouse. Freud and Tito are back seated at their table. The waitress attends to work behind the counter.

Freud: Are you too prepared to give up your life as a revolutionary as Stalin and Trotsky declare?

Tito: I've no fear of death, Freud, I just don't want to be there when it happens.

Waitress: Tito was very keen to tell Freud a story this day. They had been alone together awaiting the arrival of the other three. Unusually and without reason, they were noted to arrive quite a bit later than usual. Passing time by, Tito's story unfolds.

Tito: I was outside the Daimler factory a few weeks back: I was talking to the men about Karl Marx. General chit-chat and nothing special. Just trying to recruit for the trade union, you know, stuff like that, the norm.
I was doing all the usual speak, key facts, names, dates and places, just to demonstrate that I had knowledge worth sharing before discussing the key concepts of surplus value, class struggle, exploitation and materialism, when, he suddenly interrupted me, stopped me dead in my tracks in fact, as he then just randomly started to tell me a story.

Freud: I'm very intrigued Tito, pray tell... we've time before the other gentleman arrive.

Tito: Intrigued I was too, *he just gave me his entire life story, it went on forever, to say an hour is an under-exaggeration Sigmund, - I must tell you.*

Waitress: The man's story had begun on one unknown Christmas Eve. Tito, quite unsure which Christmas Eve the worker was referring to, explained that it had been recently, past few years, but that that lack of fine detail did not impact on the story.

Hawker: Freud had listened patiently to Tito's recollections and was, according to his journal, quite bored and frustrated with the slow pace of delivery at many points.

Tito: It was all quite surreal - I kept interrupting him and continually tried to get his focus back toward me, and the revolution, the words of Karl Marx, but he just wasn't interested – he just rambled on and on and on".

Waitress: It seemed liked the story had already gone on forever before Tito had even managed to begin to tell the story itself, finally getting down to explain that the man had been at home with his family.

Hawker: The man had had a comfortable home and what was, by all accounts, a good life. He had been an engineer. He, and family, had lived in the affluent suburb of Esterhazy Park and had all the modern trappings and worldly goods beyond others of the time.

Tito: Silver candlesticks, gas lighting and a grand piano, among many other nice things. They had just finished Christmas dinner, he had put his three children to bed at eight, and was sat in an armchair, beside the fire, his wife and he reading whilst listening to the calming tick-tock of his grandfather's old inherited Grandfather clock.

Waitress: Upon finishing this sentence Tito then randomly started to explain that there was plenty of wood in the house for Christmas, even telling Freud how many logs were placed beside the fire. 7 he had recalled the man telling him.

Hawker: Frustrated with the over and unnecessarily continued great depth and detail of the story, Freud had become quite bombastic with Tito. After one hour...

Freud: Am I ever going to hear this blasted story or are you just going to continually waffle on abut it...

Tito: If the finer details were not important, I wouldn't be telling you all about it, would I?

Freud: I despair of you, Tito. Get on with it man.

Waitress: Tito continued plodding over his words just as before, quite unaffected by his friend's apparent and obvious state of boredom and, ever increasing lack of disinterest.

Tito: There was a knock on the door; it was exactly the stroke of midnight; the clock had just announced to the second the arrival of Christmas Day. It was a cold frosty night, but they had eaten well and with the warm glow of the firelight flickering out across the room, they did not feel cold at all. He thanked his lucky stars for his fortunate life as he walked to answer -Who could it be at such a late hour - he thought. It was not a night that one wanted at all to be without warmth, sleeping on the streets amongst the many homeless peasants of Vienna's slums - It must be the poor - he concluded - They've come to ask for food again and food they shall eat – he decided. He was a good honorable man, Freud, and that's important know.

Freud: Tito explained to me how this man had risen from the comfort of his armchair, he had put down his book: A Christmas Carol by Charles Dickens, a work that many in middle-class circles had read since first published in 1843. He was utterly bewildered by Ebenezer Scrooge's absolute meanness and lack of humanity to those of lesser social strata placed unkindly below him. Upon opening the door, he found no-one. He looked round about, left to right and up and down. He found only a snail on the doormat to his feet. Without thinking, Tito explained how the man had given the snail a swift though gentle kick with the tip of his slipper, and off into the night's air it flew - far away out of site...

Tito: I'm a farmer's boy you know from a peasant family in Croatia, Kumrovec actually: I was born in 1892. My father was an alcoholic; he borrowed so much money from the banks that he used to send me to negotiate with his creditors, so they wouldn't take our land. I think he thought they would take pity on me, a child and..."

Freud: And this has got what to do with the story?

Tito: Nothing really, only to say that I've had a really hard life and thought you might show some interest in my own story first – the bankers used to ridicule and mock me. I always wanted to be so much more than I am today, when I was child, I dreamed of being a waiter, or a tailor – running away to the USA, or something grand like that.

Freud: Then why didn't you. Life is what you make of it you know.

Tito: Actually, I don't agree with you on that point, Sigmund, my father spent the family's travel money on booze, broke our hearts at the time. Promised us a new life overseas and then drank our hopes and dreams into oblivion: mother particularly. She was a good hard-working farmer's wife but... well, fate had its way, I guess.

<u>The door springs open and in walk Trotsky, Stalin & Hitler.</u>

Freud: *Thank God you're finally here, forget the revolution today, just save me from this never ending story first please gentlemen? Though after*

Freud chuckles.

Trotsky: *Well don't let us interrupt you.*

Stalin: *What's it all about then?*

Hitler: *I like stories, spit it out...*

Freud: *I fear we will never find out sirs, the snail got kicked and that is it so far.*

Waitress: *Tito seizes this moment to recap on the entire event from beginning to thus far - but we won't bore you, our dear audience, with all of that again. None other than to say that in the journal Freud later wrote: For a man of such charisma and personally, he can at times be utterly boring.*

Hawker: *Women seem to flock to him; he's informed me of a string of young fillies... and his reputation for virility and affairs is well established amongst the coffeehouses. What on earth do they see in him? I just wanted to pull my own hair out by the roots at the end of it all. Freud had concluded. The story, again after much delay, will now regain direction and pace. We thank you for your kind patience.*

Tito: *After the man had kicked the snail, everything had gone downhill from there. As he'd gone to answer the door his wife had fallen asleep with her book, knocking over a candle in the process. The chair had ignited, and after failed attempts to dowse the flames, having first awoken the children – his home had been razed to the ground by fire.*

Trotsky: *That's awful.*

Tito: *I know, but it all gets much worse I assure you.*

Stalin: *How can it get worse than that?*

Tito: *Let me explain, gentlemen he had been born the seventh of fourteen siblings and he was lucky to reach the age he is today, that being 21 years old. Only six of his siblings had lived into adulthood.*

Waitress: And then randomly Tito had started talking about how *A Christmas Tale* had at first been published by Chapman & Hall of London in 1843... It was all quite irrelevant to the story.

Stalin: So... Tito, *he kicked the snail having answered the door thinking it was the poor and then the house burns down and what?*

Tito: *After Christmas, the following year, Stalin, they had found themselves in the poor house. The man had gone from riches to rags within an instant, but they weren't yet aware of it. It seemed that every month thereafter a new horror would befall him. His life was now in ruins, a complete and total disaster.*

Stalin: So, what happened next then?

Tito: *Well - following the fire, the house next door had caught, it too being gutted along with several other adjoining apartments and tenements. The engineer had been forced to sell his business to settle multiple compensation claims. Left without home or company, the family then took up temporary rented accommodation. Though he had secured work in a local factory for himself and was in the process of obtaining a loan to start afresh. It would be a smaller, more modest affair, but in remaining creditworthy he realised that he would soon be back on his feet again. Do you know why I wanted to be a tailor or even a waiter when I was a child?*

<u>Hitler and Trotsky fall into laughter. Freud's exudes utter despair making their laughter increase in volume. Stalin is expressionless.</u>

Stalin: What the...

Waitress: *Tito interrupted Stalin by saying that he'd always wanted to wear nice clothes. It appeared to him that waiters of the day had the best cut cloth. If he couldn't be a waiter then as a tailor, he would at least learn how to make his own bespoke fits instead, and that was the reason. Eventually calm returned... so too does the story.*

Tito: Later, during January, gentlemen, having borrowed cash up to the hilt, lost his job. And in losing his job, he could not only not pay his rent but also his children's school fees. The bank foreclosed on his loans, and, now quite unworthy of credit, he relied on the generosity of friends. *So, you would think that things couldn't get any worse wouldn't you - but I assure you they did.*

Hitler: So, in December after he had kicked the snail his house burnt down, and then in January he lost his company to bankruptcy, followed by homelessness in February – is that correct?

Tito: Not quite that bad yet, Adolph, his best friend became a guarantor for the family's rent, so jobless yes, but homeless no.

Freud: Thank God for that. It's a terrible story, Tito - I do hope he finds some happiness at the end of it... for I fear you will upset my delicate sensitivities if I hear much more of this sorrow and sufferings.

Tito: You see, capitalism is the enemy of us all, we are all victims of a brutal system. That's why I was trying to tell this man of the words of Marx the day we met. The system plays us all off against each other, we are not enemies, and it's all too simplistic to say that the bourgeoisie are our enemy... they can suffer terribly too.

Trotsky: Absolutely. After all, had he not gone to the door to feed the poor none of this would have happened.

Stalin: I'm not so convinced that it was a misguided attempt to help other less fortunates' that led to this unfortunate set of circumstance, personally, I think the snail had something to do with it".

Freud: Are you suggesting that the snail possessed evil, Stalin?

Stalin: Do you not think it possible Freud? He was problem free until he kicked it. Keep your friendly snails close and your enemy snails even closer, that's what I would have suggested to him.

Tito: I used to have a beautifully cut suit, once upon a time, before I arrived in Vienna that was. I bought it in Prague. I was forced out of desperation to bed down for the night in a cattle shed, woke up the next day to find a cow had eaten it, well, most of it - at any rate.

Trotsky: Tito! Seriously! Can't you just stay focused for a moment – what happened next, we're in March now; yes?

Tito: Actually gentlemen, I owe all that I know today, my entire education that is, to the Communist Party, but as that is of no interest to you, I will tell you, for March had been appalling too. The man having now borrowed extensively from the friend who had become the willing guarantor of the family's rent tuned out to be not so much of a friend after all. He had taken liberties with his wife.

Stalin: You mean he was, shall we politely say, taking personal liberties of the flesh in romantic ways with his friend's wife?

Tito: That's exactly what I am saying - and in April, he had not only moved into the apartment with her but was now suing his former friend for the sums outstanding.

Freud: You are sickening me to the very core with this latest revelation, is there more happy news to bless my day?

Tito: Well, of course, he couldn't pay it back, Freud, the borrowed money that is, and in May he found himself incarcerated in a debtor's prison.

The room falls silent, the silence is then only broken moments later by Tito.

Tito: Hunting, fishing and horse-riding, that's the life I hope for Adolf, walking with my dogs in the countryside - and most of all I'd like to do this whilst living on an island'.

Hitler: That's the most interesting thing you've said all day, Tito, yes, dogs, it's the German shepherd breed for me on that score, not so keen on the hunting though, trying to reduce my meat intake. Not so good for the body these days. I'm more of a mountains man personally, but I agree, living on an island does appeal to the senses somewhat. I'd like to call my dog; Blondie. I knew a girl called Blondie once – quite the dog herself.

Stalin and Trotsky then shout-out in perfect unison. *June!*

Stalin: *June!*

Trotsky: *June!*

Freud: What happened in June man? – For Christ's sake Josip Broz!

Tito: I was trying to avoid June gentlemen. Terrible, terrible. Obviously, the new love affair didn't work out – how could it? I mean, you can't build happiness on someone else's unhappiness, can you? It haunted the new relationship – the debtor's prison that is. So, loverboy left her after just a handful of weeks, and she, the ex that is, well – took to the oldest profession in the world: sadly.

Freud: *It's a symptom of arrested-development, prostitution, it signals that the individual is quite unable to integrate inner conflicts. It's all about low self-esteem, gentlemen, her overall view of life's value and of course a good dose of poor self-image. If I were to treat such a wretched woman as this for the condition of prostitution, I would at first seek to resolve internal and external conflicts – focusing on her childhood relationships, that to her parents.*

Tito: *Don't need to worry about all that now, Freud - she's dead!*

A moment of silence again befalls the room.

Tito: *Anyway, concerning the milk, sugar and coffee debate yesterday, I believe that economic self- sufficiency is what a nation requires most, any dominant member of an Empire will always seek to make its lessor members contribute more of the fair share to the greater nation among them, that seems logical, doesn't it? Yes, terror as a weapon must end, we all need to find a new way, a different kind of approach – what do you think Stalin?*

Stalin: *Dead! What do you mean Dead?*

Tito: *Dead, yes, quite dead I'm afraid. Yes, in June her neck was broken – she'd gone to visit her husband in debtor's prison and…*

Freud: *And? – and what?*

Tito: *And? – well and indeed, he'd lost everything now, hadn't he? And; the family's name and honour was a step too far for him. Even from within the pitiful conditions he found himself incarcerated in, his reputation would save him, upon settling his later debts, well at least he had hope of a fresh start. But now – who would touch him? All hope had been taken away from him by his wife's treacherous act. He lunged forward; arms stretched out from the void of his cell bars and snapped her neck! Such was his rage, instantly it was, dead, yes, there was no doubt about that. So, in June, Freud, he was sentenced to death by hanging.*

Hitler: *It's the snail – you can't trust them! – They move around with their homes on their backs, like a horse and cart, transients, gypsies all of them! He needs to find that snail and deal with it! That's what I'd do.*
Stalin: *So, we're back to milk, sugar and coffee again then are we Hitler? One snail one problem, no snail no problem!*

<u>Even Freud now finds time to laugh uncontrollably before saying...</u>

Freud: *An apology is needed I feel, after all, if all this started as a result of a mere flick of the toe, one dreads to think what would have happened to this poor blighter had he chosen to stamp on it instead. I'd apologies, that's what I'd do – sorry snail!*

Trotsky: *Can this desperate man's plight get any worse, Tito? - surely not, please say no!*

Tito: *Yes, - it now worsens for him, Trotsky. His circumstances do not improve, for in July he was told that his children, desperately poor, unwashed, unfed, and unclothed, now on the street and uneducated among the squalor of the city - they were sent to the workhouse by the old back-stabbing friend. His interests were in the loins of the fairer sex, not of the children. He wiped his hands of it all.*

Hitler: *I insist upon a snail conspiracy, Gentlemen, there is probably a cult of insects who are working covertly to undermine the wealth of the state.*

Freud: *No, Hitler, it was a depth of madness, certain conditions had provoked this man to violent act, and as such, insanity surely made him do it – he must not be held accountable for his actions and be executed.*

Tito: *You've hit the snail on the head there – Sigmund old chap, nail, snail - a Freudian slip.*

Trotsky: *Jokes don't work if you have to explain them, Tito, surely you know this, anyway - do you really think that this venture is an appropriate a time for joking?*

Tito: *You're right, Trotsky, it's all very sad isn't. I'll resist and do apologies - now, where were we...*

Freud: *It's August now I believe, at the end of a long rope atop a very big drop.*

Tito: *Ah, yes, August. Well in August...*

<u>Suddenly Tito stops talking and starts to tap his fingers upon the tabletop.</u>

Tito: I love playing the piano. Just freeing up my joints a little if you don't mind gentlemen. Too much typing last night I fear, never leave Croatia without my typewriter: never know when one will need it next to knock up a one sheet for the revolution...

Stalin: If you don't get to August soon, I'll have you shot in the bloody street in front of your damned typewriter!

Tito: Shot Stalin – shot. That's not very democratic of you, is it? You're starting to sound like a fascist. That's the problem with the nationalist mindset – they don't see the need for alternate opinions – But then again, I suppose there is no need for a multi-party democratic platformed state as the Communist Party represents all the workers, doesn't it.

Stalin: August!

Tito: The whole trial had been based on the notion of his insanity, you are correct Freud, and he had suffered a total catastrophic collapse of the mind. And Adolf, you too are correct to some degree as much discussion concerning the 'apparent curse of the snail' was put forward to the judge by the man's defense team.

Trotsky: So, some good news at last then Tito. He didn't get hung after all.

Freud: Actually, it's hanged, Trotsky, and - well it's bloody obvious to me that he didn't get strung up – had he been so he would never have lived to tell Tito his tale – would he?

Stalin: I'd missed that point completely, went straight over the top of my head" – yes, so it must finally be good news then, Tito?

Tito: Not exactly good news for he still had no money; his defense team consisted of his brother; he was a local book shop owner. A clever man yes, but no experience of the legal system, especially the defense skills needed to defend a man from the crack of the noose. The insane defense all backfired, hoping to be freed he was not, and found that in August he was sent to the asylum – for life!

<u>A moment of silence again befalls the room, until...</u>

Tito: Live and let live I say, I'm not above a deal with the devil – What do you think about freedom of the press gentlemen? And of free movement too? – I'm all in favour myself... should war break-out I'd like to see an independent Yugoslavia free of its ethnic conflicts. I understand the nationalist debate but once it starts it cannot be stopped, can it? Where does all that division end?

Stalin: September Tito – September – please! Can we finish the blasted story!

Waitress: Interestingly, ladies and gentlemen of this theater, Freud's journal would later note that the story had in fact taken over three hours to deliver...

Hawker: ...a frustration that I sense that you too now share.

Tito: I was going to say that we make our own history, and I wanted to discuss the need to over-throw the monarchy, but given such tense mood of yours Stalin, I will hurry, just for you. Yes, for September arrived and this man had found out that his oldest son had died of consumption whilst in the workhouse that month. October informed him that his second youngest, also a son, was also now critically inflicted with that same dreadful, fatal condition. And in November, the poor helpless fellow now confined for life through his insanity, heard a devastating rumour passed on to him from his brother.

Trotsky: Was it a credible one'?

Tito: Yes, it was, his brother had told him during a brief fleeting visit to the asylum, this, his youngest, his only daughter, a precious beautiful young girl, well, she was now to be sold as an apprentice to Mrs. Viene, a notorious brothel owner, who, without any doubt was left of her fragile mind, and had notorious intent for her. Mrs. Viene would often recruit from the workhouse, gentlemen, by means of a subtle backhander that settled the outstanding financial accounts of her purchase's siblings, and also, paid for silence of the worker's.

<u>The room is again silent. Pouring coffee will at the very least break the silence, they pour their coffee, attending to the finer details of milk and sugar.</u>

Tito: Gentlemen, I see that you are quite distressed, do you wish me to continue into December or shall we call it a day there?

Trotsky: In all honesty, I'm not sure I can hear any more - I have nothing to say other than that.

<u>The men stir their coffee in calm contemplation of the cruelty of life.</u>

Stalin: I have not witnessed such tragedy and distress since 1905, when the Cossacks stormed the lines of demonstrators and butchered the people with swords.

Hitler: I'm not sure that Mrs. Viene is such a bad person – after all, the girl would now be saved from the fate of consumption, wouldn't she?

Freud: I fear what we hear for December will be the worst revelation of all, and I'm not sure that I have now the psychological stamina or personal resilience necessary to absorb the full impact of it, Tito, but, I sense that you will impart that it is the brother who told you of this tragic story – after all is said, how would you have come to know of it? Yes - the brother tells you, doesn't he? As, yes, this poor desperate fellow is himself found deceased, perhaps he found some peace in the end and...

Tito: Do not try to over-analyse the outcome my friend. I will explain. Yes, the brother did become involved, but he was not the one who told me the tale. For in December the brother hatched a plan to break his kin out from the confines of the asylum. He had raised enough money from his new book sales, about the story itself, to slip the guards just enough to provide freedom and silence. In December his brother was free, but on the run, homeless and hungry. If only I could return to the old family home and just collect enough to sell – I could pay for the treatment of my son, and for the return of daughter – The escaping man had said to his brother. We could flee together, abroad, to a new start. He knew the risk of being caught was considerable for he would soon be recognised amongst the neighborhood of his former street and abode, and thus returned to the asylum with short swift - but what was his freedom worth, its true value beyond the happiness of family? – That was now the burning question, gentlemen.

<u>Tito pauses to sip slowly from his coffee cup.</u>

Freud: I need to know - is it a happy ending? Does he succeed? Does he get caught? Tell me Tito – tell us all, please, and spare us of this misery.

Waitress: And accordingly, Tito obliged the men further. He explained that he had waited for the cover of darkness before creeping away from the protection and security of his brother's bookshop where he had hidden in the cellar below. The entrance to which and steps down below hidden from public view by an old wooden bookcase pushed across. The brother had collected the worst of all unsellable literature he possessed and placed it on the shelves knowing that customers would now not to bother to pay attention or scrutiny to it. It was true to say that his hide-way would never have been found. Though: against his brother's advice, he felt he could not remain there.

Tito: He arrived at his former home late in the evening, gentlemen, about 11.30 pm, it was on the following Christmas Eve. A year to the day that all this tragedy had started. He thought about the previous year's encounter with the snail as he brushed aside the ash from the fire that had raised most of the house to the ground. He dug though the filth and debris looking for anything he could sell. But all was gone, what hadn't been destroyed by fire had by now been looted: there was nothing of value to be found.

Waitress: Tito was the perfect storyteller, ladies and gentlemen, he continued to narrate to his audience just as I narrate for you.

Tito: He sat down in the earth, sobbing, a broken man – he took a glance at the pocket watch his brother had lent him. It was almost midnight – within seconds it would be Christmas Day. He thought back to the days of his former life and happiness, but he could not find any joy now. At the very pinnacle of human anguish and of despair he...

Hitler: He what? – He killed himself, didn't he? That's what I'd have done!

Tito: No! He was indeed contemplating such an act but was broken from his moment of despair by a strange feeling that suddenly came over him. Somehow unable to end his own sad bitter life, he had felt an overwhelming sense of purpose born in his suffering. That he must live to spend his entire life of his sufferings, for his sins, for kicking the snail you see, that's what he thought. An act that had doomed him to his pathetic, lonely existence. Yes: he became redemptive and sorrowful for what he had done the former year – he knelt down upon his knees and began to pray for the very first time in his life, Hitler.

Trotsky: Oh yeah, that's right, God'll save him – what God?

Waitress: Tito summed up what had happened next by saying that at exactly midnight, 12 months to the day, 12 months to the precise very second, and as his watch struck exactly the stroke of midnight as Christmas Day arrived: he heard a knock at his burnt and off the hinge, front door.

Freud: *And?*

Trotsky: *And?*

Stalin: *And?*

Hitler? *And?*

Tito: *And? – Well: he had assumed his presence had been discovered. He gave in, emotionally, psychologically, he answered the door expecting to be arrested and returned to dire conditions of the asylum, locked away for the rest of his life. Suffering for his sins as he had now resolved himself to do – but there was no-one there, not a person or cat or fox in sight, the streets were completely deserted. He looked down and there it was: he saw the snail! - that very same snail had returned exactly a year to the day - at midnight of Christmas Eve, to the very second, gentlemen.*

Freud: *And?*

Trotsky: *And?*

Stalin: *And?*

Hitler? *And – he stamped on the little so and so, didn't he?*

Tito: *No, Hitler, he didn't. The man just looked down at the little helpless creature. The snail raised its head, and in extending its fragile eyes at the end of its tender tentacles upward and outward toward him: and in a soft pathetic, squeaky little voice, which was not one as expected of great prophetical revelation – it said...*

<u>Tito breaks off to sip his coffee.</u>

Freud: *And?*

Trotsky: *And?*

Stalin: *And?*

Hitler? *And?*

Tito: And? *It was most profound gentlemen, it said: What did you do that for?*

Waitress: *Sigmund Freud went on to write: Of all those present that week; it was the man we would come to know as Marshal Josip Broz Tito who revealed himself to be the master manipulator.*

ACT SEVEN:

Waitress: By all accounts, Hitler had believed Tito's story to be one of good versus evil. He had fixated on the idea that a dark force of satanic elements was in control.

Hawker: For him, the story was no more than a fable in which a very sinister warning was present. Stalin, on the other hand, saw the tale as more straightforward.

Stalin stands.

Stalin: He should have stamped on the cursed thing the first time he saw it"

Stalin sits.

Hitler: How would you know if that was the only one? - You'd have to stamp on them all, Stalin, surely?

Stalin: No! I don't believe so, an example of might is all that would be required to send a very clear warning to any would be terrestrial pulmonated gastropod molluscs agitator! – Stamp on one and you'll soon find that you've already stamped on them all.

Trotsky: Religion, you see gentlemen, the opium of the working class – they turn to God in the hope that their poor sad existence will somehow miraculously become better: but we all know it won't- See: he turned to God in his hour of greatest need and God sent a snail...

Tito: Actually, Trotsky, that's a bit of a misquote. I think you'll find what Marx really said was; religion is the sigh of the oppressed creature, the heart of a heartless world, and the soul of soulless conditions. It is the opium of the people.

Freud: Yes, the truth young Tito, it is in Die Religion ist das Opium des Volkes of the 1844 work: A Contribution to the Critique of Hegel's Philosophy of Right.

Tito: It was a joke gentlemen...

Hitler: A joke? But it's not funny.

Stalin: Yeah, I agree – That's story was about as funny as Adolf's Oedipus complex...

Hitler: What Oedipus complex?

Stalin: Yours!

In a fit of laughter, Trotsky says in between his bouts of uncontrolled giggling...

Trotsky: I think he's referring to your mother obsession...

Stalin turns to Freud and issues a cheeky wink across the table.

Hitler: Sigmund - What mother obsession?

Freud: We'll chat later...

Hitler: What's an Oedipus complex Anyway? ...

Waitress: We do not know if the young Hitler took up Freud's invitation that day, but we do know that the offer was made, for, in his journal Freud had commented...

Freud now stands and walks across the stage to his desk, he reads as if quoting from his journal, puffing from his cigar...

Freud: The young artist demonstrates all classic symptoms of Oedipal within psychosexual stages of development. He clearly desires his mother and denigrates his father. One senses within our conversations that the child Adolf competed with his paternal role-model for possession of the matriarch, this same-sex parent is a rival to mother's attentions and affection. A theory that I closely examined in my 1899 thesis: The Interpretation of Dreams - though I did not coin the phrase Oedipus until 1910. This young man formulates perfect research material. Asked that day what an Oedipus complex was, I could do little more than offer a more private discussion... In addressing the question that day, in avoiding bitter confrontation between the two men, I merely suggested that Stalin was making folly of Adolf's continuing need to write to a young woman by the name of Geli Raubal, a half-niece. I did not impart that I observed certain sexual attraction to his opposite sex parent and the hostility noted toward the same-sex parent, which has, I believe, manifested into frustrated and inappropriate sexual fantasy toward this younger near-sibling.

Waitress: Tito liked to quote Marx, he informs that the capitalists exploit the labour force by taking advantage of the difference between the labour market and whatever the system can produce for sale in that market.

Hawker: *All successful industries followed the simple equation of surplus value.*

Tito: *Input unit-costs are lower than output unit-prices and the creation of surplus labour is the difference between the costs of keeping workers alive against the costs of what they can produce gentlemen.*

Stalin: *Yes, indeed, you understand correctly, Marx believed that capitalists are vampires sucking the worker's blood.*

Trotsky: *But Marx says that the creation of profit is by no means an injustice – he held a dual view of capitalism, and capitalists simply cannot go against the system.*

Freud returns to the table to be seated.

Freud: *Yes, it is surely not property and equipment that define capital, but the relationship between worker and owner.*

Hitler: *It's a cancerous cell - It is a problem of the economic system in general, I believe.*

Trotsky: *The workers were better off under feudalism – Under capitalism they are destined to remain impoverished.*

Tito: *Yes, I think they were Leon, they were poor but free, they had land and food a plenty. Pre-industrial Agrarian societies simply complied to the land-owners quota, once done by the end of the week, at least they could work and rest at their own leisure, but now they live ten to a room in filth and squalor, working sixty-hours per week, for what? An ever-increasing reduced mortality rate and countless deaths and injuries.*

Stalin: *Indeed! The Communist Manifesto has much to offer the proletariat, but it is only a diagnosis and not the cure.*

Trotsky: *Yes! Stalin! As if a doctor were to identify the illness without prescribing a cure.*

Freud: *So, you think that the feudal foundation stones of the past that the bourgeoisie class built itself in developing today's capital will endanger the existence of bourgeois property today, Trotsky?*

Trotsky: *Yes, I believe so, no-one is better placed to understand this phenomenon than the Russian, is that not true? - The means of production and of exchange and of the conditions under which feudal society produced and exchanged are no longer compatible with today's developed capitalist productivity. The Manifesto offers us all a social and political constitution adapted from it, the means of production have become too powerful, and they are now at the workers' disposal.*

Stalin: *All we need to do is take control, Freud, Bourgeois society may believe that the system brings order into the whole, but 1905 disproved that didn't it? They may execute us, imprison us or exile us but their greed has produced the perfect conditions for their own downfall – and that is one of workers revolution.*

Freud: *But the revolution of 1905 failed Stalin, you are in exile, I guess that makes you one of the lucky ones, doesn't it?*

Stalin: *We must teach the proletariat how to hate, to educate the masses and show them who their oppressor is. Yes, to beat your enemy you must first teach others how to hate their enemy. Prison makes the ideal school of crime for the criminal, just as it does the revolutionary; the sheer number of political prisoners ensures only that the 'lesser' learns from the 'greater' - both directly and indirectly!*

Trotsky: *A prison inmate that enters only with a basic knowledge of Marx and Lenin soon finds he will leave with an extensive one, Freud, should he first survive the ordeal of course. What else is there to do all day but to educate oneself in communist philosophy? – The more they brutalise us the more we revel in their downfall.*

Tito: *Propaganda is smuggled in Freud, and shared by the more knowledgeable amongst the faithful, it is then distributed by horse or mouse.*

Freud: *I don't follow your meaning – By horse or mouse, what do you mean?"*

Tito: *A horse is a small cloth sack or sock tide with string, Freud, easily swung from adjacent cell to cell, the mouse is a small stick, a split to one end where pages can easily be inserted and passed at reach through cell bars opposite with equal efficiency. There is the kite too, because of its triangular shape, a piece of paper folded so small it can be easily passed hand to hand, or mouth to mouth if visits are* afforded – they make think they are breaking us but in reality, they have sent us to the greatest university of all.

Trotsky: Whilst the rich live in palatial opulence and abundant luxury and the poor live on the streets like rats of an infested sewer, they serve only to radicalise us: even the minor criminal has the capacity to become a great communist leader - Marx believed that the industrial workers would rise up, and this would be an internationalist global uprising, around the whole world. The structural contradictions of capitalism will necessitate its end, from this post-capitalistic era will be born socialism within a truly equal communist utopia.

Stalin: The *bourgeoisie are their own gravediggers*, Sigmund, the fall of capitalism and the creation of squalid urbanisation will lead to the victory of the workers – this is inevitable! 1905 was not a failure, but merely the beginning of a new mass consciousness. It is the awakening!

Tito: Communism is now a real movement; we will abolish the exploiting classes and deal with the present state of things. The workers of all lands will unite, of this I am sure, we need but one nation to collapse, to implode upon itself and the rest of the world's great empires will then all fall thereafter, like dominoes.

<u>Upon a momentary pause, Freud now turns to Hitler.</u>

Freud: Marx argued in his paper: The German Ideology of 1846 - that capitalism will end, this is true gentlemen but, where will that end begin. We have not seen it of the workers of the British Empire as he first penned it to be, but of Germany, he said he was uncloaking these sheep, who take themselves and are taken for wolves; of showing how their bleating merely imitates in a philosophic form the conceptions of the German middle class; how the boasting of these philosophic commentators only mirrors the wretchedness of the real conditions in Germany – I wonder Hitler, is this new democratic society Marx predicts, enfranchising an entire population, to be born of Germany first?

Hitler: I don't see that as plausible Freud, no, the conditions for revolution may be ripe, yes, German workers surely want to end their self-alienation and be free to act without bondage to the labour market, but the notion of all united workers is surely a false premise.

Freud: Why do say that Hitler - United by what?

Hitler: *Look at the world's greatest economy shall we, the United States of America, born of colonial wars of occupation and then a war of independence, and then after that a civil war. Where today the colonialist working classes live in relative comfort whilst the Negroes as slaves sow the seeds and harvest the crops in absolute poverty: and yet today its output per capita is the world's highest. It didn't need socialism to make it a flourishing, economically advanced country did it...*

Freud: *Are you advocating slavery Adolf?*

Hitler: *No Freud, but the whole idea that workers are only separated by the shackles of their labour is utter nonsense. What I'm saying is that whilst Marx may argue that all men are equal, clearly in America they are not. Some are more equal than others: and it works does it not? Has ever before so much prosperity been attained by such a comparably large population?*

Stalin rudely interrupts...

Stalin: *I think you're being really naïve Adolf; you clearly know nothing of the desperate plight of the average American worker not to mention a nation that builds its wealth on slavery and child labour, the greed and excess of the American capitalist is boundless.*

Hitler: *I didn't say it was perfect, I'm just using it for example - Here you have a United States but no central bank or federal tax system and...*

Freud now who interrupts.

Freud: *Yes, that is correct, but there are moves I understand to change this later this year...*

Hitler: *Whatever – But we're talking about America now, today, as it stands, the wealthiest nation in the world. And should war break out tomorrow who do you suppose they would support – their trading allies, that would be the single foremost decision. Worker will gun down worker on the battlefield to protect their nation's wealth, to fight alongside their so-called capitalists, side-by-side, not the workers of other nations. What I am saying gentlemen is that the needs of the nation will come before the needs of the worker – there is no international untied workers struggle, only...*

Freud: *So, you're saying that American workers will turn on, say, German workers, or German workers will turn on Russian workers, or*

Russian workers will turn on the French or British worker to protect the wealth of the Tzars and ruling elite, the bourgeois who all treat them like filth before they will fight for the rights of each other.

Hitler: *Yes gentlemen, that is exactly what I am saying. And America is the best example of this. A country where the Jews continually condemn us, the Europeans, as anti-Semitic but condone their own racism. A country where the Negros cannot attend a white school, or travel on a white bus, walk on the same side of the road or eat in the same restaurant as the white – where the act of romance between the two races result in the lynching only of the nigger!*

Hitler starts to become ever increasingly gripped by anger.

Trotsky: *Hitler, you don't understand anything of Marx, do you? - Marx understands this point, that the proletariat is ignorant, that's why we as the intellectual Marxists must educate them, to give them the knowledge the elite deny them so that they may break their bonds, that they will identify their common oppressor, a common cause that unites them all and...*

Hitler: *And nothing! - You're living a pipe dream, and you are the one who seeks to patronise me? War, yes war, that inevitable war we all talk of, if this war broke out tomorrow what would it be over? The Workers' rights? No – ridiculous! It will be based on ethnic divisions and not the division of labour, and no doubt it will be the Slavs who...*

Tito: *Slavs Hitler? – What of the Slavs?"*

Hitler having paused on the word 'who' now sips in silent defiance from his coffee. Then replies...

Hitler: *Yes, the Slavs Tito. Isn't it Serbia who seeks independence from the Austro-Hungarian Empire? Isn't it Serbia who will bring the Empire to war? You want Slavic independence based on ethnic lines before socialism - isn't that the fact of the matter?*

Tito: *No!" - I want to see the end of the Empire, yes, but I want to see the creation of a socialist union, not an ethnic Slavic elite. You are wrong!*

Hitler: *Wrong, Tito? What do you think will happen if Serbia declares independence? War, that's what! And you seriously believe that the workers of this great Empire of ours will unite behind you? No – Germany will align itself with Austria as Germans and it will be a war between the workers, they will run to fight without question* because it is not an attack on a nation but an act of war against all non-Slavs – an attack on the both the proletariat and the Tsars – and they will all fight happily together, and not for your new socialist utopia!

Freud: So, what of the Jews then Hitler? Will they fight the Slavs too?

Hitler: You're asking the wrong question Freud; the question should be not with whom will they fight or whom they will fight against - but for what they will fight for?

Freud: They would fight for their nation, undoubtedly, they would unite against the common aggressor regardless of ethnic or religious difference, of course they would, should war break out, Austrian, German or Jew would fight in the same trenches – this is certain.

Hitler: And there it is again Freud, Jew, not German? Isn't the whole purpose of the Zionist mindset to establish an independent Jewish state based on a perceived racial dominance, built on a superiority of others?

Freud: Utter nonsense - You surely don't subscribe to that garbage, I don't want to live in a Jewish homeland any more than you want to live in a Christian homeland and, regardless, if you have not discovered Judaism within your own family tree – then I'm afraid, Adolf, you simply haven't gone back far enough.

Hitler calms himself.

Hitler: Sigmund, I don't intend to appear offensive, I am just addressing the conversation and expressing my opinion. I have no fight or quarrel with any of you, and there are many aspects of socialism to which I whole heatedly adhere. And I most certainly don't want to be a leader or a politician, so maybe I am the wrong person to ask for an opinion on such things. But if I were, I would see nothing abhorrent in the creation of a Jewish state, or a Slav state – and suspect that both you and Tito here would both want to live in them. Whether they are communist, or capitalist is not the central issue. I am merely saying that one's identity will always come before one's political persuasion and that the workers will kill other workers based on this single point. The capitalist nations will send their canon-fodder to the trenches, and they will keenly go: King and country will always prevail.

Trotsky: *If a Russian revolution should succeed, all others will see us as their vanguard and the dominoes will topple Hitler, of this I am certain. If war is inevitable, then I believe it will unite us and not divide us.*

Stalin: *The means will justify the end and if part of that process involves a lower tier of social class as; I won't say slave but cheap labour, then yes, given the American example it has its uses...*

Freud: *Yes, so you are saying I don't care whose Negro they are as long as they are my Negro...*

Stalin: *Are you sure you don't want to be a leader, Adolph? I think you have political potential and the question left in the air is one of; machines will replace manual labour, and new, even greater more efficient machines will soon replace the old machines, but men will still have to make those machines – so just who will those men be?*

Hitler: *No thank you - I am an artist and that is my passion, I believe that God has chosen me for greater things, and I have no interest in being the one that makes those machines. God has given me a unique gift and I intend to use it. I have my greatest work to yet complete; maybe one day I'll even write a book too, like you gentlemen.*

Tito: *The end justifies the means gentlemen only when the means has an end.*

ACT EIGHT:

Spotlight highlights Bucharin, centre stage, he narrates.

Bucharin: *Much discussion had centred around the work of Karl Marx and of his counterpart and great friend: Friedrich Engels. Marx's wife, Jenny, had died during the December of 1881. Developing a serious bronchial condition and overcome with grief, Marx himself would only live for just 15 months thereafter. What had initially started as catarrh developed into bronchitis and later: pleurisy. He died on 14th March 1883 at his London home aged 64 years. Marx was buried by family and friends in Highgate Cemetery: as a stateless person. 11 mourners were present at the funeral of 17th March in which his closest friends gave eulogies, these included Friedrich Engels & Wilhelm Liebknecht. Liebknecht's political career had combined Marxist revolutionary theory with legal and practical political activity. As leader of the German SPD, the new political party became Germany's largest political party of its era. Engel's eulogy included the passage:*

Hawker: *On the 14th of March, at a quarter to three in the afternoon, the greatest living thinker ceased to think. He had been left alone for scarcely two minutes, and when we came back, we found him in his armchair, peacefully gone to sleep - but forever.*

Bucharin: *The initial family burial plot was later relocated to a new plot nearby where a new memorial to his life and work was erected and inscribed with the words: "Workers of All Lands Unite" - The last line of the Communist Party Manifesto. Also inscribed are the words: "The philosophers have only interpreted the world in various ways - the point however is to change it" – of the 11th "Thesis on Feuerbach" – as edited by Engels. In 1970 a portrait bust by Laurence Bradshaw was added to the memorial by The Communist Party of Great Britain.*

Eric Hobsbawm, an eminent Marxist historian said of Marx: "One cannot say Marx died a failure" - As within 25 years of Karl Marx's death the socialist movements of both Germany and Russia had gained between "15 and 47 per cent" in representative democratic elections. Continental European socialist parties all acknowledged their Marxist origins though Marx's philosophy was, as a whole, mostly rejected in Britain.

Hawker: *Notably, unable to secure work, Marx had spent his later years relying on loans and the charity of friends in order to make ends meet.*

Bucharin exits: Spotlights highlights counter.

Waitress: *Discussions on Marxism had inevitably led to the Russian Revolution of 1905. Much of this we also find recorded in Sigmund Freud's journal of 1913. A journal simply titled by Freud as – "The Sugar Lump Club".*

Freud: *What had been the causes of the revolution in Russia?*

Stalin: *There were many, Freud, the peasants were starving, emancipated, wages were pitiful, and they were forbidden to sell or mortgage their allotted land. And then the Russification policies of the Tsars compounded this, the state brutally oppressed ethnic minorities, the repression and discrimination put them on the streets. They were forbidden to serve in the army or navy, refused schooling and denied the vote. The peasants revolted and were soon met with bans on strikes and protest – they then banned trade unions, they brutalised any worker who stood up against them – and we had a government who did nothing to protect them.*

Trotsky: *But the educated classes, the intellectuals and the students at our universities developed a new social consciousness, the more the peasants became hungry the greater the thirst for socialism and an end to the monarchy developed – 1905 was a most radical time for Russia', Sigmund.*

Freud: *I guess for Vladimir Lenin it was all about milk, sugar and coffee then?*

Trotsky: *I'm not sure I follow you Sigmund…*

Freud: *Well: didn't Lenin in his work 'Imperialism' blame certain conditions on Russia's dependence on overseas nations, did he not agitate the major powers, did he not cause all this rivalry that would ultimately lead to war?*

Stalin: *I'm not sure that war is the appropriate definition of Lenin's intent Freud, but if violent overthrow and revolution is what you refer to then I accept that we are at war - yes.*

Tito: *I don't think we can look at the causes for 1905 individually, but together as a whole, surely, they all created a perfect storm for revolt.*

Hitler: *I would agree Tito, yes, it was born of overall discontent with the dictatorship of the Tsar's and monarchy, it was inevitable given such conduct that their overthrow would be manifested in the minds of the poor.*

Trotsky: *Of course, Adolf, it all led up to great and even greater political protest that then ultimately led to rioting, all they wanted was better wages and better conditions, we as revolutionaries all sought to encourage mass strike activity and to radicalise the minds of students, and to encourage student demonstrations and...*

Stalin: *Yes, and... and as revolutionaries that included the assassination of government officials.*

Freud: *Didn't Plehve, the minister of Russian interior say in 1903: The most serious problems plaguing the country was those of the Jews, the schools, and the workers?*

Stalin: *Yes – and it was in that* order.

Trotsky: *That's why I as a Jew Freud would never be leader, anti-Semitism is as much ingrained in Russian cultural identity as it is here in Austria.*

Tito: *And the people saw prolonged problems in Russia that were not as severe in the Western economies - The Russian economy was so intertwined with others, fixed into European finances, Russia's industrial recessions lasted much longer than elsewhere, 1900 plunged Russian industry into prolonged depression, Freud. This all fanned the flames of the agrarian problem that led up to the revolution of 1905.*

Stalin: *This was allotment land Freud, and the peasants saw through it immediately. They wouldn't actually own their own plot but an assignment under an open fields' agreement. They weren't buying their freedom from serfdom, the land would not be owned by them but by a community of peasants, a cooperative if you wish, but they could not resell the land or renounce any rights to it. Instead of being enslaved to the nobles, they became enslaved by themselves. Forever: they would have to pay their fair share of rent and tax to the newly established village commune.*

Trotsky: Do you know that by 1904 peasant arrears to the communes amounted to 118 million rubles, Freud? – Their wages were so small they could buy neither food nor pay taxes, a policy that aimed to prevent the proletarianisation of peasants had now done quite the opposite. They roamed the countryside, travelling hundreds of miles to find new work. They were desperate people who would do desperate acts and their anger soon turned into violence.

Freud: Violence - So who was responsible for this violence?

Trotsky: These weren't single acts but organised masses, those who now totally ignored the restraints of authority. When you have nothing left what else have you to lose but your life? And if that life holds no value, you will easily sacrifice it.

Tito: It wasn't Lenin who inspired violence but the cruelty of a system that simply didn't care. During 1902 thousands of peasants had destroyed and looted noblemen's properties in the provinces of Kharkov and Poltava. The rebellious crowd was later brought into submission by troops who brutally punished them.

Trotsky: I'm impressed, Tito, where have you learned of this truth.

Tito: From you Trotsky my friend, I read about it in Pravda!

Stalin slaps Tito hard across the back in congratulatory.

Stalin: Well-done Leon, you see, I told you someone was reading it!

Hitler: And what did they do to try and solve the agrarian crisis Freud? I'll tell you; they blamed the Jews for it. Whilst the Tsars tolerated other faiths and culture, they never showed respect for it. They enforced that Christianity was true and progressive, they created an ethnic hierarchy. They created the myth that Jews were a special problem, enemies of Christendom, that they were the ones who exploited the peasantry and that they were the vanguard of a genuine Jewish conspiracy to over-throw the crown: they the Jews were the ones that were really in control of the revolutionary Marxist movement.

Freud: Yes, it's that deflection technique again isn't. To solve a problem, invent another one, and blame someone else entirely...

Hitler: Since I became an artist, I have always taken a tremendous interest in propagandist activity. Especially the way poster art can deliver powerful messages. And I see gentlemen that the Socialist-Marxist organisations have mastered this art too and have applied it as an instrument to your cause with astounding skill. I think that the correct use of propaganda is a true art that has remained practically unknown to the bourgeois parties. I believe it is a weapon of which is owed many of your successes in Russia.

Trotsky: It wasn't just the Jews that became targeted, but all national and religious minorities. Russian administrators couldn't even agree on a definition of 'Pole' - well not a legal definition anyway. They have made identity a matter of one's birthplace and always use the phrase 'of Polish or Russian descent' these days. They have striven to make non-Russians inferior, their propaganda is designed to aggravate feelings of disloyalty, nothing less.

Stalin: Yes, indeed - You see, post 1861, given the emancipation of the Serfs, they were forced to take into account all wider public opinion, but they failed outright to gain the peoples consent and support.

Trotsky: Russification policies directly led to the Polish uprising of 1863.

Stalin: Of course.

Trotsky: The uprising was brutally crushed; in the eyes of the Tsar the stability of the Empire was at threat.

Hitler: And distrust of Germany too. During the 1870s Russia objected to the unification of Germany by Otto von Bismarck, though by blood and iron he achieved his aim. Should you have had such character on your side in 1905 gentlemen, your revolution would have succeeded!

Tito: Yes, Hitler, a great man indeed.

Hitler: Germany, from a defensive standpoint, needed control over Prussian lands around the Rhine to the west, that is if a German Empire was ever to prove viable. And the small principalities were already destined for their own independence. What was Prussia then is now central Germany, it was great strategic thinking on Bismarck's part we must surely agree?

Stalin: And that all started the process of Russification. This upset in the balance of power between us led the Tsars to only one conclusion: Germany would use its new strength against us.

Trotsky: They needed to turn the new borderlands into Russia proper, not just in land mass but in cultural heterogeneity. Those of true Russian character, they thought, would be more likely to rise-up in defense of their motherland.

Stalin: Yes, and it was this identity crisis amongst the minorities, the so-called nationality problem, that would later plague them.

Trotsky: In understanding the revolution, Freud, you must first understand the social, political and demographical conditions the Tsars themselves had created for their own downfall. It was a grim picture of laissez-faire capitalist policies that achieved nothing. Agricultural production was stagnant, but elsewhere, in Europe, the west, internationally, the peasants saw their grain prices fall, we needed imports, and our national debt was out of control. As the people starved, they spent even more money on military preparations for war. The famine became even more widespread than ever before...

Stalin: Do you know how many died of starvation in 1891 – Freud?

<u>Freud gestures with his right hand, palm upward, to signify that he does not.</u>

Stalin: We're talking about 900,000 square miles, the previously rich fertile lands of the Volga and Nizhni-Novgorod, Riazan, Tula, Kazan, Simbirsk, Saratov, Penza, Samara and Tambov. We're talking about the malnutrition of twenty million people, all hungry and in need of food. 400,000 Freud, yes, 400,000 died from starvation and disease...

Waitress: Freud noted in his journal later - It was here, at this exact point, as Stalin finished expressing the word 'disease' that Trotsky raised himself up as he slung his right forearm hard across his chest, the sound so firm it could have been the beat of a drum, and delivered the following as if he were now attending a political rally...

Hawker: Such was his eagerness to stand bolt upright that the chair shot back out from underneath, at some speed I say, this drawing much attention to the fellow from others around us.

Trotsky: These people's efforts were in vain, who with unchanged lives, desired to come to the people's aid by distributing the wealth they have first taken from them.

Hitler: Yes, yes, impassioned poetry indeed! You deliver your words to perfection, Trotsky.

Freud: No, young Adolf – They are the words of Lev Nikolayevitch Tolstoy.

Stalin: Dissatisfaction quickly turned into despair and their strikes were banned - Impoverished workers were now sympathetic to radical socialism. The workers revolted with revolutionary protest and countless illegal strikes soon became the vanguard of revolution.

Trotsky: The Russian progressives, the Union of Zemstvo Constitutionalists and the Union of Liberation both demanded a constitutional monarchy…

Stalin: But that was not enough for us. We, as the two other main groups, the Socialist Revolutionary Party and the Marxist Russian Social Democratic Labour Party - wanted much more. The liberals were calling for freedom of religion, political reforms and a constitution, full freedom of the press, an elected national legislature. The Tsar, that scoundrel Nicholas II, sat on his arse in the grandeur of his palace only offering token improvements. They all soon started to listen when Vyacheslav von Plehve was assassinated.

Tito: I'm not sure I know who Plehve was?

Trotsky: He was the Minister of the Interior, a terrible man, a Tsarist – After the assassination they appointed a new minister, Pyotr Sviatopolk-Mirskii, he was more liberal, an attempt to appease the people's demands, but the crucial demand for a representative national legislature was still ignored.

Stalin: In 1902 the strikes started in the Caucasus', the pay disputes on the railways encouraged others, we had the general strike of Rostov-on-Don, and we were soon addressing crowds of 20,000 with revolutionary speeches, but they, the Cossacks, continued to butcher us. Political demands soon became economic ones; by 1903 the south was ready for a total over-throw of the elite ruling classes. Following citywide wage strikes in Tiflis, workers found that their working day was reduced, they got a new taste for the power the held in their own hands – we the people held our own destiny.

Trotsky: *The strikes had spread to Odessa by spring of 1904, then St. Petersburg, Baku and Kiev, by 1905 there was no stopping us.*

Tito: *It was Putilov that tipped the scales I believe - Four workers were sacked for their membership of a worker's assembly.*

Trotsky: *Yes Tito, at the Putilov ironworks, the railway and artillery supplier, yes, 1904, St. Petersburg, they refused to reinstate the four so workers downed tools, a strike was called, the Putilov strike then spread like wildfire, now we had 150,000 strikers from 382 factories on the streets – the whole city came to a standstill. And by the 8th of January 1905 – St. Petersburg fell into darkness without its electricity. No electricity, no newspaper production and all public areas were closed – By January 1905 we were unstoppable!*

Stalin: *The Cossacks would charge at us, cutting us down with their swords, slicing us up like meat, trampling us below horse charge hooves, they were relentless, but we stood our ground - but Bloody Sunday changed everything that day Freud.*

Trotsky: *If you want to understand you need to be there with us in Russia on January 22nd, it was carnage. Allowing tens of thousands of peasant agitators to starve, brutalising and cutting down Marxist sympathisers, all legitimate responses of a brutal regime, but to shoot down 1000 unarmed demonstrators led by their own church was quite another. All Father Georgy Gapon wanted to do that day was deliver a petition to Tsar Nicholas II at the Winter palace, and his response was to order his Imperial Guard to kill them. The Tsar had turned on his own church.*

Hitler had remained quiet, doodling on paper until…

Hitler: *And here you both are…*

Stalin: *Here we both are what Young Adolf?*

Hitler: *Well, you're both alive and well, living in exile having fled a failed revolution…*

Stalin: *We didn't fail, we're banished Mister Hitler, the Tsar is terrified of us!*

Hitler: *Whatever you sell it is as, you lost, didn't you? The Tsar and Imperialist Russia remain.*

Waitress: Freud had noted in his journal; Hitler behaved as if wanting to provoke an argument.'

Trotsky: We may have lost the battle, but we will win the war.

Stalin: This is just the start, Hitler, it cannot be stopped!

Freud: Now, now, gentlemen, we are all reasonable fellows are we not? Let's not get into argument or get bogged down over technicalities, shall we?

Hitler: All Russification served to do was annoy the ethnic nationalist groups amongst you. Be it the Finns or Poles or Baltic provinces, the Muslims, or the Jews, they all want the opposite to what you foresee: they want their own autonomy just as those of the Austro-Hungarian Empire today. They won't unite with you but will merely seize the opportunity to settle old scores – As your mass movements now stagnate all you will witness is a rise in terrorism upon which many more thousands will die.

Stalin: And what would you have us do then Adolf?

Hitler: I've already told you, all I want to do is paint, but I will say this: The world is not there to be possessed by the faint-hearted races.

ACT NINE:

Waitress: *Conversation would again soon turn back to the possibility of war within the Austro-Hungarian Empire.*

Hitler: *The conflict in the Balkans is the powder keg of Europe, should war break-out I believe it will start there, a war that will drag us all into a wider conflict.*

Tito: *Would you care to clarify this, Hitler?*

Hitler: *That I will. When Austro-Hungaria annexed the former Ottoman territories of Bosnia and Herzegovina during the crisis of 1908 -1909 it served only to anger the Kingdom of Serbia. After all, the Ottomans had occupied it since 1878, and, of-course, this was met by Russian political interference, the Pan-Slavic and Orthodox Russian Empire, you must see that this shattered any hope of peace gentlemen?*

Tito: *Yes - But the Ottoman territories are shrinking by the day. The Balkan League is numerically superior and, most importantly, strategically advantaged, you must see that? We will see the occupied lands of the former yoke return to European hands. The League is achieving rapid success.*

Hitler: *Do you think that Britain and France will stand by and allow the spoils of this conflict to be divided without their interference? -Do you think that had Austro-Hungaria not annexed Bosnia and Herzegovinian that Serbia would not have flexed its own muscles? It was the Treaty of Berlin that freed Bosnia and Herzegovina in the first place, and following the Empires later annexation, the Ottoman's soon sought to restore their suspended Ottoman constitution, didn't they? The great nations will always seek to maintain the status-quo and protect their Christian populations.*

Tito: *But the Ottoman's surely don't have the strength to win, it's just implausible Adolf.*

Hitler: *I'm not suggesting that at all, as the league win, they will then turn on one another, that's inevitable. There will be land grabs to restore former territories; the united will become the divided. Those minorities caught up in the middle of it will all seek their own independence and there will be yet another treaty that represents only the interests of the greater majority. All of the great Empires will want a slice; Russia, Austro-Hungaria, the British and French.*

Tito: I still don't see how this Balkan League War can affect the rest of us – the Balkan war has nothing to do with the actions of the Austro-Hungarian Empire?

Trotsky: I believe that what young Adolf is suggesting is that any new treaty will enlarge the territorial borders of Bulgaria, Serbia, Montenegro or Greece - and in doing so what will become of the former Ottoman lands of Rumelia, Thrace or Macedonia? Someone, but just who we don't know yet, yes, will want to claim it!

Hitler: I think even a monkey could have predicted this conflict.

Tito: That may well be, but even that monkey wouldn't be stupid enough to threaten the stability of Austro- Hungaria, especially given Germany's allegiance to it. It's just not possible for the Balkan conflict to spread – I simply don't see that as militarily viable – it would never succeed – total suicide.

Hitler: Generals may win battles, but it is people who win wars. When a population becomes intoxicated with hatred of another, they will soon jump as lemmings from a cliff top, that you'll see, it's an ethnic problem as much as it is a geographical one.

Trotsky: Nonsense - Soldiers win battles, but it is logistics that win wars.

Waitress: Freud wrote: The Young Turks had tried to encourage the Muslim populations of the region, especially Bosnia-Montenegro, to re-settle to the south in northern Macedonia in Ottoman controlled lands. Leon and Joseph seem to lack the significance of last year's Albanian uprisings of Spring: 1912 - in which the Albanian Muslims and existing populations of Ottoman immigrants, united together.

Hawker: Even Albanian military officials and soldiers have now switched allegiance to the Ottoman forces. This is surely to be a catastrophe for the Austro-Hungarian Empire. Especially as a policy of re-populating Macedonia where few Muslim minorities exist today is now prevalent. The Committee of Real Muslims has issued the Kararname decree.

Waitress: They have proclaimed that all Muslim peoples of northern Albania, Epirus, and Bosnia all fight. To instigate all possible means against the forces of the Bulgarian, Serbian and Montenegrin Kingdoms. It instructs all Muslims to defend the territorial integrity of their own Ottoman Empire.

Freud: *Who are you, Hitler?*

Hitler: *I'm not quite sure I fully understand the question.*

Freud: *Well, you talk like a nationalist and engage in theories of Darwinist evolution, survival of the fittest, yet on the same token you say you are a Christian? And that's all a little perplexing to me – you're a very contradictory young fellow at times, aren't you?*

Hitler: *Not at all Freud, there's only one race of people and that's the human race.*

Freud: *But there's the very issue, if you are acknowledging that we are all of the same species why do you insist on talking of racial divisions – different races?*

Hitler: *I think that one's race or identity is something that we create for ourselves, it's not necessarily purely a genetic thing but a cultural or religious badge of identity we mostly choose, Freud.*

Freud: *Exactly, so let me ask you again – who are you?*

Hitler: *Well, I guess I am Bavarian then – does that answer the question?*

Freud: *It does but then again it asks a bigger question and that is, what is a Bavarian?*

Hitler: *Then the answer to that wider question would be I'm a German then – surely?*

Freud: *So, what's a German?*

Waitress: *The two men, much to the other three's amusement and enjoyment then engaged in seeking to acquire such a definition The Neolithic period had proven, more interestingly to Freud than Hitler, evidence suggesting most of those areas known today as Austria were amenable to Neolithic agriculture.*

Hawker: *Of this there was evidence.*

Freud: *So, are you a Neolite or a Copperite?*

Hitler: *Don't be ridiculous. How can anyone know that.*

Freud: Well, how far back in one's family tree can you realistically go Adolf?

Hitler: There will be a definite problem on my father's side, Freud - I don't know who my grandfather was...

Freud: Exactly my point, there you have it! You could be a Slav, a Jew or a Pole then? At least as a Jew I can go as far back as Moses!

Hitler: I don't really care, Freud, as long as I'm not French.

<u>Tito and Trotsky are pissing themselves with laughter – Stalin just doesn't get it at all.</u>

Freud: So, let's just agree that you're a Celt for the time being then shall we, Adolf?

Hitler: I think it's you Sigmund who fails to see the wider picture. Race is not something you can prove, no more than the existence of a God, the same God that we both choose to believe in, though it be from quite different perspectives. Race is just something that is, you know who you are and to what you identify yourself as. Ask our revolutionary friends here if money exists? It doesn't, it's just pretty little pieces of printed paper with pictures on, it's of no more value than what we chose to wipe our own rear-ends with, but we believe in it because of the guarantee of payment we place on it.

Freud: Go on then - If money doesn't exist why are those three all prepared to die fighting over it?

Hitler: Race doesn't have to be a scientific fact for you to believe in it, Freud – it may be a social construct, but we all know what it is, and I am a true German!

Tito: Is now a good time to suggest that you're black then, Adolf - After all, if we go with your God theory then we all evolved from Eden, and that's now proven to have been in Africa.

Hitler: If you're going to keep forcing the issue gentlemen then I'll choose to be a Roman. Why? Because Noricum and Rome were active trading partners of the Roma era with fixed military alliances from as early as 15 BC. As Austria was annexed to the Roman Empire and endured for 500 years of so-called Austria-Romana, I guess that's a pretty healthy race to have descended from!

Freud: But your understanding of history is always written by the winning side...

Hitler: Yes, but if I were to sum up what is wrong with the Empire, I think I could do it very easily. Look around us gentlemen, there are many signs of decay which ought to be given serious thought, don't you think? As far as economics are concerned, that is, you spend far too much time concentrating on reform, if you want to win the hearts and minds of the people then you need to understand them.

Freud: Go on then...

Hitler: Well, let's take the increase of population in Germany and the question of providing their daily bread. Why do we consider the idea of acquiring fresh territory such a deplorable idea? It seems to me that the world's Empires are all seeking commercial conquest of the world over each other and at the cost of each other. This must surely lead to unlimited and injurious industrialisation. The obvious being that by weakening the agricultural classes, there is a proportionate increase in the proletariat moving into urban areas, and this can only upset the natural equilibrium and order of things. The great divide between rich and poor becomes apparent as luxury and poverty now live side by side and the deplorable consequences, the creation of slums which are infected, as a rotten apple to its core, with unemployment. This is what's causing havoc. And this is what we see in Russia isn't it? You intend to take them from the land and turn them into industrial machines, do you not?'

Stalin: Rapid industrialisation creates wealth, Adolf, wealth that we as the state share equally amongst those that have created it. We need factories, but there will be good conditions, good pay, short hours and generous holidays and health care too. By creating wealth, we create leisure time for all the people.

Hitler: Yes - But the population inevitably becomes divided into political classes. Social discontent and unrest versus commercial prosperity. Surely - things cannot go on as they are. Commerce has assumed definite control of the State, and money has become the new God whom all now serve and bow down to. We've forgotten our heavenly Gods, religion is old fashioned, and all we do today is worship mammon in a state of utter degeneration.

Freud: I don't believe this to be true Adolf. In this day and age, with science and understanding, where man created God in 'his' own image', very few people really subscribe to such nonsense. I certainly don't accept the existence of a monospherical God - And, if there were I'd certainly be asking him who elected him to rule.

Hitler: Our Majesties make a mistake when creating representatives of new finance capital to the ranks of the nobility. Ideal virtues have become secondary considerations to those of money. The nobility of the sword now ranks second to that of finance. The nobility has lost more and more of the racial qualities that those who created this Empire stood for. Disruption is being brought about by the elimination of personal control; the whole economic structure is being transferred into the hands of joint stock companies. The workers are now degraded into an object of speculation in the hands of unscrupulous exploiters who are assuming control of the whole of national life. We have given way to money-grabbing capitalism. Surely, now, national life is dependent on commerce rather than ideal values.

Trotsky: Welcome to Marxism, I had been starting to wonder how long it would take you to engage with us.

Hitler: Marxism isn't enough Trotsky - You may seek to fill the pockets of the poor and redistribute the wealth of the rich amongst them, but you create a secondary void. People want more than their daily bread on the table – they want something to believe in, something to live for.

Stalin: Are you suggesting that Socialism isn't a worthy enough cause to fill that spiritual void? It seems to me that working for all, a collective sense of duty beyond self will prevail.

Hitler: I've no desire to argue with you, but it seems to me that the Bolsheviks see themselves as replacing God. You offer the people nothing more than work and death. They as individuals just became another cog in the very machines, those mechanical apparatus they spend a lifetime servicing.

Stalin thumps his fist down onto the table.

Stalin: Utter nonsense!

Trotsky: I see the issue of religion as a means of oppression, though I accept that it is so ingrained in human culture and identity that I fear it can never be truly exorcised. You may have trained as a Priest, Stalin, and I concede you have a greater knowledge of Theology than I, but you still have that overriding need to pray – don't you?

Stalin: Trotsky, do you believe that I too am immune from Bourgeoisie conditioning? I am a product of the working classes and I too have been brainwashed into such thinking. That life is designed for the purpose of suffering and inner turmoil, that subservience on earth will be met upon death by the greatness and grandeur of heaven. I may have at times a personal need of God, but that doesn't mean to say that I would ever want to meet him!

Freud: If you feel the spiritual need to talk with God you must surely believe in him - And if you do believe then I find it hard to understand why you would never want to meet him – If God exists, then you have somewhat of a conundrum on your hands don't you Stalin?

Stalin: He doesn't, there is no God, and it's up to us to fill that void with Marxism, that's what people will now live for. I'm merely speaking aloud. If you were to put all of the sins of the Tsars and Monarchy and of the ruling classes together in one basket, that would not equate to one tenth of the sins of God. If God exists, then it is he who is the most deplorable sinner of them all, a heinous, despicable dictator who allows nothing but suffering and servitude of the poor.

Hitler: This is the problem, not whether there is a God or not, but the fact that we as people only deal with what is necessary, we live our lives born out of essentialism - our worst sin is in the decadence and habit of only doing things by halves.

Freud: And you are suggesting what Adolf? That we create a merger between God and Marxism just to fill the ignorant minds of the narrow-minded and uneducated.

Tito: It seems to me that's what Marxism already is – Christianity, but without the resurrection.

Trotsky: Maybe Lenin should become the new God then.

Freud: Are you sure he's up to the job? He's only 5 feet tall and is rather too partial to violence for me!

<u>Trotsky laughs.</u>

Stalin: So, if you too believe that Lenin is too short to be of Godly stature, Trotsky, what are you suggesting about me?

Trotsky: I'm not suggesting anything, it was a joke amongst friends. It was Sigmund who made the joke, not I – I have nothing but respect for the fine qualities of our leader, you know that.

Stalin: I think you're suggesting that you are the man for the job. So, Marxism is to become the new God, to construct its own temples of splendor and awe, and if I am to understand the thinking of our young artist correctly, half-heartedness will not suffice - Do you want the top job, Trotsky?

Trotsky: I'd rather have an icepick to the back of the head.

ACT TEN:

Waitress: The Vienna Circle was a name given to a collective of great Viennese thinkers of the time who proposed that matters of God, ethics and aesthetics were meaningless. They asserted that testable assertions about such things were wholly unverifiable, therefore, a complete waste of time. The conversations amongst the coffeehouses would focus on substantive facts – known proven existence. However, one particular event that week would question this way of thinking and that event was the Skandalkoncert.

Hawker: The Skandalkoncert (Scandal Concert) was also often referred to as the Watschenkonzert (Slap Concert). Hitler, being an admirer of Vagner, had attended this concert, one performed by the famous Jewish conductor: Arnold Schoenberg. A member of the Vienna Concert Society. Buschbeck, the event's organizer was a member of a different society: The Viennese School of Composer's and, if nothing else, he was keen to experiment. A riot had broken out with one man being slapped across the face by Buschbeck, it would come to light that the injured party was none other than Adolph Hitler himself. Buschbeck yelling at the time: "If its art, it is not for all, if it is for all, then it is not art."

Waitress: A most put out Hitler had complained of this remark the following morning to the gentlemen of the coffee house where upon hearing this, Tito had laughed at the young Adolf's pompous attitude, and merely chuckled...

Tito: Hearing you get slapped must have been the most harmonious sound of the evening, then...

Waitress: The concert had taken place in the Muzikvein (Great Hall), and by all accounts not at all to Hitler's personal tastes.

Stalin: I don't know why your laughing, Trotsky – You're nothing more than a paper tiger, nothing more than a noisy champion with fake muscles. At least Adolph has a principle at stake, he's anything but your beautiful uselessness.

<u>Trotsky is enraged and Hitler, seeing this change of mood, jumps in.</u>

Hitler: Let me explain, I went with that Klimt fellow, the one who published that series of filthy filly drawings, twenty-five of them, in the Fünfundzwanzig Handzeichnungen. So, I'm anything but narrow minded, Tito, if that it was you attempt to portray.

Tito: It was just a joke, Leon thought it was funny.

Hitler: I'd been advising Klimt on a new style, from last year - A Portrait of Adele Bloch-Bauer II, I told him, more gold Klimt, more gold. Without my talent, Tito, he would never have got that one finished in time. His Vienna's International Exhibition of Prints and Drawings this year is my doing, not his.

Freud: I know the chap well, very well, Hitler, I appreciate that he has a rather dodgy chest these days, I keep telling him to wrap up before he catches something, but to suggest he is your apprentice now is way too far beyond the pale.

Hitler: I'm not here to argue with you, Freud, the truth is truth, and we'll leave it there.

Freud: Truth? I think if you tell a big enough lie enough times it becomes your truth.

Hitler: I went to the concert last night as invited, with Gustav and his on again off again mistress, Alma Mahler. She's written dozens of books and songs, if she invited me then that alone is testament to my superior creativity, she knows everybody, and those she does not know are not worth bothering with.

Waitress: Hitler then, in underpinning his intellect, proceeded to recite the names of dozens of world-famous works of art.

Hitler: If war breaks out gentlemen, Oskar and I will both sign up. Me because I am a patriot, he because Alma wants rid of him, she told me so. If I am so talentless, why would she seek my guidance and companionship?

Trotsky: Pray tell then...

Freud: If Gustav is meeting with Alma behind Oskars back, I suggest you give such company a very wide birth in future, young Adolph.'

Hitler: I'll quote her, gentlemen, shall I? - she said - He alone seeks my destruction. One cannot cleanse what is soiled. What foul fiend sent that one to me, Adolph?

Waitress: Freud did not break confidentiality but did remark later in the journal that he knew all too well of this 'notorious' pair and of their 'Vienna couplings'. Writing: He (Oskar) has created a life size doll which Alma informs is called – 'Alma Doll'.

Hawker: She alleges it to be a true to real-life Alma, intimate in every detail and he carries around with him wherever he goes, she told me, even to parties and the opera...

Waitress: Freud knew at the very least that this part of Hitler's narration had now contained at least in part, some truth.

Hitler: So, yes, of course I wanted to impress, Gustav, Oskar and Alma, that is why I invited them there and we were seated in anticipation of a brilliant concert. I was aware that it could not compete with the brilliance of Wilhelm Richard Wagner but I did expect music, gentlemen, and they were all amateurs, and what did we get for our pennies, garbage, gentlemen, utter garbage. Not even the worst of tropes and cliches that would remotely appeal to the masses.

Tito: So, you hit the organiser because you didn't like the music - It is not for you to decide what is or what isn't music, Hitler. Buschbeck had neither sought nor asked for your advice, it is subjective only, it was his concert.

Hitler: I wasn't the only one, Tito, everybody there hated it, it was a riot, the whole place got smashed to pieces. We paid for music and what we got was noise – Yes, Stalin, it was the principal of it.

Freud: So, nothing to do with the fact that Arnold Schoenberg is a Jewish conductor then, Hitler?

Hitler: Certainly, not, what are implying?

Freud: Or is it that you seem to think that you can talk on informed behalf of everyone present last night, these matters of aesthetics are meaningless. Whether it was or wasn't and who did or did not is not testable, you make assertions about taste based on your own opinions, ones that are wholly unverifiable, and frankly, Hitler, a complete waste of my time this morning.

Hitler: How dare you, I got slapped because that man was an odious fool, an ignorant oaf who knows nothing of culture. I'll tell you this, Freud, Franz Lehar was experimental, but he managed critical success. There's nobody like him, my taste is much broader and more educated than you prescribe.

Waitress: It was Lehar who had inspired the likes of the Italian opera composer - Giacomo Puccini. Hitler was keen to stress that whilst not mainstream at the time...

Hawker: ...he was seen by many as the greatest composer of Italian opera.

Hitler: I like and respect a genuine composer that pushes his boundaries, Puccini on the influence of Franz Lehar tried his hand at creating Operetta's, Freud, and he succeeded, pure genius at every level, and what about La Rondine, one of the biggest events to take place this year, a new and pure creation, Freud, he has created an operetta of perfection.

Freud: Yes, pure. Lehar's father is an Austrian bandmaster in the Austro-Hungarian Army, and his mother, Christine Neubrandt, a Hungarian woman of German descent.

Stalin: How can you remember all this historical detail?

Freud: That's easy. Always keep one eye on the ball and one on the referee.

Hitler: So, hate the player, not the game, is it? - And what have you recently achieved Mister Sigmund Freud, a book about dreaming that finally, yes finally, got published in English only this year, and a book that you wrote over 14 years ago. You're all the same, you chosen ones', you know nothing, Sigmund Freud.

Waitress: Adolph Hitler had then by all accounts of the journal, got up and left, slamming the door of the Central Coffeehouse behind him.

Hawker: His last words upon exiting...

<u>Hitler yells back at the table from the doorway...</u>

Hitler: You're a kwakzalver.

<u>Hawker leaves the stage. On exiting shouts...</u>

Hawker: Sigmund Freud is a kwakzalver, kwakzalver Freud, read all about it...

Tito: Worry not, Freud, you won, they're all the same these Austrians, nothing but *unts and crybabies. - He'll be back tomorrow, he told me earlier that his Creditanstalt bank loan application had been turned down, yet again, apparently, it's their fault now, that's why he can't get into college. I suspect that the concert was his Achilles heel. It reminded him that art challenges and changes, and what he has to offer has been left behind. He's nothing more than an inadequate postcard seller.

Freud: *I fear that we will never hear from him again.*

Tito: *You most certainly will, not that I want to be cheeky to my elders but who else is going to pay for his coffee? I'd say bollocks to him personally but rumour is - he only has one!*

Waitress: *We know that the Rothschild family were Jewish, extremely wealthy, and originally from Frankfurt. Their banking empire, Creditanstalt Bank, was spread across Europe. Salomon Mayer von Rothschild was the first to move to Vienna establishing the first Viennese branch of the family and, by 1913, the Rothschilds firmly established Vienna as <u>the</u> European centre of finance. Louis Nathaniel de Rothschild owned the huge Vienna Palais Rothschild. The family homes would later be ceased, looted and destroyed - as 'Aryanised' by the Nazi's. The Austrian Government held on to over 200 art works belonging to the family until as late as 1998 – when they were finally returned. Later, being sold at Christie's auction house (London -1999).*

Hawker leans through the window and shouts...

Hawker: *We do know that Freud had invited his friend and mentee, Carl Jung, to meet the young artist and the other three revolutionaries of the Sugar Lump Club, but it was an invitation that was never taken up.*

Waitress: *Freud having noted: Carl would rather feed his penis into his coffee grinder than waste time on that lot.*

ACT ELEVEN:

The café is closed, late at night the waitress is busy cleaning and readying for the next day.

Waitress: Carl Jung found it difficult to follow his older mentor's doctrine at times, and as history informs us, we know they later parted ways. Jung establishing his own branch: Analytical psychology which was quite separate from Freud's original theories on psychoanalysis. Jung's 'individuation' concerns the matter of a lifelong psychological process of differentiation. An understanding of one's 'self', based on both conscious and unconscious forces. He focused on human development, describing this as: Synchronicity, archetypal phenomena, the collective unconscious, the psychological complex and extraversion and introversion. It was not that he was averse to meeting the others, Trotsky, Tito and Stalin, that he had declined Freud's invite – no, not at all, he liked to be intellectually challenged. The fact is, Jung was also an artist, a craftsman, and a prolific writer. He had met Hitler on a handful of occasions already, they had painted together, seated side-by-side, passing time and chatting. Both evidently had very different techniques and styles.

Stage lights fade, spotlight highlights Freud at his desk.

Freud: Jung had said to Hitler: As a human being, the artist may have many moods, and a will, and personal aims, but as an artist he is 'man' in a higher sense - he is 'collective man' - one who carries and shapes the unconscious, psychic life of mankind. He had gone on to share one of his many books with Hitler, but soon discovered that he was not quite as enlightened as himself. On returning the book the following day, as agreed, Hitler had said: You'll be dead before you'll ever get that pulp coffee literature published.

Stage lights return to find the waitress mopping away.

Waitress: Yes, his decline to the invitation was personal, coming to light much later on and not born of Freud's journal. It was a much later publication, The Freud/Jung Letters: The Correspondence Between Sigmund Freud and C. G. Jung (Princeton University Press, 1974). We know that most of Carl Jung's books were published posthumously and still to this day, many remain unpublished. Freud's investigations into the unconscious mind led him to believe that Adolph Hitler's sexual and aggressive impulses were in perpetual conflict. His need for a sense of supremacy over others were his *defense mechanism. Yes, Adolph Hitler was Sigmund Freud's raw material.*

Hawker leans through the window and shouts...

Hawker: Freud had felt he had somehow failed Hitler. He noted: *Upon examination, that was not handled as well as one would expect, I do feel somewhat guilty, it is true to say that this has disturbed my sleep to a degree that makes me feel uncomfortable with my retrospective actions.*

Lights fade as nighttime falls, foxes howl, a Cockrell crows as the sun begins to rise. The day begins with only Stalin and Freud at the table.

Freud: *All I have done is slight the fellow, I confronted him with the realities of his misguided values and morals, and it is I who now lacks sleep. He has all the makings of a monster, Stalin, how is it that he sleeps at night?*

Stalin: *Given everything we have come to know of Hitler this week, Mister Freud, it is clear, he doesn't drink coffee after 7pm.*

Hawker enters to stand front of stage. Waitress remains behind serving counter.

Hawker: *Stalin would then go on to offer more sound advice as we read within the journal, this would be referred to as 'the cognitive gap'. Freud summed this up as an emotional conflict between his actions and the interpretation of what others thought of his actions, the stress caused when he felt that he had let others down.*

Hawker leaves as he shouts...

Hawker: *Hear all about it! Hear all about! Freud feels guilty... A guilty Freud tells all...*

Stalin: *Most of you Europeans believe we only drink Vodka, but that's not true, you know. As Bolsheviks we prefer a fermented beverage, we call it Kvass, Freud, but these days, it's almost impossible to find a decent pint of it anywhere in Russia... that's why Vodka is taking over, it's cheap, quick, and cheerful.*

Waitress: Stalin explained that Kvass, as an old and traditional beer had been produced in Russia for well over 1,000 years, and that it was known to be the favourite beverage of Peter the Great (As Russian Emperor: 1682 - 1725.

Stalin: To make a good Kvass, Freud, you'll need rye bread, the darker the better and then season it with herbs and fruits, apples or berries are the best for flavouring, but the key ingredient is the amount of birch sap, it is this that separates the master from the novice.

Freud: That does sound rather delicious in wetting one's palette, I rather fancy some of that, you never know, it might help me to sleep.

Stalin: Oh, yes, it'll do that my friend, but it's a sweet drink, given the amount of sugar you put in your coffee, none, I'm not sure if it is the most perfect for you. It is the aroma's that do it for me, just like the coffee here does in dragging one from the street, it smells best when made with pumpernickel, brown sugar, and prunes, you should try some.

Freud: Have you found any of it in Austria?

Stalin: No, just mediocre versions, low in alcohol, suitable for children only, I tried one and it tasted just like a cheap soda. You'll only find the real thing in Russia, Moscow is best, the Yar, they say it was opened as far back as 1826, popular these days with the Russian elite but don't let that spoil the taste. I've met many famous poets, actors, writers and artists there, Friday evenings are better, for both music and for the company of...

Freud: Is it a brothel? Stalin...

Stalin: None more so than this very coffeehouse, if you want it, it is there for the taking, but most come here for the coffee as I feel certain you would agree, Freud.

Waitress: Sigmund Freud, in offering his hand in friendship explained that one day, when Trotsky and Stalin were able to safely return home again, from exile, that perhaps he could meet with them again and enjoy a pint a Kvass together. He was most keen to do this, this is certain as he noted the address of the Yar within the journal. He was shocked by Stalin's reply...

Stalin: Not possible, not now or ever, Freud, I'm banned.

Freud: *Banned? Then why build me up with all this excitement, Stalin, in my head I was already there, what a disappointment, I'm most perturbed.*

Stalin: *I wasn't offering you a holiday, Freud, the Yar and Kvass are quite irrelevant, it is the story I wished to share with you. It is your stress that requires of my attention, not your aperitifs'.*

Waitress: *As reported, Stalin had gone on to share his story, and as history also informs, we know that after leaving Vienna, he would remain in Siberia, in exile, and would not return to Russia until the revolution of 1917. Stalin explained that the story he wished to share had begun in 1910.*

Stalin: *I told Lenin I was arrested in March of 1910 for political agitation, Freud, but that wasn't quite true. I was sent back to Solvychegodsk, following an incident, you could call it a brawl it that helps to clarify, it had occurred one drunken evening, I was just young and fool hardy, and yes, I was in the Yar.*

Freud: *You lied to Lenin?*

Stalin: *Yes, not proud of it, it certainly created a sense of distrust between us when he found out the truth, perhaps to the extent that our trust in each other may never fully recover, but I wasn't trying to big myself up, absolutely not, I was genuinely too embarrassed to admit to what I had done, Sigmund, it was shameful of me, unforgivable in fact.*

Waitress: *Freud noted how Stalin had told him of this 'shameful' night on the town, one where he had been drinking to excess, and one where he would return to his favourite hord for his final beer of the evening – this, to the Yar alehouse. Stalin had demanded to drink the best pint of Yar in Moscow, and an all too eager to please landlord had served him just that. The landlord had by his account been so thrilled with Stalin's appreciation of his brewing talents, and duly served him with a pint of the best Kvass ale in Moscow.*

Hawker leans through the window and shouts...

Hawker: *The proprietor said: This is a pint of the best ale in Russia, if not the whole world.*

Waitress: *Stalin had savoured the powerful arousing aromas, the taste and the texture He congratulated the barkeeper, he was the master, of that there was no doubt. It had taken Stalin an hour to* drink as so much conversation had been shared between the patron and proprietor in exchanging views on how such perfection had been created.

Hawker leans through the window and shouts...

Hawker: Upon finishing his drink, he had then climbed onto the bar, dropped his trousers, and urinated - literally - everywhere.

Freud: Why would you do such a thing'?

Stalin: I don't know to this day. I just did, I was bursting, I felt like I was going to explode, if you have ever paid attention to the horses of Vienna, Freud, you know that it was not a halfhearted attempt, I pissed over the whole bar, soaked it, pissed like a horse and it stank.

Freud: So, what happened next'?

Stalin: Well, unsurprisingly, Freud, the Cossacks were summoned, and they beat the living daylights out of me, and as you can imagine that wasn't the first beating of the evening, they were my desert. With every punch the landlord had demanded to know why I had done such a thing, I could only reply, I don't know, I must have a problem, I begged him to stop, but no. That's really why I got arrested and sent back to Solvychegodsk.

Hawker leans through the window and shouts...

Hawker: Gossip soon spread throughout Moscow's back streets and Lenin would soon come to hear of the true circumstances of that evening's events. It would not be for an entire year that Stalin would develop the strength and stamina he needed to return.

Freud: Did you actually go back?

Stalin: I did indeed. At the very least my intention was to apologise, I felt so terribly awful about it, for the whole 12 months, I needed to get the guilt and shame of it all finally off my chest.

Caesura (dramatic pause). Stalin adjusts his posture, sits straighter and takes a deep breath, he shudders.

Stalin: I went in, it took quite some doing, believe me, but I mustered up the courage eventually and I said, a pint of the finest Kvass in Russia please landlord.

Freud: *And...*

Stalin: *He took one look at me and then punched straight on the end of my nose.*

Hawker leans through the window and shouts...

Hawker: *Graphic detail had followed concerning both the copious amounts of blood lost and the agonising pain experienced.*

Stalin: *He screamed and screamed at me, and all I wanted to do was apologise. Every time I tried, I got a swift swing toward my chin, backing up with every avoidance until I soon found myself outside in the street again. I walked around the block, gave it about an hour until I was too cold to stay on the street no more, and went back in.*

Waitress: *Freud had noted down in his texts how the landlord had finally accepted Stalin's apology. We read that the landlord had recognised him immediately, saying - Do you think that I don't remember you, last year I gave you a glass of the best beer in the entire world and in return for all of my efforts, you pissed on my bar.*

Stalin: *I did - It was me and I don't deny it, you did nothing wrong, you were nothing but kind to me, and yes, it was the best beer I have ever tasted in the entire world, but please, please, please accept my humble apology, sir, I asked.*

Hawker leans through the window and shouts...

Hawker: *Yes, after calming down, the landlord had indeed accepted that apology. Stalin had explained how shameful his behavior was, the guilt that he had felt and held on to for the last 12 months, and of his genuine and sincere need to apologise in person for such abhorrent thuggish behaviour. Stalin had accepted that he had a problem, and with his nose swollen and blooded, had told the landlord his actions were wholly unforgivable.*

Stalin: *I want to start afresh, I said, that's what I am here to do, I was wrong, and you were right. You are a good man, landlord, forgive me for my previous conduct – I must taste your ale again, for if not, my life is not worth living, I was a priest at one time, sir, I know what the wages of sin are.*

Waitress: *What else could the landlord have done, here in front of him a priest begging for his forgiveness, of course he forgave. Stalin* had accepted all responsibility for 'his problem', unconditionally, and as a Christian, the proprietor had forgiven him. He would be served not one but three beers, a Kvass to which there was no equal.

Freud: Isn't forgiveness the most beautiful of actions? I'm so pleased to hear it all ended so well for you, Stalin, a happy end is a pleasure to hear, it must be so wonderful to have finally released yourself of all that ill feeling and guilt you had carried for so long.

Stalin: Well, Freud, not exactly, I'm not the tallest man on the planet as you well know, and three pints, well, that was it. I jumped up on the bar, but this time it was different - as I only pissed in his face.

Waitress: Stalin had filled in all the gaps for the bemused and rather confused learned psychoanalysts, we know thus as Freud had reported on this discussion in vivid detail within his journal. Whilst the landlord had attempted to wash the urine from his face, in utter disgust, Stalin had fled into the dark damp of the cold night, he escaped and hid.

Stalin: As he was mopping his face with a towel, I realised immediately it was now or never, I knew what was about to unfold given my previous beatings, so I fled the Yar as if my life depended on it, and, Freud, I had no doubt it did.

Hawker leans through the window and shouts...

Hawker: Stalin clearly had a serious behavioral problem for which he had eventually sought treatment.

Stalin: I couldn't carry this pain around with me, anymore, Freud, I went to a clinic in Poland, somewhere I wouldn't be recognised, I had weeks and weeks of aversion therapy, even electricity applied to my skull, I went to confession and mass, I did everything I could to recover, but recover from my shameless condition I did, it took months but yes, eventually, I recovered...

Waitress: Stalin had written over 12 letters, one per month, over yet another 12-month period to the proprietor of the Yar. He had become obsessed with his need to again apologise and to inform of his cure.

Stalin: I wrote: I was ill sir, I know this may be impossible for you to understand, but my illness had taken over me, to behave in such a way for a second time, I have no words to offer, but I do tell you this, if it were not for those events I would have remained ill and controlled my by an inner disease, a parasite that took over me.

<u>Hawker leans through the window and shouts...</u>

Hawker: Stalin did not receive a reply to any of those most intimate letters until the very last was sent. Within his twelfth letter he had enclosed a certified confirmation as signed by his psychiatrist.

Stalin: I can confirm that this man is cured, it read. Without your forgiveness for a second time, Sir, I fear he may relapse, I stress the utter importance of this...

<u>Hawker leans through the window and shouts...</u>

Hawker: Only then had he received a reply to his correspondence, and within it an invitation to return to the Yar.

Stalin: You see, good people to exist, Freud, imagine that, how kind and compassionate that man must have to be to forgive me again, and to invite me back, I was over the moon, the best day of my life it was.

Freud: Did you go back; did you not feel it to be a trap?

Stalin: No, not for a second, I had borne my soul to him, poured out my heart, his letter was so genuine, it was pure human-to-human love, he understood me now, we both understood that we had nothing to fear of each other.

<u>Pauses to sip his coffee.</u>

Stalin: The day came, and I walked confidently back into the Yar, another full year had passed me by, and I was greeted with smiles and the warmth of the fire, he beckoned me over and offered his hand. I took it and shook it firmly, I told him just how much his forgiveness had meant to me, that life was not worth living without his finest ales a part of it. His wife made me the most delicious soup, I sat beside the fire nourishing my meal, I was in heaven.

<u>Hawker leans through the window and shouts...</u>

Hawker: The proprietor had walked over bringing Stalin's drink to his table as he had seen how much the warmth of the fireplace heat was being appreciated.

Waitress: *This brew has just won the award of best Russian Kvass, Tsar Nicolas III has personally endorsed it, we are to become the official supplier to His Majesty the King – He proudly divulged to Stalin.*

Freud: *I'm not sure most people would have been so forgiving, Stalin, forgiveness for me isn't a religious position but a practical action, I've always viewed it akin to removing your hands from around the other fellow's throat, it's about letting go and finally moving on, isn't it?*

Stalin: *Yes, Freud, and I, more than anyone, had finally moved on. I finished my soup, Borscht it was, both parsnip and hogweed, absolutely delicious, perfect in every detail, a poor man's meal but a poor man I was. I savoured the Kings pint, that too was perfect but just the one this time, stood up, adorned my cap and coat and thanked him again for his kindness.*

Freud: *He must have been very touched.*

Stalin: *Indeed, and as I was leaving, I caught a glimpse of his wife working hard away in the cookhouse, I turned and waved to her a fond farewell, too.*

Waitress: *Sigmund Freud was most impressed with Joseph Stalin's recovery, this was obvious by the excitement of his words, especially when he finally understood how this linked back to his feelings toward Hitler. As Stalin was leaving, he noticed 4 Russian men playing cards, Preferans, and large sums of money were at stake. Intuitively he walked over, introduced himself and then...*

Hawker leans through the window and shouts...

Hawker: *He pissed all over their table.*

Waitress: *As one would expect, all hell broke out, Stalin, without anytime to pull his trousers back up was punched to the floor – he was now being beaten and kicked by four very angry men.*

Stalin: *They were pulverising me, Freud. The landlord bellowed – 'get that sick, lying scoundrel off my premises, throw that garbage of a man out of here and never let him return' - and I was dragged into the street where the beating continued.*

Waitress: *The landlord had now assisted with the beating, and his wife too, striking Stalin to the legs with a steel poker. It was noted* *that had a gang of Bolsheviks not recognised him and had they not intervened in pulling them all off him...*

<u>Hawker leans through the window and shouts...</u>

Hawker: *Stalin would have most certainly been beaten to death that evening.*

Stalin: *You are a liar and a cheat, he shouted, cured my arse, you are a *astard of a man...*

<u>Hawker leans through the window and shouts...</u>

Hawker: *The insanely irate publican had continued to shout obscenities as Stalin had now stumbled back to his feet.*

Stalin: *You can call me many things, of that I am guilty, I replied to him, Freud, but a liar is not one of them.*

Waitress: *I told you I was cured and cured I am sir; he'd said in his defense.*

Stalin: *I looked him square in the eye my dearest Sigmund Freud, and said just this...*

<u>Stalin leaves the table; he stands front of stage, facing the audience as he now concludes the performance:</u>

Stalin: *I no longer feel guilty!*

DENOUEMENT:

Trotsky stands centre stage. A single spotlight highlights him as he resolves the play through the delivery of this monologue. He is reading from the now finished work: Marxism and The National Question.

Trotsky: *We finished the work, Marxism and the National Question, Bucharin, Stalin and I, ladies and gentlemen. It was a short work, more of a pamphlet than a book, but reprinted many times as a seminal contribution to Marxist analysis which conveyed our exciting new ideas. Stalin would go on to become our first People's Commissar of Nationalities after the successful Bolshevik Revolution of 1917. He would later conclude that a nation is a historically constituted, stable community of people, based on a common language, territory, economic life, and psychological make-up manifested in a common Russian culture.*

I would at this time hold the post of Commissar for Foreign Affairs, my main task was to negotiate our removal from the conflict of the Great War. I would then go on to lead the Red Army as People's Commissar for Military and Naval Affairs, throughout the civil war and until 1925. I declined the position of Deputy Chairman of the Council of People's Commissars as offered to me by Comrade Lenin in 1922, that's why Stalin got the job, and following Lenin's death in 1924, ladies and gentlemen, he would use that position against me, gradually I lost all my government positions, and Stalin's ruthlessly controlled Politburo of 1929 would eventually expel me from our Soviet Union.

As I am certain you know, I spent the rest of my life in exile, living in Mexico City, this until I as murdered on the orders of Joseph Stalin in 1940. My prolific criticisms of him seemed to have rattled his feathers, somewhat. I became lost to Soviet history whilst Tito, Stalin and Hitler would all go on to create their own historical narratives.

The spotlights now light up to focus on Stalin and Hitler, heads bowed, mournfully standing separately, silently to the stage, left and right of Trotsky.

Trotsky: *If we held a minute's silence for every victim of Hitler's Holocaust, ladies, and gentlemen, we would need to stand in silence for eleven and a half years. But I fear this also to be true, that life isn't long enough to stand in silence to the victims of the Soviet Communists. Estimates vary but alongside Lenin, I played my part in the murder of between 100,000 and 500,000 people, these mass* executions were the creation of our show trials. A further 70,000 enemies of socialism died in our forced labour camps and the mass starvation we imposed on the resisting peasant class led to the starvation of at least 3 million people. Of Stalin, we now know that official records of 799,455 mass executions exist, around 1.7 million deaths took place within the Gulag, and a further 390,000 deaths resulted from forced resettlement, and furthermore, up to 400,000 deaths of deportee's during the 1940s. The deaths of at least 5.5 to 6.5 million persons followed in the Soviet famine of 1932.

The spotlight now highlights Freud sitting at his writing desk.

Of Sigmund Freud, ladies, and gentlemen, as early back as 1897, he had described his love and addiction to cigars as a substitute for masturbation, the one great habit, he declared. In February 1923, he would detect a benign growth to his mouth. Freud was told by medical specialists to stop smoking and he would later bleed heavily during an operation to excise that growth, he narrowly escaped death. Cancer was discovered and further surgery would be required but Freud was not told – the doctor fearing that Freud would take his own life.

Hitler's Nazi Party took control of Germany in 1933. Freud remarked of the destruction of his literary works, thus; What progress we are making. In the Middle Ages they would have burned me. Now, they are content with burning my books. Austria would be annexed by Nazi Germany in 1938, violent antisemitism ensued, and Freud would flee to London. His brief home at 20 Maresfield Gardens, Hampstead, is now the UK's Freud Museum. Freud's assets had been ceased, without the help and financial support of Princess Marie Bonaparte, an eminent and wealthy French follower who had travelled to Vienna to save him, Freud, his wife Martha, and his daughter Anna would most certainly have died in Hitler's death camps.

*Aboard the Orient Express on 4th June they headed with the princess for Paris, they were accompanied by their housekeeper and family doctor. From there, traveling overnight, they arrived at **London Victoria** on 6th June.*

*By September 1939, Freud's cancer was agonising. He turned to **Max Schur,** his doctor, friend, and fellow refugee, and asked; Schur, you remember our 'contract' not to leave me in the lurch when the time had come. Now it is nothing but torture and makes no sense. Schur had not forgotten his promise. With the agreement and assistance of Freud's daughter, Anna, carefully administered doses of morphine resulting in his death at around 3am on 23rd September 1939. Schur* was not present when Sigmund Freud died, the third and final dose was administered by Dr. Josephine Stross, a friend and colleague of Anna.

The spotlight now highlights Tito.

As we conclude this evening, it goes without mention that Tito and Stalin also fell out. Having become leader of the Titoist revolutionaries, he led Yugoslavia to liberation from Nazi occupation, this with little help from the western Allies or the Red Army. Tito wanted to go his own direction, a matter that Stalin took most personally. Multiple assassination attempts were arranged but none succeeded. Yes, I know, I should have secured exile in Belgrade and not Mexico City, oh well, such is life, like an ice pick to the back of the head.

We know that Tito wrote to Stalin and said: Stop sending people to kill me. We've already captured five of them, one of them with a bomb and another with a rifle. If you don't stop sending killers, I'll send one to Moscow, and I won't have to send a second. Tito had a good innings, he died following complications of gangrene, just three days before his 88th birthday in 1980. He had married several times and engaged in multiple affairs.

The spotlight now highlights Bucharin.

Well, ladies and gentlemen, Mexico City, aside, at least I got to live for 2 years longer than my dear friend, Nikolai Bukharin. He had returned to Moscow following the October Revolution with me and took over my old post as editor of Pravda. However, Stalin's Great Purge of 1936 found that letters, conversations and tapped phone-calls implied his disloyalty to the party. He was arrested in 1937, a show trial followed, and he was executed in March 1938. His execution was a wake-up call to many Western communist sympathisers.

The spotlight now highlights the waitress.

And of this beautiful soul, our dear audience, I can reveal our waitress to be none other than: Regina Wiener. You see women were not allowed entrance to the coffeehouses of Vienna in 1913. As the daughter of the money broker Max Wiener, she used his position to obtain gainful employment upon leaving an all-girls school. Here, in the Central Coffeehouse, she continued here covert education, and she would leave this employment that very same year, 1913. This, when she married the Viennese musician Josef Zirner. Sadly, he would die on the battlefields of the war in 1915. Following her husband's death

Regina would write her first two novels, her first, The Rise, won the Theodor Fontane Prize. She was most active in the circle of literary intellectuals in Berlin and Vienna. In 1933, she too would see her books fall victim to the Nazi book burnings, thereafter, she would later flee to America via France, where she continued her work as a writer. She died in Los Angeles in 1985.

<u>The spotlight now highlights Hawker.</u>

Vienna is famous for its quirky dialect, a form of speech known to us as Wienerdeutsch. Young Hawker was a master of this quirky German dialect, ladies, and gentlemen, and as it was only spoken in the city and surrounding areas, he soon used his talents to great advantage. Wienerdeutsch features unique idioms and phrases not found in standard German, using modern Viennese inventions and many words borrowed from Hungarian, Croatian, and Slovene, our young Hawker here continued to be the most popular newspaper seller the city had ever entertained, throughout the war and beyond. For Hawker, life was simple but good. There you have it, finally, a happy ending...

<u>The spotlights fade to darkness. The stage lights take over to reveal from darkness the presence of the entire cast.</u>

Trotsky: Ladies and gentlemen, thank you!

APPENDIX

About: Jonathan R. P. Taylor

Jonathan Taylor is an award-winning 'differently able' British singer/songwriter. He is a multi-genre writer. Countless audio albums co-exist alongside his literary works. He lives in North-central Bulgaria, is Vegan, has SpLD, and is an ordained minister of the Universal Life Church. He is an LGBTQ+ ally. He is married to the Scottish photographer, Nicola Miller. If you would like to hear some of Jonathan's songs check out the Soundcloud link below.

Jonathan is a graduate of Youth & Community Studies from Bradford & Ilkley Community College (Bradford University) and teaching (P.G.C.E - Huddersfield University). He specialises (Ad.Pro.Dip -Leeds Beckett University) in Mentoring and adult education. His favourite film would probably be 'Inglorious B*stards' and of books - 'Animal Farm.'

As a new writer I have little in the way of reviews concerning my books, however as published in my lyrics song book - "This is my ministry, let there be light', I attach here the many positive reviews my songwriting has produced.

"Taylor's lyrics remain consistent in theme, his overwhelming need to lend his voice to those who remain without. Whether they're victims of the Bulgarian Communist Regime (Izvinavi) or an elegy to those lost in 9/11 ('If Only') and the messages they left behind. Again and again, he returns to his subject... You begin to get the feeling Taylor needs this kind of connection to the past and a large helping of tragedy for both sustenance and creativity. Taylor's music urges us to question why atrocities happen, whether they are individual or collective. He takes tragedy, seemingly internalising the pain and then slowly from his depths comes something beautiful, skillful, deeply memorable and strangely- immensely listenable' - Curtsy Hoppe (Freelance) 2012.

'Odd Jonathan, despite the name, offers one of the most lucid narratives folk music has produced this year, fluidly foiled by an intricate fiddle descant.' Academia (Best Folk Song Dec. 2015). His work was described by the late Tony Benn (British Politician, Author & Anti-War Activist) accordingly; 'Jonathan who has real talent has identified the crimes that are committed in our name. The songs are beautiful and the cause a worthy one'. Jonathan I'Anson, BBC Radio Leeds said; 'This song (The Holocaust Denier) was magic, In the right way the gravitas of it is completely delivered.' PM at the time, Gordon Brown wrote to thank him for it. And; Andrew Liddle, Halifax Evening Courier (Victoria Theatre Concert Review & more below) commented; 'A rare talent indeed', 'the possessor of a marvelous dusty, dusky voice full of resonance and beauty' 'writes awe-inspiring songs, both lyrics and melody' - 'deeply moving', 'iconic' and 'profound.'

Following the release of "A Useful Fool" (Jonathan's third album), Stan Graham, an award-winning songwriter himself and presenter (Community Radio & BBC Radio York) remarked; 'By far the best songs you have so far produced, melodies, recording and lyrics were brilliant. It's been on the CD player constantly, ... and I've played several tracks from it on The Akoustik Hour.' And in Bulgaria, Kiril Zdravkov, Manager of Cosmic Voices adds; 'You sound like the UK Vissotzky - accentuating on messages and lyrics, not only the music which is good.' Bands too have offered appreciation such as 'Cobario' (Florian Stradner Management – Vienna) - 'Partisan was the official song of our tour, I think we played it a hundred times in the car.' And as far away as Australia -'I also want you to know that we have been getting great feedback on your song (Valentine.) I haven't come across anyone who doesn't like it.' Gari Sullivan - Producer: The Sixteenth Touch.

In a more personal context Audience feedback (Cowling House Concerts) put forward; 'I bet lots of people say that, but you've got an amazing voice, really intense - wow!' and 'your music is inspired,' it was "simple and sincere - Fresh magic in a choking, dusty world". I've been reading a poetry anthology called 'Up the line to death 1914-18' and I've never heard songs capturing the feeling of being out there so well: Kirsten Guschal. 'Jonathan is a thoughtful and intelligent lyric writer and a superb musician. His voice ranges from Cat Stevenesque right through to smoky blues.' Richard Hollis (The Unofficial Steeleye Span Website). And forums too where 'Barry of the renowned folk one-stop talkawhile.co.uk' replied; 'Visited your website, downloaded the album (Debut - The Collection) and liked what I heard very much. I've put a little plug for it onto The Folk Corporation's forum.'

Jonathan is a cousin of Robert Johnson (Steeleye Span) of which The Country Star Page noted; 'Jonathan comes from a very talented family and talented he is!' And acts that he has supported such as State Of Undress (Dorset) - 'He has a fabulous voice, really rich and resonant and full of emotion, very distinctive.' Feedback from the same event developing this further with; 'I enjoyed your performance. I found it gritty, honest and sensitive. Thanks.' Audience Feedback (Hebden Bridge Trades Club). And of a particular song (Eene Meene Miste): 'When I saw a song had been written about the contents of Great Grandfather's box my initial reaction was - how could it possibly be done, and with a list too. Well, I think it's been done in a very clever way, and I really enjoyed it! It left me humming... Congratulations Jonathan.' - Post on the classic thread 'This Is The Secret Of Grandad's Trunk,' The Great War Forum.

On community radio it was summed up with simplicity: 'I was so mesmerised by his voice I almost forgot to line up the next track' Annie Vanders (BCB Radio).

News from The American Dyslexia Association

Jonathan Taylor, known as 'Odd Jonathan' due to his profound dyslexia and specific learning difficulties has been awarded the prestigious Best Folk Song December 2015 by top record industry executives of the Akademia Awards, Los Angeles, with the comment that judges considered it to be: "Odd Jonathan, despite the name, offers one of the most lucid narratives folk music has produced this year, fluidly foiled by an intricate fiddle descant.

The comments made by Ken Wilson, who supports musicians interested in receiving a higher degree of market exposure and recognition in the new music business era, are most appreciated by the artist. From senior posts at Arista Records, Columbia and MCA to J Records and Warner Brothers, veteran record executive Ken has shaped the careers of legendary artists such as Beyoncé, Alicia Keys, Whitney Houston, Mariah Carey, Michael Jackson, Seal, Sade, George Michael and many more, leading to record sales in excess of $2 Billion.

The winning song, "If Only (The Falling Man)," details the desperate plight of those trapped within the burning World Trade Centre following the attacks of 9/11. It was inspired when Jonathan watched the TV documentary 'Voices from The Towers' in which anguished relatives and loved ones spoke on film about how last-minute answer machines messages, from those trapped, gave them a lasting memory, a farewell and a sense of closure. The artist has never detailed which particular story the song focusses on, merely to add that he "considers the track to be for all of them, none are any more significant than the other. This is a work that remembers them all, the victims of an unspeakable horror that killed so many."

He adds; "I am delighted that this song has received such a high status of recognition from such a high-profile figure. My own experiences of profound abuse gave me a talent. I never know whether to consider my condition as a curse or a gift. Somehow, I can descend into very dark places and return again with something beautiful. In many ways this is the song that should never have been written, but if such a song should exist, then I am delighted that it be this one..."

Jonathan was born in Warwick: UK. 1966, but moved to Bulgaria in 2010 to concentrate on his writing career. He has been regularly featured on Bulgarian TV and press and is an outspoken critic of the UKIP leader, Nigel Farage which gained him much public support in his new homeland. "This is the second major recognition of my life" he states. In 1998 he was awarded, by nomination, 'The Principles' Award for Outstanding Achievement in Education' whilst studying for his youth work diploma at Bradford and Ilkley

Community College, North England. He had no previous formal school education, being placed on a supervision order at the age of 13. A persistent truant, he was quite illiterate when leaving school without qualifications. "I had not been entered for exams as all others were due to years of nonattendance. I was hated by many teachers and peers alike. I was terrified of school and was horrifically bullied and abused. You soon learn to keep away."

I returned to part time education in my late 20s and thereafter studied full-time. After nine years I eventually graduated as a teacher, how ironic now when I think of it... These days I spend most of my time teaching English and have the pleasure of writing learning materials (to music) for the Cambridge based teaching and learner resource, English Club online. The '98 award recognised my need to succeed at all costs. I was hungry for education and loved every second of mature study though had to do many re-sits, including a full year. These days I have completed 15 solo albums and have written several books: fiction novels. Sadly, upon my diagnosis for dyslexia (I had no idea what the problem was at the time but just knew I was capable of so much more) my stepfather said; "so you are still looking for excuses for being stupid?" and upon receiving my Honour's Degree, (grade 2.1), my mother added "Well anyone can get a degree there..." This was extremely hurtful.

You realise it's not what you do that matters but what people actually think about you. You just have to believe in yourself! This Akademia award means so much to me. It doesn't matter what happens now, only that somebody has acknowledged my contribution to art and culture." If Only (The Falling Man) already features as part of the artist memorial gallery of the 9/11 Memorial Museum in New York City and former English language students of Jonathan's, of The American College Arcus, Veliko Tarnovo, Bulgaria, created the accompanying video. "I told them what I wanted, and they just got on with it," he said. An American flag drifts gently in the wind as the names of all victims scroll upward across it. As the song finishes, due to the sheer volume of named victims it contains, it continues afterward for a further 15 minutes in respectful silence. The song debuted on BBC Radio Leeds and features a sample recording, of the time, from BBC news reports.

Taylor ends: "This is not just recognition of my work but recognition of the contributions that all brain damaged or disabled writers can offer. We are not disabled; we are differently able... I had always dreamed of an acting career but my short-term memory loss makes it impossible for me to remember lines... I can't even perform my own songs without lyric sheets to prompt me, so music, no matter how dark the subject matter, allows me to put the emotional expression I need into song. It's taken a while for it to be noticed and in many ways, I thank the outstanding contributions of Canadian violinist, David Copeland, for doing this. He created a violin melody that haunts you throughout and carries it to a much higher level."

Your *'first chapter only teasers'* of some of Jonathan's other novels now follow.

HOW TO BREED CHICKENS IN IOWA

A Bird in the Hand

The mind can achieve any mental-state it desires if you so want it to. We all make the most of life and lie to ourselves when needs must, to create our own false sense of happiness and to twist and contort our own sad realities; all to make life just that little bit more bearable. If this is you, then do continue to dream, go on, get on with it and bury your head in the sand for all eternity. I have no need of escape or of dreams and false hopes. I do have nightmares, why yes of course I do, we all do - but my life is already beautiful, and the sunshine of California is something to be most desired. My dreams are my reality and life is wonderful.

Leaving South Wales as a child with my mother and father, an older sister and just three old trunks could have led to disaster, this is true, but it did not. Our feverish voyage to America, as so many others did during the Californian Gold Rush, was quite the experience. Dad didn't really stop to think about the negative consequences. He had dreams and now he had hope of achieving them. Strange thing was that we never actually made it to California. We went northward to Iowa in the end.

We left Cardiff on the 24th of January, 1851, aboard a fine wooden sailing ship called the Adventurer, the name most appropriate to us. Dad had just lost his job. He was a printer for a publisher on South Street, overlooking the docks. He would look out of his workshop window and see the ships come and go. He'd watch the cargo unload and the people board most curiously as people never seemed to arrive, they just left, one after the other. '51 was a bitterly cold year and Dad's aged boss was selling up to retire. No offers to purchase the Blakeley's firm had been placed and there was to be no more work.

One of the shipping companies which transported the printed books overseas was keen to use the warehouse space for cargo storage, and as a joke Blakeley had suggested that they take the old printers' shop workers back to New York with them. The next shipment outward was a mere two days away. Although folly at first, Dad now immediately acted on the idea of a fresh start overseas. He knew that printers were in demand, but he also knew that gold had been found too. What was initially just a joke was now within a day, our reality. Blakely happily signed the rental papers over to Meridian Shipping Corp. only on the strict understanding that the rent included a one-way ticket for four.

With the bitter cold British winter behind us, we arrived in New York just 7 weeks later, and to a new form of weather, it felt much colder. From there we took an ice-cold and most torturous railway journey, slowly winding our way across four more states, Pennsylvania, Ohio, Indiana and Illinois. Our final leg and fifth state, Iowa now concluded by wagon trail, as the railway companies had not extended that far west as yet. Compared to this, our confined sea passage now felt like an absolute luxury. Explorers and soldiers came and went. So too the prospectors and all other manner of workers, but we were settlers, we were now here to stay. There was no going back now. We all knew this... and it had all started with chickens.

Dad, being the canny Welshman that he was, had sold our winter coal supply to raise money for food on the trip, and we had plenty. During this fun, but very over-tiring sail, we had become very close friends to a native-born American man called Archie Barnes. Archie was a chicken farmer and was introducing good laying breeds to the newfound lands he occupied. "Anyone can keep chickens," he would say, "but breeding them successfully, well that's a completely different concern." This is what Archie did. He bred laying hens and sold them out to numerous states, if not to them all. He had travelled back to Great Britain merely to collect six breeding pairs of Australorps as they were known. Their docility and hardiness were "an excellent addition to any ranch or homestead flock." With this in mind you will be amazed at how much I came to know about breeding chickens in Iowa, during my sea voyage west.

School had taught me many things about Australia and one of my favourite books, printed by my father whilst at Blakeley's, was the story of 'Kingston, the Friendly Kangaroo,' - though I suspect now, well out of print, for many years. But I had never thought of or read anything to suggest that Australia was becoming famous for its chickens. The Australorps were bred from original Orpingtons that were exported to the colonies from England. Australians were most impressed by its egg-production traits, and following on from outcrossing and selected breeding, the Black Orpington soon began to produce a fine quality meat yield. Another strain however was the Australian Laying Orpington. This breed was, by 1820, divergent enough to have its own classification, the all-new super laying Australorp. The bird had become so successful. The American Poultry Association accepted it as a standard breed into the country in 1829.

Archie had a plan. "I have personally travelled the Atlantic to select six pairs of the finest English-Australorps I have ever seen," he said most proudly. "With these twelve hens I am going to cross again with Campines... Let me tell you about the Campine" - he abruptly interrupted himself and added much more information to the conversation. "It is a most beautiful bird, so very attractive, in fact a direct cousin of the Braekel breed. They come from Flanders, in Belgium, do you know?" Trying to look interested I continued to smile back. "The Braekel enjoys a rich clay soil. They've been successful in Belgium since 1416. Its Dutch cousin however, the Campine, can survive on much less fertile land, such as the Kempen region." (I had already figured out that that must be the origin of the name Campine, but Archie insisted on telling us all about that as well.) "The Campine hen has been in America since 1793 but it has never really become popular, but it is an awesome layer," Archie saying, as he became more and more excited by the ongoing conversation, yet again all about chickens. "The birds over-here are just not rugged enough. Even attempts by poultry-men to breed from English stock have failed but I know that if I cross it with the new Australorps and... well, I'll be a very rich man by the turn of the decade."

My dad had become fascinated by the Archibald egg stories, and he seemed to be quite convinced that Archie's super-chicken, this amazing egg-layer with its delicious meat taste and the fact that it was the most beautiful of ornamental bird to look at too, would be a winner also.

To be fair, chickens had not been the only conversation during the seven-week voyage. Had this been the case then I fear I would not be here to tell you this story today. No – for I would have gone over-board for certain. Many of the passengers would also talk about Indians, often quite cruelly referring to them as nothing more than cold blooded savages. One story I heard was about the Tamlins of Gloucestershire. They had left Boston for California, at the start of the gold rush about two years before, 1848 or '49. The narrator of the story could be no more exact than that. This rather silly lady told of how their wagon train had been attacked, Mrs. Tamlin was brutally sexualised by several leaving the rest to our own imaginations, and that Mr. Tamlin had had his scalp cut off; the skin of his scalp cut "clean away" as she put it, "with a big knife." Mother would just grip my hand tight at such times and whisper to me, "Just ignore the silly old fool, she clucks on about it more than Archie's own chickens," reminding me that, "she's just an ignorant fool, a bigot. Listen no more to her. If there was any truth in the matter, we would have read about it back at home in Cardiff before we left."

But the truth was that my father had heard of such stories, and upon weighing up the facts, had decided that gold was out, and chickens were now in. Dad had only really joked about digging for gold. He was certain he would find work on the East Coast as a printer again; of this he had no doubt. He would turn to me and say, "What uses have I of gold, Goldie? For I have you, and you are called

Goldie because you are the most precious gift a man could ever want. Isn't that true Mrs. Davies?" Mother turning to us and adding in reply (smiling at both of us young girls with the genuine unconditional smile that came only from a mother, born out of true love of her own daughters). "Your father and I are rich beyond all imagination, for we have you two with us. Now less of this nonsense. I'd much rather talk about the chickens." My sister was only a bit older; we were both now in our late teens and to be quite honest, had made no public secret of our intention to find prospective husbands. What I hadn't realised though was that we were both about to marry into the poultry business.

"How about it, Nige?" Archie would ask again of Dad. "How about it? Come on, come west with me. I need good reliable hands, several in fact. There's work for all four of you. Good pay considering too. I've lost six of my best cowboys this year to Californian gold madness. They'll not be back for months if at all. Stay in the barns to start with. It's cosy, a stove as well, it's warm they tell me. We'll soon knock up a new cabin for y'all over spring." So that was that, Dad looking at Mum for re-assurance and Mummy laughing back, "Well I suppose so Archie, after all, a bird in the hand is worth two in the bush…"

Please Take Care of Bethany

Liverpool

I am PC 5427 Wilkinson, Police Constable Brian J.B. Wilkinson of the Drover Estate in Liverpool. My middle name is Josef-Benjamin. I was born on Merseyside during March of 1945, a small back-to-back terrace house. What today, if it still existed, well I guess you would term it a slum. That smoky, charcoal-black stained stone from the pollution of the chimneys and factories likened to the lungs of a heavy smoker. All the way over there, down the small dank, cobbled street away from the house, the toilet block. The toilet block that all twelve houses on our street shared, a most unpleasant walk during the cold Liverpool winters.

In the house opposite us, there lived a beautiful young girl called Doreen, her eyes always alight with joy and happiness. We would play marbles in the street, always such fun as the bumpy old cobbles would never allow the marbles to roll in any predictable straight line. Doreen and I were the best of friends. We would sit hand in hand on the wall at the end of the street, watching the old trolleybus go by and the old horses, the nags that dragged the coal cart, struggling to stay on their feet given the excess weight of their load. This was a Britain recovering from the war and we "made do". We were happy to be free and that's what they would say to us as kids, the grown-ups on the same street. Mr. Parker, the old storekeeper down the next road, would always say to me every time without fail as I went in to buy Mum some bread, "Freedom Brian, freedom. That is what your dad gave his life for. Be very proud of him son."

I missed my dad so very much, as I grew up without him. He went to war, and he never returned. We knew nothing of whatever really happened to him until one day long after the war had ended. The day when my mother was just stood there washing the dishes at the old Belfast sink and staring out into the yard, the day that she suddenly dropped the plate that she had in her hand. Smash! I remember the noise and Mum freezing motionless there on the spot. Then that outbreak of emotion as she fell to the floor and started crying, sobbing to herself quite uncontrollably.

I had never met my dad. He had gone to war, and I was born at home. But Dad was everywhere. He was in every conversation that we, the family, had. He was never forgotten. I never understood his sacrifice fully until this particular day, the day that the plate smashed to the ground. The knock at the door. The man I didn't know who was escorted in by one of our neighbours, a lovely lady and a dear friend to my mother, the same lady who helped my mother back to her feet. "I'll put the kettle on," she said to Mum, and I was sent out to play. I was eleven I think at this time. The year was 1956.

"Who is he?" I remember asking my Doreen, our hands as always clasped together and both of us sat up there on our favourite wall-top seat. "My dad says he's from the government," replied Doreen, giggling excitedly.

From that point in time and over the next coming few years, and as I became an independent teenager, I started to understand the magnitude and the significance of the sacrifice that Dad had made for his country; the personal sacrifice that he had made for us all, the reason that Dad had given his own life away. Just as Mr. Parker, the old shop keeper would always say to me, "He died for freedom Brian, he died for freedom!"

You see that man, the man who came to the door that day in 1956, and the man who had upset my mum so very much, this same man from the government, well he had been to our house just the once before. This government man was the man who had come to our house just two weeks before I was born to tell my mum that Dad had been shot down and killed in action. My father, RAF rear gunner 'Bull's-Eye' Brian Wilkinson, was dead. You understand now why Mum had been so very upset that day, don't you? Why she had frozen at the window, frozen at the sight of this very same man returning to the house again for a second time. He, removing that same black bowler hat again as he entered through the gate of our small stone-flagged front yard for this second visit. Bernadette, my mum's dearest and closest life-long friend, standing there at Mum's side throughout. 'Bull's-Eye' Wilkinson, my father, well his body had never been recovered until this day in 1956 and now eleven years after the end of the war with Nazi Germany my dad was coming home to us again.

I want this to be a happy story and I want there to be a happy ending but there is not one. Dad's B17 Bomber had flown low on its final returning flight and had struck head-on into the cliffs at Dover. Those beautiful White Cliffs of Dover, this first visual sight of home had probably been the very last thing that he had seen before he died. Then here we are, eleven years later, his body had been finally recovered, found to be still strapped there into his seat and entombed within the shell of the bomber, this old American B17 warplane.

Excavations had started for the building of a new terminal for shipping at Dover port, as post-war Europe had started to blossom again and economic trade with the wider world was much needed. Structural engineers and drillers had unearthed what was the crumbled wreckage of this old warplane sunken deep into the mud below the cliff-face, and the Royal Air-Force had now identified it as the Thompson. This was my dad's plane. The man from the government, the man in the black bowler hat that I clearly remember from being such a young child, had come to the house that day to make the arrangements, the arrangements with my mother Evelina for the return of my father's body back to Liverpool.

It seemed like the whole city turned out for the funeral of my dad, RAF rear gunner 'Bull's-Eye' Brian Wilkinson on this particular Sunday of April 1956, a sense that Liverpool in its entirety had come to a complete standstill. I know now as an adult that this isn't true but that's the feeling I had got as a child of just eleven and on seeing so many thousands of people there, all stood silently and respectfully as the procession drove through the city. The burial was a private family matter. Mum had wanted this, and she said to me that day, as Dad was lowered into the ground below, "I will tell you about your dad when you are old enough to understand son, but for now let's just leave him to sleep in peace."

Then the day came, the day of my eighteenth birthday and I let go of Doreen's hand to take the hand of my mother, the hand of the wonderful Evelina Wilkinson, the hand of this oh so proud war widow. I knew then that she had finally found the strength to tell me. I had never asked previously about the letter Dad had left her. I heard the family talk of it often, but I never troubled Mum as I knew this was something so dear and special to her. I knew that she would tell me in her own time and in her own way when she was ready to do so.

Today, the day I became eighteen, a man now and a man so very much in love with Doreen, Mum gave me that letter to read, a letter addressed to her, the last thing Dad had ever written down on paper and a letter found with him inside the plane. A letter sealed inside an airtight mission bag and so perfectly preserved, a letter that had somehow and almost by miracle survived all of its years below the cold strong tidal waves of the English Channel and as if it had only been written yesterday. A letter that he had penned for my mother and had then stuffed safely hidden deep down inside his flight jacket. A letter to my mum that was held close beside his heart as he breathed his last. It was this very same love letter that that government man, the man in the black bowler hat had returned to her, Evelina, on that day of 1956.

It read...

My Dearest Evelina,

I have so longed to come home to you, my dear precious Evelina. Our bombing raids over Bulgaria have ended and I no longer fly from Italy. We have for the last three months been involved in a special mission, a secret mission of which I am forbidden to speak of, but I am frightened as we all are now. I write you this letter in the hope that you will understand why I volunteered to do this and should I not return home this time, to know of my love for you: my deep, endless, undying love for you, the undying love that keeps me sane during these, the darkest of hours. You are always in my heart.

As I sat to the rear of my flying tin can, us up there so very high up in the sky, I watched our bombs fall down below onto Sofia, this once so beautiful and ancient city that had now found itself thrown into the war against us. I saw the sky light up with the blast of the bombs we dropped, and I wondered who we were killing. There were no Germans down there really. These were just people like you and me. Imagine my love, what I see in my mind, women just like you with their children queuing for the bus and then blown up, in an instant, blown into thousands of pieces of human dust by what we had just delivered to them. I am so tired and sick of this war. I am so tired of the loss of my friends. Half of us never return home. How much grief can this great nation of ours bear? They will never build a monument to remember me. Us lot, the bomber crews who kill women and children.

Do you remember Willy? Young Willy Garth from over on Sander's Fields? He killed himself last week. He was terrified and couldn't board the metal bird as ordered. I wish you could see what we see, all those planes that take off and we wait to count them back in, safely home and back at base, but they don't return anymore. We sit here strapped in with nowhere to run, nowhere to go other than downward, just sitting here waiting for our turn to be the next missing crew too, simply fall from the sky. Willy was thrown, rough-handed back into his seat by a Squadron Leader, ordered to do his duty at all cost. It was a cost to him. He jumped from the plane in flight during take-off. I think he knew he would die soon anyway and just couldn't face the fear of waiting for it to happen anymore.

We've now been given a new crate to work with, an American B17 Bomber. She's a big old heavy bird and the American pilot says, "It's like trying to steer a brick." We've had to strip it completely down. She's an amazing old bird, very strong but very heavy. She lacks the range capability we need, and we have fitted new drop tanks. We've called her the Thompson. We all named her after the guy we had down there on the ground below.

We've been in constant training for weeks. We're good now, well, I think as good as we can get given what we have to work with. I always worry about having an American pilot though, a bit too gung-ho for my liking but he's a great laugh, don't get me wrong. He's a Texan and as loud as you can imagine any Texan to be. Oh, we have a French Bombardier too, Pierre, a perfect English speaker and handpicked just like the pilot and me. We're the best in the air apparently. The lads mock us with phony salutes, funny really.

Pierre is also navigating for us. We are a jolly mix and try to have a good laugh, even if sometimes we don't quite understand each other's sense of humour. That's about it, just us three, a crew reduced by seven in this stripped-down metal brick that we can hardly believe can still fly, especially given everything we have had to take off her. We have a new nickname; they call us back at base, the Magnificent Three. I guess it's got a kind of good ring to it. The Magnificent three, imagine that?

I wanted so much to be home with you, holding your hand when Bethany was born but I volunteered to do this. I was given the choice not to do this if I so wanted, but I want to be honest with you about that fact, I have to do this for myself. Think of what they have done to your family back home and try to understand me and my motivation. Please try to understand, and remember this, I am 'Bull's-Eye' Wilkinson the best rear gunner in the sky and with me on board, well what can possibly go wrong?

I have this last mission only my love, and then I shall be home with you, at home for the birth of our child. They have promised me this. They have promised me at least two months' down leave and I can't wait to see you. I love you with all my heart,

Yours eternally, all my love, Brian xxxxx

And then, there, at the bottom of the letter and scribbled hurriedly across it, as if an afterthought, below Dad's signature it said;

"Fuel out, dropping fast, too low to bail, please take care of Bethany for me."

That's how my dad had died. He had died a war hero alongside his new crew, just the three of them alone together. My mum had known nothing of this letter or his final mission until eleven years later, and not until after the body of my dad had been recovered from beneath the sea at Dover.

The man from the government would never go on to say what the full facts of this ill-fated final secret mission were, but he did say this to Mum at the time, she recalled;

"The Thompson, a B17 Flying Fortress with a hand-picked specialist crew of three, had left an airbase in occupied British territories on February 26th, 1945, at 22.30 hours. The mission was to deliver a massive, single precision payload bomb of huge devastating capacity against a research facility beyond German held lines. Major Frank Thompson, a British officer beyond these enemy held lines had reported, before all communication with him had been lost on the 23rd of May 1944, the development of a new chemical warfare facility. 'The crew of the Thompson B17 Heavy Bomber had completed this mission with great accuracy and with great effect. They had died on their return journey having changed the course of the war. The crew were to divert and return the bomber to the UK after the payload had been delivered," he said.

The reason for this diversion was never stated. Mum explained to me that she'd asked this man what drop tanks were, as written in dad's final letter. He replied by telling her, "They are extra fuel supply tanks attached to the outside of the aircraft. They are used to increase the flying range and can be released and jettisoned by the crew when empty. The heavy bomber had been stripped down to reduce its weight load and to allow for the extra weight of the bomb and the additional fuel needed. I am so sorry, but I cannot tell you more."

Mum was so very proud of Dad and what he had done. You see my mum was of Polish origin and her grandparents, my great-grandparents, had been executed by the Nazis during the war in a reprisal attack against partisan resistance in their home village. She had survived only because her mother and father had arrived to live in Britain in 1913 and before the outbreak of the first war, World War I. She would simply smile at me and say, "Be very proud of your dad, I understand why he volunteered for this. I am very honoured to have met him and so very proud that he did so." Mum never remarried.

I have for so many years had these stories, these childhood war time fantasies, in my head about what Dad was actually doing during his final flight and I suppose that, well in the absence of the full true facts, I like these stories. Maybe they were attacked by German fighters and my dad, 'Bull's-Eye' Wilkinson shot them all out of the sky before they realised they were hit themselves and now leaking fuel? Maybe they received heavy flak over France and struggled at the controls in a desperate last-ditch attempt to reach home and clear the cliffs ahead of them?

Or maybe they just didn't have enough fuel to start with, a tragic war-time miscalculation and fatal error. What-ever the true story, my dad is a war hero and that's all that matters to me. I'm named directly after my dad, Mum told me. "We were certain you were going to be born a girl at the time, that's why we chose the name Bethany together, but the name Brian is so much more special now, don't you think so son?"

PORTHOLE (Cert. 18)

The Erotic Memoirs of RMS Fantasia

If you too have just enjoyed the magnificence of Paris, her beauty and her perfection, then I am pleased that you took such time to turn to this page. For here the story begins, but a story now told with her erotic and sensuous physique now wedged firmly in your mind. For the cover photograph of her was taken soon after we set sail and all of what I tell centres on her, for she created me for what I became. Take time for yourself, to pleasure yourself as you need, as my story unfolds before you. Place down this book as your sexual tensions deem necessary and this they will, I assure you. Look at her, she is there for you too to share and placed proudly to my masthead. Take a peep through her porthole. Play through in your own minds all that I say. For as I control all who board me, then I too shall now control you. Let go of all of your inhibitions now, whether male or female and everything in between and enjoy, just be seated, relax and relieve yourselves upon my decking.

Imagine what I first saw of her? Paris as an angel, a woman of divine grace delivered to me quayside. Her personal voyage trunk filled to overcapacity. I watched her closely. I was instantly aroused and I knew she would be the one that I wanted. The straps of her heavy trunk stretched to the limit, leather strapping that always proved so useful for restraint. That trunk, which had only one thing in mind, to now burst open and reveal all of that she had hidden inside. There, as is deliberately placed, a brief glimpse of white silk stocking trapped in its closed lid.

Why had she chosen not to reopen the trunk and push it back inside? To repack it in a more fashioned manner. Why had she left it, just the glimpse of trapped sensuality to hang down from the side? For she hadn't packed in a hurry, oh no. She and Jacques had taken all the time that they needed to pack this trunk. The stocking on show, though just no more than two or three inches, was just enough to display. As Paris was bursting, so too was her personal and delicate collection of the finest French corsetry available at the time. Both Paris and her collection were bursting-outward, exploding with her need for sexual excitement. The need to finally fulfil her deeply held fantasies and for her now liberated sexual satisfaction.

Jacques had spent his time shopping with Paris during the days before we sailed. She had always possessed the finest of silks and lingerie, her basques and corsets always hand-stitched and created by the greatest of craft-hands. Her dresses and evening wear too, were the best that France had to offer. Jacques would never allow her to be underdressed. Paris could never be understated. Money was no object and she wore only the best, for if she was aroused then Jacques was aroused, and he so adored how both men and women would stand still breathless in her shadow and in the wake of her footsteps, her scent delivering an almighty blow to any that came near and for those of generous financial means, the quality of her finest French perfume instantly recognisable.

Jacques would watch her reactions intensely when she had received the adorations of admirers. It excited her, the attention and power she seemed to hold over others. This too excited Jacques. "Are we going to do this," she would whisper into his ear, this as she felt his cum pump up inside her. "I need to," he would cry out as he ejaculated, pounding her with uncontrolled passion. They would always talk dirty to each other whilst they made love, always very dirty and content of the most extreme filth. But it was all just talk, all just dirty fantasy.

Afterwards, after sex, the conversation would soon become forgotten. Every word that they had screamed out in the heights of passion put away until the next time they needed to fuck. They both steered away from what just minutes beforehand had turned them both on so very much.

Sometimes Paris would try to return to the central issue and say, "I don't know if I could do it for real Jacques, but I know that I want to. I want you to watch me." Jacques would reply; "One day my love I hope we can. I hope that the opportunity will arise and we'll both know when that time has come. I want you to know that I want it too and that all will be OK afterwards."

Statements like this would both worry and excite Paris. "Will it really be OK?" she thought to herself. "Is he just testing me to see how I will react should this opportunity occur?" But these most personal and private thoughts of hers, held over the years of their relationship would grow stronger and stronger. Paris soon grew to long for the opportunity. She wanted it to happen. She needed to fulfil her fantasies and she needed Jacques to be in full control. Then one day, as if by magic, that perfect opportunity for the couple did so arrive. For here we all are: Jacques, Paris and I in Ireland during the spring of 1906.

So now to you, as you read this, your erection so stiff it pains you or your cunt so wet it seeps through to stain the seat beneath you. Bear only one thing in mind now my readers; you are all free to join us, to work your way free of charge and to pleasure yourselves throughout. But you must never consider Paris to be a whore, oh no not ever, for she is so much more than this. Paris cannot be purchased or bought. She is perfection and she is living art at its very best. What they both created on this journey and what they left behind for the world to hear and bear witness to is the greatest of all creations.

I, the third person within this story, would now also be known throughout the whole world as a ship of true sexual expression, a place where you can all secretly become your real selves and behave as you please. A place to fuck and be fucked to one's heart's content. A secret world upon the waves where anything can happen and where all things will. Alone at sea, your anonymity assured.

I, the RMS Fantasia, am indeed an almighty ship, but please do not get me wrong or misunderstand me. It is not so much my size that counts but the quality of the package that I offer. I am a modest ship, oh yes, a vessel of 24,000 tons and my length an impressive 167 meters. But then length isn't everything is it?

Of my beam? Well now, if you were to grip me tight within your clenched palm then a big hand 18 meters broad will surely be required. Since my very first maiden voyage from my birthplace in Belfast of 1906, I have watched them all very closely. For I too have pumped my way across the oceans for many, many years now.

For I am her, the very ship, and here I begin my story. I shall tell you all of the stories that I have collected over the years from across those oceans and seven seas. You see, in every cabin there is a traveller, and every traveller seeks that which they cannot find back at home. A journey that takes them to a place a thousand miles away, a journey in which they are surrounded by strangers and a voyage that is surrounded by the anonymous. This assurance of anonymity at sea was the perfect given opportunity for both Jacques and Paris.

So hear what I have to say, for you too will indeed enjoy such a trip. I will feed your desires just as I have facilitated theirs. You never know; you may even recognise yourself on board. Relax and lie here with me for a moment or two. Imagine you sit upon the rocks looking out across the horizon to sea. The waves are crashing at your feet. There in front of you passes me, the RMS Fantasia. In the evening's darkness the light from within my cabins draws your voyeuristic eye, and through every porthole you then take a peep.

Stay for a while here inside me and loosen up your clothing, unzip your fly or hitch up your skirt. It matters not who, what or where you are, it matters only that I please you, for this is my purpose. It matters to me that you too become a part of Paris and Jacques' story. Fear not that the price of such travel will prove too expensive for you as you will soon find out that you too are free to join us at any time and to work your passage. For I collect stories only from those who have a story worthy to tell and once upon a time - silk underwear.

COMMUNISTS IN OUTER SPACE

'The Buzludzha Files'

"Litchfield 2, Litchfield 2, do you copy? Over..." "Litchfield 2, this is Michael 3, update, update, do you receive? Over..." The base station, Michael Three, had desperately, but in vain, tried to contact the Litchfield, but now, after several hours without contact, it was all too apparent that their mission had failed. Litchfield Two, a code name used for two Anarchist Stalingus agents on Earth, had vowed to destroy the regime at all cost. Had they now paid dearly with their own lives? Michael Three, an outpost of the frozen Colne-7 within the deep Marxun space-way cc14, was now helpless to act further. Without reliable agents on Earth, who would now be able to stop the Zhivkovites, the armed guerrillas and right-hand arm of the Bulgarian Socialist and Totalitarian leader Todor Zhivkov?

Leninite had ordered the closure of the chamber, destroy if necessary, de-activate and neutralise, immediately, but contact with Earth was now over. Their Socialist revolution was failing, orders to stop de-atomisation had failed. So how? How would the Zhivkovites be stopped? Michael 3 continued to broadcast, desperately, radunas after radunas, but contact could not be re-established. Any second now they would arrive, the Socialists of Earth, free to attack and plunder. Michael 3 had issued Act 173a to decommission all receivers throughout the known galaxies, but was it too late? Had the Zhivkovite forces already transported...

It was during the early hours of Friday morning that I first heard these voices. It doesn't matter which Friday, and I don't really recall the date. My medical research at the Buzludzha facility had been stopped abruptly and I was now held in captivity. It appears that I had upset someone very powerful somewhere, over something. But when you stop working, step out of the rat race, take a moment for yourself, the peace and quiet of it all, well it is only then you start to hear things. You tune into what you were previously oblivious to before. I do swear that this is what I heard, a truth sent to me from beyond. I cannot explain further. I truly can't as I don't understand myself.

The medical field is easy. It's all about substantiating fact, medical trials, the records and statistics, and fact is the most essential part of my research. Discovering the proof needed to uphold my theories, to back them up, to make them concrete, unshakeable. It was I, yes, I Isabella Davies PhD, who first proved beyond all reasonable doubt that a psychopath cannot be created. Despite all of my hard work and efforts, no, it was impossible. It is purely a genetic thing, DNA undoubtedly, for psychopaths are born psychotic, and my psychopic husbandry studies and experiments were all too well documented, though they are no longer in my possession.

Perhaps this unexplained confinement was my destiny. As others throughout time had retreated into isolation on mountains or in deep hidden caves, on sea-locked islands to find God so now it was my turn. Had I been sealed inside my own cave, a round concrete tomb? Was Buzludzha so much more than it had at first appeared? Indeed, I questioned my own sanity as I'm sure Moses himself did, but that is where faith develops. You cannot prove it, but you know it to be true. I am sure there are many scientists out there who also believe: Christians, Muslims or Jews, even Buddhists and Hindus. For I too now believe. I believe in the final words of the Prophet, Dimitar Blagoev.

I was told how loyal members of the party, only those true to Todor Zhivkov and his regime, had paid financially for the construction of Buzludzha – and this payment was a one-way fare to another world, a right, now secured and guaranteed by the Communist Party. Many others, farmers and workers, had also donated, but these loyal Party members had paid substantially above this general requirement and way beyond the publicly acknowledged one leva donation for the cause: a public fundraising cover for something much more sinister. As Earth's socialist revolution was failing and anything other than true communists were now maintaining a stranglehold on power, the Soviets and their puppets had a much greater need to fulfil – to conquer outer space.

It was O'Neil and Richter who had discovered the bodies of the Litchfield 2. O'Neil was a technician with responsibility for the quarter, and Richter, a Charger. The Hadron accordingly was sectioned into four parts. The quarter simply referred to the first section facing northward and a charger's role was to input the collide-codes upon start-up. The discovery of the brutalised bodies was reported to command immediately – both Litchfield agents, Rebecca and Danny, had been severely beaten before being shot. Senior command consisted of House Marshall Villette and Commander-in Charge Heraud. Both were the sons of French Partisans and acknowledged heroes of World War Two. O'Neil reported on the obvious facts of the incident and Richter was more than happy to provide witness to the day's accounts. Undoubtedly, information had been sought from the victims before they were executed, but by whom?

Leach was an expert radio-hand, a decoder. He had been given the task of re-establishing a link with Marxus, a link that had been unilaterally and quite intentionally cut off by the Marxus previously. Indeed, it had been down for many years. It was not for him to reason why. This task he had only very recently achieved and since this time, most, if not all of the party elite and loyal followers had entered the chamber. De-atomisation had commenced and many, many thousands had by now, been coded down. Written documentation would later emerge in China to support this fact. Yang, an eminent female astrophysicist and writer, would add in her new book, a travel guide called 'Space-Hoppers and Inter-Stella Compression', "It is without doubt that we have succeeded, a guide such as this will soon prove itself to be vital."

Daily I fell to the floor, prostrate, receiving and bearing witness to the broadcasts of Michael 3, and what I learned of the New Truths I now document for you here. For the final transmissions of Leninite have spoken to us, the work of those Great Minds, Kötter, Tager and Massmann, as they had broadcast from Michael 3, are revealed to Earth below. If you ever take time to listen, to open your heart, mind and soul, you too will hear.

Little is known of what happened between the re-activation and de-atomisation period but folklore and belief as widely acknowledged in many Balkan households today strongly suggests that those left behind, upon realising what the Zhivkovites had achieved, completed the Litchfield mission. An old Bulgarian storyteller by the name of Hare regularly tells us, the believers amongst us, of "Communist souls now lost in space, cut-off between both worlds and forever in spiritual limbo." As if they had all somehow transported but never arrived... The regime that was left here on Earth now brought down by the forces of freedom and democracy just a mere physical duplicate, a clone of its original human-carbon-housing, but now for all eternity drifting in purgatory through outer space. For that is how the Psychopath is created, I am sure of it, that deep matter of atom-space, the soul removed, and a human shell recreated elsewhere without it. Maybe?

But for now, let me remind you that a British film-crew recently visited the site: Garrett, Archer, Florence-Mace and Woodcock, I studied them for quite some time and they too now believe. For the film 'Lost Contact' does in some way I suppose, try to explore the truth. They too must have heard the voices of the lost souls of Buzludzha. I wanted to invite them downstairs for dinner, but I think Gabriela may have eaten them...

THE GOLD STAR KID & THE DREAM ANGEL

Copper's End

"I'm so sick of chicken," said Ryan, dropping his third clean fork to the floor as he struggled to eat and play Dragon Raid at the same time. "You'll get fat!" shouted his mum, Tanya, from the kitchen as she mopped the floor. The new puppy, Thumper, had given the family yet another free gift, a small wet patch on the linoleum covering, to say thank you for its new home.

"Will you take Thumper out for a walk for me?" she asked. "I just haven't had five minutes to turn around today," she said. Muttering under his breath, Ryan reluctantly agreed.

Copper's End was a lovely quiet, rural village, and nothing much ever happened. Last week Ryan had seen a fox, and that was about it. They hadn't long lived in the countryside but it was something they had long dreamed about.

Ryan lost his father, Norman, many years ago and Copper's End would be a fresh start for them both, his mother hoped.

Norman was a soldier, a member of the Queen's Royal Lancers and he had given his life in service at the Battle of Telic, following the 2003 invasion of Iraq in the Middle East.

Ryan often thought of his dad. He was thirteen years old now and very happy to finally be a teenager at last, but being a teenager meant that he had now lived for thirteen years without ever meeting his father. Naturally this saddened Ryan a great deal. What saddened him even more was that now they had moved from the city to Copper's End, he could only visit his father's grave following trips back to see his grandparents in Warwick every four weeks or so.

The family had not coped well with the tragedy of Norman's loss. Initially it was very difficult and painful, but as time passed, and with only happy memories to talk of, they eventually decided they had to move away and make a fresh start for themselves.

Thirteen years in mourning had now proved to be enough. The wider family: aunts, uncles, cousins and grandparents were happy for them too. Granddad said to Ryan; "Your mother has always wanted to live in the country. I think this new beginning will be great for you both."

Norman had always dreamed of buying a house in the country for them all, after Ryan was born, but sadly it would never happen. Tanya had always dreamed of owning her own horse.

As Ryan walked Thumper in the woods, continually fetching her ball back and forth as Ryan would throw it, and occasionally chasing the odd wood pigeon or two that, startled, would now take to flight, he wondered what life would be like if his dad were still alive today. "What would having a father be like?" he thought to himself. He thought too about what he would actually do if "this stupid dog ever managed to actually catch one of the pigeons it so eagerly chased." Though this was most unlikely to ever happen.

After finishing the dog walk he went promptly back home. It was almost five thirty on a Friday afternoon and this meant that later on that evening mother and son would enjoy a fish and chip supper together. "I've only got five pounds and twenty pence in my purse," Tanya said. "I'll tell you what: we either have chips and make a chip butty each, there'll be enough for that, and some mushy peas too, or we can wait until tomorrow for a change and I'll treat you to supper out at that new restaurant in town." Ryan had tried to remind his mum to take some money out of the ATM during their last shopping outing but, as usual, her mind had been miles away. Living out in the country miles from a bank meant that the normal things they would take for granted, such as access to cash machines, needed more planning.

"Okay Mum, that's great," he said. "Let's wait until tomorrow then." He was of course a little disappointed. He loved his special treat, his weekly chip supper, but he would never want to upset his mother over such small things. Being brought up without his father had made him value the good things in life, his family and friends, and never to take anything else, no matter how small, for granted.

Ryan's mobile rang. "It's Asan," said the caller. "We're all going to watch a new DVD tonight, and my dad said you can come over too, do you want to?"

Ryan paused, turned to his mum and asked, "Can I Mum, please?" Asan's dad was called Iqbal and he was a teacher at the local school. Both Ryan and Asan studied there together and were the greatest of friends. Tanya knew that Asan's family had taken pity on her son, and that Iqbal had tried to be a father figure as well as a teacher to the boy. She did appreciate the family's kindness.

When the family had first moved into the village six months earlier, it was he who had taken the time to stop by and introduce the locals; this by means of countless never-ending stories that caused much folly and laughter. Iqbal was a good, honest man. "Go and have a great time Ryan," she said, and "I'll pick you up around 10."

After Ryan had ran through the village and, as arranged, waited to meet Asan outside Rayner's, the local grocery shop to buy crisps and pop for the evening's viewing, something caught his eye. As he had sat waiting on the wall opposite the shop he noticed a twenty pound note on the ground below him. He had to look several times before he realised it really was a twenty pound note and not just a figment of his own, over-excited imagination. He jumped down and picked it up. "Who could it belong to?" he thought.

He told Asan of his find and decided it was best to hand it in to the shopkeeper. After all, it must have belonged to somebody who had been shopping earlier that day, mustn't it? He explained to Mrs. Rayner what had happened. "You two must be the most honest boys in this village, that's for sure," she said.

Ryan explained that he had not kept the money as he knew many people in the village were very old and relied only on their pensions from the government, and this was not a lot of money to live on, this his mother had told him.

Mrs. Rayner shouted for her husband, Bill. "Come downstairs. The young ones have found some money outside. Do you know anything about it?" She most loudly called up to him as he was somewhat a little deaf these days after years of working down the West Midland pits. Arriving promptly out of curiosity, Bill said, "Nobody's been in asking about a twenty, that I'm sure of Mrs. Rayner." - "Then here's what we'll do with it," she said in reply. "I'm going to give you this note to keep. You deserve it for your honesty and there's not a cat in hell's chance of anybody coming back for that now. Lord knows who it belongs to, and if I give it to the local policeman, he'll not be happy about all the paperwork, of that I'm sure."

She continued: "I'll tell him what I've done and if anyone by an angel's miracle does come looking for it, I'll give it back out of my own pocket. That's the deal son." Mrs. Rayner was also all too aware of how difficult life must be for Tanya, the boy's mother, struggling to cope alone on her war widow's pension from the army, but she did not embarrass Ryan by adding such a comment to the conversation. "I'll tell you what," Bill uttered, certain that his wife was correct and that nobody would ever come back to claim the money. "I second that. Make that ten pounds from each of us if they do. It'll be a blinking miracle if anybody comes in for it, for sure."

THE MAN WHO BURIED HIMSELF

Mrs. Stinchcombe

I was first introduced to Mrs. Stinchcombe the day she barged into my office. With two plastic carrier bags almost bursting at the seams, she had charged in, quite unannounced, and shouted at me, "He's gone! That was it. "He's gone..." - "Who's gone?" I replied. "Him, the Vicar, Walton, he's gone," to which she volunteered no more.

I sat startled, looking out across my desk at the rather plump, ageing woman, quite bemused by the whole thing, and asked astonishingly, "Is that it? Is there anything else you wish to add?" And that was my big mistake. For over a four-hour period, way into the late afternoon, she told me this most incredible story. So intriguing it was, I quite forgot to take lunch.

She was a retired nurse and had moved up north to the village of Stretton three years ago. She had arrived to care for an elderly man, apparently a retired Vicar, Reverend Jeremy Walton. He was described as being in his mid-sixties, of very good health and stamina, but possessed of the disorder agoraphobia, a fear of open spaces which, sometimes, looked as if he had a fear of meeting people simply because he never left the house. How strange I thought, but there it was. The Vicar had lived, during the complete employment of Mrs. Stinchcombe, inside a single bedroom. She had never met or seen him.

"Madam, I don't wish to appear rude, but you are telling me that a man you've never met, or even seen before who you say has employed you as a private nurse for three years, has now disappeared?" "Yes, and it's about bloody time someone started listening to me," her anguished reply. The tormented lady began to sob. WPC, Karen Kneed soon assisted with tissues and a good cup of tea, served with a cup and saucer as demanded and two sugars. "My dear, why have you travelled all this way to Merseyside to tell me this when you could have easily gone directly to Stretton Village police station and saved yourself all this bother - you've travelled quite a distance haven't you?" "Yes, indeed Mr. Wilkinson, but they refuse to listen to me, and I saw you in the paper, all about that Bethany thing, clearly you are the only man who can help."

I began to listen more closely to her words. She seemed believable, adamant, asserting herself and backing up what she was saying with stories that were not possible to make up in such an impromptu way. Above all, she appeared credible.

Today's date was 26th August 2008. Having left London three years earlier, in January 2005, following her successful application for the post of Personal Carer, she had now left Kent. She was widowed, had committed her entire life to nursing and had no children or family of her own to speak of: just one sister, Anne, who had died many years ago at a tender young age. This had been a wonderful opportunity for her and she was very keen to move to Cheshire, a small village known locally as Stretton, with a pond, a pub and a post office. The Police Station was much as you would expect to find, located in the front room of the local officer's house. But none-the-less, it was always available to her. Stretton's full title was Stretton Bank Willowfields. I telephoned the local station, keen to get to the bottom of this story. My call was promptly answered. "Good afternoon, 4452 Totwell here, how may I help you?" I explained the problem.

I held the phone as close as I could to my ear to protect Mrs. Stinchcombe from hearing what was now being said, this in between bouts of uncontrolled folly and laughter. "That bloody old fool," Totwell added. "I must apologise Brian. I made a joke and clearly she has taken it seriously. She's been in and out of my office countless times over the last ten days, stating that her employer has disappeared without trace. I merely suggested, given your reputation as the British Columbo, that maybe you could solve this mystery for her, just like the one in your book. I didn't think for a minute she would seriously go all that way to find you." I accepted the apology and engaged further. "Has she got two plastic shopping bags with her Brian?" "Yes," I said, "and apparently they are quite full." "Okay, here it is," and he continued...

"The Vicar has never been identified, traced or even any confirmation offered that confirms that he ever lived in that house... All I have is the nurse's word for it, and as convincing as she is, that's it! How can I possibly investigate the disappearance of a man who never existed in the first place? I would be the laughingstock Mr. Wilkinson, you do understand don't you?" "Of course," I agreed. The call ended politely.

"Mrs. Stinchcombe, may I please address you by your first name?" "If you must," she abruptly replied. "It's Clara, and you're about to patronise me, aren't you?" I had no intention of doing so, and genuinely felt quite sorry for this silly old bugger, but what could I do? "Stop it right there Brian!" And without further ado, she tipped out the entire contents of both plastic bags onto my desk. The first bag had contained all of her medical notes and a journal of activity, her log, in various bound forms, and as eccentric as it all appeared, very well written and informative. The second bag contained his notes; the Vicars rantings as she put it. These were all loose scattered papers with no apparent order. "He used to slip them under the door to me when I left his food," she added. "This all began about a year ago. He was always odd, don't get me wrong, but he'd never been mad that I was aware of."

"Brian, I've read your book 'Please Take Care of Bethany'. Did anybody ever believe you at first? Well, no, of course they didn't. This is what happens isn't it. They convince you that you're mad, don't they? Well, you've got the reputation as quite the sleuth now, and I damn well suggest you've earned it!" And with that she stood up, turned around and stormed out.

It was 1 am the following morning before I had finally finished reading through the contents of both piles of paperwork. She was obviously well organised and highly professional in her dealings with Walton.

"Tuesday 14th March"

Have been here for three months and have never set eyes on my employer. All dirty linen is left in a pile, weekly, outside his door. His room has apparently been fitted with an en-suite. I do hear the noise of running and flushing water in the pipework from time to time. Notes with my instructions are still left daily, as ever, with his dirty plates and cutlery etc. after dinner, as usual outside of the same bedroom door.

I read on. Everything was there, a very accurate account of her daily practical encounters covering the entire period of her employment. But there was no description of the Vicar or any evidence of any personal interaction. On the whole a most professional relationship between nurse and patient had taken place although it was entirely through a locked door. She obviously believed he existed. There had been no sightings, but there had been countless active conversations.

"One Journal entry of May 2006, read:"

I told him that the internet connection was very slow this morning. He assured me he had emailed the company directly and they'd increased the bandwidth. There has not been a problem with the connection since. He sounded very tired and I suggested he sleep. I apologised for my knock having woken him."

It became apparent that her salary had always been paid directly into her bank account by BACs transfer. I noted a sum of one thousand and eighty-six pounds was paid in every four weeks; in fact, on the 15th of every month, regularly, like clockwork without fail. Curiosity got the better of me. After a good night's sleep, I asked the appropriate colleague, Sheila (from CID) who held security clearance to telephone the Cooperative Bank's local branch in the town of Morton. After her initial enquiries on my behalf, Sheila told me something even more intriguing. The manager had been most helpful to her. This sum had been paid into Clara's account for three years without fail, until quite recently that was. It had now stopped following a huge sum that was finally and inexplicably transferred - Two hundred and seventy-four thousand pounds, twenty six pence. Further, there was no record of a Vicar or Reverend Jeremy Walton ever making these transfers. Strangely, there was no explanation at all. The funds were in her account as demonstrated, and the address of the account holder was Mrs. C. M Stinchcombe. She was indeed a resident at the address given; The Old Bore Hole, 14 Willow Rd, Stretton Bank Willowfields, Cheshire.

So, what was she up to? What on earth did she think she had been playing at? I didn't want to accuse her of wasting my time or of dishonesty. Perhaps she was ill? She was evidently aged and it could, after all, just be a simple case of Alzheimer's. I needed further evidence before I telephoned her and confronted her with my findings.

Pre-Installed Navigational Guidance (PING)

"We are Bradley Manning"

On August 21st, 2013, Bradley Manning was sentenced to 35 years in prison. The US prosecution team had called for at least 75. He lost all army privileges, pay and allowances, and was dishonourably discharged with immediate effect. He is required to serve at least one third of his sentence before being eligible for parole. Considering time served and good behaviour he could be released after eight years – but this is highly unlikely...

ARAT can never be identified for this very reason. Too many people have too much to lose. But look here. They chose to release details previously unknown and obtained as a direct consequence of Edward Snowden and the associated WikiLeaks scandal. Pre-Installed Navigational Guidance is now uncovered and exposes those directly connected to the PING conspiracy; a flight control system with only one purpose in mind; to take control of the cockpit for most sinister and covert operations.

Quotes of Interest

"Some even believe we are part of a secret cabal working against the best interests of the United States, characterizing my family and me as internationalists and of conspiring with others around the world to build a more integrated global political and economic structure – one world, if you will. If that's the charge, I stand guilty, and I am proud of it" - Memoirs: David Rockefeller

"If my sons did not want wars, there would be none" Gutle Schnaper Rothschild

"There's a plot in this country to enslave every man, woman, and child. Before I leave this high and noble office, I intend to expose this plot" -President John F. Kennedy

"Anything you can imagine, we already know how to do" - Lockheed CEO: Ben Rich

It was at 1.30 pm on Saturday May 25th, 2015, when police officials forcibly entered the apartment of Brian Wilkinson CBE. This well-loved but now retired police officer had disappeared without trace. A manuscript was found, a new title, a book by the name of 'The Man Who Buried Himself'. Beside it, an all too familiar note, it stated "Publish or die." Both Brian and I were involved, though quite unwillingly, in the Interpol investigation concerning the sadistic death cult, the Gabrielites, and these instructions were followed to the letter. Brittunculi adding this newly discovered title to the existing series; 'Meat: Memoirs of a Psychopath, The Definitive Edition' 2015). Nothing more had been heard of this old, now battle frail former police officer since. That was until now; Part Four has been received.

I had remained in Police protection. My defiance and confrontation of the sect leader, Gabriela 13, had put my own life at immediate risk. I had defied her orders. I had mocked her and publicly humiliated her. Her divine work – a series of religious instructions was now a proverbial laughingstock: her masterpiece; a mere comedic farce with a rather opportune happy ending. I now apologise to you all for this irresponsibility. Has my own arrogance now cost Brian his life? I was foolish – I take responsibility for this. As Gabriela confirms that she will now provide further instruction under the guise of Part Four, I fear for so many others and I apologise to you all. But here we are; Part Four now seems to be the appropriate place to commence this journey.

PING (Aviation, Mind control and the Illuminati) will, I hope in many ways, correct my misgivings. Here you will find exposed for the first time a solid link between the activities of the Gabriel Sect (the Gabrielites) and the old established hierarchy of the ancient Illuminati. This book is based on fact, irrefutable and undeniable. Open your mind and expand it at your peril. The ARAT findings are conclusive proof of a bond that seals the two like glue – they cannot be separated. One and the other are the same thing. You'll find the contents herein underpinned through solid referencing, research and much recommended further reading. I've met many celebrities in the music industry who claim to be members of the Illuminati; I do not.

David Icke, in The Biggest Secret (1999) puts forward his argument that all humankind is ruled by reptilian descendants from the planet Draco; this he refers to as his "reptoid hypothesis theory." He argues that reptilians, Gods known as the Anunnaki (which first appear in ancient Babylonian creation myths), are lizards that walk on two legs and appear to be human. Our ancestors, these so-called inner earth reptilians live in complex tunnel systems, the natural caves found in the earth below our feet.

Icke was born in England, 29th April 1952. His full name is David Vaughan Icke. He has concentrated his writing career on political conspiracy theory since retiring as a professional football player. He has worked extensively in sports journalism and public speaking. As well as working for the BBC, he was briefly a spokesperson for the Green Party, a British fringe movement at the time promoting ecological and sustainable change. It was during his time in local politics (1990) that he befriended a psychic who informed him that; "he was on Earth for a purpose, and that the spirit world would soon channel messages through him." He later declared himself to be "Son of The Godhead" at a press conference in March 1991. He acknowledged that an appearance on BBC television's Wogan Show had now turned him from a respectable household name to the status of village idiot. He published four books during the following seven years; The Robots' Rebellion (1994), Truth Shall Set You Free (1995), The Biggest Secret (1999), and the Children of the Matrix (2001). His core belief is that "a secret group of reptilian humanoids (the Babylonian Brotherhood) controls all of humanity." He stated that many public personalities are indeed reptilian in disguise. He named names: George W. Bush, Queen Elizabeth II, Kris Kristofferson and even Boxcar Willie, to name but a few. He said that the moon as we know it is "probably a hollowed-out planetoid" and that it is from there that the reptilians broadcast an "artificial sense of self and the world." We, the humans of Earth, mistakenly perceive this as our "true reality." Enter stage left a most impressive science fiction film, The Matrix, as good example.

Whilst this book about aviation, mind control and the Illuminati is based on solid fact, Icke's contemporary adaptation of the "ancient astronaut" is not. It's pure fiction, the product of certain mental illness and delusion. His reptoid hypothesis is nothing more than a narrative from the Israeli-American writer, Zecharia Sitchin. He (Sitchin) argued in his work, The Divine Encounters (1995) that the Anunnaki came to Earth for its precious metals. In contrast, Icke states that they arrived to collect "monatomic gold."

The Anunnaki have now, throughout modern evolution, interbred. The line of descendants, their reproductive copulates, are chosen carefully to maintain political and social control over us. Icke argues that the biblical figure and first son of God, Adam, was created some 200,000 or 300,000 years ago and was a pure Anunnaki. There were two other breeding programs: 30,000 and more recently, 7,000 years ago. It is the latter period that contains the "bloodlines of the modern evolved Anunnaki (now more human than reptilian) who control the world" - Icke states. They have a powerful, hypnotic stare, and believe that the origin of the idiom 'to give someone the evil eye,' is born of firsthand encounters with them. He also believes that their advanced alien DNA allows them to shapeshift following the consumption of human blood.

In the Children of the Matrix (2001), Icke adds that the Anunnaki have now bred with another extra-terrestrial race which he refers to as the Nordics – and they in-turn created the Aryans; a group of white supremacists with a tendency toward fascism, this due to their "cold-blooded attitudes, and desire for top-down control." He adds to this; "an obsession with ritualism, nationalism and racism." As we know, and understand consistently throughout known history, the far right has declared the supremacy of its own Aryan bloodline.

To suggest that the reptilians are merely aliens in human form that have now settled on Earth is not sufficient. You must also consider the evidence that they come from within a different dimension. Icke describes this as "the lower level of the Fourth Dimension, the one nearest the physical world." We all live together, sharing a universe that is nothing more than an infinite number of frequencies. Just as radio or television signals are found, some humans have the ability to tune into them. This is what he believes to be psychic power. But in turn, the reptilians of this Lower Fourth are now controlled by a fifth dimension.

The lower level of the fourth dimension is the lower astral dimension. This is where demons and other entities live, the dark forces that Satanists summon during black magic and rituals – And it is at this point that I too tune into my reader's laughter and folly. I too, though previously amused, am now bored to the point of suicide. So, the next time you see a horror film, and in it they awaken your worst nightmare entity, do just remember, it is really only just a lizard in a zip-up humanoid suit!

Neither I nor this book has time for conspiracy theorists who believe in the lizards from outer space. If this is you then please move swiftly on as you, sadly, will swallow anything. There is little point in trying to enlighten you further. Those who make that huge leap of faith in joining reptoid hypothesis with the true origins of the Illuminati have no place here. Please step aside into the fiction aisle. But, if you believe that as David Icke puts forward in Tales from the Time Loop (2003) - that Queen Elizabeth II, George W. Bush and Tony Blair are Red Dresses, the highest level of the Brotherhood, you may stay! Though if you believe them to be lizards too, then alas, you have no place here. Organised religion, Judaism, Christianity and Islam are all creations of a genuine ancient Illuminati hierarchy with sole purpose to divide and conquer. This you will come to understand as you read on.

Icke introduces the idea of reptilian software in 'Love is the Only Truth (2005)', He states three levels of humanoid existence. The highest level in the Brotherhood is the Red Dresses, and these are our rulers. They are reptilian software, constructs of our minds - their human bodies are mere holographic veils and they are absent of free will and conscience. They are here to conquer the human race through endless conflict; 9/11 an example of a catastrophic world changing event perpetrated by a global elite. Icke calls this process "order out of chaos," or "problem-reaction-solution." Many such events, if not engineered by the Brotherhood, are at the very least hijacked by them for political ends.

The sheeple are identified as the second group and consist of the vast majority. Icke informs us that we have only a "back seat consciousness." We do whatever we are told to do. We are the Repeaters, and our journalists are considered to be the greatest repeaters of all as they perpetrate the lies of the third group; the mad and the insane - The dangerous ones amongst us. The Red Dress genetic lines are required to obsessively interbreed to ensure that bloodlines are not weakened by the "second or third levels of consciousness." They must be careful as "consciousness can rewrite the software."

David Icke simply refuses to go away, and today still maintains a small but significant cult following. In Human Race Get Off Your Knees: The Lion Sleeps No More (2010) he introduces his contemporary belief that the "human body-computer," noted to be located in the left hemisphere of the brain, receives broadcasts from spaceships that present to us our sense of reality. "We are living in a dream world within a dream world – a Matrix within the virtual reality universe." It is being "broadcast from the Moon," he states. He builds further on this in 'Remember Who You Are: Remember Where You Are and Where You 'Come From', 2012. Saturn's rings are artificial platforms created by reptilian spacecraft and are the "ultimate source of the signal." The Moon is, "merely a sort of amplifier."

Icke continues to pursue his 'New World Order' conspiracy theory. The old arguments that networks of secret alien societies, the Babylonian Brotherhood (who are predominantly male populated) control the world order are as fresh today as it ever was. The Brotherhood includes 43 American presidents, 5 Commonwealth Prime Ministers and too many Sumerian Kings and Egyptian Pharaohs to mention. Icke also includes in this world order list a handful of household celebrities, including Bob Hope. Yes; you did read correctly - Bob Hope.

Essential bloodlines also include the Rockefellers, the Rothschilds and other European royal and aristocratic families such as the House of Winsor. Icke stated that the Queen Mother was "seriously reptilian" during an interview with the press in 2001. He wrongly associates his reptoid hypothesis with the Illuminati, who in turn control the Round Table, the Trilateral Commission, the Bilderberg Group, and Council on Foreign Relations, Chatham House, the International Monetary Fund and the United Nations. Also controlled by the Illuminati are the media, the armed forces, all spy agencies including the CIA and Mossad; and of course, science, religion and the Internet.

Icke rejects the findings and interpretations as we are informed of by ARAT, in that at the top of the apex of the Brotherhood now stands the Gabrielites, a death cult that has most successfully, as the new global elite, taken control of the ancient and historic administration of the Illuminati. Icke and ARAT separate here. He argues that the Global Elite are prison wardens; their goal is nothing less than "world domination and a micro-chipped population." For ARAT this far too simplistic; the goal is to exterminate all human race through genetic modification of the food chain, and to re-create a new world order based on the Gospel of Gabriela. You will find out more about returning to the darkness in the epic biographical work; 'Meat: Memoirs of A Psychopath, The Definitive Edition' 2015) as you read on.

...Beam me up Icke!

MEAT: MEMOIRS OF A PSYCHOPATH

INTRODUCTION

When I first telephoned Brian Wilkinson during the summer of 2012 to discuss the publication of these memoirs, I was met with an uncomfortable silence. Brian told me he was not going to talk with me and remarked, "Why would you publish such horrors? What possible reason could there be to publish this filth?" I apologised for having troubled him so and explained my reasoning.

An extract from 'Meat: Memoirs of a Psychopath' had been published previously by the UK journal Personality and Mind on the 3rd of November 2011; the professional, subscription-only magazine of the mental health community. During my downtime (the usual coffee and cigarette following one particularly trying day) I had read the extract 'In Finding a Victim'. I read it from professional curiosity only. But what I read filled me with disbelief, and I was driven by curiosity to obtain a complete copy of the memoirs.

My first question though was, were they authentic? I hadn't even been aware of the existence of the memoirs until I read the journal that day. I had just so many questions! No doubt it was because the questions it would raise with the profession... not least of which being that the journal must have chosen to publish in the first place. We are a small community in mental health, and we hear the strangest of stories and meet the strangest of patients. Publication of the memoirs had only been made following a long and drawn-out consultation process with Merseyside Police, so a secondary purpose for publication was by way of an appeal for information. Somewhere, somebody had to know who this man was.

Brian Wilkinson had not been too difficult to find. He was recently retired and very well liked. A few choice phones calls from my practice in Cardiff by my very committed receptionist, Annie, and she had soon found him. The Merseyside Review, a weekly independent newspaper, had published an interview with Brian shortly after he had retired in January 2010. By all accounts he was an everyday bobby. He took a great interest in his local community and would be sadly missed by the residents of the Drover Estate and surrounding beat. The community had rallied around and had thrown a party in the Ferguson Community Centre. Everything I read from the internet said Brian is a good policeman, faultless, hardworking and sincere, a real stalwart and a decent nice guy. After my initial conversation, I left Brian with my telephone number and an invitation to get back to me if he felt able to discuss the matter further.

Two days passed and then the phone call came. Brian had thought over our previous conversation, short though it had been, and said, "How can I help?" We talked for a while and agreed to meet. I drove up to Liverpool the following Sunday. We met as arranged, for a coffee at a motorway service station, (easy to find) and we talked. Brian was now in his early sixties, plump and with a silver beard just like any other old, retired copper you could bring to mind. He wore a suit and tie and explained how difficult he had found it to settle into retirement. He would dress up, always smart, he said, and visit the older people on the estate. "I need to be doing something positive," he said. Brian's wife Doreen had died several years before and you could feel his sense of loneliness. Following Doreen's death he had filled his time with a passion; a passion of his he held dear, a passion for military history. He would tell me wartime stories about his father during the World War II. Brian had self-published his wartime story in 2005 and was very proud of it.

On the memoirs he said, "I never had anyone to talk to, no one to listen. I just had to deal with it and this has been so very hard." You could see straight through Brian when the memoirs took hold of the conversation. You could sense his fear and feel the chill, as if the temperature had suddenly dropped to below zero. But most of all you could see that this was a man, a man who was haunted by his find; a man who had never recovered from it nor had been helped to move on. I would remain in continual contact with Brian and help him to rebuild his sense of self-esteem afterwards. I would later get assistance for him.

Brian was a tough old bugger, didn't like discussing his feelings at all and a gentle gradual path to recovery was much needed. Brian today is receiving counselling from the Merseyside Police Psychology Services. I had worked with them all closely for many years but it was finally nice to meet them and put a face to all the names. "I can talk about it now," he would later tell me.

The police inquiry in regard to the discovery of the memoirs remains open and ongoing. They are looking for a killer; a serial killer and a known psychopath. Science moves on very fast and DNA printing techniques break new boundaries almost on a daily basis. They have the killers DNA profile taken from three victims and one day somewhere this killer will be caught. They are adamant about this, unequivocal. "Just one small crime, shoplifting or drink driving, anything that will result in a personal smear... saliva from the mouth and we have him," Brian told me.

And so now we move to the memoirs. Brian told me how it was all just so routine. A beautiful night and he was happy to be out and about on his beat. He recalled that the moon that evening was crescent shaped and the sky so clear. "I was just doing my thing, walking the beat and then the radio went," he said. "Concern had been raised by a local resident about youths entering and possibly vandalising an old, abandoned house. I knew the house immediately; I had walked this beat for so many years, 16 Veron Road: a lovely old house; not a bad part of town. Not part of the estates; professionals and student lets mainly and close to the university campus. This is the kind of house you always wanted to live in; big and expensive but left to decay as so many are in the area," he said.

"There was a procedure. We didn't put ourselves at any unnecessary risk, resources were tight, low police morale and few new officers," he told me. "I was happy to work alone. I had had a long time on the job. I was counting my days down to retirement. The people here were good people," he remarked. "Back up was usually available but you just didn't want to waste time and money. My old favourite, the procedure, had taken care of me for 29 years. I never felt frightened. Like I say, it was all just so routine," he concluded.

Brian's procedure, a standard police tactic, was to arrive noisily. "It was just youths vandalising an old house and, as ever, routine,' he said. The police were simply not in a position to arrest every wayward kid. This was Liverpool after all, and homelessness and drug addiction were commonplace. Crack cocaine, the biggest single destroyer of any small inner-city community, was abundant," he confirmed.

He would arrive noisily, banging the fence or the bins with his truncheon, perhaps a window or anything else that made a sudden shocking noise. He would shout, "Police Officer in attendance" and then wait for 3 minutes before entering. "The kids would just scarper," he said, "and any users inside, the addicts that is would just jump out of the windows and leg it." There were so many old rundown Victorian and Georgian houses like this in Liverpool and we couldn't stop the vandalism. "We couldn't stop the drug dens popping up," he said, "but we just made our presence known and they would move on."

"I went in. The place stank of excrement and urine, the damp, the usual smells. My hand on my emergency assistance button (on every copper's radio), and my heavy metal torch held up to the right of my head and gripped tightly. Just as I would with my old faithful truncheon to my left if needed. One blow and that hurts," he smiled. "You would hold it at the front, by the bulb end and you could swing down very quickly," he told me. "There was no one there, nothing unusual but yes, all the drug paraphernalia you are used to seeing 3ethe bottles turned into home-made hash or crack smoking pipes, but nothing I didn't expect to see. Old mattresses spread out across the floor and numerous used condoms, all just everyday stuff. But I did smell a candle," he said to me.

He told me how the smell of the candle was fresh, a smell that told you that it had just been extinguished. That hot wax smell he had found was very recent. He had looked around for the candle but it was nowhere to be found. He was just doing his job and making sure some idiot bored kids hadn't somewhere started a fire. "And then I went into the cellar. It was the last place to check and the last place I wanted to check. You see there is no way out in the cellar. You have to give them chance to run if they can. Always check upstairs first and make lots of noise. Give the little buggers a chance to get out," he said proudly. "And then I saw them, these memoirs, saw them placed on a table beside this recently used candle. It was just an old orange card covered folder, a student kind of thing." He stopped, silent. He had got to know me by now and trusted me. We talked a lot and often, nonsense usually and just day-to-day chit chat, but now Brian was suddenly and totally silent.

"What on earth is wrong?" I said. He exclaimed, "You have to understand the fear. I just read the note on the cover that was just stuck there like a reminder, handwritten below a big bold title in black felt pen. It said 'Meat: Memoirs of a Psychopath'. I froze cold, so very cold at what I saw. This wasn't routine anymore, anything but," he said. He told me how he had read the cover, maybe it was some kind of sick joke, maybe it had been stolen from some would-be author's car and just dumped there, but no, nothing about the find made any sense.

It was in perfect condition, undamaged and no rips. Something like this could not have been here long. The kids would have burnt it and the druggies would have most certainly used it as toilet paper,' he told me. No, Brian had found it: the memoirs perfectly placed on an old wooden table that was spotlessly washed cleaned and the candle beside still warm. "I opened the cover with a pencil, a policeman's nose, you know that this is something important. You sense it," he said. "I read it in disbelief. Was this real? I didn't want to call it in and make a fool of myself," he said. "It was sick what I saw. I mean sicker than anything else I had come across in my life. Just so sick and I felt quite nauseous because of it. I could read no more of it. This was something that I had never seen before in my entire career. I'm just an old beat bobby you see, that's all, but this was so twisted."

Brian later called the find in and within minutes he told me, the entire team was there. The entire team consisting of everybody, and the house was locked down for forensic testing for many days. "I was just a handful of weeks away from retiring and I am left with this," he said in a dampened voice. "It was weeks later before all of us lads down at the station got to read the whole thing."

"Can people like this really exist?" he asked me. All I could offer him at this stage and in reply, was that you could never trust anybody really. People are capable of anything, as experience had shown me. "I have never recovered from the fear," he said to me, "that fear, that gut churning fear I got knowing that I had been maybe just inches away from this sick, twisted bastard." I had never heard Brian use profanity before, because by nature he was a real gent and always so polite. But now, and only now, did I begin to understand his fear and his absolute revulsion at his find. Brian clearly needed clinical help to move on from it. "It haunts me, the stuff of nightmares," he said, "and that's why I rang you back after you telephoned me. We have to catch him." "That's why I am here Brian," I told him. "I am sure you are all very close."

The resulting investigation and my conclusion form the appendix of this book, 'The Police Investigation.' Each chapter of 'Meat' will be followed by my reflections on what has gone before, both in terms of psychological profiling and personal opinion. You may find these memoirs both disturbing and horrifying. My own texts are both my attempt to bring a clinical focus on the subject matter, and to offer the reader some respite from the otherwise gruelling content. These anonymous memoirs are printed in full, unabridged and unedited. They are at times chaotic, unreadable and, some might say, written out of pure madness. Is this a work of fact or fiction? At this stage only you, the reader, can decide...

Words At War: Adolf Hitler (Book of Horror)

Audio Book Index

Book Track One: 1939. Lord Chamberlain (Declaration of War)

Book Track Two: 1939. CBS News(Followed by Extraordinary Session of US Congress)

Book track Three: 1940. BBC Lord Chamberlain (Resignation speech)

Book Track Four: 1940 BBC Bernard Stubbs (On the B.E.F advance into Belgium)

Book track Five: 1940. BBC Winston Churchill (First speech as Prime-minister)

Intro - Historical Context / The Secrets of Mien Kampf: Free Documentary courtesy of The History Channel - History is dedicated to bringing high-class documentaries to you on YouTube for free.

Mein Kampf: Adolf Hitler: A Retrospect

Chapter One: In the Home of My Parents

Pre-Introduction: Westerbrook (3). Leon Greenman's Holocaust testimonial.

'An Englishman in Auschwitz.'

Book track 1: Die Herst Wessel Lied (The fascist anthem of Nazi Germany)

Introduction: Mein Kamphf for anti fascists. Track dedication: The Holocaust Denier.

Book track 2: 1940. RRG. Adolph Hitler (If our will is strong enough)

Book track 3: 1940. Winston Churchill (Fight on the beeches)

Book track 4: 1944. Eisenhower. (D-day broadcast to Western Europe)

Book track 5: 1940. RRG (British troops in full retreat)

Mein Kamph: Author's introduction. Translator's (Murphy 1939) introduction & chapter 1

Book track 6: 1940. BBC Bernard Stubbs (On the evacuation of troops from Dunkirk) Book track 7: 1940.

BBC Alver Liddell (On the invasion of Denmark & Norway)

Chapter Two: Years of Study & Suffering in Vienna

Book track 1: 1940. BBC Winston Churchill (On the capitulation of Belgium)

Book track 2: 1940: BBC (German advance on Antwerp)

Chapter Three: Political Reflections out of my Sojourn in Vienna

Book track 1: 1940, Last Marseillaise broadcast (As Paris falls)

Book track 2: 1940: CAN Eric Savereldon (The fall of Paris)

Book track 3: 1940. RRG Nazi radio (Announcement on the fall of Paris)

Book track 4: Winston Cuirchill (Pledge to free France)

Book track 5: 1940. William C Kirker (On French armistice)

Book track 6: 1940. ETAR Benito Mussolini (Italy declares war)

Book track 7: 1940. RDN Marchal Petain (On collaboration of France)

Chapter Four: Munich

Book Track 1: 1940. CBS Elmer Davies (Reporting on the first day of the Blitzkrieg)

Book Track Two: 1940. RSH Lord Haw Haw - British traitor (British Minister of misinformation)

Chapter Five: The World War

Book Track 1: 1940. BBC Sec. State Anthony Eden (Calls for local defence)

Book Track Two: 1940. BBC Charles Gardner (on

convoy attack and dogfight) Book Track Three:

1940. BBC A 'Londoner' (On shelters & The Blitz)

Book Track Four: 1940. BBC Charles Gardner (Continues reports on dogfight)

Book Track Five: 1940. BBC Sec. State for War Anthony Eden (On the Battle of Britain)

Book Track Six: 1940. CBS Edward Murrow (On London rooftop during The Blitz)

Book Track Seven: 1940. BBC Alver Liddell (Reports on 175 German aircraft shot down)

Chapter Six. Propaganda

Book Track 1: 1940. BBC Robin Duff (Sees London burning)

Book Track Two: 1940. BBC Very Reverend R.T Howard (On Coventry Cathedral)

Book Track Three: 1940 RSH British traitor Lord Haw Haw (British invasion looms)

Chapter Seven: The Revolution

Book Track One: 1940. BBC Winston Churchill (A sterner war)

Book Track Two: 1940. CBS: Today In Europe

Chapter Eight: The Beginning
of my Political Activities Book

Track One: 1940. BBC 'Russell'

(Interviews a bomb victim)

Book Track Two: 1940. BBC Gillard takes cover...

Book Track Three: 1940. Albert Einstein 'on the bomb'

Book Track Four: 1940. BBC Robin Duff (In an air-raid shelter)

Book Track Five: 1940. J. Edgar Hoover (On the opponents of war)

Book Track Six: 1940. BBC Blitz Emergency Services

Book Track Seven: 1940. BBC Girl talks of bomb shelters

Book Track Eight: 1941. BBC Winston Churchill (Give Us The Tools)

Chapter Nine: The 'German Labour Party'

Book Track One: 1940. BBC Herbert Morrison. Minister for Home Security

Book Track Two: 1940. US Sec. State Cordell Hull (On the need for)

Book Track Three: 1940. BBC Winston Churchill (House of Commons secret)

Book Track Four: 1941. BBC Alan Howland (On German air attacks)

Book Track Five: 1940. Coventry - Loudspeaker announcement

Book Track Six: 1941. BBC Winston Churchill (War production)

Chapter Ten: Why the Second Reich Collapsed

Book Track One: 1940. BBC Winston Churchill (The navy is here)

Book Track Two: 1940. Princess Elizabeth & Princess Margaret (Speak to evacuees)

Book Track Three: 1940. 1941. BBC (Clothes rationing)

Book Track Four: 1941. BBC Alan Howland (On German air attacks)

Book Track Five: 1941. FDR (On the Land-lease Act)

Book Track Six: 1941. FDR (Fireside chat on the Pan-American Unity)

Audio Interjection: Mein Kampf (The Bloody Time - 1960)

Having finally completed this audio book presentation, and having added comment to Chapter 12 concerning my feelings regarding Chapter 11 (Race & People) – I felt it necessary to return again and add this interjection. Placed between chapter 10 and 11; the listener now finds the above work of documentary film-maker - Erwin Leiser. Historic Nazi speeches have been translated and minimal comment made. I considered it essential, as a final afterthought, that before Chapter 11 be accessed, the rise of The Third Reich and the crimes against humanity committed should be appropriately addressed.

The Audio soundtrack of the US military footage (presented at The Nuremberg Trials: 1945) appears as an Appendix: The Final Solution. Erwin Leiser was born on May 16th 1923. He was German-born director, writer, and actor best known for his film-documentary Mein Kamphf - often referred to as The Bloody Time (1960). Utilising original Nazi film archives he skilfully captures previously unseen footage of the atrocities committed. He fled from Nazi persecution; leaving his city of birth behind (Berlin) arriving in Sweden at the age of 15. He completed many notable works on the rise and fall of the Third Reich. Following his death (August 22nd, 1996) he was buried in Zürich's Israelitischer Friedhof Oberer Friesenberg.

Book Track One: 1941. NBC Bulletin on capture of blockade runner

Book Track Two: 1941. BBC Winston Churchill (Do Your Worst and We'll Do Our Best)

Book Track Three: 1960. Erwin Leiser: Mein Kamphf (The Bloody Time)

Book Track Four: WW2. Onward Christian Soldiers (Wartime Propaganda Song: In

German)

Book Track Five: 1940. BBC Winston Churchill (Our Finest Hour)

Book Track Six: 1944. NBC Poem and Prayer (For invading army)

Chapter Eleven: Race and People

Book Track One: 1941. BBC Winston Churchill (Broadcasts to America)

Book Track Two: 1941. Wendell Wilkie (Calls for end of US isolotation)

Book Track Three: 1941. RRG German radio (Announces sinking of HMS Hood)

Book Track Four: 1941. BBC First Sea-Lord A V Alexander (On the sinking of The

Bismark)

Book Track Five: 1941. PCPT Josef Stalin (Adresses the nation)

Book Track Six: 1941. PCPT Russian radio (Reports on German invasion)

Book Track Seven: 1941. BBC General De'Gaulle

(Urges America to join the Allies) Book Track Eight:

1941. MBS Wise Williams (On fighting in Russia)

Chapter Twelve: The First Stage in the Development of The German National Socialist Labour Party.

Book Track One: 1941. BBC Robert Dougal (With convoy in The Atlantic)

Book Track Two: 1941. NBCR (First bulletin on pearl Harbour attack)

Book Track Three: 1941. NBCR (Manila bombed)

Book Track Four: 1941. MBS Football match (Interrupted)

Book Track Five: 1941. CBS New York Philharmonic Concert (Interrupted)

Book Track Six: 1941. NBC (Burma bombed)

Book Track Seven: 1941. NBCR (KGU Honolulu report)

Book Track Eight: 1941. NBC Bulletin US Congress: Declaration of War (on Japan)

Book Track Nine: CBS Bulletin: US Declaration of War (On Germany & Italy)

Charlie & His Orchestra: Charlie and his Orchestra (also referred to as the "Templin band" and "Bruno and His Swinging Tigers") were a Nazi-sponsored German propaganda swing band. Jazz music styles were seen by Nazi authorities as rebellious but, ironically, propaganda minister Joseph Goebbels conceived of using the style in shortwave radio broadcasts aimed at the United States and (particularly) the United Kingdom. British listeners heard the band every Wednesday and Saturday at about 9 pm. The importance of the band in the propaganda war was underscored by a BBC survey released after World War II, which indicated that 26.5 percent of all British listeners had at some point heard programmes from Germany] The German Propaganda Ministry also distributed their music on 78 rpm records to POW camps and occupied countries.

1) Who'll Buy My Bublitchky

2) Double Dare You

3) FDR Jones

4) Hold Me

5) I'll Never Say never Again

6) Japanese Sandman

7) Makin' Whoopee

8) United Nations Airmen

9) Want To Be Happy

10) Lili Marlene

11) St Louise Blues

Broadcasts of Lord Haw Haw: Lord Haw-Haw was a nickname applied to wartime broadcaster William Joyce, remembered for his propaganda broadcasts that opened with "Germany calling, Germany calling", spoken in an upper-class accent. The same nickname was also applied to some other broadcasters of English-language propaganda from Germany, but it is Joyce with whom the name is now overwhelmingly identified. There are various theories about its origin. The Englishlanguage propaganda radio programme Germany Calling was broadcast to audiences in the United Kingdom on the medium wave station Reichssender Hamburg and by shortwave to the United States. The programme started on 18 September 1939 and continued until 30 April 1945, when the British Army overran Hamburg. The next scheduled broadcast was made by Horst Pinschewer (aka Geoffrey Perry), a German refugee serving in the British Army who announced the British takeover. Pinschewer was later responsible for the capture of William Joyce.

1) 1940: Diplomatic Correspondent

2) 9.4.40: Denmark and Norway Part One

3) 1940: Height of Cynicism

4) 1940: Cruiser Exeter

5) 27.2.40: British Minister of Misinformation

6) 16.2.40: The Altmark Incident

7) 1940: Minster of Misinformation

8) 1940: Lord Haw Haw (unknown title)

9) 28.6.40: British Invasion Looms

10) 21.6.40: The Fall of France

11) 28.5.40: Holland and Belgium Invaded

12) 9.4.40: Denmark and Norway Part Two

13) 16.4.40: Scandinavian Update 'Scmidt'

14) 13.4.40: Russo-Finnish War Concluded

15) Date-Unknown: Haw Haw - Last Known Broadcast

WORDS AT WAR: Old Time Radio Broadcasts (1943-1945)

Produced in cooperation with the Council on Books in Wartime the NBC (USA) episodes of Words at War were based on literature created during the war by a variety of authors. Words at War is a glimpse of the beliefs (with a sprinkle of wartime propaganda), and fears of (predominantly) American authors during the last great war. These recording appear as 'Part Two' attachments to each chapter.

1) Combined Operations (43.06.24)

2) They Call It Pacific (43.07.10)

3) The Last Days of Sevestopol (43.0.17)

4) The Ship (43.07.24)

5) Firm Hands, Silent People (43.07.31)

6) Prisoner of The Japs (43.07.07)

7) Love At First Flight (43.06.24)

8) Malta Spitfire (43.08.25)

9) Dynamite Cargo (43.09.02)

10) Since You Went Away (43.09.16)

11) They Shall Not Have Me (43.09.23)

12) Battle Hymn of China (43.09.30)

13) Eighty Three Days (43.10.05)

14) Paris Underground (43.10.12)

15) Shortcut to Tokyo (43.10.19)

16) Who Dare to Live (43.10.26)

17) Here is Your War (43.11.02)

18) To All Hands (43.11.09)

19) Escape from The Balkans (43.11.23)

20) Hail Ceasor - El Duce (43.11.30)

21) Book of War Letters (43.12.07)

22) Mother America (43.12.14)

23) Logbook British Merchant Marine (43.12.21)

24) 9th Command - Holland Invasion (43.12.28)

25) The Ninth Commandment (43.12.28)

26) They Shall Inherit the Earth (44.01.04)

27) War Tide (44.01.18)

28) Condition Red (44.01.10)

29) White Brigade (44.02.01)

30) George Washington Carver (44.02.08)

31) The New Sun (44.02.15)

32) Assignment USA (44.02.22)

33) Weeping Wood (44.03.07)

34) Science at War (44.03.14)

35) Der Fuhrer (44.03.21)

36) A Bell for Adano (44.03.28)

37) Wild River (44.04.11)

38) Silence of The Seas (44.04.18)

39) Curtain Rises (44.05.02)

40) Gunners get Glory (44.05.09)

41) Life Line (44.05.16)

42) Land Lease - Weapons of Glory (44.05.23)

43) The Navy Hunts the Cgr-3070 (44.05.30)

44) War Criminals and Punishment (44.07.04)

45) Captain Retread (44.07.11)

46) War Below Zero (44.07.18)

47) Lost Island (44.07.25)

48) Head Quarters Budapest (44.08.01)

49) The Nazis Go Underground (44.08.08)

50) Simone (44.08.29)

51) The Veteran Comes Back (44.09.05)

52) One Man Air force (44.09.12)

53) Journey Through Chaos (44.09.26)

54) Pacific Victory, 1945 (44.08.01)

55) Still Time To Die (44.10.23)

56) One Thing After Another (44.11.14)

57) Barriers Down (44.11.21)

58) Camp Follower (44.11.28)

59) The Guys On The Ground (44.12.05)

60) Your School Your Children (44.12.0112)

61) The Cross and The Arrow (44.12.19)

62) The Scape Goats in History - History of Bigo (44.12.26)

63) It's Always Bright Tomorrow (45.01.02)

64) Borrowed Nights (45.01.09)

65) Verdict India (45.01.16)

66) The Story of A Secret State (45.01.23)

67) What To Do With Germany (45.02.13)

68) Battle Report - Pearl Harbour to The Congress (45.02.20)

69) Faith of Our Fathers (45.02.27)

70) Rainbow (45.03.08)

71) Can Do (45.03.13)

72) Tomorrow We'll See (45.03.20)

73) Banshee Harvest (45.03.27)

74) Full Employment in a Free Society (45.04.03)

75) Apartment in Athens (45.04.10)

76) They Left the Back Door Open (45.04.17)

77) Brave Men (45.04.24)

78) The Hide Out (45.04.01)

79) The Road to Serfdom (45.05.15)

80) Wartime Racketeers (45.05.22)

81) Soldier to Civilian (45.05.29)

82) My Country (45.06.29)

83) Fair Stood The Wind of France (44.06.28)

Interview with the narrator:

84) The Holocaust Denier. BBC Radio Leeds (UK); 22nd Dec: 2009. Jonathan I'anson & Jonathan Taylor

Part Thirteen: Nurenberg: US Army Public Interest 1946 (Audio and/or Video)

Part Fourteen: Nurenberg: USSR: The Trials 1946 (Audio and/or Video)

Part Fithteen: Nurenberg (15th Oct.1946) Arthur Gaeth reports (Audio and/or Video)

Appendix

Book Track One: 1945. Hitler's last broadcast

Book Track Two: Voices: (date unknown) Hitler Youth Song

Book Track Three: 1943. Lancaster Crew over Berlin (Drop fighter)

Book Track Four: 1.5.1945. BBC First announcement of Hitler's death

Book Track Five: 1945. BBC Voices: First memorial service at Belsen Concentration Camp

Book Track Six: 1945. BBC Voices: Ravensbruck Concentration Camp (Reportage)

Book Track Seven: 1945. US Military: Judgement at Nuremberg (Audio only)

Book Track Eight: 1945. BBC Voices Hiroshima news bulletin

Book Track Nine: Atomic Bomb destroys Hiroshima.

Milton Keynes UK
Ingram Content Group UK Ltd.
UKHW041134030624
443552UK00001B/107

9 781312 432048